Faster

We

Burn

a novel

Chelsea M. Cameron

chelseamcameron.com

One

Katie

I told myself that I wasn't attracted to Stryker Grant the first time I saw him. Between the pierced lip and eyebrow, his torn (not on purpose) jeans, and his bleached hair, he was the opposite of every guy I'd ever wanted. Plus, he was dressed as a vampire, fake fangs and all.

My boyfriend, Zack, and I were on again, and I was enjoying being in the center of so much activity, so much life. Then Zack did what he always did and pushed it too far. In the middle of a crowded Halloween party, no less. I tried to chalk it up to him being drunk, but that was quickly becoming an overused excuse.

Stryker was there quicker than you could say "damsel in distress." I totally had Zack handled, but Stryker wouldn't let it go.

Plus, there was the whole drama of Zan, Zack's brother, getting Zack home and everyone fussing over me like I was five. Then, Stryker called me "sweetheart" in a way that made me clench my teeth.

Even without the fake fangs, I didn't see it.

I didn't figure it out until he showed up at my door the next day, asking for the stupid vampire cape he'd given me the night before when I was cold.

—

5

"Here," I said, shoving it at him. He took it, but didn't leave. Audrey had finally gotten me out of my pink dress and into my sweats, and I wasn't in the mood to entertain; especially after the look on Lottie's face when I told her I'd slept with her boyfriend. But, they couldn't watch me 24 hours a day.

"Listen," he said, and I knew where this was going. I was going to put a stop to it before anything happened. He chewed the side of his lip that was pierced with a silver ring. His clothes were filthy, and his boots were so covered in dirt I didn't know what color they were originally. Not that I was one to talk. I didn't even have contacts in, displaying instead the dorky glasses I wouldn't be caught dead wearing in public.

"Look, you saved me; you made sure I didn't freeze to death. Congratulations. You can go now." I moved to shut the door in his face, but he put his arm out to stop me.

"That wasn't what I was going to say." He put his foot in the doorway, and leaned into the room. "What I was going to say is that you're an idiot." He folded the cape over his arm.

"Excuse me?"

"You heard what I said. You're. An. Idiot." He enunciated the last three words and leaned closer to me until our faces were only separated by a few inches. For the first time, I met his eyes and saw they were green. How had I not noticed that before?

"And what makes you qualified to say that? You don't even *know* me." Seriously, who did he think he was?

"I may not know you, specifically, but I've known girls just like you before. You're the girl who has what everyone thinks is this perfect pink life. The girl who spends all her time trying to be something she's not. The girl who's barely hanging on. You're an idiot because you think you can keep it up, and you're an idiot to think that you have to." I watched the lip ring move as he talked so I wouldn't look into his eyes again.

"Whatever." I tried to shove the door closed again, but he was still in my way. "Get out of my room." I was so done with guys and their testosterone trips.

He held up his hands and backed away, as if I were freaking out for no reason.

"I'm not telling you anything you don't already know, sweetheart." The way he said "sweetheart" pissed me off, just like it had the first time.

He pivoted on his heel.

"See you around," he said with a wave over one shoulder.

"Never would be too soon," I yelled at his back. I could still hear the sound of his laughter, even after I'd slammed the door and pressed my forehead against it so I could just breathe for a second.

The last thing I needed in my life was another guy. Especially one that told me I was an idiot.

But, of course, that was exactly why I opened my door and dashed down the stairs until I found him in the lobby, leaning against the wall beside the door to the stairs. As if he had been waiting for me.

He was messing with his lip ring again, but other than that, he was all swagger. He raised his pierced eyebrow.

"Is this never?" he said.

I shook my head.

"You're wrong. About me. I'm not pretending to be anything," I said.

"Sure," he said, a smile playing on his lips.

I took a step toward him and he moved away from the wall and toward me. "I don't owe you anything."

"No, you don't."

"Good. Now we've got that straight –" I grabbed his shirt and yanked him toward my mouth. Luckily, I'd had a lot of practice, so my aim was good, and his lips crashed against mine perfectly. He froze for a moment in surprise, but that didn't last long. The cape fell to the floor as his arms captured me, pulling me close. It wasn't a sweet kiss; it was a demanding, get-your-clothes-off kind of kiss. It was a kiss that made me want to wrap my legs around him and take him back to my room.

I heard people walking by and making comments, but I was too preoccupied with the feel of his velvety mouth on mine and how the metal of his lip ring warmed with the contact from my lips.

He slowed the kiss and finally we broke apart. Both of us were breathing heavily. Green eyes seared into mine, locking me in place.

"What was that for?" He took a step back, but didn't let go of me.

I shrugged one shoulder as I tried to get my breath back. "I've never kissed a guy with a lip ring. I was curious."

A pucker formed between his eyebrows as he studied me, searching for the real reason. He wasn't going to find it because I didn't even know the reason.

"And?" he finally said.

"And now I know." I tried to back away, but he had both arms wrapped around me, trapping me.

"You ever fucked a guy with a lip ring?" he said.

I shook my head side to side once. "Nope."

He raised his pierced eyebrow again. "Want to try?"

I fisted my hands in his shirt and gave him another fierce kiss.

"Absolutely. Just don't call me an idiot *ever* again."

Stryker

I wasn't planning on getting laid when I went to see her, but I sure as hell wasn't going to say no when she kissed me like that. Plus, I had a thing for girls with glasses, and she still had that whole damaged thing going for her. I finally let her go, and she grabbed my hand and dragged me up the stairs to her room.

"We don't have much time, they're watching me like I'm going to lose it," she said, making sure the door was closed before she ripped the elastic band out of her hair and pulled her sweatshirt off. Underneath she was just wearing a tank top, no bra. "I'm not going to lose it. I'm *not* going to lose it." She pulled her pants off in one quick motion and I realized I was just standing there, still fully-clothed. I also realized she had a shit ton of pink things. In fact, there were so many pillows on the bed, I wasn't sure if there would be room for me.

She walked until she was right in front of me and grabbed the bottom of my shirt. "I'm not going to lose it, got it?"

"Got it," I said. She pulled my shirt up and I helped her get it over my head. After only a moment to assess my tattoos, her hands were on my belt.

"Good." She kissed me again, and we fell onto her bed.

"Too many pillows," I said against her mouth as I reached behind and chucked some of them on the floor.

"Mmm," she said, pulling off her tank top. I tossed more pillows until I could finally flip her over so she was on her back under me. She broke the kiss. "Condom?"

"Don't have one." I had one in the truck, but I didn't think I needed to put it in my pocket like I would have if I'd gone out to a bar.

"Top drawer," she said pointing over her head at her desk. I reached and pulled one out, ignoring the fact that the condoms were probably left over from Zack.

We both got the rest of the way naked and the sex was quick and hot and hard. I knew her neighbors were probably getting an earful, but the sounds she made were so sweet as her fingernails dug into my back and she begged me for more. Her legs wrapped around me and she rose up to meet me, demanding more, faster, harder. There was also a hint of desperation in it. Of hurt. Of anger.

Of pain.

I finally felt her come around me and I held out for as long as I could after her, but it wasn't very long.

"*Fuck*," I groaned, holding myself up so I didn't collapse on her. Our eyes locked and she gave me a quick kiss. She moved so I could lie on my back beside her on the small bed. I turned so I could look at her.

She had a beautiful body. Sweet curves and soft angles. A few freckles dotted their way along her stomach. I hadn't gotten to taste them. Yet. I reached out to trace them but she grabbed my wrist.

"Don't. Just because we had sex doesn't mean I want you to touch me." She let me have my wrist back and I moved farther from her as she crossed her arms over her chest.

"Do you want me to go?" I said.

"Yes." I sighed and sat up so I could climb over her, but she put her hand on my shoulder. "No."

"Which is it? Yes or no?"

She took a shaky breath and stared at the ceiling again. As if she didn't want to look at me anymore now that it was over. A tear slid down her cheek, followed by another. She tried to wipe them away so I wouldn't see, but I did. It wasn't the first time a girl had cried after sex with me, but this time hit me like a truck.

"Hey," I said reaching down to wipe one for her, but she moved her face. Fine. I tried to go again, but I couldn't leave a crying girl. I pulled my boxers and pants back up, found a blanket on the end of the bed and covered her with it.

"I'm sorry I called you an idiot. Even though you were being one," I said. I knew that wasn't the reason she was crying, but I still felt like a dick for adding insult to injury.

"I'm not crying because you called me an idiot," she said between sobs. "I don't know why I'm crying."

I grabbed a tissue from a box that was covered in fuzzy pink material. "Yeah, you do."

"Shut up," she said, blowing her nose. "You've fucked me, now you can go. I just wanted to get laid, I didn't want to have a heart-to-heart with a guy I don't even know or like."

"Fine. If that's what you want." I pulled my pants up, climbed over her and found my shirt. I'd never even taken my shoes off.

She sobbed again, but she'd asked me to leave and that was what I was going to do. You fuck a girl and she asks you to leave, you get your ass out the door.

I looked back once at Katie curled up under the blanket, holding onto herself as if she was going to break apart. Her wide, wet eyes found mine and begged.

"Just. Go."

I nodded and shut the door behind me as she tried to cry quietly. I fished in my pockets and found a receipt from the gas station. There was a little board on Katie's door with a marker to leave messages for Lottie and vice versa. I scrawled my cell phone number and the words *call me if you need anything* on the receipt and shoved it under her door.

I'd probably never hear from her, but I did it anyway. Call it one lost cause reaching out to another.

Two

Katie

After Stryker left, I got myself up and dressed and to the shower. Trish and Audrey were coming over to babysit me and I would rather have burned the dorm down than tell them that I'd had sex with Stryker, or that I'd had a meltdown and cried afterwards.

I cleaned up the evidence of our escapade, changed the sheets and sprayed the room with vanilla cinnamon room spray to get rid of his scent. He smelled like . . . something clean but spicy with hints of cigarettes and gasoline.

My skin tingled as if it were remembering his touch. I shouldn't have done that, but sometimes I made bad life decisions. Sleeping with Stryker was one of those on a looonnnngggg list. I found the receipt with his number on it that he'd shoved under the door. If I was going to call someone to talk about my feelings, it wasn't going to be him. Still, I put the piece of paper in my desk drawer instead of throwing it away.

I berated myself the entire time I showered and cleaned, so by the time Audrey and Trish showed up with movies and ice cream I had already lectured myself a hundred times.

"You guys don't have to stay with me, you know," I said as Trish handed me a pint of Cherry Garcia and Audrey slipped off her shoes before flopping on my bed.

"We're not babysitting you. We're concerned friends who want to hang out with you," Audrey said, arranging some of the pillows. Stryker had thrown all of them on the floor when

. . .

"You okay?" Trish said as she popped in *Bridesmaids*. I knew my face was red, so I stared into the ice cream container to try to hide it as I sat next to Audrey.

"Yeah, fine." Trish looked at me suspiciously, but Audrey started tossing pillows at her so she could make a little couch of them on the floor.

I didn't pay attention to the movies and just laughed when Trish and Audrey did. My mind was occupied with remembering what I'd done with Stryker and trying to forget it at the same time.

It didn't matter how good it was, or how right it had felt at the time. It had been a bad idea that I'd acted on and it wasn't going to happen again. Especially after my little breakdown.

The last time I had sex with Zack, he'd made me cry, too. Maybe it was a conditioned reaction for me now. Sex and crying.

"Are you sure you're okay?" Audrey asked as she handed me her empty container at the end of the second movie. I didn't know how she ate so much ice cream and still kept that thin. Good genetics, probably. I got up to toss the ice cream containers and took a deep breath so I wouldn't say something I would later regret.

"I love you guys. Both of you. But if you don't stop asking me if I'm okay, I'm going to freak out, and I really can't handle that right now. Zack and I broke up, I'm moving on. Got it?"

They both nodded like bobble head dolls.

"I'm not trying to be a bitch, because it's so sweet that you care and that you're willing to give up your lives to make sure I don't go off the deep end, but enough is enough. I need some air."

Audrey spoke first, her eyes not meeting mine.

"We're sorry. We just didn't know what else to do." Yup, I felt like a bitch anyway.

"It was Lottie's idea. Blame her," Trish added. I wished she hadn't mentioned Lottie. She was off on a date with Zan, even though she knew he and I had slept together. She must really love him.

"I hope she doesn't hate me," I said, sitting next to Audrey again.

"It's not like you could have known," Audrey said

"Not to be creepy or anything, but how did it happen?" Trish said. "I just don't see the two of you hitting it off."

"It was one of those really, really stupid decisions you regret the second after you make it, but it's too late. Let's just say I'd had a really bad week, it was summer, I was drunk and he was willing. I don't remember much of it, but enough to know that it happened. And then Zack noticed me and that was it."

When it came to charm, Zack had it in spades. He'd said all the right things that made me feel all warm and fluttery inside, and before I knew it, we were going at in the bed of his truck, and then we were just together. And now we weren't.

I shrugged because it seemed so minor now. None of it mattered anymore.

We got through another movie and made nachos before Lottie came back from her date with Zan. She should have been spending the night in his room, but she probably wanted to make sure I was okay, which made me feel even more like a bitch.

"Hey, how was your date?" Audrey said, yawning.

"Good. Really good. How are you?" The last part was directed toward the group, but meant for me.

"I'm fine." She nodded and I could sense one of her famous word volcanoes was about to erupt. She always took a deep breath before she started one so she could talk without having to interrupt the flow by breathing. It was annoying at first, but I'd gotten used to it.

"Okay good. Because I know it's weird that you had sex with him and now I'm dating him, but I don't want things to be weird because it's not your fault. I mean, you didn't know me and you didn't know that he and I were going to end up together. So it's okay. Just so you know." She looked scared after she finished, as if she was worried about how I would respond. I sighed and tossed the empty bag of tortilla chips in the trash.

"It's fine, Lot. If anyone should be apologizing, it should be me. I shouldn't have told you like that. I should have told you a long time ago, but I was afraid you'd hate me."

Trish and Audrey looked like they felt uncomfortable, but Lottie and I needed to do this now to clear the air. She took everything so personally and I wanted her to know that I was fine with her and Zan, as long as she was happy. My mistakes with the Parker brothers weren't hers.

"I don't hate you. I just didn't want things to be weird," she said.

"Come on ladies, hug it out," Trish said, getting up and pulling Lottie across the room. "Come on, roommate hug."

Lottie and I hugged, which ended up with us giggling, rocking back and forth, trying to tip the other one over.

"See? Works every time," Trish said, patting both of us on the back as if we'd just won a football game.

"Okay, okay," I said, rolling my eyes. "It's late and I'm tired."

"We'll get going," Audrey said, gathering her movies and her coat. "See you tomorrow? Library date?"

"You're on," I said, giving her a salute. Trish waved goodbye as well, and then it was just Lottie and me.

"Have you heard from Zack?" Lottie said as she cleared up the rest of the refuse from our little Katie pity party. I could tell she'd been waiting until we were alone.

"Yeah, he's left me a million messages. I'm just waiting for the "sorry I fucked up" gifts to start coming in." I'd already put the necklace he'd given me from the last screw-up in my jewelry box.

"Maybe you should change your cell number or something."

If only it were that easy. Something that simple wouldn't stop Zack from finding another way to contact me. I'd take a million voicemails over him doing something really crazy, like showing up in one of my classes, or waiting at my car, or something else like that. Phone calls were harmless.

I gave her a look.

"Sorry. You probably don't want to talk about him."

I stacked the pillows back on my bed for something to do. "Not really."

She handed me two more pillows. "I'm sorry, I shouldn't have asked."

"It's okay." I should just record myself saying that and 'I'm fine' so I could play them back whenever I needed to.

"You sure?" I grabbed the last pillow and placed it in the middle of the rest.

"Yup."

She gave me another look and went to brush her teeth. I lay back on my bed and tried to forget that only a few hours ago, I'd been fucking Stryker in it. Tried, but did not succeed.

Stryker

"How is Lottie going to keep this a secret from Will? They have that creepy twin thing," I said as I worked on replacing the clutch Zan had burned out while learning how to drive a standard on Will's truck. The weather was getting colder and soon it would be nearly impossible to work outside without the potential risk of losing a few fingers or my nose to frostbite.

"I don't know, honestly. I'm shocked she's managed to keep us a secret this long."

I wiped my hands on a rag and slid out from under the truck. Zan sat on a folding chair and worked on his banjo picking. The rest of the driveway was filled with some of my other car projects. It was a decent way to make a few bucks and my landlord didn't seem to mind that I took up three times the spaces as long as I kept his car tuned up and running like a champ. I also bartended here and there when I got really strapped for cash, but I'd been doing better at saving money. Being dirt poor also meant you got great financial aid. I still had no clue what I'd do when I graduated, but I had plenty of options, thanks to being, what I told Zan, "a fucking genius".

"So you two are serious?" I said.

He looked up from the banjo.

"I love her. I thought I did before, but it was just an infatuation. This is different."

I leaned against the truck and shaded my eyes from the afternoon sun. "How?"

"I used to think she was this perfect person. That everything she did was right. Now I know that she's got flaws, but I love those flaws. She's not perfect and I love her the way she is. She makes me want to be a better person, and she doesn't care about everything in my past. How could I not fall for that?"

Jesus, it was so simple for him.

I'd never told a girl I loved her. Probably because I'd never loved one. At least not in the way Zan was talking. His past was dark, yes, but it was a temporary darkness. He hadn't been born to it, hadn't been raised in it. His parents were generally decent, and his brother, however fucked up he was, loved him too. He'd had money and second chances and people who'd pulled him through the dark.

I shoved my past aside and went to help him with some of his fingering.

Katie had been ignoring me and I'd been letting her, out of respect. She probably never wanted to see me again, and I was fine with that. Not that I wouldn't have picked up the phone if she'd called me. I would have. The sex was great and I would be more than happy to let it happen again, if she wanted it to. I just wasn't into forcing girls like some guys.

I was about to answer Zan when my phone rang from my back pocket. I looked at the screen and it was an unknown number. It could have been someone calling my phone with a wrong number, but I didn't think so.

"Hello?" My greeting was met with silence and I was about to hang up when she spoke.

"Hey," Katie said after a long pause. "You said if I needed anything to call. I need a distraction. Of the physical variety."

"Mhm," I said, fully aware that Zan was sitting right in front of me and Katie would not want him knowing. "When?"

"Right now. Can I come to your place?"

"I'm fixing a friend's truck right now, but maybe in an hour?"

She sighed.

"Okay, fine. But don't tell anyone."

"You got it," I said and hung up.

"Who was that?" Zan said.

"Just a friend who wanted to look at that extra guitar I've been trying to sell. He's coming over in an hour."

"Can you finish in time? I have to get this back to Lottie so Will doesn't kill me."

"Sure thing." I got on my back and slid back under the truck, trying not to grin too much.

***

Zan left ten minutes before Katie's Mazda pulled into the lot next to my apartment. She'd never been here, but she clearly knew where it was anyway.

She was visibly upset when I opened the door at the bottom of the stairs. I was on the second floor, but the first floor apartment was vacant, so I just treated the whole space as mine.

"You okay?" I said, taking in her puffy red eyes and the fact that she hadn't made much of an effort with her appearance again.

She laughed without humor.

"I wish everyone would stop asking me that. I'm so tired of saying 'I'm fine.' I didn't come here for that."

Jesus, calm down. We signed up for a hookup, not a therapy session. "Okay. From now on I will not ask you if you're okay. Deal?"

She inhaled.

"Deal."

"Any other requests?"

She thought for a moment and stepped over the threshold until we were chest to chest.

"Yes. Don't call me babe."

"You got it," I said before I picked her up and kissed her so hard our teeth collided. I nearly broke both our necks getting us up the stairs and through my front door, but somehow I managed it.

At least this time I got my pants all the way off. She was no less frantic as she stripped me down and shoved me toward the couch. I had to toss the banjo on the floor, hoping it didn't get damaged. She straddled me and this time at least, I was prepared with a condom. She tore the package with her teeth and rolled it on, like someone who had had a lot of practice, before sliding down on me.

Neither of us spoke.

I let her take the lead this time, picking up her quick and vicious rhythm. My hands dug into her ass as she found her pleasure and then I found mine. We both panted as she climbed off of me and started getting dressed. I went to take care of the condom and when I came back she had folded my clothes and left them on the couch for me.

"So what are you escaping from this time?" I said as she pulled her shirt over her head.

"Zack sent me a bunch of stuff and wrote me a note saying he wants to talk." I put my boxers on. The tag was sticking out of the back of her shirt, so I put it back in for her, even though she flinched at the simple gesture.

"Don't do it," I said.

She turned her head to look at me, her eyes blazing and her cheeks still flushed from the sex.

"Don't tell me what to do," she snapped.

Christ, I needed to wave a white flag with this girl every time I opened my mouth. "I'm not. Just advising. It isn't a good idea."

"Well thank you so much for your concern, guy I just fucked, but I've got plenty of concern and I don't need it from you." She pulled on her boots and smoothed her hair, re-doing her ponytail. "I don't need anything from you except a physical distraction, and now that I've got it I'm going to go back to my room to watch movies with my friends and smile and be fine. Because I am."

I smiled at her. "Okay, sweetheart. You're fine."

She glared at me and put her purse over her shoulder and pulled out her keys.

"Don't patronize me."

I shook my shirt out and pulled it over my head.

"Sorry. My mistake." Upon further inspection, the banjo seemed to be unscathed, so I set it on my lap and played a little tune.

"Sooo, bye. I'll call you." She paused for just a moment with the door half-open.

I grinned at her. "Me and my dick are looking forward to it."

She glared again and shook her head before slamming the door.

Three

Katie

Saying something and doing it are two different things. I hadn't thought about Stryker much since our little tryst, but when I got back to my room Friday afternoon to find a pile of gifts and a note from Zack taped to my door, I lost it.

The note was all hearts and flowers and things he thought I wanted to hear. He was sorry, and he missed me and he loved me.

I crumpled up the note and threw it in the trash before I pulled Stryker's number from my desk drawer. I didn't even hesitate before I dialed.

The hour of waiting to go over there nearly killed me. I spent it opening Zack's presents and figuring out how much they cost him by looking them up online. At least this time he was keeping his distance. I knew I had Zan to thank for that.

I was actually a little shocked that Stryker was willing to give it a go again, but then he was a guy and I was a girl who was willing to have sex with him. No attachment, no feelings, no clingy girlfriend behavior. Most guys dreamed of that. The only thing that bothered me about our arrangement was the fact that he'd started giving me his opinion. I should probably institute a no-talking rule.

Lottie was reading when I came back from Stryker's, feeling satisfied physically, but shitty otherwise.

"Hey, where have you been? I wanted to know if you were coming to dinner." She put a bookmark in the book and set it down on her desk. *To Kill A Mockingbird*, of course.

"Just went out for a little while. I needed a breather after finding all of this," I waved my hand at the presents.

"Yeah I was going to ask, but then I figured it out. He's getting good with the grand gestures, isn't he? I guess he's had lots of practice."

"Whatever." I gathered up the stuff and shoved it under my bed.

Out of sight, out of mind.

Stryker was out of my sight, but he wasn't out of my mind.

That night Lottie went to stay with Zan and I was alone, I found a *Law and Order* marathon and put that on, but the room felt too big. Like it was going to swallow me whole. I paced and bit my nails and picked up my phone and scrolled through the numbers. I couldn't call Britt or Karina or Ashley. Speaking of them, I still had a wall full of pictures of all of us, and quite a few of me with Zack. No, I couldn't call them. Those girls who would have told me, once again, that Zack was a great guy and I should figure out how to make it work. Their grinning faces mocked me, so I turned my back on the wall.

I also couldn't call Audrey or Trish. They'd drop everything and come over and be all comforting and hover like helicopters, and that wasn't what I needed either. I was surrounded by a whole bunch of people and I'd never felt more alone.

I'd known before I picked up my phone who I was going to call. I also knew that he'd pick up.

"Hi," I said when he answered after the second ring.

"Hey. Is something wrong? I can ask you that when you call me in the middle of the night, right?" He only sounded half-awake, his voice husky.

"No, nothing's wrong, per se. I'm just here. Alone." I laughed a little. It seemed like a stupid reason to call when I said it out loud. "I'm sorry for calling you."

"Don't hang up," he said, as if he sensed that I was going to. "I wasn't asleep, if that's what you're worried about." Liar, liar, pants on fire. No, I did not need to think about Stryker's pants, or what was in them.

"Oh, good." We both breathed in unison for a moment.

"What *were* you doing?" Maybe I didn't want to know the answer. I almost heard him formulating a snarky response, but he chose the truth instead.

"Drawing."

"Drawing?" I could see that, I guess. With the tattoos and everything.

"Yeah. I'll show sometime. If you decide you want whatever this is to extend beyond merely a physical distraction."

I shook my head, even though he couldn't see me. "Right now I don't need a physical distraction. Just a verbal one."

I heard the smile in his voice. "I think I can do that."

So he started talking. About how he still didn't know what he wanted to do when he graduated, even though he'd already gotten internship offers from more than a few companies. About his favorite bands and how he felt the first time he heard The Beatles and how he'd taught himself to play most of his instruments and read music. I listened as he talked and the passion in his voice was so strong that it made me sad, and jealous that I didn't feel like that about anything.

I remembered feeling that way about things in the past, but it had been years. I missed it.

"What's your favorite song?" I said to try to distract myself from my depressing lack of passion.

"I don't have a favorite song. I have a current favorite song. It changes a lot. I have different favorite songs for different situations."

"What's your favorite song right now?"

He answered without hesitation.

"'Demons' by Imagine Dragons."

"I've never heard it," I said. I thought I'd heard Lottie mention the band once or twice, but it didn't sound like anything I would listen to.

"I'll play it for you." I heard him set the phone down and put it on speaker. "Can you hear me?"

"Yeah." Of course he had a guitar. I would have been surprised if he didn't.

"I'll be right back. Hold on." I waited and heard him crashing around getting something. "Sorry about that. Needed to find the right instrument. Haven't quite learned this one on the violin yet, so you get the boring guitar version."

"I'm fine with that." He played the violin? Now that was a shocker.

He laughed before he started strumming, and then he began to sing. His voice had a rough quality that pulled at something inside me. I found myself breathing quieter, clutching the phone to my ear and turning the volume all the way up so I could hear him better.

Since I'd never heard the original, I didn't know how his version compared, but it sounded damn good to me. I heard him put aside the guitar and pick up the phone again.

"So that's my favorite song. Sorry about those little screw ups on the second chorus. I'm still working on the arrangement."

"What screw ups?" I honestly hadn't heard any. He'd been flawless.

He laughed.

"Never mind. So how am I doing on verbal distracting?"

I didn't want to blow up his ego too much. "I'm impressed with your skills."

"If you ever want to experience more of my skills in the physical distracting department, I'd be more than happy to share them with you."

I rolled my eyes, which he couldn't see, but he probably knew I was doing it anyway. "Yeah, I bet you do. Guys always talk a big game but when the time comes to deliver, they can't."

"Don't worry, sweetheart. I can walk the walk." There was a fluttering below my waist that I tried to ignore. That lasted about five seconds.

"Come over. Right now." The words were out of my mouth before I even knew I was saying them.

He paused before he said, "No."

"No?"

"No. I'm not just some guy you can call for a fuck anytime you want. You called me for verbal distractions and you want physical ones in the same night? Sorry, sweetheart. You don't always get what you want."

I was about to say something, but the call cut off. He hung up on me. I hit redial right away. What the hell?

No answer.

I tried again.

No answer.

I texted him and got back a response a second later.

I'm going to bed. You probably should too. Get your beauty sleep. To be continued

I typed an angry response and then deleted it before typing something else.

Dot dot dot.

Stryker

It was only a matter of time before I got into bed with Katie again, and it was only a matter of time before we got caught. We were in the thick of it when Katie's door opened and I head the gasp of surprise.

As expected, Lottie gave both of us a talking to. For a tiny girl, she sure knew how to make you feel like you were even shorter. Zan didn't seem either surprised or upset, which led me to believe he'd known all along. I was an idiot to think I could put it past him. He noticed everything. I apologized and tried not to be a dick about it, but I knew that I was going to be on Lottie's shit list for a little while.

After Lottie dragged Zan down to his room for the night, Katie dragged me back to her room.

"Shit. Shit, shit, shit," she said as she tried to put her clothes back on with shaking hands. "Now she's going to hate me and Zack is going to find out. Shit, shit, shit!" She tried to get her panties on, but tripped, and I caught her.

"Here." I pushed her onto the bed and got them over her feet and pulled them up for her, following them with her jeans.

"You don't have to baby me," she said, snatching her bra from the bedpost and putting it on.

"I'm not trying to. I was just trying to help." I backed off and dressed myself. It never bothered me when Katie talked like that to me. I was pretty sure I was the only person who saw this side of her. To everyone else she was sweetness and light. I got the sarcastic side. But sarcasm was often tinged with truth. More so than niceness.

"I shouldn't have done this. I should have done what they said and taken some time alone instead of fucking you a bunch of times. I always *do* this and it never ends up working out."

"It's fine, Katie. It doesn't matter to me either way."

She looked up from adjusting the buttons on her pink shirt. I'd become immune to the amount of pink she surrounded herself with. Somehow.

"It doesn't matter?"

"No. This was never anything special. Just two people having sex." I zipped my pants and did my belt. Getting caught had totally killed my buzz, at least for a moment.

"Then what was all that about your music and singing me that song? What the hell was that?"

I shrugged. We hadn't had any more late night conversations, and I regretted that one. I'd let her get too close. I should have just come over and fucked her like she wanted and then she wouldn't be looking at me like this. All sweet and hurt. "A verbal distraction, like you said. You said you needed something to distract you. I provided it. You're welcome."

She stood up, hands on hips. "Are you fucking serious?"

"Why, what did you think this was?"

"I don't know," she snapped. "Just go. I can deal with this by myself."

"I told you that you don't always get what you want, but you asked for this. You said sex with no strings. Don't get mad at me for giving you what you asked for. If you want more, you have to tell me. I'm not a fucking mind reader." I wasn't sure if she even wanted more. I probably was just a distraction for her until someone better came along. That hurt more than I thought it would.

She opened and closed her mouth, and I could tell she wanted to scream at me and probably slap me in the face.

"Go ahead. Let me have it," I said, holding my arms out so she could get a good shot.

She swallowed and I swore I saw some moisture in her eyes. She was hurt, but she wasn't going to admit it. "Just get out of my room, Stryker."

A few weeks ago, I would have left, but I couldn't. I'd left her crying once and I was going to do it again. This damn girl had actually gotten to me.

"You don't always get what you want. So no, I'm not going to leave. Not until we sort this out."

"What do you want from me, Stryker?" She tried to push me aside, as if she was going to storm out of her own room.

"I don't want anything from you. I'm not Zack." Just saying his name made me want to hit something.

She inhaled sharply, as if I'd punched her. That shock was replaced with anger in a blink.

"Screw you." Tears dripped down her cheeks and onto her chin. I reached up to wipe them away and she didn't stop me.

"Hey. I just wanted you to know that I'm not him. And I will never be like him."

She tried to pull away, but held her chin so she couldn't.

"I. Am. Not. Zack. Got it?" Her eyes finally met mine. She sniffed and nodded.

"I know you're not him. You're . . . you're nothing like him." She gripped my wrists, but didn't pull them away from her face. "Who are you Stryker Grant?"

I said the first thing that came to my mind. "I'm a guy who wants to toss you back in bed and finish what we started."

So we did.

It was a little slower this time, a little sweeter. She let me kiss her stomach and she kissed mine. Afterward, I didn't get up right away to put my clothes on and she didn't either.

"Do you want me to stay?" She was on her stomach and I was on my back, one of her blankets covering us.

She folded her arms under her chin and turned her head toward me. "You don't have to."

"I'm not asking if I have to. I'm asking if you *want* me to."

She smiled. "As long as you don't mind sleeping in a pink bed."

"I'm confident enough in my manhood to sleep in a pink bed, thank you very much. You are talking to a guy who used to paint his fingernails." I held up my now-unpainted hands. They almost always had grease under them from working on one car project or another, and my fingers were all covered in callouses from playing various instruments.

"You did?"

"Yeah, in high school. Got pretty good at it." I also had spiked hair and wore a lot of chains, but I didn't tell her that. I wasn't proud of that phase of my life. There was no way that Katie would have fucked that guy. Plus, that guy wouldn't have been caught dead with a girl who surrounded herself with so much pink. We would have dined on opposite sides of the cafeteria and only crossed paths in homeroom. She would have called me a freak and I would have called her a mindless Barbie.

"I can always do my left hand, but I suck at my right." She held put her hand up and I met her palm with mine.

"I could do them for you, if you want. If that wouldn't be absolutely weird."

She laughed. "It's a little weird, but I'm okay with that."

We spent the rest of the night talking while I painted first her fingernails and then her toenails with pink and used a toothpick to add little white dots.

"You're good at that," she said as I blew on her toes to dry them.

"Thank you." I screwed the caps back on the polish bottles and put them on her desk as she inspected my work.

"I know you're not Zack. That was never a question. Just so you know," she said.

I crawled back under the blanket.

"Are you sure you want me to stay?" She traced the treble clef on my shoulder.

"Yes," she said, getting under the blanket with me.

Four

Katie

Stryker never asked me for a definition of our relationship status and I didn't feel the need for one. He was different. I didn't want to put him in the relationship column with all the other guys I'd dated. Not that I was or was ever going to date Stryker. He wasn't the boyfriend type. He was type-less. Not a friend, not a boyfriend. He was a guy. A guy I had sex with and who painted my toenails and let me bitch about my problems and took my sarcasm and thought I was funny.

Stryker was right; he wasn't Zack.

I was still dealing with presents and calls and notes from Zack. Surprisingly, he hadn't shown up at my door, so maybe he was finally getting the hint. Or maybe I was just being naïve. I hung out with Britt and Karina, but they just told me I should forgive Zack and let it go. Not fucking likely. But I smiled and told them I had homework to do and just ignored their texts after that. They didn't understand.

More often than not, I came home to find Lottie and at least one member of our little group deep in conversation that cut off the second I opened the door. I pretended not to notice and they started getting more stealthy about it. As November wore on, the presents piled up, taking up more and more space under my bed. By this time I had at least a couple hundred dollars' worth of fuck-up gifts, but I just kicked them further under and blasted Miranda Lambert's "Mama's Broken Heart" when I thought about them.

I was holding things mostly together, or at least giving the appearance of it, until one Friday afternoon when I came home early from class with an upset stomach–I suspected the shrimp scampi from the cafeteria–and was all set to crawl into bed and die, when I noticed there was someone standing in front of my door, waiting for me. He smiled the second he saw me. Yeah, no more, buddy. That shit doesn't work on this girl anymore.

"Hey, babe." He was freshly-showered and wearing the shirt I'd gotten him for our one month anniversary, and standing in front of my door holding a bouquet of yellow roses that still had moisture on the petals from the florist.

"What are you doing here, Zack? I don't want to talk to you." I thought he was going to keep blocking my door, but he moved aside so I could swipe my card.

"I know, I know. I brought you these. Yellow roses mean 'I'm sorry'. I looked it up." He gave me the knee-weakening smile that had found me across a crowded room at that party last summer. I looked away from it, like looking away from the sun so you didn't burn your retinas.

"I'm sorry, Zack. I don't want to talk to you." I tried to push the door open, but he stopped me.

"Please. I know you don't want to be with me, but I just miss you. I want to tell you how sorry I am. I need to make this right. Please." He held the flowers out to me and I reluctantly took them. They were beautiful. His words were soft and sincere and I saw a glimpse of the guy I'd fallen in love with. And if I was honest, a guy I was still a little in love with.

He stroked the side of my face with one finger. "Please, babe. I just want to talk to you."

I took a deep breath and his familiar smell brought back memories of the summer, of lying in his truck bed and looking at the stars as he pointed out the constellations.

I pushed the memory aside. "Fine. When?" Definitely not until I stopped feeling like I was going to puke any second. Although I wasn't sure if it was the shrimp anymore, or if it was the thought of being alone with him. Stryker's warning went through my mind. Screw him! I could handle this. One last time and then he'd leave me alone and I could start selling the crap he'd gotten me and finally burn all the pictures of the two of us. This would be the period at the end of our relationship.

"Tonight? Can we go somewhere? Just for a little drive like we used to. I need to get off campus for a little while. How about it?" He leaned into me, making it hard to think. Why did he have to smell so good?

"Okay, okay."

"Look, I have this thing I need to do, but I'll text you?"

I nodded and he let go of my door. "Sure."

"See you later, babe." His fingers brushed my shoulder and he disappeared down the hall. I opened my door and shut it, hard, leaning against it to make sure it was closed. I threw the roses on the floor.

Yellow roses my ass.

***

He didn't text me until late. Zan and Lottie were having a movie night and everyone else had plans of some sort. I was on the phone with Stryker when Zack texted me.

"I have to go," I said, sighing. He'd been playing me "Imagine", by John Lennon on his banjo.

"Where to?" I wasn't going to be able to lie to him. I passed the phone to my other hand so I could put on my jacket. We hadn't had snow yet, but it was definitely coming.

"I'm having a chat with Zack."

He paused for so long that I thought the call had dropped. Finally he spoke, and it sounded like he was gritting his teeth on every word.

"I'm not going to call you an idiot, but you will be if you go. Don't do it, Katie."

"Don't tell me what to do, Stryker."

"The only reason I'm telling you what to do right now is because you know that you shouldn't go. I *know* you know that you're going to regret it." The only thing I'd regret was not getting the last word, but I wasn't completely immune to the fact that Zack had hurt me in the past, physically, and he could again. It was a risk I'd be willing to take to have this over.

"I can hear you thinking," he said.

"Shut up." I grabbed my key card and my purse. "I'm going. I'm going to make a clean break with him, that's all. The end." The roses were already history; torn and bruised at the bottom of the trash can. I'd taken great pleasure in tearing off each individual petal. My stomach had gotten over whatever had affected me and my head was clear. I was doing this.

His voice was soft and insistent. "Don't do it, Katie. Please."

"Why do you care?"

"Because I care about you!" he yelled. "Christ, how can you not know that?" I stopped, my hand on the doorknob. He wasn't supposed to care. That wasn't part of our deal, not that we'd sat down and really talked about it, but I assumed that was implied. I shouldn't have let him sing to me, or talk so much. I should have made a "just sex" line.

I didn't have time to think about this.

"Then if you care about me, you have to let me make my own decisions. I'll call you after and you can gloat all you want when you're right, but I'm going. End of story. Bye."

I shut my phone off and walked down to meet Zack in the lobby.

***

Stryker was right. I realized it the moment I got into Zack's truck and he started driving. His energy was different from the afternoon. I didn't know if he'd been drinking, but I'd seen this side of him before. This was the Zack Parker that scared me. He turned off the main road and into a deserted parking lot.

He hit the automatic locks on the door and his smile dropped.

"So I heard you're seeing that freak who tried to beat me up at the Kappa party." All my confidence and bravado deserted me.

The key to dealing with this Zack was to speak calmly and slowly until I could get out of the truck. He wasn't going to let me go until he'd had his say.

"I'm not seeing him Zack. We're just friends." Stryker and I weren't even friends. I still wasn't sure if I even liked him or not. But Zack wouldn't understand that, so I had to simplify it.

He smashed his hands on the steering wheel.

"Don't fucking lie to me!"

The parking lot was dark; there was no one around. I just had to let him have his say and then he'd let me go.

I took a breath to steady myself and try to calm down. My enemy right now was panic. "I'm sorry, I'm not lying to you. I'm not seeing him. I'm not with anyone. Look, you said you wanted to clear the air, so let's do that."

"Oh no, you're not getting off that easy." He turned slowly and the streetlight I saw the gleam in his eyes. The heart-melting smile was gone, replaced by something I'd never seen before.

The next moment my head hit the dashboard and I screamed.

The moments after that were a blur of yelling and pain and desperation followed by quiet as he drove me back to campus. I didn't even realize he'd shoved me out of the truck and onto the ground until I felt the cold pavement under my fingers.

I couldn't speak. I couldn't think. Tires squealed and then I was left in silence. My head was too heavy to lift, so I lay there with my cheek mashed against the ground, doing my best to just keep breathing.

"Katie?" A voice called my name and I tried to move, but it hurt too much. "Oh my God, Katie!"

Will crouched down in front of me and touched my shoulder.

"Who did this to you?" I still couldn't answer. "It's okay, I'll get you out of here. Come on." He took my arm and put it over his shoulder, then lifted me into his arms. I wanted to cry out, but my vocal chords wouldn't work right.

"It's okay, we're almost there. Just hold on." I bounced in his arms as he walked as fast as he could to the elevator and then to my room. He put me in bed and got on his phone.

"Audrey's on her way, okay?" He crouched in front of me and touched my head. "You don't have to talk if you don't want to, okay? How many fingers am I holding up?" He held up four.

"Four," I said, my voice rough, as if I was recovering from strep throat. I cleared it and looked down at my shaking hands. I could feel blood on my face.

"Good. I should probably know what to do, but I honestly don't. I should call 9-1-1, shouldn't I?" He seemed to be talking to himself more than me.

"Don't. Please don't." I didn't want to go the hospital. I just wanted to crawl into bed and go to sleep.

"I have to. You need to see a doctor."

"No!" My voice didn't have much power, but I got my point across. He nodded.

"Okay, okay. Let's just wait for Audrey, okay?"

***

The next few hours were chaotic. I didn't get my wish of not going to the hospital, and I didn't get my wish of not pressing charges on Zack. My parents came and Mom got hysterical all over me.

Everyone from my dad to Lottie to Zan to Stryker blamed themselves. If the blame could be baked into bread, we could have fed the world.

It took every ounce of restraint I had to not scream at all of them and say that it wasn't their fault. I was the one who had made the decision to see Zack when I knew I shouldn't have.

My parents fought on the way home from the hospital the next morning. I didn't want to go, but I didn't have a choice. Coming home used to feel comforting, like I was finally in a safe place, but all I wanted when we pulled into the driveway was to go back to school and watch *Law and Order* and eat ice cream with the girls.

Mom fussed over me, getting me settled on the couch with a bowl of soup, as if I was five again and had a cold. It took Dad yelling at her before she would move even a few feet away from me. I wished Kayla, my sister, was home, but she was off saving starving orphans in Africa and only had contact with us via an email once a week. She was Mom and Dad's golden child and I was the baby who couldn't get anything right.

"Gina, let her be." Dad always found a way to get Mom to chill out. Eventually. It was going to take a lot of effort on his part this time, though. When it came to Mom, there was only one person who knew how to stop her from pushing the panic button and that was Dad. They were perfectly suited for one another, as weird as that was.

They took their fight to the kitchen and I stole a moment to call Lottie and give her an update, but she wasn't the only one I needed to talk to. I shifted on the couch, the movement giving me a twinge of pain. The nurses said I was lucky that I didn't have any internal bleeding. Yeah, lucky was the right word. Fucking stupid was more accurate.

I needed to talk to Stryker, and not just to tell him he was right. I just . . . I needed to talk to him.

"Hey, are you okay?" Stryker said after Lottie handed him the phone. I heard him walking and then a door closed.

"You're not supposed to ask me that," I said.

"Katie."

"You were right. Is that what you wanted to hear?" I curled my feet up under the blanket.

"I didn't want to be right like this. I *never* wanted this to happen to you. If he wasn't in jail I would have killed him myself. Or at least maimed him so he would have to crawl through the rest of his life. I still could. I've beat the shit out of more than one asshole in my life, although I think Zack deserves his own category."

"You don't have to do that."

"Do what?"

"Be all mad at him for me. Be mad at me for being an idiot."

He sighed heavily. "I'm not mad at you, Katie."

I heard Mom's voice coming back from the kitchen. Probably bringing me a plate of cookies or something.

"Look, I have to go, but I'm coming back on Monday. Bye," I whispered before I shoved my phone under the blanket.

"Who were you talking to?" Yes, it was a plate of cookies, but store bought. She hadn't had time to make her traditional crisis oatmeal cookies. She held the plate out to me, but I shook my head.

"Lottie. She wanted to know when I was coming back."

Mom pursed her lips and sat down on the edge of the couch.

"Maybe you shouldn't go back for a while."

"Gina," Dad snapped from the kitchen. "Let her be."

Mom glared at him. "Don't tell me what to do, Glenn." Didn't that sound familiar?

I put my hand on my head. Where the hell was that pain medication? "Please, can you just leave me alone? I'm tired."

Mom started to protest, but when I closed my eyes, she sighed and got up.

"Let me know if you need anything, okay baby?" she said, kissing the un-scratched part of my forehead.

"I will. Thanks, Mom." I watched as she went back into the kitchen and I scrunched back down on the couch.

"It's okay," I heard Dad say.

She sighed. "I know, I'm just so worried."

"I know, Gina, but she's strong. Like you." I could hear him smiling and I could imagine her smiling back. A second later I heard him humming and the shuffling of feet as they danced in the kitchen and mom laughed softly.

***

By Sunday night I was so ready to get back to school I almost stole my mother's car to drive back myself. She worked the night shift managing the bakery at a grocery store, so Dad drove me back early Monday morning before he had to work.

"Are you sure you're going to be okay?"

"Yeah, Dad. I'll be fine." I barely put any effort into saying it.

"You know you can talk to me about anything, right Katiebug?" I cringed at the nickname.

"Yeah, Dad. I know." Been there, said that. All he and Mom had done was talk at me. Not to me. They'd lectured me, even though they said they weren't going to do that. They were parents and they had to do their thing. The problem was that everything they said I'd said to myself at least a hundred times. They also got me appointments with a therapist back at school and there was no way I was getting out of that because they were going to call and check after every session.

Mom also couldn't hide that she was devastated about Zack. He'd charmed her, and that was going to be a hard habit to break. She wouldn't shut up about how every time he brought me flowers before a date, or chocolates, he'd bring her a little something. She thought it was sweet. I saw it for what it was. Buttering her up so she wouldn't mind when he brought me home late, or decided to spend the night. At the time I hadn't cared.

Dad gave me a huge hug when he dropped me off, being careful not to hold me too tight. He had to bend down pretty far.

"Call me tonight, Katiebug. I love you."

"Love you too, Dad."

I glanced up at the dorm and realized I didn't want to go in. Just moments ago, I'd been so eager to get back, but now that I was here, I wanted to be anywhere else.

A few people walked by me on their way to and from breakfast or class. Some of them were laughing, and all of them looked so free. Careless and young.

I felt old and bitter. God, what had happened to me? Just a few months ago, all I'd been thinking about was how great college would be, how much fun I'd have and how many parties I'd go to. Now it all seemed . . . pointless. A few of them glanced at my face, which was still splotched with bruises that I hadn't bothered to use makeup on.

Turning from the building, I got my keys out of my purse and headed for my car. I was still stiff and my face was anything but pretty, but he wouldn't care. I needed to see him.

I didn't even know if he would be home, but his current car project was parked in the driveway. I walked up the porch and banged on the downstairs door. He shared the entrance with the tenant on the first floor, but I'd never seen or heard anyone coming or going.

It took two tries before the door opened.

"You're back." He was just pulling a shirt over his head, so I must have woken him up. His hair was all over the place and it made me think about sex.

"I didn't mean to wake you up. I just wanted to see you."

"Come in." He waved me in and we walked up the stairs as he wiped his eyes and yawned.

"Late night?"

He glanced over his shoulder at me. "Something like that." The way he said it made me uneasy, and I didn't know why.

"How are you feeling?" he said as he opened his front door. I shrugged as an answer.

"My parents are making me see a therapist," I said.

"I figured," he said as he shut the door behind me. I'd been here before, but I hadn't really been paying attention to the room at the time.

The space was wide and open, almost like a loft. Only furniture separated the living room from the kitchen and dining area. Two doors at the other end of the room were his bedroom and bathroom. Stryker had a sparse style when it came to furniture, except for the fact that there were musical instruments and books and other crap piled everywhere. Drum kit, standing bass, a ukulele on the coffee table. There were also a lot of empty cans and bottles and trash around. Like he'd had a party.

He rubbed his head, messing his hair even further. "I wasn't expecting you, or I would have cleaned up. I had a little session last night and haven't had a chance to recover."

"Session?"

"Music. I had some friends over and we played for a while. I had to get my mind off things."

He went to the kitchen and started pulling things out of the cabinet.

"Coffee? I think I've got some cereal here somewhere, too." He held a cup up to illustrate.

"You don't have to do that. Feed me and take care of me and everything. I just came to say that you were right and I don't think we should see each other anymore. At least not like this. I'll still have sex with you, but the talking and the soul-sharing and all that? I can't do it anymore. I've got friends and a new therapist for that."

He paused, the cup in his hand.

"Is that really what you want, Katie?"

I hovered in the doorway. I couldn't do this if I came all the way in and sat on the couch. I knew I wouldn't want to get up again. "Why does it matter what I want? I'm only using you."

"If I really believed that, I wouldn't be making you coffee right now when I'm horribly hung over." He took a box of Cinnamon Toast Crunch down from a cabinet and grabbed two bowls. I almost laughed at the silliness of this tatted-up, pierced guy eating Cinnamon Toast Crunch.

"You need to get your head on straight, sweetheart. I get that. You need some time. I get that, too. I'm more than willing to have sex with you, no strings, if that's what you want."

"Okay."

"Fine." He poured cereal into both bowls and I unstuck my feet from the floor and went to the fridge to get the milk.

Five

Stryker

Katie and I ate cereal and drank our coffee in almost total silence. I should have been pissed at her for not telling me she was coming over so I could have cleaned, but then I realized she wasn't my girlfriend. I didn't have to impress her so I stopped caring. Almost.

She looked like shit, if I was being brutally honest. Her face was puffy and patterned with bluish marks and still-red scratches. She also hadn't washed her hair and her nail polish was chipping. The girl who sat at my table and stared blankly at the wall was not the girl I'd seen in the pink dress that night at the party. This girl had "damaged goods" written all over her.

"Thanks for breakfast," she said, putting her bowl and cup in the sink. "I have to get back so Lottie and everyone can fuss over me and make sure I'm not going to slit my wrists like in some tragic TV drama."

"Slitting your wrists really isn't an effective way to kill yourself. Too many things can go wrong. You're better off shooting yourself or taking cyanide. Or being hit by a train," I said, draining my coffee cup. It was going to take more than one cup to get me back in fighting shape again. I massaged my pounding forehead with one hand, wishing I had listened to my intuition last night.

She froze and stared at me for a moment.

"I wasn't asking for tips, but thanks. I'll keep that in mind. How the hell do you know that?" she said.

I joined her at the sink with my dishes.

"Morbid curiosity," I said turning on the water and grabbing a sponge. Ouch, even that hurt.

"Have you ever . . . "

"Obviously not, but that doesn't mean I haven't tried. When I was seven I found a knife and tried to stab myself. Still have the scar." I put the sponge down and lifted up my shirt, pointing to the thin white line on my stomach that marked my first, and least-successful, attempt. There had been others, but Trish had always thwarted those.

She looked anywhere but at the scar.

I stepped closer to her and she backed up. "Does it scare you?"

"No."

"Then why won't you look at it?"

"Because I don't want to." She pushed me away and rushed to the door. "I told you. Sex only. None of that other stuff. I'll call you."

With that, she yanked the door open and rushed down the stairs. I really knew how to clear a room.

***

Katie didn't call me for "just sex" for a week. In that time I didn't see her at all. I only had secondary information about how she was from Zan and Trish. I also got a lecture of epic proportions from Trish about respecting women. It was one of her more-impassioned speeches. I always thought she would make a good politician or leader of some sort of political group, but she thought all those people were self-righteous losers. I told her to look in the mirror and then we ended up fighting until one of us stormed out. We would meet up later and things would be normal again.

When I did finally see Katie, she looked marginally better. Her hair was clean and pulled back, and her pinks all matched again. We met at my place, which I had since picked up a little.

She attacked my mouth and my body with more ferocity than the first time, if that was possible. The sex was quick and angry and when it was over we were both panting. She'd kept her eyes closed nearly the entire time.

"Why the fuck do you wear so much pink?" I said as she pulled her pink underwear off the lamp where I'd tossed it.

"Why do you care? I told you, just sex. No chitchat." She covered my mouth and I licked her palm.

"Ugh!" She pulled her hand away and wiped it on the couch.

"You'll take my dick inside you and my tongue down your throat, but some of my spit on your hand grosses you out?"

"Stop asking so many fucking questions!" She fastened her bra and grabbed the rest of her clothes as she headed for the bathroom.

"Crazy girl," I muttered.

She came back fully-dressed with her hair smoothed.

"Look, I don't need a boyfriend. I don't need a friend. I just need someone to fuck me. That's you."

I have her a thumbs up. "I'm your fuck guy. Got it."

"Good." She reached for her purse but in her hurry, it upended and everything went flying. "Shit," she said, scrambling to get her stuff. "Everything is just so screwed up."

I got up and tried to help her, but she put her hands out to stop me. "Don't touch my stuff."

"Jesus Christ, Katie. I'm doing what a stranger would do if you were in a public place and this happened."

I crouched next to her and waited patiently until she looked at me. She chucked some makeup into the bag and I saw a tear drop into the bag along with it.

"I'm such a bitch to you. Why are you so nice to me?"

"I could be a douche if you want. I have a pretty good track record of douchery." I also had a list of witnesses that would swear to it under oath.

She giggled as another tear fell.

"Get your shit together and get the fuck out of my apartment," I said, standing up and kicking her wallet out of my way. "I don't want all that shit on my floor."

She looked up in shock and then I smiled.

"See? Now get your pink ass out of here."

She shoved the rest of her stuff away and hurried to get out the door.

"I'll call you. Asshole," she added at the end.

I laughed after she shut the door and I swore I heard her laughing as she jogged down the stairs.

Katie

After much begging, Lottie finally agreed to my makeover idea. I was looking forward to it until Trish started grilling me about Stryker.

I didn't know how much of what we were doing she knew, but from the way Lottie and Audrey talked, they'd put him in my 'boyfriend' box already. I didn't tell them it wasn't like that because, to be honest, I didn't want them to think less of me. They were both so sweet and innocent when it came to that. I couldn't imagine Lottie ever having a strictly physical relationship and Audrey had been engaged for Christ's sake. Commitment wasn't one of her problems.

They'd been treating me with delicacy ever since the whole Zack thing. If I thought they talked about me behind my back before, that was nothing compared to after, especially when I was always going over to Stryker's.

So I settled on the 'it's complicated' box and let them think what they wanted. They always thought the best of me, which was part of the problem. I hated that they saw the best in me, expected the best, because inevitably I would disappoint them. It always happened.

I was having trouble sleeping, and kept waking Lottie up from nightmares about Zack. I had a voicemail from his mother saying how sorry she was for everything. I wanted to delete it, but I couldn't. It wasn't really her fault her son was an abusive, psychotic d-bag.

Stryker honored my request that our relationship be 'just sex.' I would text him or call him, we'd meet somewhere, fuck and then one of us would leave. Sometimes we wouldn't say a word. I liked it better that way. No talking, no music, no soul-sharing. The one thing I wished I could get him to stop doing was look at me. Those damn green eyes had this way of searing into me like a searchlight. I never felt more naked than when he was looking directly at me.

The therapist, Dr. Sandrich, turned out to be a pretty decent guy. He didn't push me to talk about anything I didn't want to, so I was free to make things up and pretend I was talking about my feelings. He knew, but he just listened and after my hour was over he shook my hand and let me go. I was always waiting for him to call me on my bullshit, but he never did.

I had to go to court to talk about what Zack did to me. It was humiliating and traumatic and all the worse because my parents were there and they both cried and all I wanted was for the courthouse to catch fire and destroy us all. The only good part was seeing Zack in handcuffs. Of course, his stepfather had bailed him out so he was free from jail for now, but on a tight leash, and he'd been kicked out of school. I took comfort in the hour of driving that separated us now.

One way or another, Zack and I were done, period. I was moving forward, or at least taking one step forward for every two steps back, until I saw that I had a missed call from Lottie after my anthropology class one afternoon. I'd started getting involved in my classes again, and I'd come to find I actually enjoyed most of them. There was something comforting about sitting in a lecture hall, listening to someone else speak, taking notes, letting the information wash over you. I didn't have to think about anything else. Just listen.

"Hey, what's up?" It wasn't like her to call me in the middle of the day for something silly. She usually just texted me for stuff like that.

"Hey, I just wanted to let you know what's going on. Zack called Zan and he's drunk and he's in a park somewhere and Zan called the police so Zack is getting arrested. Again." I stopped walking, causing a pileup on the sidewalk that got me nasty looks and more than a few curse words thrown at me.

"What?"

"Yeah, I debated about calling you, but I didn't want you to be out of the loop. We're going back to the dorm now. Where are you?" I heard Zan and Will talking in the background. Arguing, it sounded like.

"I just left anthro. I'll be there in five," I said, picking up my pace. That guy just didn't know when to say when, the fucker. Maybe this time they'd put him in jail and he'd stay there, where he belonged. The Zack I knew, the one who pointed out the constellations and made me all knee-watery wasn't real. I'd probably known that all along, but it took him punching me in the face for me to really see it, once and for all.

No wonder my parents thought I needed therapy.

Lottie hug-attacked me the second I opened the door to our room, nearly knocking the wind out of me.

"Are you okay? I know you're probably not and that's a stupid question to ask, but I have to ask because I care about you and I'm your friend." I patted her back and she let me go.

"I'm fine," I said in a voice that didn't sound like mine. In reality, I didn't really care. He could rot in jail for the rest of his natural life. I didn't know why they'd involved me, honestly. I was trying to move on, and this wasn't helping. I almost said something to Lottie, but she looked so concerned that I swallowed my bitter words.

She kept rubbing my shoulder and sat down with me on my bed. Will was furiously texting Audrey and Zan was staring at me with eyes that burned almost as intensely as Stryker's. They were two of a kind. They saw what you tried to hide, but at least they kept their mouths shut about it. Most of the time.

"I think we need to go out," Lottie announced, standing up. We all looked at her as if she'd lost her damn mind, me included. A second ago, she'd been whispering soothing things like I was going to have a mental breakdown or something.

"Now?" Will said, his fingers still flying. "You really think now is a good time?"

"Well, not *right* now. Tonight. If we all sit around here thinking about this we're going to go crazy. Am I right?" Zan put his hand on her shoulder and kissed her cheek. How was it that he and Zack shared so much DNA, but they'd turned out two completely different people? The more I lived, the more I decided life didn't make any sense.

"I think it's a good idea. You in, Will?" Zan said, putting his arm around Lottie.

Will nodded, not looking up from his phone. "Just let me ask Aud."

"And we can bring Simon. He's been dying to show off his new boyfriend. And we can have Trish and Stryker." Lottie looked at me when she said his name, and emphasized both syllables. Not this again.

He was the last person I wanted to see right now, but I shut my mouth and let them chatter away. Maybe it could be good. Going out in a group. Normal. I could be normal. Or at least pretend. Just because we were going out in a group and there would be talking, didn't mean our relationship would change from our current "just sex" arrangement. No, we would put on a show for our friends and then go back to the way it had been.

"Sounds great," I said with a smile that felt almost real. I waited until after Lottie told me was coming and then escaped to the bathroom to call him.

"Hey. I'm not calling you for sex. I just want to set some ground rules for this group thing," I said before he could get a word in.

"Hello to you, too. If you're going to ask me to be a douchebag in front of my friends, the answer is no."

I took a breath, hoping he didn't take it the wrong way. "I wasn't going to ask that, actually. I was going to ask if we could put that on hold for tonight. You can be nice to me in front of everyone. I don't want them to know that we're just having sex, even if that's what we're doing."

"Why not?"

"Because . . . "

"Because you don't want them to think less of you. I get it, Katie. Jesus, you drive a hard bargain. What if I wasn't so compliant to your wishes? I mean, you say, 'Jump,' and I ask how high, and then you say, 'Stand still,' and I stand still. Not that I don't get anything out of it, but damn."

"Then why do you do it?"

"I'm still figuring that out. Can't the sex be enough of a reason right now?"

"Sure. Fine. Just don't think this is an invitation to change our current arrangement. I'm fine with it."

He paused for a long time before he said, "Me too."

The door to the bathroom opened and I stopped talking.

"Katie?" Lottie's voice echoed off the tile floor.

"Yeah?" I said, hoping Stryker would get the hint. I could hear him listening intently.

"You okay? Are you talking to someone?"

"My mom just called. I was just filling her in. She's freaking out."

He laughed a little and I had to fight the urge to shush him. "Oh, so I'm your mother now, am I? I can handle being a douche, but that's a stretch, even for me."

"Shut up," I hissed at him and he laughed again.

"What?" Lottie said.

"Nothing. Bye, *Mom*. I'll call you later."

"Bye, sweetheart. Make sure to do your homework and eat all your vegetables," Stryker said in a falsetto that sounded scarily like my mother. I rolled my eyes and hung up on him.

***

Lottie let me do her up for our little evening out, which gave me a distraction from thinking about everything I didn't want to think about. That didn't mean that I could completely stop, because everyone else was talking about it.

"I hope they put him in jail for the rest of his life. That's where he belongs," Trish said as I braided Lottie's hair back from her face.

"Trish, maybe we shouldn't be talking about this," Audrey said, glancing at me. "How are you doing?"

"I'm fine," I said with a smile. The guys were all down in Will's room playing *Minecraft* and the girls were in ours "getting pretty" as Simon said. He was practically gleeful about inviting his new boyfriend on our 'group hang' as he called it. I just hoped Stryker would play his part. I was just pinning one of the braids to Lottie's head when my phone buzzed with a picture message from Stryker. I hesitated a second before I clicked on it.

He was standing in his kitchen, wearing a frilly apron and holding a spatula, one arm extended out so he could take the picture.

A mother's work is never done.

I snorted with suppressed laughter. I messaged him back asking where he'd gotten the apron and set my phone back on Lottie's desk.

"What's that?" Lottie said as I resumed doing her hair. "What's so funny?"

"Nothing," I said in what I hoped was a convincing voice.

"I'll guess it begins with a Stryk and ends with an er," Trish said, doing the patented Grant eyebrow raise.

"It's nothing. Just let it go." All the ladies in the room shared a collective look at my expense.

"Whatever. Just whatever." I finished another braid and pulled the rest of Lottie's hair into a low, loose bun and secured it with an elastic band and some pins.

"There. You're perfect," I said, tapping Lottie on the shoulder to tell her she could get up. She did and stood right in front of me.

"He's a good guy. You deserve a good guy who makes you laugh." She grinned and went to admire her hair in the mirror with Trish and Audrey.

I just nodded. He was a good guy, but I didn't deserve him at all.

***

"Okay, you two need to stop taking up all the cute. Leave some for the rest of us," Trish said as Brady and Simon argued about what kind of pasta they were going to share at the restaurant. Brady was shorter than Simon, but just as adorable with blond-tipped hair and a preppy fashion sense. They held hands, swinging them as they walked, and I couldn't help but smile. I was still laughing to myself about Stryker's little picture message. Already this 'group hang' was turning out much different than I expected.

When Will had suggested the place I hadn't objected, but being in the same restaurant I'd once been to on a date with Zack turned out to be a not so great idea the minute I walked in, and then my smile about Brady and Simon froze on my face. Shit. I'd been doing so well.

Stryker's hand rested lightly on my back as we went inside. "I hope I'm supposed to ask you if you're okay tonight, because I'm going to. Are you okay?"

"Not really. But keep that to yourself. Please." I looked over my shoulder at him and met his eyes. He toyed with his lip ring and that made me think about kissing him.

"Sure thing."

We pushed three small tables together to get all of us in. Simon wouldn't settle for us being in separate booths. The waitress turned out to be a girl from my anthro class, but I couldn't remember her name until I read "Carrie" on her nametag.

It was complete chaos with everyone talking at once and she looked overwhelmed. Of course they had all engineered it so I had Stryker on one side and Lottie on the other. Trish was right across from me and looking grumpy about the fact that she was the only one who didn't have "someone"'. Stryker's foot kept bumping against mine under the table and I knew it was deliberate, so I banged my foot against his, only harder. I had heels on, so if worse came to worse, I could always stab him with one.

It was completely different from the last time I'd been here with Zack, and I tried to relax and let myself sink into the moment.

"Be nice," he muttered at me when Carrie brought our drinks. He ordered a beer since he was the only one who was old enough. "Want a sip?"

"No, thanks."

"So I think we should toast," Simon said, standing up. Brady tried to get him to sit down since the entire place was staring at us, but he wouldn't.

"I think we need to toast to friends and good people and love and . . . anyone?"

"New beginnings," Will said as he stared at Audrey.

"To Rumi and escapes and Pop Tarts," Lottie said, winking at Zan.

"Okay, sure. Anyone else?" Simon said, looking around.

"To drugs and sex and rock and roll," Stryker said, raising his beer mug.

"I second that," Trish said, raising her glass. Stryker put his other hand on my leg and squeezed.

"To assholes getting put back in prison where they belong," I said. Everyone cheered at that and we drank.

I was pretty sure the restaurant was regretting letting us sit down because we were the loudest group in the place. Volume control wasn't one of our strong suits as a group.

I hated to admit it, but Lottie had the right idea. It was impossible not to smile and laugh when Simon started doing impressions of Will and then Lottie and when Stryker kept making silly little comments that only I could hear.

"Will is going to touch Audrey's hair in three, two, one. See?" He was right. Audrey blushed as Will made sure her hair didn't fall into her pizza.

"And Simon is going to kiss Brady in three, two, one." There was a collective 'aw,' when they did kiss. Even Trish had a wistful look on her face.

"How are you doing?" It was a different question than asking if I was okay.

"I can truthfully say that I'm enjoying myself," I said.

"I can tell."

"Don't." He'd been walking his hands up and down my leg. Not in a sexual way, but in a way that told me he was aware that I was sitting next to him and he wanted me to be aware of it, too. I'd told him to not be an asshole, but that didn't mean I wanted him to treat me like . . . like we were dating.

"I have no idea what you're talking about," he said, marching his fingers as if they were feet.

"Stryker, stop it." I made sure I wasn't looking at him when I said it so no one would get any ideas.

"Fine." He removed his hand and started drumming it on the table with the rhythm of the song that played over the speakers hidden behind tacky plastic plants that were supposed to look like olive vines. "Then I'll tell you that it's not just the sex."

"What?" Everyone else was distracted by Will and Lottie team-telling a story about how they were when they were growing up and she knew he'd fallen out of a tree. That twindar really freaked me out.

I looked up to meet his eyes. He'd been waiting for that.

"It might not just about the sex, although that is nice." I stared at him and then my eyes moved down to his lips. The memory of kissing him that first time and feeling his lip ring press into my mouth was fresh and delicious.

I'd been afraid of that. The moment this crossed into boyfriend/girlfriend territory, I was going to bail.

"It has to be this way, Stryker," I said, touching his lip ring and remembering how nice it felt to talk to him and listen to him sing.

"But we can talk. And I can sing to you. And paint your nails, right?" he said.

I nodded. I'd miss those things too much.

"Good."

Six

Stryker

After the group thing Katie relaxed her rules a little bit. I didn't mind her constant rule changes because they never stuck for that long. She got mad when I asked her to write them down one afternoon while I was working on Zan's present for Lottie, a 1970 red Datsun we'd bought for next to nothing.

"I just think we need to set some rules when it comes to sex. What is so crazy about that?" I lifted my head from the engine I was cajoling into both running and passing a state inspection. Katie'd been sitting in the driver's seat with the door open, wrapped up in a blanket. November was turning out to be especially harsh in Maine this year.

"Because it's just weird. It makes it into something that it's not," she said.

"Then what is it? To you?"

I took my gloves off and blew on my hands.

She shook her head, as if she'd changed her mind. "I don't know. I was just saying."

"No, I knew what you were doing. I find it interesting, Katie, that you can have casual sex, but you can't really talk about it."

"Whatever. Forget about it."

"Like, for example what would you say if I wanted to go down on you? Or kiss your stomach? Or even just take it slow? Not that angry revenge sex isn't great." I'd tried all of those things, but she'd always stopped me.

"Angry revenge sex?"

I sighed and closed the hood of the car. I wasn't going to get anything more done today until we got everything out in the open.

"You have sex with me because you're hurt and you're mad and you're looking for a distraction. You even said so yourself. A physical distraction."

"And your point is?"

I leaned on the door and stared down at her.

"My point is that just because you say you're going to have casual sex with no attachment, that doesn't mean it's going to happen."

She pulled the blanket tighter. "So, what? You want to be my boyfriend now?"

I shook my head. I'd really walked into that one. "I don't know what I'm saying. Forget it. You hungry?" I grabbed my tools and started to walk back upstairs, but she stopped me.

"I can't do non-angry revenge sex. I can't. I can barely do . . . whatever this is we're doing. Not after everything with Zack."

I put the tools down and swung to face her.

"See? That's your problem. I've told you. I'm not him. Stop treating me like I'm going to beat the shit out of you and leave you in a fucking parking lot. I've never hit a woman. Not even Trish. You think that everyone is going to screw you over. It's a bad way to live, sweetheart."

She glared at me. "Aren't you? Aren't you going to screw me over?"

"I might. But that doesn't mean you shouldn't let me in. You have some really good people in your life and all you do is wait for them to hurt you instead of enjoying it. God, I don't know how you got started on this fucked-up path, but I wish I could kick his teeth in."

"What about you? You show me your suicide scar and tell me that you've tried more than once? What the fuck is up with that?" We were both in each other's faces.

"Do you really want to know? Because I thought we weren't doing that heart-to-heart shit. If you want to know, I'll tell you."

She jutted her chin out and met my eyes.

"I want to know."

"Fine, but let's go inside. I'll make you some coffee." Her teeth had started to chatter.

She nodded and let me lead her inside. I got her on the couch with another blanket and a hot mug of coffee in her hands before I sat down next to her.

"So, where do you want me to start?" She swirled the cup and stared into it.

"What were you like as a kid?"

We were starting at the beginning. They said it was a good place to start, but not for me.

"My parents were both drug addicts. Meth heads. They had a lab in our basement. Trish and I used to play with some of the equipment. It's a miracle the place didn't blow up. There were always people coming and going and I remember not eating a whole lot. Dad split pretty early on and Mom was high or drunk or both most of the time."

I'd been prepared for her sharp intake of breath.

"Then she got busted so we bounced around for a few years. First to our relatives, no matter how distant they were. We switched schools and states. I had to teach Trish how to read and do math because of how many times we moved." One of the worst places had been with our Mom's brother and his wife. He took a liking to Trish and I had to beat him off her one night with a baseball bat. I also tried to kill myself for the second time in that house by swallowing a bunch of aspirin, but it made me sick and I'd just ended up in the hospital and we'd gotten moved to a new home afterward. I didn't give Katie those details. She didn't need them and I didn't want to give them to her.

"Then, when we'd exhausted all our relatives' hospitality, we got put in the foster care system. After that it was just a merry-go-round of houses. Some were good, some were bad, but we left all of them eventually. Our last one was especially bad, so when I turned eighteen I got custody of Trish. Despite moving so much I had really good grades, so I got into college and even though I didn't look responsible, they let me have her. We had a social worker that went up to bat for us. Trish finished up high school and then enrolled here. We fought like cats and dogs, so as soon as she could, she moved out. Fast forward a few years and here we are."

Katie sipped her coffee through my story and put the empty mug down when I finished.

"I'm sorry you had to go through that, Stryker. I had no idea." No, but she'd had her own crosses to bear.

"Everybody goes through hard shit in their lives. It's how you deal with it that determines what kind of person you are."

She picked at the edge of the blanket. "What kind of person am I?"

"You're a girl who's been trying to be something she's not for her whole life and it finally stopped working for you. Now you've got a chance to be who you really are."

"Who is that?" She brought her knees up under the blanket and put her chin on them.

"A girl who does makeovers for her friends and puts on a brave face for them, and cares so much about people that she can't even see it." There was a hell of a lot more than that, but that was enough for now.

"Is that what you see when you look at me?"

"I also see a lot of pink," I said, leaning back and putting my arm around her, hoping she wouldn't bite my hand off for doing so.

"I really like pink." She brought her head up and moved her face closer to mine.

"I know," I said, moving until our faces were only a millimeter apart.

She pressed her lips together and shook her head back and forth.

"I should go. Thanks for . . . all that."

"You're going to leave me after I unburdened my soul?" I said, clutching my chest. "I'm hurt, Katie."

She rolled her eyes and stood up, handing me back my blanket.

"You'll get over it. See you later."

I got up and caught her before she got all the way out the door.

"I don't know if this fits into the "things we're not supposed to do" category, but do you want to come over tonight? I'm having some friends over to have a session and I would like to invite you to come. As a friend." I didn't stop to think about the consequences of inviting her to hang out with my friends. If I did, I probably wouldn't have invited her. Too late now.

She toyed with her keys. "A friend? Is that what I am?"

"I told you, you can be whatever you want to be." She leaned in the doorway.

"I guess I can be your friend. If you want me to be."

"I want you to be what you want. You have enough expectations already."

She looked down with a little smile.

"You're right. And yes. I will be your friend. At least for tonight. What time?"

"Around six?"

"Sure." I waited for her to move, but she seemed conflicted.

"We can still screw each other if we're friends, right?" she said.

She leaned closer and touched my belt.

"I have absolutely no problem with that definition." I moved closer to her and I was about to yank her in for a kiss when she took a step back.

"No. I shouldn't. I have to go. I'll see you tonight."

She skipped down the stairs and I was left with a hard dick and no one but myself to take care of it for me.

Katie

"What are you doing?" Lottie said as I went through my closet, trying to find something that would work for a music "session." I'd gone to plenty of concerts, but this was totally different. I didn't think my pink glittery cowboy hat would be welcome. Or maybe it would. I had no idea, which was what made it so hard to choose.

"Looking for something to wear. Stryker invited me to one of his music things and I don't know what to wear. Ugh, I have nothing!" I threw everything off my bed onto the floor.

"You have more shirts than I have books," Lottie said, getting up to help. "And that's saying something."

"I just don't want to look like an idiot."

"You could never, ever look like that. Well, maybe if you wore this," she said, holding up a pink shirt that said STAY CALM AND WAIT FOR PRINCE CHARMING. It had actually been a sarcastic gift from Kayla. I'd forgotten that I even had it.

"You're the makeover queen. Look at what you did with the red dress."

"I know, but it's one of those things that I can do for other people, but not for myself." Lottie started folding shirts and putting them back on my bed.

"You're overthinking, which means you care. A lot. Stryker isn't going to care what you wear. I've seen the way he looks at you."

"It's not him I'm worried about." It was his friends. I knew pretty much nothing about them, except a few of their names and that they played instruments. Other than that, I was shooting blind.

"How about this?" She found a soft t-shirt with little pink flowers and a grabbed one of my pink cardigans.

"Super cute," she said, holding it up to me.

"Hey, you're stealing my makeover thunder," I said, pulling the shirt I'd been wearing over my head and putting on the t-shirt.

"Here, take these," she said, handing me one of the only pairs of earrings she owned. "Will had a weird moment and bought me these last Birthmas." They were dainty drop pearls, and not the cheap ones either. I had a pair that were pink, but I'd forgotten them at home.

"There. You're perfect," she said after I'd added some make up. "Now get out of here, you crazy kid. Have fun."

I'd never been nervous going to Stryker's apartment, so this was a first. I had to park on the street because his lot was taken up by an assortment of cars that all looked like something he'd probably worked on at one time or another.

My heels clicked on the porch and I took another breath before I knocked.

"It's open!" a voice that wasn't Stryker's yelled down the stairs. Once I opened the front door I wondered how they'd even heard me knocking because of the noise that came from his open door at the top of the stairs. I wouldn't exactly call it music. My mother would have been horrified.

I took my time getting to the top step and poked my head into the open doorway. Five guys and three girls were crammed on and around the couch and on the futon, some of them with instruments, some of them with bottles, but all of them staring at me. Stryker was in the exact middle of it and smiled when he looked up from tuning his mandolin.

"Hey, I hope I'm not late," I said, waving and wishing I could just vanish. Or at least melt into the floor. It was just like that nightmare where you walk into class and realize you're naked, only I could feel my heart pounding and my mouth went completely dry and I knew I was awake.

"Hey, you're right on time. We haven't started yet," Stryker said, getting up and stepping over a few people to get to me. "I'm glad you came. Everyone, this is Katie." He dragged me into the room and eight sets of eyes gave me the once over.

"Katie, this is Perry, Cort, Baxter, Ric, Pepper, Zoey, Allan and Theo. Yes, there will be a test on this later. Say hello everyone. I've told them to be on their best behavior." The girl I thought he'd pointed out as 'Ric' rolled her eyes, but I thought I was the only one who noticed. She had two-tone black and blonde hair and was draped over the guy named Baxter, who had gigantic gauged ears and snakebite piercings in his bottom lip.

"So this is where you've been when we called you to go out," Allan said. He got up from his position on the coffee table and came forward to shake my hand. He bent over and kissed it and I met gray/blue eyes in a face with a crooked nose that had been broken more than once. "Nice to meet you, little lady."

"Hey, man. Hands off," Stryker said, shoving Allan away so he let go of my hand. Then everyone else got up and shook my hand. There were definitely more piercings, tattoos and other body modifications than I was used to, which, I had to admit, was intimidating. I was also the only one wearing pink, but that was no shock.

Stryker led me to the couch and shoved Perry aside so I could sit. I was still getting a lot of stares.

"You don't have to move," I said, but he waved me off. I squished in next to Stryker and he gave me a little smile before picking up the mandolin again.

"Okay, let's take "Devil's Tattoo" from the beginning." Allan sat back on the coffee table and picked up a guitar, as did Perry and Baxter. Cort seated himself at the drums and Pepper had Stryker's banjo. Theo went to the standing bass and they all waited for Stryker to count.

"One, two, three . . . " They launched into a song I didn't know, with Stryker, Allan, Ric and Zoey singing. Even with the mandolin, the song was raw and had a heavy beat that made me move with it. The group throbbed with the song and I was in the middle of it.

It was like diving into a pool of music. It was everywhere, soaking into my skin and driving me crazy, consuming me.

I'd never seen Stryker play in person, it had always been over the phone, so I watched him. He kept his eyes closed most of the time, but every now and then he would open them. Once or twice they searched and found me and he smiled a little.

I closed my eyes too and gave myself over to it. They all played harder and faster, and the energy was almost too much to take. I was afraid it was going to crush me and then it ended.

"Not bad, not bad. What did you think?" Stryker turned to me and everyone waited for my response.

"Wow. That was . . . Wow. What song is that?"

"'Beat the Devil's Tattoo', by Black Rebel Motorcycle Club," Ric said, leaning back against Baxter. "Ever heard of it?" I almost laughed at her attempt to make me feel like a moron.

Yes, I was intimidated in this foreign environment, and yes, I wanted them to like me, but I wasn't going to get into some sort of stupid girl fight. She had no idea how easy she was to read. Despite her attempt to show everyone that she was totally into Baxter, her eyes never strayed far from Stryker. She was jealous.

"No," I said, giving her a sweet smile. "But I really like it."

"Be gentle with her. Her musical education is in the beginning stages," Stryker said, giving her a look. "Sorry, sweetheart, but it's true. We need to wean you of your Swift addiction." Jesus, listen to one song and you're branded a fan. Not that I wasn't a fan. I'd just denied it when Stryker had asked.

"Hey man, don't disrespect the Swifties," Allan said with a serious face. "They are a force to be reckoned with."

"We, are never, ever, ever getting back together!" Perry sang in a loud, off-key voice which made everyone laugh.

"That's gold, man. You just don't understand," Allan said, shaking his head sadly. "You get it, right Pinky?"

"Oh, I get a nickname?" I said.

"Everyone who joins The Band gets a nickname," Perry said. "Especially if your real name sucks."

"So you're saying Katie sucks?" I said, turning to him. He was paler than Lottie, as if he spent all day in his basement, but he had deep brown eyes and the cheekbones of a model under a mop of dishwater blond hair.

"No, I wouldn't say that it sucks. It's just really common. So is Christopher, which is my real name."

"Nice save, Per," Stryker said, giving him a thumbs up. "So you want a drink before we do another?"

"Yeah, sure," I said.

"Okay, take five," Stryker said in a mock serious voice. Everyone broke up, and some went outside to smoke while Stryker took me into the kitchen and handed me a beer from the fridge. I felt Ric's eyes following my every move.

—

"So what do you think?" he said as I popped the top and took a swig. Beer wasn't really my drink of choice, but I wasn't going to turn it down.

"You guys are amazing. I feel intimidated by your talent."

He grabbed another drink and leaned against the counter.

"Are they what you expected?" That was a loaded question.

"Honestly, I was expecting more tattoos, scary guys with motorcycles and girls who looked like they could rip my spleen out with one hand."

He raised his pierced eyebrow. "So you thought my friends would be scary?"

I leaned next to him on the counter, our shoulders touching, and sighed.

"I don't know. Are you mad at me?" I swirled the bottle in my hand.

"Hey," he said, bumping my shoulder lightly. "Do you think I'm scary?"

"Well, the first time I met you, you did have fake fangs on, sooo . . ." I bumped him back.

"Haha," he said. "That is true."

"I'm not scared of you," I said, lying through my teeth. I was terrified of him, but not in the way he thought. I was scared of how I felt around him.

"I'm not scared of you, either." Our eyes met and I thought he was going to kiss me, but a voice invaded our moment.

"Hey, Stryk, do you think you could give my engine a look? It started making this noise on the way over, and you know that Baxter wouldn't know a spark plug if it bit him on the ass," Ric said with a little grin, appearing out of absolutely nowhere.

"Yeah, sure. I'll be right back." He touched my shoulder and whispered in my ear, "Don't get scared while I'm gone."

"I won't," I whispered back. Ric saw the exchange, and gave me the briefest of glares before turning on the charm with Stryker again.

"Soooo, Pinky. Where the hell did you come from?" Allan said, coming back in with the smoking group.

"Just ignore him," Zoey said, going to the fridge. Out of all the girls, she was the least 'modified,' and just had a nose ring and had her light brown hair chopped into a messy bob. "That's what I do."

"Oh, come on Zo. You know you want me," he said, coming up behind her and pretending to kiss her neck. She jammed her elbow back, getting him in the gut, and he doubled over falling to the floor, groaning while everyone else laughed.

Zoey put her foot on his chest, as if she was going to stomp on it. "For the millionth time, Allan, it's *never* going to happen."

"Because I have a penis," he moaned, still on the floor.

"Yes, because you have a penis and you're also a dick." She ground her foot back and forth and then lifted it off him. He grinned up at her.

"Not always."

85

She rolled her eyes and stepped over him, going back to the couch.

"Are you okay?" I said. No one else seemed concerned about Allan, who was still writhing on the floor.

"Yeah, I'm good." He pushed himself up, using the counter to get fully vertical again. "She just shuts me down every time. I'm not a dick. Well, at least not most of the time."

"I'm reserving judgment," I said, crossing my arms.

He laughed, pointing at me. "I like you. I hope you stick around. Do you sing or play or anything?"

"Ah, no. I'm just here as a groupie, I guess." Stryker came back in, and it wasn't my imagination that his eyes searched the room until he found me.

"You have any sisters? Friends?" He winked and that made me laugh.

"They're taken. But nice try," I said, walking past him and patting him on the shoulder. "There is a lid for every pot."

I sat down next to Stryker again.

"How was the engine problem?" I said, resisting putting sarcastic emphasis on "engine problem."

His eyes widened in mock surprise. "There didn't seem to be a problem. Can you imagine that?" I pretended to gasp.

"I cannot." We both laughed as everyone settled back into their spots.

"Don't worry about Ric. She's not the one I want to fuck on this couch after I kick everyone out," he whispered in my ear before swapping his mandolin with Zoey for his banjo.

I'd said no this afternoon, but maybe it was the combination of the alcohol burning in my veins or the music burning in my ears, but I wanted him to throw everyone out right then and there and have my way with him. Not angry-revenge sex. Just hot, sweaty, passionate sex.

They played "Beat The Devil's Tattoo" again, followed by "Demons", by Imagine Dragons and then "Letter to the President", by a Maine band, The Rustic Overtones, followed by a crazy time when someone would yell out a random song and they'd all attempt to play it. Anything from commercial jingles to cheesy pop songs. Then Allan yelled out "We Are Never Getting Back Together!" and they started playing it.

They didn't quite know the lyrics, but that made it all the more entertaining.

"Sing it out, Pinky!" Allan yelled as they mumbled their way through the verses. I'd finished my first drink and was on my second, so my walls were down a bit. I sang the words, and somehow my voice carried and everyone followed me. I didn't try to do anything fancy, but somehow I was able to blend with the rest of them and sound okay. At least, not like an injured whale or one of those horrible tone-deaf people on American Idol.

They ended the song with a bang and everyone laughed.

"I knew you had it in you, girl," Allan said, holding his fist out. I bumped it and got fist bumps from everyone else. Except Ric, of course.

"You can sing," Stryker said, looking at me as if I'd revealed that I had a box full of treasure hidden in my dorm room. I heard a scoffing sound coming from Ric's direction.

"I wouldn't exactly call it that. I just like to sing in the car when I drive," I said, shrugging. "Oh, and I was in chorus in sixth grade and I totally rocked 'Jingle Bells' at the holiday concert."

Everyone laughed.

"Well, it's getting late," Stryker said, glancing at the clock on the DVD player. "You guys should probably get home. Don't you all have things to do early tomorrow morning that you need to go to bed for?"

"All right, all right. Stryker wants to get laid, everyone out," Allan said, putting his guitar back in its case. "Some of us don't get to have sex with the girls we want to all the time."

"Oh shut up, Allan," Zoey said, getting her coat. "I am only giving you a ride if you are silent the entire way."

"I don't know if I can promise that," he said seriously. "Please?"

She rolled her eyes.

"Fine. It was nice to meet you, Katie." She waved and gave Allan a look.

"Nice to meet you, too."

"Bye, Pinky!" Allan yelled from partway down the stairs.

"Next week it's your turn to host, Allan!" Stryker called as he helped everyone get their instruments back into their cases. I got good-byes and smiles and invitations to come back again. Ric looked like her teeth hurt when she said she wanted to see me again. I just gave her a sweet smile and shut the door behind her.

"You can sing?" Stryker said, and I jumped because he was right behind me. I turned to face him.

"I wouldn't really call it that. It's just something I do in the car. And the shower. And sometimes when I'm alone." He held my face in both hands and did that deep eye stare thing that made me want to slam my body up against him and kiss him until we couldn't breathe.

"Sweetheart. You. Can. Sing." We slammed against the door as he attacked me with his mouth.

Seven

Stryker

Not that her talking voice wasn't sexy, but when she opened her mouth and vocalized those awful lyrics, I almost fell off the couch. Somehow she'd been hiding the sexiest, sweetest, lilting singing voice. Most girls would spend hours trying to get their voice to yodel at the end like that. She probably wasn't even aware that she was doing it, which made me want her all the more.

I wanted to fuck her singing voice, but I settled for kissing her instead, plunging my tongue inside her mouth.

Her back crashed against my door as we frantically tried to get our clothes off. I didn't mind doing it with clothes on, but I liked seeing her body and tasting her skin if she let me.

"Slow down," I said as she went for my belt. "Slow down, sweetheart."

"You attacked me first," she gasped as I kissed her neck, pulling her cardigan aside.

"True," I said, blowing on her skin until goosebumps formed. "But I changed my mind. Let's do this slow." I started with the cardigan, slowly unbuttoning it as her hands moved under my shirt and up and down my back.

"No angry revenge sex?" I could tell she was having a hard time standing still.

I got to the last button and pulled the fabric off one shoulder, kissing the skin it revealed. "No. Just you and me sex."

She smiled and laughed as I used the hem of her t-shirt to drag her back to the couch. I pushed aside cups and bottles and lay her down.

"If we're going to take this slow, I think we need some music. Be right back." I went to my stereo and plugged in my iPod, switching to a playlist I'd made before I met her. Ed Sheeran's "Give Me Love" was the first song.

I glanced at her and walked back to the couch with the slow beat of the music. I kissed her mouth softly, brushing back her hair with both hands. She kissed me easily and it gave me some time to tease her, to try some things and learn if she liked them based on her response. It was like it was our first time.

Our clothes came off, layer by layer, piece by piece. She kissed my tattoos, and I kissed her freckles. I made my way down her stomach and paused with my face between her thighs.

"You don't have to. Zack always said no."

"I'm. Not. Zack," I said planting a kiss with every word on the inside of her left thigh. "So I'm going to kiss you here. And here. And here."

"Fuuuuccckkk," she moaned, grabbing onto my ears.

"Easy, girl." I backed off a little and started slower. Clearly, she hadn't had a lot of oral experience, which was a damn shame. It didn't take too much to get her off, so I decided to go for round two, and then round three. I added my fingers and absolutely wrecked her until her entire body convulsed and she cried out. I wished she could see what she looked like, lost in ecstasy.

I kissed my way back up her body and reached for the condom I'd stuffed behind the couch cushion before she'd come over.

"You really didn't have to do that, but I'm so glad you did. I owe you at least two blow jobs for that. Would you like the first one now?" Her hand wrapped around my dick and moved up and down.

"Maybe later," I said. "I want to be inside you." I handed her the condom and she got it on with her usual swiftness.

"There's something crazy sexy about a girl who can roll a condom like you." I moved and then thrust into her so fast she wasn't expecting it. She gasped and then pulled me close.

"I thought we were taking it slow?" She wrapped her legs around me and waited for me to go again.

"We are." As slow as I could I pulled almost all the way out and then pounded into her again. We set a syncopated rhythm that drove us both over the edge.

I looked down at her to find her looking at me. Usually she turned her head, but finally, I got to stare into those wide brown eyes. I thrust into her again and held still, kissing her hard. I was shaking with the effort of doing it, but she was shaking too.

I finally couldn't hold out any longer and I came, saying her name.

We were both still shaking as I lay my head on her chest.

"That was anything but slow," she said, her fingers threading through my hair. I lifted my head up and propped my chin between her breasts.

"That was nice. Not angry or revenge-y at all."

"Nope. Just you and me."

***

"So what's the deal with you and Ric?" she said as we lay on the couch. She was wearing my shirt and I just had my boxers on and we were sharing a bottle of beer, passing it back and forth.

I shrugged and handed the bottle back to her.

"I've known her for a couple of years. We met at a concert and she's been a little obsessed with me ever since."

"Obsessed? Don't we think highly of ourselves." She took a swig and handed it back to me.

"You have no idea. She's showed up here in the middle of the night before. I'm actually scared of her." Katie kissed my shoulder.

"Don't worry, I'll protect you."

"I bet you will." I kissed her nose and she giggled. "So my friends aren't scary, are they?"

"Not really. As long as Ric keeps her paws off you, we'll be good."

"And as long as you keep your paws *on* me, we'll be good."

She rolled her eyes and drained the rest of the bottle.

***

Katie stayed the night after texting Lottie and saying that she was sleeping over. I dragged her to my bedroom and we both passed out, her head on my chest, her hair all around me.

Her eyes were open when I woke up the next morning.

"Are you watching me sleep?" I said, admiring the way her hair was all over the place. That girl knew how to rock sex hair.

"Maybe."

I gave her a quick kiss that turned into something more before she pulled away.

"What are you doing for Thanksgiving?" she said.

The question seemed to come out of nowhere, but I could tell she'd been thinking about it.

"I usually just spend it with Trish, or go to Allan's house. His mom always invites me and sends him to come get me if I try to bail. Why?"

"Do you want to come home with me?"

I leaned back so I could see her face better. "Are you serious?"

"Yeah. I mean, if you want to. You'll have to deal with my family, and my sister won't be there, but I want you to come."

"Why?"

"Because I can't stand being around all my relatives without wanting to kill myself and I need someone to take the fork out of my hand if I try."

I gave her a look.

"Oh shit. That was meant to be a joke and I –"

I put my finger on her lips.

"It's okay. I actually enjoy a little suicide humor now and then. If you can't laugh about death, then you end up worrying about it all the time and that can consume you. Trust me."

She pressed her lips against my finger and I moved it away so she could talk.

"It's okay if you have plans."

"Katie. I would be happy to come to your Thanksgiving with you."

Her face lit up. "Really?"

"Really. I'm just not sure if your parents are going to like it. Have you ever brought anyone like me home before?"

She tapped her chin and squinted at the ceiling as if she was thinking really hard about it.

"Uh, no."

"Have you asked your parents if you can do this yet? Your dad doesn't have a lot of firearms, does he?"

"No, and just a few hunting rifles. He likes to go moose hunting." Like nearly every man in Maine.

Fantastic, that was just what I needed. "Jesus, Katie."

She patted my cheek and then got up. "Oh come on. You're a big boy. You can handle it. Breakfast?"

"Yeah, sure. Be right there." She skipped out of the room and I heard the fridge opening a second later.

I shook my head at myself. What the hell was I thinking? I knew what would happen if Katie brought me home. I'd been down that road before. It never led anywhere good. I was about to tell her no way when I heard her singing as she cracked some eggs into a pan.

I leaned out of the doorway and watched her in the kitchen. She was singing the Taylor Swift song again and dancing a little as she minded the eggs. My shirt just barely covered her ass, but she didn't seem aware.

I couldn't say no to her. At least not about this.

"What about Trish?" I said. She looked up and stopped singing.

"She can come too, if you want. The more the merrier."

I walked until I was standing behind her. "I really feel like you should check with your parents first." I put my arms around her waist and rested my chin on her shoulder.

"It's fine. Trust me. They love having people join. They're always telling me to invite people. My mom always cooks too much and we end up foisting it off on the neighbors." She flipped the eggs over gently and turned in the circle of my arms.

"It'll be great. I swear. I hope you like pie."

"Who doesn't like pie?" I said.

"No one."

Katie

"Are you seriously taking him home?" Audrey said as we rested our eyes for a moment after a marathon study session. It was just the two of us since Lottie was out with Zan and Trish had to work and the guys always studied in their room. In my opinion, it was just an excuse for them to say they were going to study and then play video games instead.

"Yes, I am. He doesn't have anyplace to go," I said, stretching my neck. I was still a little haunted about what Stryker had told me about his past. I knew it was worse than he let on, but he glossed over it. I wasn't sure if that was for me or for him, so I didn't push.

"What are your parents going to say about that?" she said.

"Honestly? I don't know. It's going to be interesting." Understatement.

"And you're bringing Trish, too?" She put the cap on her highlighter, setting it back beside her pen. That girl had studying down to a science. I wished I could emulate her, but I knew that wasn't going to happen.

I shook my head. "I was going to, but she's actually going home with Lottie. We're all going to rendezvous the day after and have dinner together."

"Well, I want a phone call, or at least text updates. Things are going to be really dull at my place."

"What about Will?"

She sighed and blushed at the same time. If my relationship with Stryker was complicated, I knew that Audrey's and Will's was, too, only I couldn't figure out why. Obviously they liked each other and I didn't think either of them had massive baggage, but I couldn't see the hold-up.

Audrey rolled the highlighter back and forth on the fake mahogany table. DU was a state school, so everything was meant to look real, but it was only a painted or varnished façade. "He asked me to come home with him, but I felt weird about it. My parents are big on family and all that, so there's no way I can miss my family thing. He was so sweet when he asked, though."

"He's a really great guy."

"I know." She looked down at her book.

"So what's the problem?"

She looked like she was going to say something and then shook her head.

"Nothing. Absolutely nothing. Hey, you want to get some coffee or something?" It was classic deflection, but I let it go. Maybe she did have something dark in her past, although she hid it much better than I did. Audrey was one of those beautiful girls who looked like they had all their shit together, but maybe not. Huh.

***

Simon decided to have another huge dinner the Tuesday night before Thanksgiving break started, and Stryker volunteered his apartment as a gathering place.

"Does this mean you're going to wear that lovely apron again?" I said as we dragged grocery bags full of food up the stairs.

"The first rule of cooking is: Don't speak of the apron. It is sacred and no one must know about it," he said in a serious voice. "Never speak of it again."

"Okay, rule one: Don't speak of the apron. Any other rules?"

We set our bags down on the kitchen floor and I stretched my back.

"Don't mess with my spice rack. If you take something out, put it back." He opened one of the cabinets and showed me an epic spice rack with everything alphabetically organized. I'd seen it once before, but hadn't mentioned it to him. Stryker just didn't seem like a spice rack kind of guy. I figured it was a gift from someone.

"You're a closet foodie. I knew it," I said, pointing at the spice rack. "Nice try, Mr. Cinnamon Toast Crunch, but you couldn't fool me for long."

He shut the cupboard.

"Don't tell anyone," he whispered, leaning in and kissing me on the cheek. "Or I might have to kill you."

I moved to kiss his lips but someone knocked.

"Damn," he said, brushing the side of my face with his hand. "They have the worst timing."

"Knock, knock!" Simon yelled. "You'd better be decent." Stryker gave me a look and went to open the door and everyone piled in, also carrying bags.

We ended up making the most random, weird dinner ever. From pancakes to steak tips to pizza, with chocolate covered pretzels and white chocolate raspberry cookies for desert. There were way too many cooks in the kitchen, and Stryker tried to rein everyone in, shouting orders like a general and trying to organize the chaos that refused to let itself be organized. We didn't even bother to take everything over to the couch and futon, we just stood around and piled our plates high, stuffing our faces until we'd had enough and we had to sit down.

"I don't think I can move," Will said, putting his hands on his stomach.

"Ditto," Lottie said, her head lolling on Zan's shoulder.

"Who knew pancakes and pizza made such a good combination?" Simon said. Brady raised his hand.

"I did."

"Sure you did," Simon said, honking his nose.

Stryker had found a pen and was busy drawing something on my arm as I sat in his lap. He wouldn't let me look at it until it was done, so I was just watching everyone else as they debated about the best Thanksgiving side dishes.

I'd told my parents I was bringing a guy home, but I hadn't told them much more than that. Trish had accused me of being ashamed of Stryker, but it wasn't true. I knew if I went into too much detail, they'd either tell me that he couldn't come, or read too much into our relationship.

Yes, I liked him. I could no longer deny that. Yes, I enjoyed spending time with him and yes, that included having sex with him.

No, I did not want him to be my boyfriend. Things were fine the way they were, and besides, we weren't headed for commitment. Boyfriend came before fiancé came before husband. I wasn't going to marry Stryker, so why even go down that road?

"You can look now," he said, holding up my arm. He'd drawn a silhouette of my face with a frame around it, like a picture. "What do you think?"

"It's beautiful." I turned my arm to see it better. "Now I've got ink, too."

"Would you ever get a tattoo?"

"I've thought about it, but I could never decide what I wanted."

"They say you should sit on a tattoo idea for two years before you get it."

"Is that what you do?"

"Not exactly, but it's a good idea. At least for your first one."

"If I make up my mind, I'll let you know and you can go with me. Deal?" I held up my hand and he shook it.

"Deal." He capped the pen. "So I was thinking I should bring something."

"You don't have to do that, I swear."

"Still, it is a tradition in polite society to bring the hostess gift at least."

"Well, I have the green bean casserole covered, and Mom always does potatoes, squash and sweet potatoes."

"How about a baked brie?"

"A what?" I'd never heard of such a thing.

"It's cheese baked in a crust with jam. It's delicious. I swear, you'll love it."

"Brie? The boy with the banjo, tattoos and lip ring eats brie?" He leaned in and snuffled my neck, making me giggle.

"Shhh, that's the third rule of cooking: Don't speak of the brie," he whispered in my ear before biting my earlobe.

"Okay, I won't speak of it." I slid my hand down and squeezed his dick once when no one was looking. He made a little sound of surprise and shifted under me.

"Dirty. You play dirty, sweetheart."

***

Mom was in full panic mode when I got home on Wednesday night, and I could hear her fighting with Dad all the way from the front door. They'd put the turkey flag outside and I knew the house was going to be dripping in leaf cutouts and various other Thanksgiving memorabilia. My mother had an entire room in the house reserved for her various holiday decorations.

"Gina, you need to calm down. You do this every year and it always turns out fine," Dad said in a soothing voice. "Hey, Katiebug!" His face broke into a smile.

"Hi, Dad." I set my bags down in the doorway and headed into the warzone, otherwise known as the kitchen. The table was set with the maple leaf placemats and a Yankee Candle store's worth of spice-scented candles were burning. And, of course, Mom had her traditional rust-colored turtleneck on. Dad leaned down from his towering height to give me a hug.

"How is she?" I whispered.

"I've hidden the coffee so she won't get crazy on caffeine. So far we haven't hit panic mode," Dad whispered back before letting me go.

"Hey, Mom. Do you need any help?" The counter was covered in cans and bags of flour and cooking spray and spices galore. Stryker would have been horrified at their disorganization.

I'd said good-bye to him this morning and I was already itching to text him. I'd put my phone in my glove box so I wouldn't be tempted to look down at it while I was driving.

"No, I'm fine. Just trying to get organized. When is that guy coming?" As far as my parents knew, Stryker was a friend who was also a guy who didn't have a home to go to on Thanksgiving. Granted, this was true, but I knew my mother was painting an Oliver Twist-like picture in her head that the reality was going to shatter.

"Um, I told him to be here by eleven." We usually ate around one, so that would give my parents enough time to get used to Stryker before we all sat down to dinner. It would also give my relatives enough time to properly embarrass me in front of him.

"That sounds good. Is he staying the night?" She wiped the counter down with a leaf-shaped sponge. I had no idea where she got this stuff from, but she always managed to find things to fit the holiday.

"Uhh," I said, stuttering. I hadn't anticipated that. "I don't think he'd planned on it."

"Well, didn't you say he was a couple hours away? We could always make up the extra room for him." She rinsed the sponge out and I could feel Dad staring intently at me. Normally Mom was the one who read too much into situations with boys.

"I'll ask him," I said, getting out my phone.

My mom wants to know if u'll stay the night. In the guest room. I think she thinks ur a loser I'm being nice 2.

He responded immediately.

Can I sneak into your room for pity sex?

I had to stop myself from rolling my eyes because both my parents were watching.

I told you, my dad has guns.

I could almost hear his sigh through the text.

Fine. We can rendezvous in the shower. To be continued

I smiled as I typed **dot dot dot**

"Yeah, he's going to stay."

"What did you say his major was?" Mom said, fiddling with the oven.

"He's a double mechanical and environmental science major." Stryker's majors painted the picture of a helpless dork, complete with glasses and a pocket protector.

"Impressive. He must be really smart." Dad was still giving me a searching look.

"He is. He's also musically inclined, and may or may not bring a guitar with him. He usually always has one in his car." I didn't know which car he'd be bringing, because he was always working on two at once.

"And he doesn't have any family?" Mom said.

"His sister is going with Lottie, actually. Their parents abandoned them and they don't have any relatives they're close to."

Mom shook her head sadly. Oh, how her delusions were going to be smashed tomorrow.

"That's such a shame. Well, he's more than welcome."

"He's really grateful," I said, which wasn't complete bullshit. "So, I'm going to go take my stuff to my room."

I scurried away before Dad could intercept me, and shut the door. So far, so good.

Eight

Stryker

If I said I wasn't nervous, I would have been lying. I panicked and wrapped the container I put the baked brie in with towels so even if it bounced, nothing would happen to it and checked my appearance in the mirror more times than I had in all the previous years of my life, combined.

I'd even made Trish help me pick out a tie, which was like making a really grumpy cat take a bath.

I'd debated about taking out my piercings, which was another first, but I left them in. I didn't care what they thought about those. I did, however, wear a long-sleeved shirt that hid my tattoos.

Luckily, I had a nice long drive to panic and try to rehearse what I was going to say.

I texted Katie when I was a few minutes away, realizing that in my nervousness, I was pretty early. My GPS directed me that her house was my next right in a lovely calm robotic voice.

Katie's neighborhood looked like the set of a quintessential American town. It was a development with houses that all had the exact same-sized lawns and evenly-spaced trees. I'd lived in a lot of places, but definitely none like this. This was a place with snowblowers and riding lawnmowers and potted shrubs and white fences. It was so . . . clean.

There were at least six cars parked in the driveway and in front of the house, so I had to park on the street in front, partially blocking the neighbor's driveway.

I unwrapped the casserole dish from the towels, grabbed the bag with my hostess/suck up gift and walked up to the front door. There was a flag shaped like a turkey hanging from the eaves of the porch. Wow. They were *those* kind of people. The kind of people who had boxes of decorations for every holiday, even the holidays that weren't really holidays. Like President's Day. Katie hadn't mentioned that.

I rang the doorbell and crossed my fingers that Katie would answer. I heard pounding footsteps, which probably meant she was trying to beat someone else to the door. Smart girl.

"Hey," I said, giving her what I hoped was a confident smile.

"Did you do something to your hair?" She said after staring at me for a full thirty seconds.

"Yeah, I actually brushed it today." This was partially true. I'd also put some gel in it to make it behave.

"You look, wow." She blinked, but didn't move to let me in. She didn't look so bad herself. I didn't know anyone who could pull off pink jeans with a white sweater, but she could. Behind her I could hear the hum of people talking and laughing. Panic tried to claw its way into my brain, but I pushed it back. There was no need to panic.

I held out the brie. "I come bearing gifts. Do you, um, think I could come in?"

She blinked again and shook her head, as if to clear it.

"Um, yeah. Come on in."

"Thanks." I stepped over the threshold, but she grabbed my arm and leaned to whisper in my ear.

"Are you sure about this?"

"Now isn't really the time to be asking me that, sweetheart," I said.

"I know, but—" I stepped around her. No, I hadn't spent the two-hour-drive-in-the-car-practicing-for-this time for nothing. We were doing this.

"I'm here, Katie. It's too late now."

She nodded and dived in front of me so she could make the introductions. I followed in her wake and tried not to drop the casserole dish. I also tried not to watch her ass as she walked away.

At least I didn't drop the dish.

Her voice made me look up and realize I was in the kitchen and everyone was staring at me.

"Mom, Dad, this is Stryker Grant," Katie said as I walked behind her and set the casserole dish down on the already-crowded counter. Katie had her mom's wide eyes, but that was about the only similarity they shared. Katie was very much her father's daughter, except for the fact that he was about as tall as Zack.

"Mr. and Mrs. Hallman, thank you so much for inviting me. I really appreciate it." I set the bag with a bottle of wine and a bunch of flowers down so I could hold out my hand for her father, who was standing closer to me. He was the first one to unfreeze from his shock. Yeah, I'd expected that, and I was used to it.

"It's nice to meet you, Stryker. Please, call me Glenn." He gave me a firm shake. Maybe a little too firm. I let go and looked at Katie's Mom.

"Mom?" Katie said. For a second, I thought she was going to snap her fingers in front of her mom's face.

"You're Stryker?" Mrs. Hallman said, her eyes flitting from my eyebrow ring, to my lip ring and to my earring.

"You have a beautiful home," I said, picking up the gifts. "I brought you some wine, and this," I said taking out the flowers.

"Uh, thank you, they're beautiful." She took them but didn't stop looking at me. She finally shook my hand, but it was limp and she let go as quickly as she could. Ah, so that was how it was going to be. This would be interesting.

"I also brought a little something. It's a baked brie. I tried to keep it warm on the way over, but it might need to sit in the oven for a few minutes to warm up.

"Right this way," Katie said, glaring at her mother and grabbing the casserole dish. This was also a house with two ovens, apparently, because there was a turkey in one, but the bottom oven was unoccupied.

"I knew she was going to do this," she whispered as she set the oven and shoved the dish in.

"It's okay," I said back as everyone else broke into chatter again. There was a microscopic part of me that wanted to shut the oven and run out the front door to my car, but one thing kept me from doing it.

Katie. Her fingers dug into my arm, and I could feel she was as nervous as I was, maybe even more so. She cared if her parents liked me or not.

"What am I, chopped liver?" An older man wearing a flannel shirt with more than a few holes in it marched over, his hand out.

"Stryker, Grampa Jack. Grampa Jack, this is my *friend*, Stryker." I shook his hand and he winked at me.

"Welcome to the family, son."

"Oh, he's not—" Katie said at the same time I said, "I'm not—"

He laughed, wheezing. Clearly, he'd smoked more than a few cigars in his life. He crooked his finger for me to lean in.

"Just be careful with my granddaughter," he said, giving me a roguish wink from under his unruly white eyebrows. He only gave my appearance a quick glance, but I still felt like I wanted to crawl into a hole and hide. I wasn't afraid of a whole lot of people, but this guy scared me. Katie had barely mentioned him when I'd asked about who I'd be meeting, but I did remember her saying he was ex-military, which sounded less intimidating when the guy wasn't standing in front of me.

I looked at Katie and she rolled her eyes.

"I will. Thank you, sir," I said, wishing I'd taken my piercings out. Too late now.

He clapped me on the shoulder and wheezy-laughed again.

"Come and sit next to me. I want to hear all about you." He grabbed my shoulder and steered me toward the living room as a few kids ran by screaming. I sort of wished I could join them.

Katie was right behind me when I heard her mom say, "Katie, can you help me with something?" She gave me an angry look and then smoothed a smile over it.

"Sure, Mom." *Be right back,* she mouthed at me before going back into the kitchen.

Great. I had to face the grandfather interrogation alone. There was no choice but to let the man with the iron grip steer me into the next room.

The living room was beige with more beige and simple furnishings, which I guessed made a nice canvas for all the Thanksgiving things. I moved a stuffed cornucopia pillow so I could sit on one end of the massive sectional. He took the other end, and sat back.

"Why did you do that to your face?" he said, pointing at his own lip and eyebrow. It took me a second to get enough moisture in my mouth to talk.

"What?"

"You've got metal in your face. How do you go through one of those detectors at the airport?"

For about five seconds, I had no idea what to say. Then he started laughing as if it was the funniest thing he'd said in his entire life. The laugh turned into a cough and I wondered if I should get off the couch and bang on his back or something.

"You okay, sir?"

"I'm fine, son. The look on your face was priceless." He wiped tears from his eyes and slapped his knee with one hand.

"So, what are your intentions with my granddaughter?"

I was about to form some sort of response that wasn't *She's using me for sex* when the front door opened and someone called out, "Surprise!" The talking stopped as everyone rushed to the door to see who it was.

"Oh my God, Kayla?" Katie shrieked and ran from the kitchen, launching herself into the arms of a girl who had to be her sister. They both hugged, rocking back and forth and I was afraid they were going to tip over in their enthusiasm. Guess it was genetic.

"Hey, Katiebug!" Kayla said, pulling out of the hug, but not letting go of Katie's hands.

"What are you doing here?" Katie said, her face lit up like a kid on Christmas morning. Christ, she was beautiful.

"It's Thanksgiving and I got on a plane. Hey, Mom." There was a flurry of hugging and tears and laughter as the family welcomed their new guest. I stayed in the living room and watched it all. Katie beamed and kept her arm around her sister. Even though Kayla was taller, you'd have to be blind not to see that they were two peas in a pod, with identical brown hair and eyes.

Kayla cleared her throat and then whistled to get everybody to shut up. "Um, so everyone, I have someone I want you to meet." She opened the door again and grabbed the hand of a tall black guy who looked like he wanted to get back in the car, and led him in. Kayla threaded her hand with his and gave him an encouraging smile that he somehow returned.

"This is Adam, and um, we're getting married." She held up her left hand to show a simple gold band and beamed at the terrified-but-trying-to-hide-it Adam.

There was a half-second of stunned silence and then house exploded with noise as everyone started talking and yelling at once.

Katie

I couldn't *believe* her. She'd mentioned a guy in a few of her emails, but never his name and never that she was serious about him.

I was torn between being so happy to see her and super pissed that she didn't tell me, but that was just like her. She'd been all set to get her Master's degree, but then she decided that helping people in third world countries was more important. She didn't tell us she'd dropped out of school until the night before she was set to get on a plane.

"What the hell, Kayla?" I said when Mom finally stopped freaking out. I felt bad for Stryker. He sat in the living room by himself and I could tell he was regretting that he'd come. Poor guy.

"I'm sorry, it just happened so fast." She glanced over at Adam, who was getting grilled by Dad, and then her eyes found Stryker. Everyone else was talking to Adam all at once, including Grampa Jack, who'd levered himself off the couch to come and inspect his soon-to-be grandson-in-law.

"Who's that guy?" she said, loud enough for him to hear. He pretended to be very interested in the couch.

"Ah, that's Stryker. He's a friend," I whispered.

She crossed her arms and gave me a look.

"Now who's keeping a secret guy?"

"It's not like that, Kayla. It's more of a . . . friend's with benefits thing," I said even lower so only Kayla could hear, my face turning red despite my best efforts.

Kayla gave me a knowing smile. "Of course it is. Come on," she said, linking her arm with mine. "I wanna meet this guy." There was no way I was going to win that battle so I let her drag me to the living room. I tried to give Stryker a look to warn him, but he was still staring at the couch. He got up when he saw us coming for him, his hands making sure his shirt was tucked in the right way. He really looked damn good all cleaned up like that.

"Well, well, well, look at you," she said, giving him the once over as he stood still, awaiting her inspection. I had to give him credit; he didn't even flinch. They stared at each other in complete silence and I could sense they were having a conversation without saying a word. Stryker's jaw tensed and Kayla's eyes narrowed before she slowly smiled at him.

It was one of the weirdest non-conversations I'd ever seen, and I'd watched Lottie and Will do their twindar thing any number of times.

"Stryker, this is my sister Kayla, Kayla, this is Stryker," I said, to try to break up some of the tension. They shook hands and Kayla's gaze went back and forth between us a few times.

"So, what are your intentions with my sister?" Stryker thought about it for a moment, leaned in and winked at me.

"I'm just using her for sex," he whispered. Kayla's eyes went wide and then she started laughing. Stryker relaxed a fraction. He'd taken a risk, saying something like that. It sounded more like the Stryker I was used to.

"I like him. He's not a douchebag. That's a first." Stryker nodded at Kayla and his lips twitched as if he was trying not to smile.

Seriously? "He just said he's using me for sex and you think he's not a douchebag?"

She shrugged. "How do you think Adam and I got together? Nice to meet you, Stryker" she said, patting him on the shoulder and going to rescue Adam from my dad.

I stared after her, shaking my head. "I don't understand what just happened," I said.

"Go with it. We should probably check the brie," Stryker said, stepping around me to go to the oven.

"Right, brie."

***

Kayla definitely took the heat off Stryker, which was a good thing. Mom was too busy gushing over Kayla's announcement to worry anymore about Stryker's appearance. She was shocked for as much time as it took Kayla to tell her that Adam was in medical school and was on his way to being a doctor with a huge salary and then she was ready to throw them a wedding in our living room right then and there. Dad just laughed and shook his head and told her not to get carried away.

Adam was quiet initially, but Kayla got him talking about their time in Africa and how they met and all the adventures they'd had with food poisoning, lions and droughts. Hearing them talk about it made me ache, and after a few minutes, I just wanted them to shut up. They were just so . . . goddamn happy. Kayla was glowing with it, like a firefly. I'd been so happy to see her, but we'd barely had a chance to talk about anything because everyone was so eager to hear about the engagement plans and all that. I just wanted a chance to talk to her, just us, away from everyone else.

But I was trapped at the table with them, Stryker on my right and Grampa Jack on my left. My parents ended up having to bring in another table to fit everyone, including my Aunt Carol, Uncle Clay, their kids Jackson, Ruthie and Andy, my Uncle Ray, Aunt Linda and their kids Bailey and Brandon, our neighbors Poppy, and Ron and their daughter Rosalee.

The dinner was a flurry of passing plates and the salt and everyone trying to cram their plates full. I took a huge helping of Stryker's baked cheese thing, which turned out to be mind-blowingly good. I would have licked my plate if I was alone.

Mom was busy with Kayla and Adam, so I chatted with Grampa Jack and Stryker. The latter kept touching my feet with his under the table and shooting me little smiles every now and then. I wished he would be less obvious, but he didn't seem to see the glares I was shooting him back and he ignored it when I kicked him under the table.

Finally, everyone had stuffed themselves and Mom brought out the pies.

"You still have room?" Stryker said, raising his pierced eyebrow. "Where's it gonna go?" Jesus, I wasn't that skinny. I'd definitely been smaller in high school, but that was because all my stupid friends were skinny bitches and I didn't want to be their one fat friend.

"Oh, I can put away some pie. You just watch."

He leaned toward me, brushing some hair off my shoulder. "Is that a challenge I hear in your voice? Because I bet you can't finish an entire slice of pie. With ice cream."

"What do I get if I win?" I said, turning in my chair.

"How about I take you to dinner?"

Oh, I'd make that worth my while. "Deal."

"What do I get if I win?" he said, running his finger down my arm. I hoped no one was looking.

"What do you want?"

His smile was slow and sexy. "I want you to sing a song with me at the next Band meeting."

I could agree to that because it wasn't going to happen. There was no way I'd lose. "Deal."

Mom passed the pie around the table and finally got to me.

"Apple, pumpkin or cherry?" she said.

"Apple."

"Ice cream?" she paused, the scoop in the tub of ice cream. I looked right at Stryker. "Yup."

The plate was passed down to me and then it was Stryker's turn.

"Cherry, please. With ice cream." I handed his plate to him and we clinked our forks together. Everyone else was attempting their own slices of pie, including Kayla and Adam who seemed to be having a similar contest.

My baby cousin, Andy, started to wail, so Aunt Carol went change him as the other kids had an impromptu pie-eating contest while their parents weren't looking, ending up with most of the pie on their faces and not in their mouths.

"So. Where are you taking me?" I said when I held up my clean plate a few minutes later. "It better be somewhere nice."

"We'll see, sweetheart."

"Shh," I said, looking around to make sure no one had overheard. Grampa Jack was snoozing in his chair, his pie only half-eaten and everyone else was focused on something else. "Let's keep that on the down low, okay?"

"Sure thing." We got up from the table and he grabbed my plates and his and took them to the sink.

"Katie, can I talk to you for a minute?" Mom had finally let Kayla off the hook, and she escaped to the living room with Adam, probably to cuddle and whisper adorable nothings in each other's ears. I'd never seen my sister so . . . disgustingly in love.

"Yeah, sure." I gave Stryker a look and he went to the living room to chat with them. Mom steered me down the hallway toward her bedroom. She made sure that no one followed us and then turned on me. Her face went from happy hostess to pissed-off mom in about half a second. Like flipping a switch.

119

"What is wrong with you?" she said, putting her hands on her hips. She had a smear of what looked like cherry pie on the front of her shirt. She'd have a hissy fit when she found out.

"What are you talking about?" I had some idea, but I wanted her to say it out loud.

"Bringing a boy like that into this house? With the kids?" My mouth popped open. I couldn't believe she was actually saying this. I'd thought they'd be upset about Stryker and maybe think he was just a slacker, or a loser. Not someone who would actually hurt children. I worried about how her mind had made that leap with Stryker when she'd let Zack into her house with open arms.

"Are you hearing yourself right now? You think that just because he's got a few piercings and tattoos and doesn't look like an all-American college boy that he's some kind of criminal? Because I have news for you: That guy? Zack? He's a criminal. Just in case you forgot, he beat the shit out of me." Every now and then, I still had a twinge of pain as a reminder.

"Keep your voice down," she hissed, glancing down the hall to make sure no one had heard my unseemly outburst. "That is an entirely different situation." I didn't see how.

"Oh, and what about Adam, huh? You know *nothing* about him and you're ready to let Kayla marry him just because he's going to be a doctor. For all we know, he could be a serial killer." I was pretty sure Kayla wouldn't be engaged to a serial killer, but I had to make my point somehow. Mom's face went red and I prepared for another verbal assault.

We both shut up when Kayla came walking down the hallway, the happiness fading from her face.

"Look, if you two are going to have a fight, you should probably be more quiet about it. I can't hear exactly what you're saying, but everyone can hear that you're fighting. Seriously? You can't even let it ride for one day?" Mom and I had a habit of choosing the holidays to have our knock-down-drag-outs.

At least Mom had the sense to look guilty for being admonished by her own daughter. She dropped her angry face.

"I'm sorry. I was just worried about your sister after everything she's been through."

Kayla put her hand on Mom's shoulder. "I know, Mom, but you really have to stop being so judgmental. I mean, I have a tattoo."

"Oh my God, Kayla. You didn't." Mom clutched her heart. You'd think Kayla announcing she was marrying a guy Mom had never met would cause that reaction, but no, it was the tattoo.

Kayla rolled her eyes like she did when she used to come home after her curfew and Mom would ask her where she'd been. "Jesus, Mom. Everyone has tattoos now."

Mom started looking Kayla over, walking around her, searching for the tattoo. It was kind of funny. "Where is it? How big is it?"

Kayla looked over her shoulder and then walked toward my parents' bedroom. Mom and I followed, and Kayla closed the door behind us.

"I just didn't want everyone to see," she said, pulling her shirt over her head. On her left shoulder was a quote and a picture of a dandelion blowing in the wind, the fluff floating toward her spine.

Not all those who wander are lost.

"It's awesome, Kayla. When did you get it?" I said. It rivaled Stryker's for the intricacy of the work. She must have gone to someone really talented.

She smiled back at me. "Few months ago. It was a present from Adam."

Mom was still looking horrified.

"It's nice lettering, I guess. And it isn't too big." Wow, big compliment Mom.

Kayla pulled her shirt down again and put one hand on my shoulder and one on Mom's.

"So, now that we've got that out of the way, can you two call a truce, just for today? After that you can go back to normal."

I would if she would.

Nine

Stryker

"What do you think they're talking about?" Adam said to me as we waited in the living room for our respective girls to come back. He'd gravitated toward me, since we were both outsiders. He'd found some beer in the fridge and had brought one back for me. Normally I would have turned it down since I wanted to make a good impression on Katie's parents, but I could use a little liquid courage right about now.

"Probably not recipes," I said. The rest of Katie's family and neighbors gave Adam and me some space, including Katie's Dad, who was busy dealing with the dishes.

"So what's your story?" he said, sitting down on the couch. I joined him, setting my beer bottle on a leaf-shaped coaster.

I shrugged. "Katie took pity on a guy who didn't have a family to spend Thanksgiving with." More or less.

He smiled and shook his head. "Yeah, I'm not buying that. You're into her."

"Well, we do have a sort of . . . arrangement." I figured he was a smart enough guy to read between the lines.

"Arrangements often turn into something else. Be careful, kid. Those Hallman women have a way of infiltrating your life until you can't see anything but them. How do you think Kayla got that ring on her finger?" He took another swig and looked at me.

I was saved from forming an answer with the arrival of a grumpy-faced Katie.

"Did you bring your stuff to stay the night?" she said, leaning on the back of the couch.

"Yeah, it's in my car."

She gave me a tight smile.

"Great, I'll help you bring it in." She pivoted on her heel and headed for the front door.

"Better get on that," Adam said to me as Kayla walked over and gave him a kiss on the cheek.

I nodded and walked toward the front door where Katie was waiting for me.

"What was that about?" I said.

"Oh, nothing. Just my mom being judgmental." She wrenched the door open and stomped down the porch. I grabbed her arm and made her sit down on the steps.

"It's about me, isn't it?" It was only a matter of time. I was surprised it hadn't come up earlier. I guess I had Kayla and her announcement to thank for that.

Katie growled and banged her hand on the step. I'd never seen her this frustrated before. It was kind of cute and also a huge turn-on. Frustrated sex was something we hadn't tried. Yet.

"She just pisses me off. When I dated Zack she rolled out the red carpet for him. He brought her flowers and kissed her ass and she bought every second of it. You know, she doesn't really believe that he hurt me as bad as he did. Even though she saw it." I couldn't believe that. It just wasn't possible.

"So she thinks you're lying? That you did it to yourself? Because that's pretty fucked up."

"No." She dug her fingers into her eyes, and I pulled her hands away and held onto them. "She just bought what he sold her. This all-American guy who was going to be my one true love. The perfect boyfriend. I guess she's just having a hard time letting go of that."

"But why? Why does she want that for you so much?" I rubbed my thumbs over the backs of her hands, trying to do anything I could to make this better for her.

"Because that's what she and Dad were. High school sweethearts. Captain of the football team and the captain of the cheering squad. It sounds like a movie, but that's how it happened for them. I know they fight a lot, but they really love each other. It's not crazy that she would want that for me." No, it wasn't, I guess.

"But what about what you want?" I let go of one of her hands, pulled a pen out of my back pocket where I always kept one and started doodling on the back of her hand. She looked down for a second, but didn't stop me. Her sleeves hid the place where I'd done the drawing before, but I was sure she'd probably already washed it off.

"That doesn't factor in as much," she said, holding still.

"That's a shame."

I could feel her watching me as I swept the tip of the pen across her skin.

"I shouldn't be bitching about my parents, especially in front of you."

I shook my head.

"It's okay, Katie. I want you to tell me what you're feeling. Whatever that is. Your feelings are important. Never forget that." I looked up from my drawing and gave her a quick smile before going back to work.

"Adam seems nice," I said, trying to shift the conversation onto less-volatile ground.

"I knew she was seeing some guy, but I had no idea it was this serious. Mom's thrilled that he's going to be a doctor, of course. But seriously, who does that? She's only known him for a few months." She shifted closer to me, using me as a shield to block some of the wind that was whipping leftover leaves around the yard.

"Maybe it's real," I said, moving the design up to her wrist.

"I should hope it's real. She's marrying him."

Leaning her head down to see the design better, she breathed in my ear.

"You're really talented, Stryker."

"Thanks, sweetheart. You make a good canvas." I tilted my head and found her mouth nearly touching mine. She smiled slowly and pressed her lips against mine tentatively. As if she'd never kissed me before. As if we were two teenagers coming home after a date and neither of us had the guts to kiss the other, but she decided to go for it anyway.

Instead of attacking her, I stayed perfectly still, letting her skin melt into mine. I kept my hands and tongue to themselves and just savored the sweetest and softest of kisses.

And then the door opened and I heard a gasp.

Katie pulled away and we both looked over our shoulders and I met the livid eyes of Mrs. Hallman.

"Mom," Katie said, scrambling to her feet. "This isn't what it looks like."

"Really? Because what I saw was you kissing a guy you claimed was just a friend who needed a family to spend Thanksgiving with, who happens to look like he just got out of prison."

"Mrs. Hallman—" I started to say, but a single glare from her shut me up. Mr. Hallman was right behind her, putting his hand on her shoulder and talking softly in her ear. That was my cue to make myself scarce.

"I'll give you a minute," I said, heading for my car.

Katie tried to stop me, but this wasn't my place. She had some issues to work out, and my being there wasn't going to help. I didn't know if I should still get my stuff or not.

I couldn't count the number of times I'd been kicked out of a house, but this one felt shittier than any time before.

Deciding I should give them a few minutes, I got in my backseat and stretched out, grabbing the violin I'd brought. It seemed like a better choice than the guitar or my uke.

I plucked a few strings and wondered how the conversation with Katie and her parents was going. I really shouldn't have let Katie convince me to come. I also shouldn't have kissed her, but what was done was done.

I'd had a lot of "shouldn't haves" with Katie.

I pulled out my bow, swiped some rosin across it and started playing. I started with "Holding On and Letting Go", by Ross Copperman and moved to "Hysteria", by Muse and then to "I Want You", by Andrew Allen.

Every song made me think of Katie. I poked my head up and glanced at the porch where they were still talking. It didn't look good, because Katie was using her hands while she spoke. She only did that when she was especially pissed. She was also leaning heavily on one hip, which was another bad sign.

The thing that almost made me laugh was that her mother was doing the same thing. Guess the apple didn't fall far from that tree. Mr. Hallman looked like a referee who was trying to let both sides win.

My phone chose that moment to chime with a call from Trish.

"Hey, how's Thanksgiving with the Cleavers?" she said, sounding quite cheerful, for Trish.

"It's been . . . interesting. How's yours?"

"Well, I've been invited to move in, so that's good, I guess. Lottie's parents are pretty cool. They're both seriously smart though. You'd fit right in."

"Probably better than I do here," I said under my breath.

"Her mom's freaking out, isn't she?"

"Just a bit, but she did catch us kissing on the porch after Katie told her I was just a friend."

She snorted. "Dude, can't you keep it in your pants for one day?"

"It wasn't that kind of kiss."

"What kind of kiss was it, lover boy?"

"Look, I'm not discussing this with you right now." Out of the corner of my eye, I saw Katie storm off the porch and march her way toward my car, her face as dark as a hurricane. "Gotta go. Say hi to everyone for me."

"Will do. Bye."

Katie wrenched open the car door and climbed in without further ado.

"How did it go?" I said. She pushed my violin out of the way and lay on top of me. That was unexpected, but it didn't mean my dick didn't respond accordingly.

"Will you take me somewhere so we can fuck?" Her hands started working on my shirt and it took every ounce of willpower I had to grab them and make them stop.

"Now? You want to fuck in the middle of your family's Thanksgiving dinner?" Even for me, that was a little extreme.

"Not in the middle of it. I just . . . I need to get away for a little while. I need a physical distraction."

She tried to wrench her hands away from my grip, but I wouldn't let her, so she started grinding her hips against me. Damn, she knew how to push all the right buttons.

"Katie, stop. Seriously. We can't fuck every time you have a problem and don't want to deal with it. Not that I don't enjoy every second of it, but it never solves anything."

She looked down at me and I watched her face break and the tears start to fall on my shirt. I let her have her hands back so she could wipe them away.

"I'm being stupid," she said, moving so I could get out from under her. "I'm sorry. That was impulsive and stupid." She pulled her knees up on the seat and I sat beside her.

"Look, you may think that your mom is being crazy, but everything she's doing is because she loves you. She loves you so much she's trying to protect you from the scary pierced and tattooed guy. Most mothers would have the same reaction."

"You're not scary."

"To a mother with a daughter, I am. To be fair, you didn't give her a good warning about who was going to show up. You could have given her a heads up. Why didn't you?"

She shook her head.

"I don't know." Refusing to look at me, she just stared at the half-finished drawing on her hand and wrist.

"Tell me the truth, Katie. Did you not tell her about me on purpose to make a point? To piss her off?"

Her head rose and her red eyes met mine.

"Is that what you think of me?" she whispered.

"Is it true?" It wouldn't have surprised me if it was, even if she wasn't aware that was what she'd been doing.

She shook her head and put her hands in the air.

"I don't know, Stryker. Maybe a little. She just made me so mad about Zack. But it's not just that. Not anymore."

She traced one finger on the design I'd made.

"But I told you, I can't do this. The relationship thing. Not with you. Yes, maybe I was using you, and I'm sorry. I guess I get the douche award today."

I nodded, since I'd expected as much. So why did it bother me? I slid away from her and got out, pulling open the driver's side door.

"Are you leaving?" she said, getting out of the backseat and standing behind me.

"I don't belong here, Katie. I don't want to cause problems between you and your family." I should have turned around the second I walked in the door, but I'd thought maybe I could make it work, but I'd been fooling myself. For a few moments, I'd imagined what it would be like to be a member of her family, but it would never happen. Could never happen.

"Why did you come?" She put her hand on the door so I couldn't move it.

"Because you invited me and I thought it would be nice to see what a Thanksgiving is supposed to look like. I've never had one before."

She pulled in a quick breath, as if I'd said something that shocked her.

"Way to make me feel like shit, Stryker." She stepped back and looked up at the sky. "Why do you put up with me?"

"I ask myself that question a lot. I still haven't come up with an answer."

She tipped her head to the side and squinted at me.

"Come on. Let's go back inside. Dad's probably got mom under control enough. Why don't you bring your violin? You'll seduce everyone with your musical genius. You don't have to stay the night. Just for an hour."

She gave me a smile and it was the kind that a girl could use to sweet talk her way out of a speeding ticket, or out of paying the cover at a club, or to get the codes for a top-secret government facility. Christ, she could make me do anything.

"Please?" Little did she know, if she asked me to cut off my right arm with a rusty saw, I would have done it for that smile and that little 'please.'

I could do this. It didn't have to be a big deal.

"Fine. But if your mom takes me out to the backyard and shoots me, it's your fault."

"She doesn't even know how to use a gun. It's my dad you have to worry about when it comes to using firearms."

"Good to know," I said as she pulled my violin out of the back and handed it to me.

Katie

Stryker stayed. Mom got herself together with the help of Dad, and everyone else warmed to him after he started interacting, and especially after he played a heartbreaking rendition of "Brown Eyed Girl". Dad belted it out and danced her around the living room and she laughed as he dipped her. I rolled my brown eyes when I recognized the song, but Grampa Jack just laughed and joined Dad with his baritone voice.

Kayla got me aside for a few minutes as Mom served everyone coffee and Grampa Jack told stories about the Vietnam War.

"You like him, Katiebug. Admit it."

"Keep your voice down," I said, glancing at the group in the living room. "It's complicated. He's just a distraction."

"Yeah, okay. You just keep telling yourself that."

Adam walked into the kitchen and Kayla wrapped her arms around him.

"Hey, husband."

"Hey, wife," he said and they shared a quick kiss. "Sorry to break up the sisterly moment, but I wanted to have a chance to talk to the girl who's going to be my new little sister."

"First of all, the way to butter me up isn't to call me 'little sister', okay?" I said.

Adam just grinned a wide smile and looked at Kayla.

"Yeah, she's exactly like you said she would be," he said.

I was at a loss for something to say, so Kayla just honked my nose.

"Well, you didn't tell me anything about him, sooo . . ." I said, poking her in the ribs.

"Hey, that's not fair," Kayla said. Adam jumped into to rescue her.

"It's my fault. I told her not to say anything. I didn't know how your family would react, seeing as how they hadn't even met me yet. I wanted her to keep the engagement a secret, but I lost that fight. It will be the first of many, I'm sure."

"Yes, yes you did." Kayla twisted the ring on her finger.

"Couldn't spring for the big rock, Adam?" I said, but this time Kayla saved him from answering.

"I didn't want one. There's no point in having a huge diamond when we're going to be going into areas where people don't even have drinking water. It seemed extravagant. Plus, it would get stolen quicker than you could say, 'stick 'em up.'"

"So what are you two going to do after you get married?"

"I still have to get through medical school, so I'll be doing that and then I want to join Doctors Without Borders and travel around the world. I'm lucky I found a girl who wants to go with me," Adam said as Kayla rocked back and forth, taking him with her.

"Now you're stuck with me, husband."

"Wouldn't have it any other way, wife."

"Get a room," I said, pretending to be disgusted. I'd never seen her like this.

Kayla had always been selfless. Between starting a penny drive that raised thousands of dollars for the food pantry when she was seven to the hundreds of hours of community service she'd put in, to volunteering to go places other people would avoid so she could build wells and deliver mosquito nets and help anyone who needed it.

My parents secretly wished her altruistic values would rub off on me, but no such luck. Attempting to be better than Kayla was something I didn't even want to try. Plus, I was a self-centered brat almost half of the time. Some people would say it was more.

"We're just going to do whatever feels right. You know?"

"Yeah," I said, even though I had no idea what she was talking about.

She sighed and looked at the clock. "We should get going soon," Kayla said. "We're flying back on Saturday."

"Where are you staying?"

"We haven't figured that out yet," Kayla said.

"You can stay in the basement," Dad said, jumping into the conversation. For a tall guy, he was really good at sneaking up on people. "There's that extra bed down there. We got brand new sheets and everything." I shared a look with Kayla. The basement hadn't changed much from when she'd moved out, and she knew that.

"Oh, that's fine Dad, I'm sure we can just get a hotel room or something."

"Absolutely not." Mom wasn't as quiet as Dad. Especially because she was wearing her ugliest and most-comfortable shoes, which made her sound like a Clydesdale when she walked. "You are staying here. I haven't seen you in months, and we need to get wedding planning."

"Oh, Mom, that's not –" Kayla was interrupted by Mom grabbing her and dragging her away.

I'm so sorry, Adam mouthed at Kayla as she was led away.

"She's been planning a wedding since we knew we were having at least one daughter," Dad said to Adam. "It's pointless fighting it."

"I hope Kayla's going to tell her that we didn't want a huge thing. Just my family and hers and a few of our friends. It's going to be expensive enough flying them all in to wherever we're going to have it, even though I don't have a huge family," Adam said. He didn't know my mother at all.

"I hate to break it to you, but I think she's already got a venue chosen," Dad said. "I've tried to stop her, but once she gets something into her head she just goes for it."

"See? This is what you get to look forward to," I said to Adam as Stryker started taking requests and I moved toward the living room.

"Hey, Katiebug, can you come help me set up the bed downstairs?" Dad gave me a look that meant he wanted to talk. At least he was more subtle about it than Mom.

"See you later, future big brother," I said to Adam as I followed Dad down the stairs to the basement. The violin music faded behind us, and I hoped Stryker would be okay on his own for a few minutes. My mom had a serious problem collecting furniture, bordering on an obsession, and most of it was stored in the basement. Since I'd been at school they'd painted the walls and moved some of it out of the way so you could at least walk from one side of the room to the other without climbing over something. Sort of.

The bed for Kayla and Adam to share was shoved in a corner, so Dad and I moved it out a bit so they could at least get in and out of it without crashing into one of the lamps Mom couldn't say no to, or the gigantic chest that could have passed for a coffin.

"He's an interesting young man you brought home, Katiebug. Is he your boyfriend?" He pulled a sheet set out of the 'rustic' dresser Mom had paid an arm and a leg for.

"Well, Dad don't beat around the bush." We shook the sheets and set about making up the bed. "No, he's not my boyfriend."

"But you want him to be."

I wished everyone would stop asking me that. "I don't know what I want. Right now, after everything with Zack, I can't really think about dating. It's just too complicated."

"I think that's a good plan, but that doesn't mean it's going to work. Sometimes life gets in the way."

"Hmm," I said tucking a corner of the fitted sheet over the mattress.

"Mom doesn't like him, does she?" I said.

Dad spread the flat sheet out and started tucking it in, looking down at the drawing Stryker had done. He really was crazy talented.

"I'm not so sure about him myself, Katie. He's not who I would have chosen for you."

"I'm not *choosing* him. He's just a guy I'm hanging out with." That was all he needed to know. I would rather dive naked into a volcano than admit to Dad that Stryker and I were having casual sex. Hell, my parents hadn't even had 'the talk' with me. They'd handed me one of those books with graphic anatomically correct drawings and said to come to them with any questions. Little did they know that Britt's Dad had a secret porn collection we'd sampled during junior high sleepovers when her parents went to bed.

"Have you heard from Zack?" Dad said as we tucked the quilt over the flat sheet. I knew he wouldn't have brought it up, so Mom must have convinced him to do it.

"Not really. I think his parents are keeping him on a short leash. I'll have to see him soon enough." Bless our legal system for drawing this whole thing out longer and longer.

"He's talented." Dad tossed a pillowcase at me and I slid it over one of the pillows. It took me a second to shift gears and realize he wasn't talking about Zack.

"Yeah, he is." I sighed. "He intimidates me."

"He is, ah," he said, coughing, "intimidating." Our eyes met and he smiled.

"You really like him, don't you?"

I shrugged.

"I don't know what I feel anymore." We finished with the bed and I glanced back up the stairs. "We should get back before Mom plans Kayla's entire wedding."

"I never really liked Zack. Just so you know." He put his arm around me and pulled me in for a hug, placing a kiss on the top of my head. "You know how you feel, I think. You're just scared because you're hurt, but that will pass. You'll figure it out."

"Thanks, Dad." I hugged him back and we walked up the stairs together.

Ten

Stryker

As the day wore on, the relatives departed, including Grampa Jack who gave me a hearty handshake, another wink, and a bit of advice.

"Treat that girl right, you hear?"

"Yes, sir." He wheezed all the way down the steps as Katie's Aunt Carol helped him into the backseat of the car.

Mrs. Hallman was still shooting me disapproving looks whenever she could, and I had about had it. Yes, there were those people who were into body modification that got mad when people stared at them, but I wasn't one of them. People stared. Get over it. If you didn't like it, don't go out, or don't get modified.

I'd told Zan that people judged you and put you in a box when they first met you. Mrs. Hallman had seen me, and put me in the "troublemakers who shouldn't be allowed near my precious daughter" box. It was both scary and disconcerting that she hadn't put Zack in that box.

I'd put my violin away, and Katie and Kayla were catching up while Adam listened, when I saw my chance. Mrs. Hallman was cleaning the kitchen, again, and Mr. Hallman had manufactured some excuse to leave the house. Smart man.

"Mrs. Hallman?" I wasn't going to buy her telling me I could call her Regina. "Could I talk to you for a moment?" She paused as she wiped the counter with a sponge, her back to me. I probably shouldn't have snuck up on her. Bad idea.

She stiffened, as if what I was asking was a huge inconvenience. I wasn't going to beg, so I waited.

"Fine." She put the sponge in the sink and faced me, crossing her arms.

"You don't like me, and I get that, but I just wanted to thank you for opening up your home to me and letting me stay. You could have shut the door in my face. I know you wanted to."

She tried to hide her shock, but it still took over her face for a few seconds.

"I know you judge me by the way I look, and the funny thing is that you're wrong. You let that monster, Zack, near your daughter and the first time I saw him, I knew what he was. That night that she went to see him, I told her not to go. She probably didn't tell you that, but I knew. I *knew* he would do this to her." Her face went white and then red with the speed of a traffic signal.

"How *dare* you? How dare you accuse me of putting my daughter in danger? I'm only letting you be here to keep the peace with Katie, but I'm not so sure I want you spending the night in my home. I would appreciate if you would just leave." She crossed her arms, standing her ground.

This had been a mistake. A huge mistake.

"How dare *you*?" I hadn't heard Katie come up behind me. "Mom, seriously? Just give it a rest."

I jumped in before they could lunge at each other's throats. I'd done enough damage already. "No, it's fine. Thank you for the lovely meal, Mrs. Hallman." I went to the living room and grabbed my violin and then to the guest room to pick up my coat where Katie had left it earlier.

"You're not leaving, are you?" Katie followed me.

"I shouldn't be here. I'm just causing problems for you, and I don't want that. You shouldn't have asked me to come. I don't want to be the guy who makes you fight with your mom, so I'm going to go."

"You're just going to leave because my mom doesn't like you? I don't care what she thinks."

She sat down on the bed, and tried to take my coat from me.

"Yeah, I think you do. She's your mom, Katie. Even if you have a fight, you know she'll always love you and always be on your side. My mom tried to sell me for drugs once."

"Stryker." Her wide brown eyes begged me and I wanted so much to give in and stay. Oh, I wanted to, but I couldn't. I didn't belong here.

"Just let me go, Katie," I said, yanking the coat away from her and put it on. She wasn't going to make this easy on me. I was going to have to go into dick mode. "Leave me the fuck alone. Don't call me for sex anymore, because I can't do it. I'm not your slave, and I'm not a guy to bring home just to piss your parents off. Just leave me the fuck alone." I slammed the door open and stomped through the house and out the front door. Katie tried to catch me, but I was peeling away from the house before she even got down the porch. I'd done a quick getaway more times than she could imagine.

As I accelerated down the street, I turned on my radio and found the loudest, most obnoxious music I could, which turned out to be some weird punk version of a popular song. I hit the gas even though the speed limit was 25. I was probably going to get a speeding ticket, but I didn't give a shit. I realized too late that I'd driven the wrong way from Katie's house, but I wasn't going to turn around so I just kept driving.

My GPS was yelling at me, but I ripped it off the dashboard and threw it in the back. I'd find my way back. My phone started blowing up, so I grabbed that, turned it off and tossed it in the back as well.

I hadn't been this pissed in a long time. I hadn't fucking *cared* this much in a long time, if I was being honest.

Realizing how *much* I cared caused me to blow a stop sign and get an angry honk from another driver. I saw a sign for the highway and turned. I had no fucking clue where I was.

I followed the signs and got onto the highway going in the right direction to get back to school. I pushed the accelerator and got in the passing lane.

"Get fuck out of my way," I growled at everyone who wasn't driving at least seventy-five miles an hour.

The faster I drove, the more I realized how much I wanted to go back and apologize and tell her we could work it out. That we'd find a way. That we could go back to just being fuck buddies, if nothing else.

But I couldn't, because I wanted more, even though it would never, ever work.

I was a guy who she'd fool around with in college before meeting someone better and then she'd tell her own daughter stories about me when she was doing the same thing. I was the cautionary tale.

I wasn't husband material. I wasn't boyfriend material. I wasn't forever love material. I was 'guy you fuck' material.

It wasn't until I realized that I was nearly out of gas that I pulled into a gas station and stopped. I had a moment of weakness and found my phone in the backseat and turned it back on. Yep, I had a million texts and messages from Katie. I couldn't read them, because I knew they would pull me back.

"You fucking idiot!" I said, banging my hand on the hood of my car. That earned me a nasty look from a mother walking by with her two young children. She hurried to get them into the car as if I was going to come over and try to kidnap them, or sell them drugs.

"Yup, that's right. I was totally going to steal your obnoxious kids and do really bad things to them," I said to myself.

The pump clicked off and I screwed the cap back on my gas tank. I knew what awaited me back at my apartment. Nothing. No one. Trish was with Lottie, Zan had gone home to his parents and everyone else was with their families.

I was fine with being alone.

I threw my phone in the backseat, but something caught my attention, so I picked it up. It was one of Katie's pink pearl drop earrings. Her dad had gotten them for her birthday, and I knew how much she loved them.

The earring glinted under the fluorescent light of the gas station. The pearl was perfectly round and unblemished. I shoved it in my pocket and got back in my car.

Katie

I sat on the porch after Stryker left me, wondering what to do. Half of me wanted to get in my car and go after him and beg him to come back, and the other half wanted to find him and beat him senseless.

As the two different instincts wrestled, I called his phone. It went straight to voicemail.

"Look, I'm super pissed at you right now, and that was a dick move leaving like that so would you please come back so I can yell at you and then we can be friends again?" I paused, unsure of what to say that would make him reconsider. "It would suck if we weren't friends anymore. It's not just about the sex. I'd miss you."

I hung up before I said anything else. I also texted him a few times for good measure. I was freezing my ass off, but I didn't want to go inside because I knew they were all talking about me and Stryker. The front door opened and I turned my head to make sure it wasn't Mom. I couldn't talk to her right now without saying something I would regret later.

"Hey, Katiebug," Kayla said, throwing a blanket over my shoulders. "You wanna talk?"

"Nope," I said popping my lips on the 'p.'

"I figured. I know everyone's been giving you advice and I know how much that pisses you off, so I'm not going to give you advice."

"Good."

She sat down next to me and I held out the blanket so we could share it.

"You know, the first time I met Adam, I was trying to hook up with his friend?"

"Really?"

She laughed and shook her head. "Yeah. It was the night before we were leaving on our plane and we all decided to go out. I was totally crushing on his friend Robbie, but he didn't seem to be into me. Then I just started talking to Adam because he was standing right next to him. He seemed so cocky that I was totally turned off at first, but then a few hours later I couldn't get him into bed fast enough."

I really didn't need that part of the story. "Ugh, too much information."

She continued. "So anyway, I thought I didn't like him. I kept telling myself that I didn't like him, that I just liked how I felt when we hooked up. It took me an entire week to realize that the feeling I had when we hooked up was no different than the feeling I had when he made me laugh, or said my name, or even when he was in the same room. It was love. Yes, it started out as lust, but that changed pretty fast."

"You said you weren't going to give me any advice," I said, moving closer to her. My fingers were numb and any moment, my teeth were going to start chattering.

Her eyes went wide an innocent. "I have no idea what you're talking about. I was just telling you about the first time I met Adam."

I rolled my eyes and wrapped the blanket tighter.

"We should go inside. My ass is officially frozen," Kayla said, getting up. "Come on. You can hide downstairs with me and Adam. We could play Hot Lava."

Mom's furniture obsession had started before she had us, so when we were kids we assumed everyone else had a basement full of furniture they couldn't use. We often spent rainy afternoons hopping from chairs to dressers to get from one side of the room to the other, pretending the floor was lava.

"I think we're both a little too big for that. I'm not sure Mom's new table, oh excuse me, sideboard, could take us standing on it."

"I think she has a problem," Kayla said as we walked slowly back into the house. The blast of warm air was so shocking compared to the air outside that it almost hurt. I flexed my red fingers to try to get some feeling back into them.

The living room was quiet except for Adam humming to himself while reading a book that I knew didn't come from my house.

"Where's Mom and Dad?" Kayla said, rubbing her arms.

"They went to their room. A little chilly out there?" He closed the book and took Kayla into his arms.

"I'm going to my room," I said. I wanted to try Stryker again, but I didn't want an audience.

"I'll bring you some tea or something," Kayla said.

"Thanks."

I heard Mom and Dad talking softly in their room as I went upstairs. I shut the door and called Stryker again, sitting back on my now-bare bed. Nearly all of my pillows were on my bed at school.

"Hey, it's me again. I just wish you would come back. Or I could come to you. Did you go back to school? I really wish you'd answer your phone. I really wish you were here. I really wish things could have been different. I wish we could back to when you dared me to eat the pie. You still owe me a date, by the way. So just . . . call me back. Even if it's to tell me to leave you the fuck alone. I just don't want it to end like this. It can't end like this."

I ended the call and looked around my room. Stryker was always asking me why I was obsessed with pink.

Yeah, I had to stop thinking about him. I grabbed my phone again and called Lottie.

"Hey, roomie! Are you in a turkey coma yet?" Her Thanksgiving had obviously been better than mine.

"Well, it kind of blew up in my face and Stryker stormed out."

"He did what? What happened?" I heard Trish talking behind her, asking if she was talking to me because Stryker hadn't called her back.

"Trish, seriously. I can't hear her when you're yelling in my ear," Lottie said, and moved away from the noise.

"Okay, I'm alone now. So what happened?"

"It was so stupid. My mom was completely unprepared for him, and I knew she was going to freak out, but I hoped she wouldn't and then she did, and then I tried to fix it and we ended up fighting and he got pissed and left. I've called him a million times, but he's gone. I'm such an idiot."

"What did your mom say?"

150

"Oh, she didn't really say anything specific. She just treated him like he'd just gotten out of prison, and wouldn't stop glaring at him. Honestly, I don't blame him for leaving. He wanted this perfect Thanksgiving and it got ruined."

"That's not your fault."

"Yeah, it kind of is. I shouldn't have let him come in the first place. I knew Mom would react like that. I should have told her, but what then? She wouldn't have let him come, so then I would have told him he couldn't come, and I couldn't do that. Lottie, what am I going to do?"

"I'll get Trish to call him and see where he is. He'll probably answer for her. Let me tell her the situation and I'll call you back, okay? Don't worry, this is fixable."

I said goodbye to Lottie and stared at the pictures of my high school friends and me that were plastered all over my wall. I took a shit ton of pictures, I realized. I got up and looked at them. God, there were a bunch with Zack in them. I pulled one after the other off the walls, scattering them on the floor like leaves ripped from the branches of a tree.

I looked at my face in picture form, grinning back at me. I didn't know that girl. The girl who smiled at Zack like he'd found the world and handed it to her. Fuck. Him.

I tore down the rest of the pictures until my walls were mostly bare.

My phone rang, interrupting my redecorating.

"Hey, so Trish can't get a hold of him either. He's gone off the grid," Lottie said, a little out of breath.

"Shit," I said, letting my back slide down my bare wall until I was sitting on the floor. "He's probably on his way back to his place. I should go apologize."

Someone knocked on my door.

"Yeah?" I said, putting my hand over the phone. Kayla poked her head in the door, only glancing at the pictures that littered the floor.

"Brought you some tea." She held a mug out and I took it, setting it next to me.

"Thanks."

"You should come talk to Mom. She's really upset."

Yeah, I bet she was.

"I'll be there in a second." Kayla nodded and waited in the doorway.

Lottie had been waiting patiently, but I could hear her talking to Trish as well. I banged the back of my head against the wall.

"I don't know what to do, Lot."

"Just fix things with your mom and deal with him tomorrow. He just needs some time to cool off. Okay, Trish, you can talk to her. Here's Trish."

The phone was passed as Kayla gave me a look that said she was waiting for me to come with her.

"Look, he does this. He runs and then he feels bad about it and comes back the next day. Trust me, he'll be back. This is his thing. The best way to deal with it is to let him have his time. You don't want to chase after him, because he'll just run away again. But he always comes back if you let him. Like a boomerang."

"If you say so," I said.

"I do say so."

"Trish, I'm sorry."

She scoffed. "Why are you apologizing to me? Save it for him. Not that he'll let you. He hates apologies."

"Great."

"I'm telling you, this is not a big deal. He's done worse. Many times. Be glad he's not still going through his binge drinking phase. That was a great time."

"You don't think he would do anything stupid?" I said softly.

"Over this? No way. This is nothing. Relax, girl. He just needs a breather."

"Okay."

"Okie dokie, here's Lottie. Don't worry, bye."

Lottie came back on and I told her that I had to deal with my mom so she agreed to give me updates if Stryker contacted Trish back.

I grabbed my tea and walked into the kitchen where Mom was sitting at the dining table, her eyes blotched from crying.

"I'm sorry, Katie."

That made two of us.

Eleven

Stryker

I got back to my apartment and it was just as I'd left it. Cold and quiet. I turned on some music, but it turned out to be the playlist I'd come to think of as "Katie songs" so I switched it out for something harsher.

I tore through my cupboards and found the bottle of whiskey Allan had stashed for his own personal use. There was still plenty left so I grabbed a shot glass and downed one. It wasn't the cheap stuff, either. Allan was a total alcohol snob, especially when it came to whiskey.

I paced the apartment, searching for something to get me out of my own head. I picked up each and every one of my instruments, but I couldn't play them. I downed another shot.

It was way too cold and dark to work on my car. I poured another shot, but didn't drink it. I put my chin on the counter and squinted at the clear brown liquid. It used to solve all my problems. At least until I woke up with a raging hangover and realized my problems were still right where I left them when I started drinking.

Back and forth I pushed the shot glass across the counter. Pulling out the pearl earring from my pocket, I set it next to the glass.

I should call her and tell her I had it. I should call her and apologize for bailing and for saying "fuck" in her parents' house.

Cage the Elephant's "Ain't No Rest for the Wicked" came on and I tapped my hand on the counter with the beat of the song.

Before I could second guess myself, I took out my phone and downed the third shot.

"Hey, you," she said, the sweetness dripping from her voice. "What are you up to?" I heard voices in the background and soft music, so she was probably out somewhere. Big surprise.

I tossed the shot glass up in the air and caught it. "Nothing, just hanging out at home. You want to come over?"

"I'd love to. Be there in ten."

She hung up and I set my phone down, got a second shot glass from my cupboard and filled it up, pouring another one for myself. If I didn't want to end up in the hospital, I was going to have to pace myself. Trish wasn't here to save my sorry ass this time.

I put the earring back in my pocket and waited.

There was a knock at my door less than seven minutes later. I got up and answered it. She was dressed in a miniskirt with fishnets and a ripped tank top, as per usual.

She put one hand up and leaned in the doorway seductively. Yep, I was drunk. "Hey, Stryk."

"Hey, Ric."

She gave me a kiss on the cheek that lingered. Her breath already smelled like alcohol, and I could tell she'd just put out a cigarette. God, I hadn't smoked in a long time.

"Ooohh, are we taking shots?" she said, seeing the drinks on the counter.

"Yeah, I just need a smoke first. Come with me?"

She smiled slow and stepped toward me, walking her fingers up and down my shirt.

"Absolutely."

That was what Katie had said when I'd asked her if she wanted to fuck me the first time. The word hit me in the chest. I paused for a second, and Ric put her arm around me.

"Something wrong, babe?"

I looked down at her face, and picked it apart. Her eyes were too close together, her smile was too wide, her cheekbones too sharp. She was also too tall.

She wasn't Katie.

I shut my eyes for a second and then opened them.

"Nope."

Katie

The 'little chat' with Mom turned into one of our yelling matches, as it always did. Kayla and Dad tried to stop it, but there was only so much they could do before we were both screaming at each other. Like a hurricane, they knew they just had to sit back, board up the doors and windows and wait for it to be over.

"Say it, just come out and say it. You judged him the moment he walked in. You made up some image of what he would look like in your head and when he didn't match that you freaked out, proving you are just as judgmental as I knew you were."

We were standing in the spotless kitchen now, having already taken the fight around the rest of the house. Dad and Kayla watched from the safety of the dining room table, ready to come in and referee if things got really bad.

"That isn't fair, Katie. You gave me no warning. What was I supposed to think?"

I threw up my hands. "You weren't supposed to think anything! You were supposed to wait and see what kind of guy he is."

She smashed her hands down on the counter with a slap. "How was I supposed to do that? You didn't tell me anything about him."

"Would you have let him come if you knew?"

She started to protest, but it was a second too late.

"Yeah, that's what I thought. God, Mom." I stalked toward the living room. I couldn't fight with her anymore. "Congratulations, you win. He's gone and I'm going, too." More often than not, our fights only ended when one of us stormed out.

"Katiebug, don't leave like this," Dad said. "Don't leave angry."

"I'm sorry I brought him here and ruined Thanksgiving. I'm sorry that I ruin everything. It seems to be my thing." I ran to my room so I wouldn't break down in front of them. I slipped on the photographs that were still all over the floor and landed hard on my side.

"Shit!" I rolled over on my back, massaging my hip.

"You're being a brat, you know," Kayla said, pushing my door open.

"Yes, I am, but that's what I do. I'm the screw-up little sister." Kayla crouched down next to me where I still lay on the floor. I turned onto my back and glanced at her, wiping tears away.

"That's not true and you know it. Mom and Dad worship the ground you walk on. I used to hate you," she said, lying on her back next to me.

What in the what was she talking about? "Are you serious? You're their golden child."

Kayla laughed as if that were genuinely funny.

"It's all about perspective."

"Whatever," I said. She was nuts.

Kayla picked up one of the pictures and it happened to be of Zack and me at a party. He had his arm around me, a bottle of beer just out of view. He was looking at the camera and I was looking at him.

"I never understood what you saw in this douchebag." She studied the picture for another moment, then ripped it in half. Before I could say anything, she picked up another picture of Zack and me and ripped that too.

"Here," she said, handing me another one, where Zack was giving me a sloppy kiss and not even trying to hide his beer bottle anymore.

I stared at my giggling face for a second and then tore it apart and threw it back on my floor. Kayla found another one, and then another, and another. We got up and played a twisted version of 'Where's Waldo', trying to find any picture that had Zack in it. There were quite a few.

When we'd ripped up all of those, I started on the other pictures. Kayla sat back and let me go at those ones. She pulled the trash can over and we piled the torn pictures of my former self up and then dumped them in.

When the floor was bare and the trash can was full, I stopped and sat back, bracing myself against the wall.

"Thought you were leaving," Kayla said.

"I was. I am. I just wish he would call me. Trish said he hates apologies and that I need to let him cool off, but I just want him to contact me in some way."

She came to sit next to me against the wall. "You'll work it out. I swear."

"I wish I had your confidence."

"Comes from being the older sister. So, are you going to stay or go?"

I shook my head. "I have to go. I can't stay here with Mom."

"She'll come around."

Not likely. "I wish I had your confidence about that too."

***

It was nearly ten when I pulled up in front of Stryker's apartment. He wasn't alone. There was another car there, but I didn't know whose it was.

I tried calling him one more time before I knocked, but he didn't answer, so I knocked and waited.

No answer.

The lights were on upstairs, so he must be home. I stepped back and saw someone peek through the curtains, but they were gone before I could see who it was.

I banged on the door again and footsteps pounded down the stairs.

"Katie," Stryker said as he yanked the door open. No, he didn't just say it. He breathed it. In those two syllables I heard hope and shock and even a little anger.

"Who is it?" A female voice said from his open door at the top of the stairs. I heard her start walking and when she came into view I had to swallow hard.

Ric.

"What are you doing here? I thought you were home with your happy little family," she said, coming to stand behind Stryker and putting her hand on his shoulder. Marking what she thought was her territory. It only took me a second to assess the situation and know that Stryker had done this on purpose. Not that I was that cocky, but I knew he thought this would piss me off, which was the exact reason I wasn't. Nice try, Stryker Grant, but I don't play that game.

Stryker smoothed his expression and spoke in the hard voice he'd used when he stormed out of my house earlier. His douchebag voice.

"I thought I told you to leave me alone."

"Yeah, and I thought I told you it wasn't just the sex, so we're even."

Ric's eyes narrowed when I mentioned the sex. They both smelled heavily of alcohol, but they were both fully-clothed. Well, Stryker was. Ric looked like she'd just come from clubbing.

"Yeah, well, I changed my mind. I don't want to do this anymore, Katie." If he clenched his jaw any tighter, he was going to damage some of his teeth.

"I didn't come here for that. I came to say I'm sorry. I know you hate apologies, so I hope you like grand gestures instead." Without another word, I went to my car and grabbed two grocery bags. My trunk was full, so it was going to take a few trips to bring everything in.

In my head this had gone different, mostly because I expected him to be home alone. I'd written out this whole script on my way up, and he'd decided not to follow it.

"I'm making you dinner," I said when I came back holding the bags. "So let me in because I need to preheat the oven if we're going to eat before the sun comes up."

Stryker stared at me as if he couldn't figure me out.

"You're not pissed that Ric is here and I'm drunk and we might have messed around?" Ric smirked at me from over his shoulder.

"Not really. You gonna let me in or not?"

He moved aside and I pushed past him and Ric and marched up the stairs. I heard her saying something to him, but I couldn't make it out. I set the bags down on the kitchen floor and started unpacking them.

Finding a turkey *on* Thanksgiving was something I deserved a medal for. I had to go to three grocery stores and finally found a fresh one in an organic market. It was tiny, but it would do for my purposes, and it didn't need to be thawed.

I plunked it on the counter and pulled out a bag of potatoes.

"You're cooking me an apology turkey?" Stryker said, waiting in the doorway, as if he was nervous to come in his own apartment.

I slammed down a can of cranberry sauce. "Yup."

"This is so weird," Ric muttered.

"You can stay if you want," I said, giving her a dripping sweet smile. "The more the merrier."

"Yeah, I'll pass," Ric said, edging down the stairs. "You, um, have a good time."

"Are you sure?" I said, pulling out an acorn squash. "Well, see you at Band." I smiled as wide as I could and slammed the squash down, making her jump. She gave Stryker a look and scurried away.

"Aw, shame she couldn't stay," I said, pulling out some rolls. "I wasn't sure if you liked this kind or this kind." I pulled out another bag. "So I got both."

"Katie, what are you doing?" He finally came all the way inside.

"I'm making up for the shitty reception you got at my house. You wanted a perfect Thanksgiving, so I'm giving you a perfect fucking Thanksgiving. Now, could you be a gentleman and go get the rest of the bags from the car? Please and thank you."

Twelve

Stryker

I stumbled out to her car and found the trunk absolutely bursting with anything and everything you could make a Thanksgiving with. I grabbed some more of the bags and hauled them back up the stairs. It took a while because my balance wasn't at its finest.

When I opened the door and saw her, I was almost relieved. I thought she'd see me with Ric and that would be it. She'd yell and scream at me, call me an asshole and never want to speak to me again.

But, no. Katherine Ann Hallman had found a way to surprise me again.

It took me two more trips to get everything upstairs. Katie set it all out on my counter, and then when she ran out of room, she lined the boxes and cans up on the coffee table.

It was enough food to feed at least twelve people, but she also had other things. Placemats shaped like leaves and red, orange and yellow plates and even a paper fold-out turkey.

She didn't say a word as she rooted around in my drawers and found the apron I'd put on when I'd sent her that funny picture.

"Give me a hand?" She turned her back and held out the strings so I could tie them behind her back.

I tied a bow and moved away from her as quick as I could, resisting the urge to wrap my hands around her waist and pull her body toward me.

She stepped around me and went to my television, going for the instant movies. She did some searching and selected one that turned out to be *Charlie Brown*.

"Sit. Watch. Enjoy," she commanded, pointing to the couch. I did as I was told and she pulled out a very old and stained cookbook, flipping the pages until she found the right one. I glanced at her out of the corner of my eye while I watched the *Peanuts* gang's antics.

I knew there was no way she could singlehandedly make all that food, but I kept my mouth shut. To be honest, I was a little terrified of her at the moment.

"Oh, I almost forgot," she said, picking up one of the bags and rooting through it. "Here. Make some paper turkeys." She threw a box of markers, some scissors, glue and construction paper at me. The fact that she was pretending not to be pissed at me told me that she was, she was just trying to hide it.

"What?" I said, looking at the supplies.

"Haven't you ever made a paper turkey?"

I shook my head.

"Not in school or anything?"

"Nope."

She glanced at the mountain of yet-to-be-peeled potatoes and reluctantly sat down next to me.

"Okay, so you trace your hand like this." She traced her hand on an orange piece of construction paper. "Then you cut it out and do a few more and then you make a body and a head with the brown and glue it together. Presto, hand turkey."

She handed me the marker and I saw that the design I'd drawn on her hand this afternoon was still there. I'd expected her to wash it off.

"Okay, I need to get back to work. I expect at least two decent hand turkeys by the time I come and check on you again."

When she tried to get up, I took her arm to stop her.

"Why are you doing this for me? You don't care that I was getting drunk with Ric?"

She didn't pull away. "Did you have sex with her?"

"No, but I was going to."

She met my eyes without fear.

"Why? Because if it was to push me away, you failed. I'm still here."

"I'm still trying to figure that out." She put both hands on my shoulders and leaned in as if to kiss me.

"I've told you. It's not just the sex." Using my shoulders as leverage, she pushed herself to her feet. "Now don't disturb me. I'm cooking, and the first rule of cooking with Katie is that you keep your ass out of the kitchen."

"Yes, ma'am," I said, turning my focus back to the hand turkeys.

I got a little artistic with my hand turkey, putting texture on the feathers and giving the turkeys interesting facial expressions. Katie banged around the kitchen, peeling things and boiling water and rubbing butter on the turkey and raiding my spice cabinet. I couldn't help but notice that she put everything back where it should be when she was done.

If she didn't know what she was doing, she was really putting on a good show. The *Peanuts* show ended and Katie came and chose another show, *Addams Family Values*.

"It qualifies as a Thanksgiving movie," she said before I could even comment.

"I didn't say anything."

"How are those turkeys coming?" I held one up that was nearly dry.

"Very nice." I guess that was as good as it was going to get. I went back to making turkeys and she went back to cooking.

I didn't glance back until she swore loudly.

"What happened?" I didn't move from the couch, worried she'd throw something at me.

"Cut myself. I'm fine." She ran it under the water. "Do you have any Band-Aids?"

"Yeah, sure. Can I move from the couch to get them?" She glared at me. "I'll take that as a yes."

I dashed to the bathroom and came back with a Band-Aid and some ointment.

"Here," I said, coming up behind her while she was still at the sink. She jumped a little, but I'd been counting on that.

167

"Rule number two about cooking with Katie is that you don't sneak up behind her like a creeper." She snatched the Band-Aid and the tube of ointment from me and slid sideways, so I wasn't behind her.

"Get back to your turkeys."

I did as I was told, but not before brushing my fingers along her back where the apron was tied.

"Careful, sweetheart. Don't want you chopping off any of those fingers." She chucked an empty can at me, but missed.

***

Four hours later, my eyes were heavy, but my apartment had never smelled so delicious. There was so much food she had to be creative with containers to put it in. The mashed potatoes were in a metal ice bucket, the squash was in a mixing bowl and she'd put the cranberry sauce into a few of my shot glasses.

As I taped the paper turkeys all around, she threw a white lace-edge tablecloth on my coffee table and set it with the plates and new silverware and cloth napkins before placing the paper stand-up turkey in the middle.

I looked at the plates and bowls mounded with food.

"I am never going to eat all this," I said.

"Don't worry about that. Here." She handed me a serrated knife. "You get to carve the turkey."

I did my best and started putting pieces on her plate.

"I'll be totally honest," I said as she spooned some mashed potatoes onto her plate, "I didn't think you were going to pull this off."

"Well, that just goes to show you don't know me and what I'm capable of." Our hands brushed as we both went for the rolls. I moved my hand back and let her go first.

"That was a dick move, though. You should apologize to Ric. I'm not her biggest fan but it still wasn't nice," she said.

"I know." She poured gravy over her potatoes and turkey and went to sit on the couch. "Oh, crap, I forgot the wine."

"I've got something better." I searched the bottom of my liquor cabinet and found a bottle of spiced rum Allan had forgotten about that I'd been saving.

"You trying to get me drunk, Stryker?" she said when I held up the bottle.

"I was already drunk. I'm on my way to sober, but if you want to venture into drunk territory with me, I wouldn't say no."

"Well, seeing as how I can't go back to the dorm since it's closed up for the holiday, and I have nowhere else to go, I might as well." I grabbed my plate and the rum and joined her on the couch.

She held out her glass and I poured a little in and then poured myself some.

"To the perfect Thanksgiving," she said, clinking her glass with mine. We both drank and she chose another movie. *Planes, Trains and Automobiles* with Steve Martin and John Candy.

She smiled at me and we dug in to *Thanksgiving 2.0, The Middle of the Night Edition.*

"How is it?" she said after only my first bite.

"Fantastic," I said, my mouth full. It was even better than her mom's and that was saying something.

"Thanks." We both ate and watched the movie, laughing at the same parts. I hadn't seen this movie for years. Trish was a John Hughes fan. She only loved Nicholas Sparks more.

Everything was fabulous, and I was thrilled I didn't have to lie and pretend I liked it. I would have, but I was glad I didn't have to.

The rum made me warm and relaxed, and hearing Katie's laughter made everything even better.

She made everything better. Food, music, kissing. Hell, she made breathing better because every time I breathed, I got a little bit of her scent.

I glanced at her out of the corner of my eye and found she was doing the same thing. We both looked away and put our attention back on our plates.

No girl had ever done something like this for me. Not even close. I still didn't know how I should react. Did this mean she had *feelings* feelings for me? Yes, she'd said it was about more than the sex, but how much more?

I'd never been this fucking neurotic about a girl and it was freaking me out. She shifted and her leg brushed against mine.

"Sorry," she said.

"It's fine."

She was still wearing the apron and I had to stop myself from picturing her wearing that and nothing else.

I cleared my throat and took a sip of rum, but I choked on it.

"You okay there?" she said, raising her hand to bang me on the back.

I waved her off. "Yeah, fine."

She must have thought I was being a moron because I was drunk.

Katie

What the hell was wrong with me? Just sitting next to him on the couch was proving to be more difficult than I thought. I'd always taken it for granted that when I wanted to have sex with him, we'd just do it.

Holding off was *hard*. I couldn't help but notice how the tattoos on his arm flexed when he moved his fork, or how his hair was different, swept to the sides of his face. His leg brushed mine, sending chills up and down my spine.

I tried to watch the movie, but I kept catching myself looking at him instead. It was shocking to think that I hadn't thought he was attractive when I'd first met him, even after he took off the stupid fangs.

Now I couldn't stop myself from wanting to stare at him all night. This realization made me blush with embarrassment, as if I'd said it out loud.

"You did a good job with the turkeys," I said, pointing my fork at one he'd taped to the door. He'd drawn it with an eye patch, and the one taped to the window behind the television was winking.

"What's that one supposed to be?" It had hollow dead-looking eyes and a gaping beak.

"Zombie turkey," he said, as if it was obvious.

"Got it." Now that I thought about it, zombie was the most obvious conclusion. "Oh my God!"

"What?" He put down his fork as if I'd seen a robber and he was getting ready to protect me.

"We forgot to say what we're thankful for. Shit, I can't believe I left that out." I blamed the rum. And him. It was totally his fault for being so . . . him.

"It's not too late. We haven't had the pie yet." I'd been a slacker and bought a frozen pie, but he didn't seem to mind. "Do you want me to go first?"

"If you want me to."

He poured some more rum into his glass and took a sip.

"I'm thankful for music and art and friends who stand by me even when I screw things up and Trish and broken cars that I get to fix and tricky equations I get to solve and that everyone I care about is healthy and for a girl who wears too much pink, doesn't take no for an answer and tells me that it isn't just about the sex."

He took another sip of rum and I blushed at the end of his speech. I hadn't blushed at something in a long, long time.

"How can I follow that?"

"I'm sure you'll do okay," he said, patting my knee. His hand lingered for just a second before he moved it.

"Okay, I'm also thankful for friends who stand by me even when I screw things up and also pink and roommates and my sister and my parents and Grampa Jack and for everyone being healthy and . . . and for a boy who took pity on a girl with a broken heart and showed her that all guys aren't douchebags and who makes her feel happy again."

I took a swallow of rum and waited for him to say something.

"Seems like we have a lot to be thankful for," he said, swirling the liquid in his glass. All the things unsaid between us hung in the air like smoke.

"Oh, I'm also thankful that I'm alive. I don't know how I forgot that," I said. "Being alive is important. Unless you're a vampire."

"Haha."

He put his glass down on the table and sighed.

"I'm sorry about the Ric thing. I feel even shittier about it now that you've done all this." He waved his arm around.

"It's okay. I forgive you, and I'm pretty sure she's scared of me now, so that's not a bad thing."

"Was your mom pissed that you came back?" I wished he hadn't changed the subject. I'd rather talk about Ric.

I shrugged. "I don't know. I didn't talk to her before I left. We had our usual yelling match and then I went to my room with Kayla and then I left. I just couldn't be in that house anymore with her. I'll call her tomorrow."

"You think she'll ever see me as anything other than a troublemaker?"

Probably never. "She might. We'll see," I lied.

"So are you telling me that I have to take out my eyebrow ring, and my lip ring and cover my tattoos and dye my hair a respectable color?"

"No!" I couldn't even imagine him that way.

"Oh, so you're saying that you like all of this," he gestured up and down. "Interesting."

"It's not that I don't like it, it's just that I can't imagine you being like that. Being like everyone else. You're not like everyone else." I leaned closer and put my hand on his arm.

"You're not like everyone else either, sweetheart," he said, leaning in as well.

We both paused with our faces about a foot apart.

"So," I said.

"So," he said coming an inch closer. "There's one more thing I want to be thankful for."

"And what's that?" I came closer so that when he exhaled, it moved my hair.

"This." He put his hand under my chin and brought my face to his and gave me a sweet, soft kiss. Like the one we'd shared this afternoon, before we'd gotten interrupted.

Funny, that kiss had led directly to this one.

I leaned into him and kissed him slowly. No biting, no tongue. Just two sets of lips trying each other out. Testing. Teasing. I took my hands and put them on his upper arms, pulling him a fraction closer.

He tasted like the spiced rum and faintly of cigarettes. He must have smoked one with Ric. I really wished he'd quit, but I wasn't going to quibble about something like that right now.

Stryker leaned back on the couch, taking me with him. I braced my hands on his chest as he moved his hands from my chin to my hair, wrapping it around his fingers and tugging it just a bit. The kiss got a little bit more intense, and he took the invitation to slip his tongue into my mouth. I touched his with mine and we began an exquisite slow dance, giving and taking, back and forth, him and me, me and him.

I pressed my body against his and felt him getting hard. He pulled his tongue back and broke the kiss. Both of us took a moment to breathe, and he put his hands under my chin again.

"I'm thankful for that."

"Just the kissing?"

"For everything. For the way that you feel against me, and for the way you get this little pucker between your eyes when you kiss me hard. For the way you taste and you smell and for . . . you."

"I'm thankful for you, too."

He took his hands and squeezed my boobs.

"These are pretty great, too."

I tried to be shocked, but he didn't move his hands away, and started stroking my nipples. Despite having a shirt and a bra between his fingers and my skin, his touch was still setting me on fire.

"This wasn't some elaborate plan to seduce me, was it?" he said, moving his hands down to my stomach and moving his thumbs in circular motions. It was very hard to think.

"No. I honestly wanted to apologize and Trish said you hated apologies, so I figured food was in order to help you swallow it. Besides, I don't have to do much to seduce you, do I?" I squeezed his dick once and gave him a satisfied smirk.

He closed his eyes and breathed through his nose.

"We should get to bed," he said.

"What?"

"It's nearly six in the morning. Do you really want to start this now?"

"I wasn't the one who started it. You did."

"Sweetheart, you started it that first day when you ran after me and kissed me. I've only been following your lead since then."

I turned my head to the side and put it on his chest so the temptation to kiss him again wasn't so strong.

"So this is all my fault?"

"Pretty much." He stroked my hair and I listened to the syncopated rhythm of his heart. I could still feel his desire against me, but I wasn't going to do anything about it until he asked me to. I'd been in charge, and now it was his turn.

"Did you even bring anything to wear?" he said.

"Not really." I hadn't thought about that when I'd stormed out. My stuff was still back at the house.

"So what are you going to wear?"

"Your clothes."

He exhaled loudly and laughed a little. "Jesus, Katie."

"What?"

"There's nothing sexier to a guy than a girl wearing his clothes."

"Well, then what would make me un-sexy?"

He screwed his face up as if he was thinking really hard about it.

"Nothing."

Thirteen

Stryker

Between the rum and the fact that she was talking about wearing my clothes, I was seconds away from throwing her over my shoulder, taking her to bed and ravaging her, but I held off.

We'd always just given in to our desire for each other, one way or another. Maybe there was something to be said for anticipation.

So, I moved out from under her, giving her one last little kiss on her chin.

"Where are you going?" she said, confused.

"To clean up and to find somewhere to put all the leftovers in my fridge." I grabbed both our plates and dumped them in the sink. It was going to take at least an hour just to clean up everything, but at least she'd started by putting some of the utensils in the sink.

"You're not avoiding having sex with me, are you?" she said.

"No," I lied. She got up and brought some of the dishes over.

"Then why do I get the feeling you're avoiding having sex with me?"

"I'm not avoiding it, I'm just . . . not giving in to the urge."
Same difference.

"Why not?"

I turned around and faced her. "Because we always do. You say, 'let's have sex' and I'm all for it. I've never said no to sex. Well, except for Ric, but that doesn't really count. I've never said no, and I just think we need to . . . back off a bit."

"Why the change all of a sudden?" Her eyes narrowed.

"I just think we should take a step back. Jesus, the second time I met you we had sex. That's not exactly how things usually go."

"So, are you saying that you want to rewind and start over? That you want to be my boyfriend? Because that's not what I want."

I shook my head quickly. That was definitely not what I wanted. "No, that's not what I want, either. I just think we should maybe put the brakes on. Just for a little while."

"Okay," she said, coming to stand next to me at the sink and grabbing a sponge. "We'll slow down."

***

In the spirit of slowing down, I slept on the couch and let Katie have my bed. Yes, we had slept in the same bed multiple times before, but that was always after sex. I couldn't handle being in the same bed with her all night, I knew that much, and when she came out of my bathroom wearing a ratty OAR t-shirt that was too big for her and a pair of my boxers, I nearly said "screw slowing down", but I took my desire to peel the t-shirt from her skin and shoved it deep down and started doing quadratic equations in my head.

"Are you sure you're okay taking the couch?" she said, pulling on the hem of the shirt so it skimmed her thighs. It took me a second to realize what she was saying because I was too busy picturing those thighs spread wide and her head thrown back in ecstasy.

"It's fine, Katie. I've passed out there more than once." It seemed dumb to say goodnight because it was actually morning by the time we got the kitchen in order and all the leftovers stored somewhere. Fortunately, neither of us had to be anywhere. She was completely and totally running away from her problems, but that seemed to be her thing, and I wasn't going to tell her what to do. Not this time. I'd told her not to go see Zack and she'd done it anyway, and look where that had gotten her.

Even though she closed the door, I could still hear every move she made. Every time she turned over, which was quite frequently, I wanted to get up and go climb in bed with her. All I could think about was how perfectly her back fit against my front, how perfectly my arms fit around her and how perfect her head felt when it was tucked into my shoulder.

I'd closed all the curtains, but daylight still invaded the apartment, and since I couldn't sleep, I spent the time I wanted to be sleeping telling myself all the reasons Katie and I would never work. Yes, I'd said I didn't want to be her boyfriend, but that didn't mean that I wanted to say goodbye to her. She'd sort of dropped into my life and now I couldn't see going back to a time without her.

"Stryker?" her soft voice called to me from a crack in my bedroom door.

I didn't roll over because I knew I would somehow find her eyes, and if I did, I was a goner. "Yeah?"

"I can't sleep." That made two of us.

"Normally people go to bed when it's dark, but we were too busy with our second Thanksgiving." Shit, that was mean. "I'm sorry; I didn't mean it that way. I'm just really tired, Katie."

"Me too."

"Then go to sleep." Her soft footsteps were like drumbeats as she crossed the floor and stood behind the couch. I turned my head and there she was in all her gorgeous wearing-my-clothes-and-sexy-bedhead glory. She leaned her forearms over the edge of the couch and it was all I could do not to grab them and yank her on top of me.

"I can't. Every time I do, I just remember all the things I've fucked up lately."

I wanted her to go away. I wanted her to go back in her room so I couldn't smell her skin or watch her breathe or see her wide brown eyes.

"Well count some fucking sheep then, Katie."

She was only shocked for a second.

"You're pushing me away and I want to know why, Stryker."

"Maybe because I just want to get some sleep, Katherine." I'd never used her full first name, but I knew it would get her attention. A little smirk tugged at her lips and she leaned further over the couch so I could feel her every breath on my bare chest. I only had my boxers on, but at least my lower half was covered with a bit of a blanket that Trish had made me. I was going to have to shift positions very soon so she wouldn't see my hard on.

"There you go again, Stryker Abraham Grant." I had no idea who the hell had told her my middle name, but I was going to strangle them the first chance I got. I re-arranged the blanket so it covered more of my chest and glared at her.

"Why are you pushing me away now? Is it because you're scared that you feel something for me? Because . . . you're not the only one." She looked down when she said the last part, which was why I knew it was true, and not just a way to get me admit something.

"It's crazy, I know. You and me, we don't make sense. At all," she whispered.

"No, we don't." I could agree with her on that.

"But I've been thinking about something you said to me. About the fact that I was trying to be something I wasn't. It's not completely true, but it's not completely untrue, either. I've lived my whole life under the shadow of my sister, and I guess I never really stopped to think about who I was. I was always trying to not be her, but wanting desperately to be her at the same time. That makes absolutely no sense at all." She shook her head, and it fell over her shoulders and in her face. I pushed some of it back.

"No, it makes complete sense."

She leaned her head against my hand. "I knew you'd understand."

"So now you have to figure out who you are, Katherine Ann Hallman. When you do, let me know." I took my hand away and rolled over, putting my back to her.

I heard her sharp exhale, as if I'd thrown cold water on her. She waited for a moment, as if I was going to roll back over with a smile and tell her I was kidding. I stayed as still as I could, holding my breath. After a moment, I heard her take her hands away and stand up straight.

"Happy Thanksgiving, asshole."

She marched back to my room and slammed the door.

Finally.

***

Somehow I got to sleep and when I opened my eyes, it must have been almost noon. I stretched a kink out of my back and rubbed my eyes. I listened for any sounds from my bedroom, but all was quiet. I sat up and noticed something on my chest.

Writing.

There was a discarded marker on my coffee table. Someone had written something on my chest while I was sleeping, and they'd written it upside down so I could read it when I woke up. I only needed one guess to figure out who had done it, but the question was how she'd done it without waking me up. That took talent.

I know you're being a jerk because you're pushing me away. You should have just been a jerk from the beginning and I might have believed you last night. That's fine. I don't want to force myself into someone's life. I'm off to go find myself, or some such crap like that. Call me if you want to have sex. I'm always open for that with you.

-Katherine.

She'd signed it with a flourish, right at the top of my chest. How the hell that had not woken me up, or at least woken my dick up was a mystery I didn't think I would ever solve.

I got up and went to my bedroom, but my bed was made and her things were gone. She'd even carefully folded the clothes she'd worn last night. Before I could stop myself, I reached for the shirt and inhaled her scent. Katie always smelled sweet, like frosting, or cotton candy or a lollipop. I dropped the clothes in my hamper on my way to the shower. I'd have to wash those ASAP.

Katie

Since Stryker didn't want me at his place, I had no choice but to go back home. I briefly considered asking Lottie if I could crash with her, but that would have been asking too much. Lottie had bailed me out of too many situations already.

I made it to my house at ten the next morning. After Stryker had pushed me away, I'd spent the rest of the night-slash-morning figuring out what I was going to do. So far, I didn't have any answers, but the first step was going home and trying to make things right with my mom. Stryker had told me it was time to get my shit together, and he was right. It pissed me off that it took him saying that to me to get me to believe it for the first time in my life.

I thought back to that night in the hospital, when I'd begged them not to press charges against Zack. If he had walked into that room and told me it was all a mistake, I would have taken him back. Realizing that made me feel sick, but I couldn't hide from it anymore.

I opened the front door slowly, wondering what I would find.

"Where have you been?" Mom was in the midst of putting away the Thanksgiving stuff. Once a holiday was over, she was onto the next. I'd always hated having Christmas decorations up in November. She put her hands on her hips, bracing for another fight. Well, I wasn't going to give her one.

"I stayed with a friend for the night." She didn't need to know it was Stryker.

"You might be over eighteen, Katie, but you still live under this roof and you can't go running off whenever you feel like it. We were worried sick."

I swallowed. Yes, I'd prepared for this reaction, but it still made me feel like a shitty daughter.

"I'm sorry. I shouldn't have left. I'm sorry about everything."

She almost seemed shocked at my willingness to apologize. I usually put up more of a fight.

"Katiebug!" Kayla came up from downstairs, her hand in Adam's. She rushed to hug me. "I knew you'd come back," she whispered in my ear. I wasn't going to tell her that it was because I had no place to go, and not just because I wanted to make things right.

I hugged her back and said hi to Adam.

"Where's Dad?"

"He wasn't feeling that great, so I sent him to lie down," Mom said, folding the blanket covered in a leaf pattern over her arm and then putting it in the Thanksgiving decoration tub.

"Hey, you want to go to the movies or something? I was thinking about showing Adam our awesome town. He's a city boy," Kayla said.

"Guilty," he said, raising his hand. "I don't trust any place that doesn't have public transportation."

"You are so weird," Kayla said.

"Hey, you want to marry me. I'd say that makes you the weird one."

She beamed at him. "True."

"That sounds great," I said to interrupt their couple's banter. Mom just watched with a smile on her face. "I'm going to put my stuff in my room."

I threw my purse back on my bed and saw that my trash can was empty of all the pictures that had filled it the day before. My bare walls were still a shock. I was going to have to do something about that. After changing my clothes, I tiptoed down the stairs to my parents' bedroom. Dad was watching golf and still had his PJs on.

"Hey, Dad." He smiled and turned the television off.

"You make up with your mother?" Geez, don't beat around the bush much.

"Sort of." He moved over and I sat next to him on the bed. "How are you feeling?"

"It's nothing."

187

"It must be something if you got out of helping Mom dismantle the Thanksgiving decorations."

"Shhhh," he said, winking. "I may be laying it on a bit thick. Nothing to worry about, Katiebug. I probably got something from one of the kids."

"Probably."

"What's this?" He pointed to the fading drawing Stryker had made on my hand. I'd thought about scrubbing it off when I was in his bathroom this morning, but couldn't bring myself to do it.

"Just a doodle. Got bored."

"But this is your right hand." He pulled my hand closer so he could get a better look.

"It's nothing." I took my arm back and tried to pull my sleeve down to cover it as I searched for a way to deflect his attention. "So what do you think of Adam?"

"He seems like a very nice guy, but I'm not sure how I feel about your sister getting engaged to him so quick. Even if he did ask my permission after the fact."

"He did?"

Dad nodded.

"This morning. Said he wished he could have done it sooner, but he didn't think he could do it before I'd really had a chance to meet him."

"Wow."

He moved over some more and held his arm out so I could cuddle against him like I did when I was younger. I couldn't remember the last time I'd done that. His hand went to my hair, pulling it through his fingers.

"You've grown up so fast, Katiebug. All I did was blink and here you are, a young woman. How did that happen?"

"Well, those growth hormones you fed me probably had something to do with it."

"Yeah, probably." He kissed my forehead and I snuggled closer. He smelled like Old Spice and a little bit of sweat and furniture polish.

"Dad?"

"Mmhm?"

"Do you think I'm a good person? And don't give me a dad answer."

He moved so he could look at my face.

"Why would you even ask a question like that?"

"Because of all the stupid things I've done. I loved this awful guy who beat me up and I didn't even want to press charges against him. I've made so many mistakes with guys and fighting with mom and school and everything."

"I want you to listen to me," he said, sitting up. "You did not ask for what happened to you. You are not responsible for Zack and his sick mind. To even blame yourself for one single second is wrong. Everyone makes mistakes, Katiebug, but we learn from them. We move on. That's the key. It's not that you made the mistake in the first place, but what you do with the result. You are a smart, strong, beautiful young woman and I am proud that you are my daughter. If you believe anything, believe that."

It was a total dad answer, but that was what I expected. My dad seemed to see the best in me and my mom saw that I wasn't what she wanted me to be.

"Thanks, Dad," I said, hugging him tight. "I love you."

"Love you too, Katiebug."

He waited until I left before turning the television back on.

***

Kayla was supposed to go back with Adam, but she ended up staying for the rest of my break. She said it was because she wanted to show Adam everything, and have home-cooked food, but I knew she was trying to be a buffer between Mom and me. For the next couple of days I tried my best not to get under Mom's skin. I helped out around the house more than I would have, and volunteered to get groceries.

I was constantly checking my phone for any message from Stryker. I was curious about the effect of my little note on him. I'd been about to leave him one on paper, but he was sacked out on the couch and his chest was exposed, so I figured it was only fitting that I draw it on him as payback for the times he'd drawn stuff on me. He almost woke up a bunch of times, but I was able to complete it. Somehow.

I had a long chat with Lottie one night when Kayla and Adam had gone out, and I didn't feel like being the third wheel again. Dad was still under the weather, so Mom was busy nursing him and I was holed up in my room.

"Still haven't heard from him?" she said.

"Nope." I'd filled her in on the note, and she thought it was hilarious.

"Well, he's alive, according to Trish. She's talked with him a few times."

"Has he . . . has he said anything?"

I could hear Trish's voice in the background answering.

"Nada. He's being like a clam with a pearl. The penis effect and all that."

I sighed. "Got it." I hadn't expected anything less. When Stryker didn't want to talk about something, there was little you could do to get him to open up. That was fine with me.

"So, you ready to get back to normal?"

"If by normal you mean losing *Law and Order* bets and eating our weight in ice cream, then yes, I am ready for that." So freaking ready.

I could almost hear her rolling her eyes. "At least your mother hasn't grilled you about your boyfriend's favorite books and then made conclusions about him based on those books."

At least her mother hadn't made her boyfriend so uncomfortable that he stormed out. Not that Stryker was my boyfriend.

"True. Hey, I'll see you tomorrow, okay? Bye, roomie." Will and Trish must have been playing a game because I could hear both of them yelling in the background.

"I'm coming, I'm coming," Lottie shouted at them. "Sorry, I have to go help judge which is more sympathetic, pirates or volcanoes. I swear, these two are going to kill each other over a game of Apples to Apples. Bye, roomie."

She hung up and I was left in silence in my empty room. I twirled my phone in my hand, restless.

My bare walls were really pissing me off for some odd reason. I looked around and found a cup full of markers. I grabbed a pink one and stared at the wall right across from my bed. Mom was going to have a coronary if I drew on my walls.

I made one little dot. Ha.

Then I made another, and another. I connected them with a swirly line and kept going, making more lines and more swirls. It was very similar to the design Stryker had drawn on my hand. I added some circles in between, moving the drawing from one side of the wall to the other, and then down to the floor. Once the design was done, I felt like it needed something. I turned on my iPod and looked for some of the music Stryker had given me, searching for one song in particular. "Endlessly", by Green River Ordinance. It was softer than most of the stuff Stryker listened to, which was why I thought it was so odd when he gave it to me.

Slowly, I wrote random words on the wall. "Love" and "Happiness" and "Beauty" and "Fun" and "Surprises" and "Music" and "Laughter" and "Magic". I just wrote what came to mind, and it wasn't until I'd written "Love" over and over that I realized these were all the things I wanted out of life. My wall had become some twisted version of a vision board. I'd thought those things were totally stupid, but somehow seeing the words written out like that made sense.

"Oh my God. Mom is going to murder you." I paused in the act of finishing a letter and looked over my shoulder to find Kayla gaping at me and my newly-decorated wall.

"Yeah, well, wouldn't be the first time." I wrote "Love" again and glanced back at Kayla. "Where's Adam?"

"Just making some coffee. You want some?"

"Sure."

"We were going to watch a movie if you want to join us." She hovered in the doorway.

"Sure." I capped the marker. One wall was enough for tonight. I took out my phone and snapped a picture of it, just in case.

Fourteen

Stryker

I almost called her or texted her so many times I lost count. But I didn't know what to say after I'd given her the cold shoulder. If I called her and she came over and we had sex, we'd be back to square one, only I couldn't go back to that place. The place where I didn't care so fucking much. Really, though, I'd never been there. That first night when I saw her, I'd cared. When I'd seen her eyes scared and wide, I'd felt something that was stronger than just a guy wanting to help a girl out of a bad situation. Even then, I'd felt it. I'd never had a chance, really.

I spent the days without her eating leftovers and learning new songs and working as many hours in the frigid temperatures as I could on rebuilding a few engines. I skipped out on Band, much to the anger of everyone. It was Allan's turn to host, and he was the most upset. I pretended I had food poisoning, but I was sure none of them bought it. Trish called me to basically tell me to get my head out of my ass, which was less than helpful.

The night before classes started back up, there was a knock at my door. My heart did a funny little lurch and I told myself over and over as I walked down the stairs it wouldn't be Katie.

It wasn't.

Allan leaned on my porch, holding a bottle of scotch and two cups.

"Figured you could use it," he said with a lopsided grin.

"I told you, I'm not feeling that great. I don't think scotch is going to help that situation."

"You know, food poisoning is often code for: I got dumped." He shoved his way past me and jogged up the stairs. Nothing I could do to stop him, so I closed the door and followed him.

"I didn't get dumped."

"The Stryker I know wouldn't let anything get in the way of Band. Except a girl." He set the cups down and poured a little into each, holding one out to me. "I don't need the details, but I figured you could use a friend and a drink. So here I am."

I hesitated, but took the cup from him and took a sip. Damn. This was good stuff. Allan might be poor as shit, but he always found money for good alcohol.

"I'm not going to get drunk and spill all my feelings," I said, savoring the sweet burn.

"Who am I, Oprah? I don't want to know your feelings. But if you feel the need to share them with me, I'm your man, buddy." He banged his hand on my back and went to make himself comfortable on the couch.

"We're both unlucky in love, man. I'm crazy about a girl who doesn't like penises and you're in love with a girl who is completely, totally and utterly out of your league."

"Out of my league?"

Allan looked up from the couch.

"Uh, yeah. Like, you two aren't even on the same planet."

I sat down next to him. "At least she's interested in my anatomy."

"Ouch, burn." He held his heart as if I'd stabbed him. I took another sip and sat down next to him on the couch.

"You'll live."

Allan and I sat in silence, drinking and wallowing. I'd never wallowed about a girl before. It felt like shit.

He poured more scotch and I started to feel the effect.

"Do you really think she's out of my league?" I said.

"Well, yeah. Katie is like . . . Miss America and you're . . . you."

"Thanks, Allan that really clears things up."

"No, no, that came out wrong. It's not that she's better than you; it's just that you're not the kind of guy a girl like her would go for. She goes for football players and guys with money and guys with clean criminal records."

"Wow, Allan. You've managed to insult both her and me all at once. Thanks, that was so helpful." I patted his leg. He threw his head back in frustration.

"Shit. You know I'm bad at this. I told you I wasn't Oprah. But you know what I mean, right?"

I did. I knew just what he was saying. It was what everyone said when I left the room. It was the reason Katie's mother hadn't wanted me to stay. I would contaminate her pure daughter.

If only she knew that her pure daughter was the one who fucked so many times.

I nodded and swallowed another mouthful of the scotch. Tonight was a night for getting drunk. Blessedly, mind-numblingly drunk.

So I did.

***

Right around the time Allan started crying about how much he loved Zoey, I decided to call him a cab. It was a miracle I could even dial the number on my phone. He nearly fell down the stairs, and I wasn't much better, but I got him inside and gave the guy the address, slurring my way through it.

"I've taken a lot of drunk directions, kid," he said and I shut the door as Allan started wailing again.

I crawled all the way back up the stairs and collapsed on my couch. Allan had left the bottle of scotch, so I poured myself another drink. The bottle nearly slipped from my hands, but I caught it in time. My reflexes weren't drunk enough yet.

A knock made me look up. Probably Allan. He'd been thrown out of more than one cab before.

I stumbled to my feet and went to my door to find someone standing there, but it wasn't Allan.

"Your front door was open," she said, giving me the once over.

"Ric." This time she had a thin t-shirt on, thin enough for me to see her nipples, under a leather jacket, with a pair of jeans that were so ripped they could hardly be called pants. There was one particular rip on her thigh that showed a pair of black lace panties.

"Looks like you've had a rough night." She strolled in and spun around to face me. "So I heard you and the pink bitch are on the outs."

"Don't call her that," I said, walking past her, but I misjudged how close she was and our shoulders bumped.

"Hey," she said, putting her hand on my chest to stop me. "I'm sorry. I just came over to see if you're okay." She sniffed, smelling the scotch on my breath.

"Looks like Allan already beat me to it. Scotch?"

"Yep," I said, stepping away from her hand. "So, I'm fine."

"Hey." She reached for me again, putting her arms around me. "It sucks, okay? It's okay to talk about it." Her hair smelled like cigarettes and some sort of spicy perfume.

She didn't smell like Katie.

Hesitantly, I returned the hug and she pressed herself against me and I could feel her tits pressed into my chest. Her hands meandered up and down my back and she breathed softly.

I dropped my arms and broke the hug.

"I don't want to fucking talk about it."

Her blue eyes widened for just a moment.

"Then we don't have to talk," she said, her hand moving down my back and dancing on the hem of my shirt. "We can forget all about it."

"What about Baxter?" I said as she started to pull at my shirt and move closer to me.

"We broke up. He's not the one I want." She lifted her chin and I couldn't look her in the eye. Blue eyes. Not brown.

Not Katie's eyes.

Her lips were close to mine and I could feel the heat coming off her skin. She was taller than Katie, so I wouldn't have to bend as much to kiss her.

"You're the one I want," she said just before she closed that last whisper of space between us and placed a kiss on my lips. They were dry, and didn't fit my mouth quite right, but after a moment, I gave in, putting my hand on the back of her head and holding her in place. Her hands went to my shirt, pulling it over my head and throwing it on the floor. Hers was next, and no, she wasn't wearing anything under her t-shirt.

"Finally," she said, hooking her fingers into my belt loops and pulling me toward the couch. I kissed her again and let my eyes close as I fell on top of her. Her hands ripped at my belt as her lips tried to devour me. Our noses crashed a couple of times, and she couldn't seem to get the belt undone, which was odd, because she was the sober one.

"Got it," I said, taking her hands away from it as she worked at her own pants and I heard a tearing sound as she ripped them even more in her hurry to get them off. Raking her hands on my chest, she yanked me down for another kiss. I shoved my pants and boxers down to my ankles and paused for a second above her.

"Fuck me hard, Stryker. I've wanted you for so long."

Her boobs were too small and her hips too narrow and her legs too long and her lips to thin and her eyes not brown.

Not Katie.

She put both hands on my dick and guided me down.

"Fuck me hard."

I plunged into her and her eyes went wide and she made a little grunt. I only gave her a second to adjust before I pulled back and slammed again. Her hands went around my neck and she tried to kiss me. I let her because I didn't want to look into her not-brown eyes.

Over and over I pounded into her as she urged me on.

Not. Katie. Not. Katie. Not. Katie.

Her ankles didn't wrap around me, she didn't make those sweet little sounds, she didn't dig her fingers into my back.

Not. Katie. Not. Katie. Not. Katie.

"Yes, yes, fuck me harder." Her voice invaded my mind and I tried to shut her out by kissing her again so she'd stop talking.

Thankfully, I was able to finish a second later. I pulled out immediately, yanked up my pants and stumbled to the bathroom to turn on the shower.

Katie

Mom didn't discover my wall until the next morning when she snuck in to clean. I never kept anything secretive in my room because she snooped through all of my drawers. My secret hiding place was in Kayla's room, under a floorboard.

Her shriek carried all the way down the stairs. "Katie! What did you do?"

I looked at Kayla and Adam. We'd been having a discussion about the worst ways to die. I thought drowning, but Adam was all for fire.

"Looks like I'm in trouble, as usual," I said, getting up from the couch and walking up the stairs to face my doom.

"What is this?" Seeing her face made me reconsider the drowning thing as the worst way to die. Getting glared to death by my mother had moved its way to the top of the list. She waved her hand at my wall.

"It's art." Okay, okay, it was a snarky response and totally set me up for pissing her off more, but I couldn't help it. Holding back from fighting with her all week hadn't been easy.

"This is not art. This is graffiti. This is going to take forever to wash off, Katie." She put her hand to her forehead, like I was giving her a migraine. If I hadn't already, what I was about to say definitely would set her off.

"I don't want to wash it off." I moved to stand in front of the wall, as if I was protecting it. In a way, I guess I was.

"Katie, be serious. You're not five years old anymore. I will not have this crap all over my walls."

"Well, it's not crap, and it's on my wall. If you don't like it, don't look at it."

Mom's glare got narrower and meaner and she put her hands on her hips.

"Katherine Ann, you are acting like a child."

I most certainly was, but it was my go-to defense mechanism when I fought with my mother.

We faced each other, at an impasse.

"I don't know who you are anymore." Her voice was more frustrated than mad.

I started laughing, thinking about what Stryker had said.

"Yeah, me neither." Once the giggling started, it was hard to stop. Now Mom looked worried.

"Are you okay?"

"Yeah, just great." I gave her a thumbs up as I tried to stop laughing. She backed away from me and picked up the duster she'd been using as an excuse to come into my room.

"Well, when you get yourself together, I want that cleaned off before you go back to school. Don't make me ask you again." She closed the door with authority and I leaned back against the wall.

The laughter slowed and I caught my breath. Turning my head, I saw the word "Love" and traced it with my finger.

I should have used paint instead of marker.

Fifteen

Stryker

"Stryker?" Ric's voice, not Katie's said to me through the closed bathroom door. I'd gotten into the shower without even taking my jeans off. The urge to wash myself off was so powerful after . . . after everything with Ric that I couldn't be bothered to get them off.

I didn't answer her, and I didn't hear her footsteps so I knew she was still waiting.

Not Katie. Not Katie. Not Katie.

"Are you okay?"

Fuck no.

I braced my hand on the wall of a shower, feeling how solid it was. I needed something to hold me up, brace my shaking body. The hot water coursed down my back, pattering on the floor of the shower. Each little splash said something to me, blurring together until I couldn't tell them apart.

NotKatienotKatienotKatienotKatie.

"Look, I'm sorry about that. It's just that I've been in love with you for so long and I took my chance." Ric wasn't in love with me. Not really. She'd just told herself she loved me so many times that she'd started believing it.

"Go away, Ric."

"Stryker, I —"

"Just . . . leave." I spat the words out through my clenched jaw.

I was being a dick to her, but that was what I did. I was a dick. I pushed people away. It was so much easier than caring.

"Well, um, thanks for . . . thanks." Her footsteps retreated and a few moments later my door closed.

I stood in the shower until the hot water turned cold, but I didn't move. It was like, if I moved, the reality of what I'd done would see me out of the corner of its eye and come rip my throat out. Part of me wished it would so I would stop thinking about it.

When my shivers became too much, I shut off the shower and finally took my pants off and grabbed a towel. I rubbed myself dry, wishing I actually felt clean. My fingers had pruned up from being in the shower so long. Avoiding the couch because it still smelled like sex, I grabbed the bottle of scotch and headed to my bedroom.

I pulled on a pair of boxers, realizing only after I got them on that they were the ones Katie had worn just a few days before. I'd only washed them when her scent had faded, but somehow, I could still almost smell her.

I took another hit off the scotch bottle and lay back on my bed. The apartment was too quiet, but if I put on any music, I would think of her, so I didn't.

I'd literally tried to fuck my sorrows away, and now it was time to try to drink them away instead. It was no use, because they'd find me eventually, but maybe I could avoid them for a few more hours.

Maybe.

I lit a cigarette, even though I never smoked inside. The glow of it and the haze of the smoke were comforting.

Not. Katie. Not. Katie. Not. Katie.

Katie

I had no doubt in my mind that the second I left the house, my mother would have a scrub brush and a bucket of industrial strength cleaner out quicker than you could say, "Mr. Clean". That was fine. Next time I was home, I'd do the same thing again. What was she going to do? Scrub my walls every time? Remove all the markers like I was five?

Dad was feeling better and up and about, and gave me a nice long hug before I left.

"Believe in yourself, Katiebug. I know I do."

Mom's hug was quick and limp. She was still pissed about the cleaning, but she told me she loved me and I said it back, because, at the end of the day, I did love her.

Kayla had left the day before with Adam because they had to get back to Africa. She'd given me a gigantic hug and said that she was planning to buy a computer so we could Skype. Adam also gave me a hug and a wink and said he'd see me on the flipside. I gave Kayla a look, but she just gazed adoringly at him.

My drive back to school seemed to take longer than normal, and it wasn't because I drove slower. Or maybe I did, unconsciously. I was more than eager to get back to the dorm, back to my life, or whatever it was now, but there was just one little thing holding me back. Well, one big thing. Named Stryker Abraham Grant.

I had no idea what his parents were thinking when they named him, but for some reason, his name made complete sense.

I turned on the radio, irritated at myself for thinking about him. Why did I feel like I'd just been through another breakup? We weren't even together. Stryker and I . . . we weren't even friends. So why did I feel like I wanted to wallow in misery and never leave my bed again?

Stupid boy. Stupid boy and his stupid blond hair and his green eyes and his musical talent and his lips that kissed like he was trying to put out a fire and his smirk and his tattoos and his hips and his hands and . . .

Stupid, stupid, stupid boy.

***

"I've missed you so much. Is that weird? I know I just saw you a few days ago, and we talked on the phone, but it feels like forever and I'm just really glad you're back," Lottie said the second I walked into our room and dropped my bag. Damn, I'd even missed her verbal vomit.

My face cracked into a smile before I realized what I was doing.

"So how were things at casa Hallman?"

207

"Faaaabulous," I said, rolling my eyes. "I managed to piss my mom off at least once a day."

"Yeah, well I thought Trish and Will were going to kill each other over a simple game of Monopoly, so I get it." No, she didn't. Everyone loved Lottie. Even when she wouldn't stop talking. It added to her adorably awkward personality.

I shoved aside my problems and we caught up. God, I'd missed her so much.

"So what happened with Stryker? With the whole apology thing?" I had been vague on the details of my little Thanksgiving stunt. Especially since it ended up blowing up in my face.

"I drove my ass back to his apartment and cooked him dinner in the middle of the night. Then we went to bed and when we got up he said he didn't want to see me anymore, which is dumb, because we weren't dating."

Her expression was confused. I hadn't told her I was dating him, but I hadn't told her I wasn't. It was exactly as Stryker said. I didn't want her to think less of me.

"You weren't?"

"Not really." I sunk back into the mountain of pillows on my bed. I'd missed that too. There was nothing quite like falling into them after a shitty day.

"So you guys weren't dating, but you broke up?"

"I guess. All I know is that he doesn't want to see me anymore. So I'm not going to see him anymore."

"By see him you mean . . . "

I started laughing again.

"I don't even know what that means either."

A loud and frantic knock put pause on that conversation. Audrey and Trish burst in, Will, Simon and Zan following along behind a little less enthusiastically.

I was hugged and I couldn't help but hug and smile back. I'd missed them. I didn't know how much until I saw all of them standing in front of me. Even Zan, who gave me a semi-hug and a smile. I almost asked him about Zack. Almost.

The words drowned in my throat and I wasn't going to bail them out.

We all ended up sitting on our floor, passing around the leftover pies Audrey brought up, eating straight from the pans, all our forks fighting for the best bites, and swapping holiday stories. I sat back against a pile of my pillows and listened. It was such a relief to fall back into this life, into this place where I was surrounded by people who cared about me and missed me and wanted to share things with me.

Not that my family wasn't like that, but this group was different. They didn't have to like me. They chose to spend time with me. They showed up at the hospital and sat and waited for me. I still wanted to cry every time I thought about that.

"So what did you do to my brother?" Trish said, scraping the last bits out of one of the pie pans. "Because he's like, so emo right now, I'm afraid he's going to start painting his nails black and only listening to really crappy music."

Every set of eyes swiveled in my direction and every voice went quiet. Fantastic.

"I didn't do anything to him." I readjusted the pillows behind my back so I wouldn't have to focus on them all.

"Well, something happened because he drunk-texted me late last night telling me that he loved me. Actually, he said he "lobed" me, but that's beside the point. Stryker never uses that word unless he's wasted. So. What happened?"

"Trish," Lottie said, making her name two syllables. "This probably isn't the right venue."

"Oh, whatever," Trish said, tossing the fork in the pie pan and setting it on the floor. Will cleared his throat and Simon looked around, as if the room was really interesting. Zan just kept rubbing Lottie's back. Audrey gave me a sympathetic look and I wanted to melt into the floor and sink into the linoleum.

"Just let me say one more thing. I know he's my brother and all and I give him shit a lot, but he's actually a decent guy, and I think you two are great together. Okay, I'm done."

Will coughed again and the topic changed to bitching about how much we didn't want to start classes the next day.

***

"What happened with Stryker? I know you didn't want to say in front of everyone, but you can talk about it. You know, if you want. No pressure." Sure there was pressure. There was so much pressure I could feel its hands around my neck, and its insistent voice in my ear.

"Okay, but this falls under the roommate umbrella of secrecy. No twindar, or any of that."

"If there's one thing that Will doesn't want to know about, it's other people's relationship drama, so no worries. He'll probably beg me not to tell him anyway. So, your secret is safe."

"So I didn't want to tell you this, but Stryker and I weren't dating, but that doesn't mean we weren't having sex." I paused, waiting for her reaction. I expected surprise, not for her to snort and say, "And?"

"You knew?"

"First, I'm not blind, and second," she said, holding up one, then two fingers, "I'm not an idiot. We all knew."

Now I was the one surprised.

"Everyone?"

She nodded. Well, shit. I guess we weren't as covert as I thought.

"Great. They must all think I'm a slut."

Lottie scoffed, making this little snorting noise.

"No one would think that."

I gave her a look. "Not even after everything I did with Zack?"

She shook her head again.

"We just want you to be happy, and it seems like Stryker makes you happy. So what happened?"

I took a deep breath and went into the whole story, giving her every detail from the Thanksgiving dinner I cooked, to our kiss to when he told me he wanted to wait to have sex. She was uncharacteristically silent the entire time, and her silence reeled the story out of me, including tearing up the pictures with Kayla and writing on my wall and the fight I'd had with my mom. I kept talking and talking, the words spilling out of me and into the air, filling the room up with my voice and my insecurity and my confusion and my hurt.

"And I have no idea what to do. None," I said, finally done.

"You, my dear," she said, raising her hands above her head to stretch, "are in a pickle."

"I guess that's one way of thinking about it. 'I'm fucked' seems more appropriate."

"Well, if you want my two cents, I'd say you give him his space. He'll come to his senses."

I inhaled and said the one thing that scared me the most. "What if he doesn't want to be with me anymore and he's trying to let me down easy?"

Lottie laughed, throwing her head back.

"Yeah, I don't think so," she said, shaking her head as if I'd said something absurd.

"Maybe he realized that he just wants to be friends."

"Listen," she said, coming over to sit next to me on my bed and putting her arm around my shoulder. "No guy who looks at you the way Stryker does wants to be just friends. He looks at you like no one else is around and he wants to throw you down on the table, right there, right then. Like you're the only girl in the entire world and he's ready to worship you."

If it wasn't Lottie saying it, I would have thought she was mocking me, but she said it with such sincerity that I believed her.

"Well Zan looks at you like he's dying and you're standing there holding the cure to whatever's killing him."

She blushed and giggled.

"Listen, we can trade these back and forth all night, but we should probably go to bed." Giving me a quick shoulder squeeze, she got up and went to her dresser to get her PJs.

"Speaking of Zan, why aren't you staying the night with him?"

"Because I figured he could deal with one more night without me. I don't want to be one of those girls who can't breathe without a man around all the time. Even if I do find it hard to breathe without him." She traced the edge of a picture Zan had taken of the two of them. One of those where he had to hold the camera at arm's length and they had to squish their faces together to get them both in the shot.

Yeah, I wasn't buying it. She was staying for me. She knew I knew, but I wasn't going to say anything. So we got into bed and said goodnight and I closed my eyes and tried to think of anything but how much I wanted to call Stryker and talk to him. Even if he wouldn't talk back.

Sixteen

Stryker

I knew I was going to see Zan the next day and I knew he would be able to see what I'd done written on my face, so I skipped class and stayed at my apartment. Not that I would have been able to go, even if I'd wanted to. "Hung over" was an understatement. I was still hanging. I was also still hating myself for the night before. I checked my phone, but there were no messages from Ric, which was good, and there were a lot of messages from Trish, Zan and the rest of the crew, which was bad.

I wasn't going to be able to avoid them forever, but maybe I could get one more day.

That one day lasted until two in the afternoon when my sister burst through my door and slammed it shut behind her.

"You have got to be out of your fucking mind," she said storming over the couch where I'd been tuning my violin. Hurricane Trish had arrived and she was pissed. Nostril-flaringly, violet eye-buggingly pissed.

"You *slept* with *Ric*?" That didn't take long to get out. Trish came over and smacked me on the chest.

"Ouch," I said, putting my violin back in the case. I didn't want it to get damaged.

"That's all you have to say, asshole?" She smacked me again and crashed down next to me on the couch.

"Who told you?"

"Well Ric couldn't keep her mouth shut, and she told Zo and Zo told me. I wanted to believe it wasn't true, but even Ric couldn't make that up. Please tell me you've been to the doctor and that you have multiple personalities, or brain damage, or something to explain this excessively stupid thing you've done."

"Nope." I flinched back before she could hit me again. "Just doing what I do best."

Trish glared at me so hard her eyes were just slits. I stared right back at her, not breaking eye contact. Her eyes widened suddenly, snapping open like shades being yanked upward.

"You have *got* to be kidding me." She got a hit in this time. Her jaw dropped as I tried to figure out what had gotten her so shocked. It couldn't have been what I just said. There was something else she'd seen that had shocked her.

"What?" I said, not sure if I wanted to know what revelation had made her look like that.

And then she opened her mouth and said the last thing I ever thought she would say. "Oh. My. GOD. You *love* her. You fucking love her."

I nearly fell off the couch. It was a good thing I'd put the violin away because I might have crushed it in my hand.

"W-what?" I stuttered. Trish leaned over and grabbed my face between her hands and stared into my eyes, searching for something. I was too out of it to stop her.

"You. Love. Her." Each word was like a punch she delivered to my brain with brass knuckles.

Those three words made me come to my senses. I shoved Trish away and got off the couch. I didn't know where I was going, but I had to get away from her and what she was saying. I stumbled backward, nearly crashing into my standing bass.

"Aha!" Trish said, pointing my finger as if she was accusing me of a crime. "You love Katie. That's why you slept with Ric. Oh, Stryk. You are in so much trouble." She shook her head sadly and then grinned at me.

"I do not love her," I said, nearly choking on the words.

"Yeah, you do, brother. We may not have twindar, but I I know you pretty well and I know what I see and I know how your mind works."

"It's not like that, Trish. I just fucked her a bunch of times and got tired of it. That's all."

She smirked at me and ran her fingers through her hair, which was fading and needed to be re-colored.

"Wow. You are so gone. I knew it. I *knew* it."

"You can think whatever you want to think, Trishella, but you're way off." I knew using her full name would piss her off and might change the subject.

"You said you would never call me that again." Her eyes had gone back to dangerous and narrow. "You swore."

"Yeah, well, I lied. Look, I have somewhere to be, so if you don't mind." I didn't, but even if I had to get in my car and drive somewhere random to get rid of her, I'd do it.

"Okay, okay. Don't worry, bro, your secret is safe with me." She got to her feet, and I could hear her laughing to herself as she walked out the door. "By the way, we're doing a welcome back dinner this weekend, and your attendance is required. See yah." She wiggled her fingers and vanished down the stairs.

"Son of a *bitch*," I said.

Her laugher echoed until I heard the front door close.

I wasn't in love with Katie. Okay, I liked having sex with her and laughing with her and that apology dinner had been so sweet. No one had ever done something like that for me. And I still couldn't get the image of her wearing my shirt and boxers out of my head. But none of that meant I was in love with her.

I stared around my apartment, and I knew I had to get out of it. I didn't know where I was going, but I had to get out. To a place that didn't make me think of Katie.

***

I ended up at a park downtown. Mostly so I could smoke and walk around without people staring at me. A homeless man shivered on a bench, a woman walked her dog, and a mom played with her kids on the swing set. I huddled in my jacket, pulling the collar up and lit another cigarette.

My mind ran in circles, and more often than not, those circles led back to one thing.

Katie.

What Trish had said pissed me off. What I had done with Ric pissed me off. What Katie had written on my chest pissed me off.

Everything was pissing me off. One of the kids screamed as his mom gave him a big push. He threw his head back and his arms out, like he was flying. I remembered doing the same thing, only I didn't have anyone to push me. I'd pushed Trish more times than I could count. Just like the little boy on the swing, she always screamed for me to push her higher. I always did and she'd laugh and pretend she was scared.

"Don't worry," I always told her, "I'll catch you."

The mother caught me watching and her eyebrows knit together in concern. I blew out a smoke ring and walked away from them so she wouldn't think I was some sort of threat. I paced the park in circles. It seemed like everything was going in circles.

I'd think I was moving toward something new, something different and I always ended up at the same place, back at the beginning.

Damn motherfucking circles.

Katie

It was a relief to get back to classes and homework and things that didn't involve Stryker or feelings or fighting with my mother. My study habits left a lot to be desired, and I knew I had to change. Again.

"Library?" Lottie said after dinner as we were walking back to the dorm. "Aud's going to meet us." She gave Will a look, but he just kept walking, whistling a tune.

"Yeah, I'm in." If there was anyone who could push me to stop being a slacker, it was Audrey.

"You in, Zan?" She tugged on his hand, as if she was trying to get his attention. As if it wasn't already on her.

"Sure thing, L." He tucked her under his arm, and she let herself sink into him, as if he was protecting her from something.

Maybe he was.

"You talked to Stryker yet?" she said innocently. I knew she'd been itching to ask me all day.

"Nope. The point of giving him space is to put space between us, which means not contacting him. So that's what I'm doing."

"Have you talked to him?" She turned her attention to Zan and I breathed a little sigh of relief.

"No, he skipped class today." Zan's eyes were on me, and I pretended to be really interested in a sign on the door advertising a band named Peach Pit Apocalypse that was playing the next weekend on campus.

She kept prodding. "You text him?"

"Yeah, he never got back to me."

"You think he's okay?" We headed for the stairs because we couldn't all fit on the elevator.

"Yeah, I asked Trish and she said she'd stop over to see if he was still alive and she messaged me that he was still breathing."

"Such a way with words, that girl," Lottie said, shaking her head.

I wasn't interested in Stryker skipping class. It made no difference to me if he went to class or not. It made no difference to me that I hadn't heard a single peep from him in days. It made no difference that sleeping alone sucked worse than sleeping on the ground at summer camp, with part of a stump up my butt and a rock under my head.

Nope. Made no difference to me what he did or didn't do.

***

"You know what I think you need?" Lottie said as we walked back later that night from the library. For the first time since everything happened with Zack, I was back on track with my homework and assignments. It actually felt good, like something I could control.

"What do I need?" I said, thinking that I probably wouldn't like the answer.

"A makeover." Her eyes sparkled under the orange glow of the streetlight.

"A makeover?" Usually I was the one suggesting that, but I had the feeling that Lottie wasn't suggesting the kind of makeover I usually did.

"Not like, with clothes or anything. More like . . . a life makeover? Wow, that sounds bad. Like there's something wrong with you. I mean . . . "

I decided to stop her there because even though I couldn't see her blushing, I could hear the embarrassment in her voice.

"No, I knew what you meant. My life could use some . . . making over." More like a complete overhaul. A do over. Like that was actually possible.

Stryker's words came back to me: *So now you have to figure out who you are, Katherine Ann Hallman. When you do, let me know.*

Screw him.

"What did you have in mind?" I said, shoving Stryker out of my mind and turning to Lottie.

"I was thinking," she said, preparing as if she was about to insult me, "that you could pick a major. We're going to be signing up for classes soon, so now would be the best time."

It wasn't as bad as I thought it would be, but that didn't mean it was something I thought I could do.

"Do you have anything in mind?" Zan walked beside Lottie, his arm linked with hers as if they were a couple out of an old movie and he was escorting her to a ball.

I shook my head. The truth, the thing I didn't want them to know was that I had no idea what I wanted to do. Not a clue. Sure, Lottie was only majoring in marine bio to make her dad happy, but at least she had that, and she could always be a writer, or a librarian or a teacher or . . . anything. She could do anything.

I couldn't do anything. When other little girls wanted to be ballerinas or astronauts or presidents I never knew what to say. I always just said an actress or something so at least I'd have something to say. I'd thought about singing once, but that dream was long gone.

"What about fashion?" Lottie and I had had this conversation more times than I could count. Yes, I enjoyed giving makeovers, but that didn't mean I wanted to do it for a living, or even attempt it. The world of fashion was cutthroat and you had to want it more than you wanted anything else. You had to devote your life to it, and I didn't know if I was ready to do that.

What did I want to devote my life to?

I came up completely blank. *When I grow up, I want to be . . .* I had nothing to fill the rest of that sentence.

"I don't know," I said, wishing I could change the subject.

"You should make a list or something. You know, all the things you like to do and then careers you could do with that." I wasn't going to tell her that I'd done the same thing in high school and I never came up with any answers.

"Look, you can do whatever you want. You're smart and strong. Not everyone gets the chances you do," Lottie said, the smile fading from her face. I knew that she was thinking about her friend Lexie and that made me feel even worse.

I had all the chances in the world. I had parents who were footing the bill for my college education and I was wasting it. I knew I was wasting it.

Zan swooped in and changed the subject, saying something about an assignment from the class that he and Lottie shared.

I didn't give him enough credit, but he was really a decent guy. Even after everything he'd done, he'd found a way to start over, start fresh. So why was it so hard for me?

Seventeen

Stryker

"Long time no see," Zan said when I walked into class on Wednesday. I kept my face neutral.

"Wasn't feeling that great."

"Rough weekend?"

"Something like that."

I'd timed it so that I would get to class right before Quan started, and I planned on bolting as soon as I could. I pulled out my notebook and started drawing like I always did in this class. If attendance didn't count toward my grade, I would skip every class but the test.

I let my pen take over, drawing random designs on a fresh page instead of adding to another drawing I'd already started.

It wasn't until class was over and half the page was filled that I realized I'd done a duplicate of the drawing on Katie's wrist.

"That's nice," Zan said, shoving his books in his bag while I tried to hide the drawing.

"Thanks." I fished in my pocket, but I couldn't find my lighter. It was a way to try to prevent myself from smoking. I had the cigarettes, but if I couldn't light them, I couldn't smoke them. In theory it worked, but not so much in practice. Zan always had that old Zippo on him.

"Can I borrow your lighter?" He handed it over and followed me to the designated smoking area outside the building. I always offered him one, but he always refused and today was no exception.

He watched me smoke, silently waiting for me to start talking. There was something so unnerving about a silent person.

"I had sex with someone else," I blurted out after about thirty seconds of silence. Zan took the lighter back and flicked it in his hand out of habit. On. Off. On. Off.

He waited for me to elaborate.

"It was a mistake and I was drunk, but to be fair, I did break it off with Katie before it happened."

"Then why are you hiding it?" He flipped the lighter off and put it back in his pocket.

I shook my head and tipped my face up, blowing the smoke toward the clouds.

"I don't know." Trish's words came back with a vengeance.

"Look, I know I'm not good at talking, or giving advice, but this is my two cents," he said, leaning next to me against the building. He had to tip his head down to meet my eyes.

"You and Katie have something together. We all saw it that night at the party. Whether you want to admit it or not, there is something there, and it's not just attraction or lust. It's something more. Something deeper. You care about her and she cares about you, despite everything she's been through. You're both trying to stop it, but here's the thing. It's going to happen anyway. Something that powerful is like a speeding train. You can slow it down, but it's never going to stop." That's how it felt with Katie. Like I was standing on the train tracks, waiting to be demolished by a thousand pounds of metal coming at me.

"When it's real like that, you can't fight it. I know what you're going through." He looked up at the sky. "I tried to fight it with Lottie, but we just kept getting pulled together. And then the reasons I was keeping her away dissolved and they didn't seem like reasons anymore, just roadblocks on our way to finding one another."

I thought there would be more to the speech, but he just exhaled and looked back down at me. I stubbed out the rest of my cigarette and shoved my hands in my pockets.

"For a guy who's not good with words, you sure sound like a fucking poet. If only you could make that shit rhyme, and you'd be the next Shakespeare."

Zan gave me a brief smile and shrugged.

"I have to get to class. You wanna hang out this weekend? Banjo session?"

"Yeah, sure thing. I'll let you know."

He nodded again and went to walk to his next class as I pulled out another cigarette and stared at it wishing I'd brought my lighter.

***

Katie had banged on my door so many times, I figured it was time to return the favor. I had no idea if she'd be there, but it was her face that I saw when she opened the door. She seemed surprised for a moment and I thought she was going to slam it in my face.

"I thought my people were going to call your people when I 'found myself.'" She put air quotes around the "found myself" part.

"Yeah, well, I figured you'd showed up unannounced at my place enough times that I should see what it's like on the other side." She leaned against the half-open door as if she wasn't sure if she should let me in.

After a moment of deliberation she rolled her eyes back and sighed as if I was a huge inconvenience.

"Come on." She flung the door wide and I stepped in behind her. I would have thought my eyes had adjusted to the amount of pink from being around her, but it was like I was being eye raped by it. She never had given me an answer on why she was obsessed with it.

She spun to face me, her arms crossed over the pink shirt that draped over her shoulders and hung long over her black pants. "So, what do you want?"

I swallowed, trying to bring moisture into my dry throat.

"I got your little note. Took me two showers to wash it off," I said, gesturing to my chest.

"That was why I used permanent marker," she said, her voice icy, but I could see the shadow of a smile tugging at her lips. She leaned back against her bed and sat down. I remained standing.

Something that powerful is like a speeding train. You can slow it down, but it's never going to stop.

I had to keep my distance from her. Even just being in her room and being submerged in her scent was making my head buzz.

"So what do you want? If you're here to fuck me, sorry, not in the mood."

"I'm not here for that," I said, although if she would have said, *hey, let's go for it,* I wouldn't have said no. Not this time.

"Then why are you here, Stryker Abraham Grant?" She stood up and walked until there was only a breath of space between us, our chests almost touching.

"I have something I have to tell you," I said, but I was interrupted by her cell phone ringing. I wanted to tell her to ignore it, but she snatched it and was answering before I could form the words.

"Hey, Kayla. What's up?" I watched as her eyes went wide, her other hand went to her mouth and she let out a sound as if someone had stabbed her.

And then she was falling to the floor, as if her legs had decided they didn't want to support her anymore and had gone on strike. I caught her just in time.

The phone slipped from her hands and she screamed. No, it wasn't a scream. It was the sound of a soul ripping itself in half. Pure agony.

I was finally able to speak.

"What happened?"

She was only able to get out two words.

"My. Dad."

I looked down and realized Kayla was still on the other end of the phone call. I picked the phone up.

"Hello?"

"Who's this?" She sounded stuffed up, and I could tell she'd been crying.

"Stryker. What happened?" I was still trying to hold Katie up. She was silent, as if she'd gone into shock, but her body shook, like she was freezing. I had to figure out what was going on.

Now.

Katie

Kayla's words banged in my head over and over like a sledgehammer. I heard them over Stryker talking to me, and Stryker talking to Kayla and trying to figure out what had happened to me.

Dad had a heart attack.

We took him to the hospital.

He didn't make it.

Words strung together in a particular order that had dropped me to my knees. Words that made sense, but didn't.

"Katie!" Stryker waved his hand in front of my face and then smacked me in the cheek. The little sting of pain brought me around.

"I have to go home. Right now." I used his arms to pull myself to my shaky feet. "Where are my keys?" I knew I'd just seen them a moment ago. They had a stupid pink elephant on the keychain that Kayla had gotten for me.

Stryker wouldn't let go of me.

"Let go. I have to go home." I thrashed, but he wouldn't budge.

He shook his head and blinked, as if he was stunned himself.

"No, I'll drive you."

More words strung together.

"I have to get there now. We're wasting time."

He didn't make it.

He blinked rapidly. "It's okay, I'll drive you. Right now. Let's go."

Before I could protest, he was shoving my arms into my coat, grabbing my purse, throwing my phone in it, and dragging me down the stairs. The next thing I knew he was putting me in his car and buckling my seatbelt with hands that shook just a little before peeling out of the visitor's parking lot.

"Shit," he said, trying to fiddle with the GPS. "Can you give me directions to the hospital?"

"Yeah," I said, and my voice didn't sound like mine. It sounded like it belonged to someone else.

"Are you okay?" Before I could answer he swore again.

"I shouldn't have asked you that," he said under his breath as he took a corner too fast and almost hit another car. "Shit, shit, shit."

"Slow down," I said.

He was still muttering to himself, and every other word was a curse. I took my coat off and rolled down the window.

"What are you doing?"

"It's hot in here." I fanned my hands, trying to get some cool air into the car. I couldn't breathe. My skin was on fire. I was on fire. "Why is it so hot in here?"

"Katie!" he said, his voice cracking like a whip in the confines of his car.

"What?"

He blinked a bunch of times and slammed his foot on the gas to pass a car he perceived to be going too slow.

"You have to calm down, because I'm freaking out, and I should be the calm one in this situation. Because I don't know if I can handle this." His voice was controlled; too controlled.

"Pull over," I said, feeling my stomach heave once.

"We have to get there, we can't stop," he said, pushing the accelerator to the max.

"Pull over!" I screamed, and he pulled into the breakdown lane. Even before the car stopped, I had the door open and was crashing to my knees, my body deciding it was going to be sick.

I choked and coughed, but nothing came out. The sound of the highway was muted in my ears, as if they were stuffed with something. A hand touched my shoulder.

"Are you okay?"

No, I wasn't fucking okay. How could I be okay?

"You're not supposed to ask me that question. Ever."

"Shit," he said, rubbing my shoulder as he crouched down beside me. "Listen, we need to go. You need to get there. I need to get you to your family. I'm not the person you should be with right now. I suck at this. Anyone would be better than me."

His hands were finally steady, and he put them on my shoulders. They were strong, and his grip was firm.

"I can't believe this is happening. How come I'm not crying?"

"I'm not a doctor, but I think you're in shock."

"Oh."

That made sense, except shock wasn't the right word. I didn't feel shock. I didn't feel anything, except for Stryker's hands on my shoulders. They were the only things that felt real in this moment.

"Let's get you in the car, sweetheart. Come on." His arms went under my armpits, sort of getting me partially to my feet before he swept one arm under my legs and another behind my shoulders.

He tucked me in the passenger seat, rolling it down so I could lie back instead of sit up. He buckled me in again, this time more gently. I looked up to meet his eyes, which, I decided were exactly the color of a stone I'd seen in a ring once in a little shop Kayla had dragged me into. A color midway between green and yellow, if there was such a thing.

My dad.

I shouldn't be thinking about Stryker's eyes. He blinked and closed the door softly before getting in himself.

"Thank you," I said as he put on his blinker and waited for someone to let him get back onto the highway.

Eighteen

Stryker

I didn't freak out often. After everything I'd seen and been through, I'd learned freaking out was a waste of time and didn't get anything done.

I was freaking out.

It was a struggle just to focus on the road and which exit I was supposed to take, and trying not to crash into the car in front of me.

One word just kept repeating in my head.

Fffffffuuuuuuuucccccckkkkkkk.

This was not my territory. I didn't do grief. Yes, if I found out that my mother had died, I probably would feel a moment of sadness. My dad, not so much.

I tried to find some words to say to break up the overwhelming silence in the car, but every single one I chose sounded stupid in my head, so it would sound even worse out loud.

Even Trish, as tactless as she was, would have been better at this. Lottie would have been amazing. So would Zan.

Not me.

She was in shock, and I knew that could be dangerous, but I had no idea what to do about it.

I didn't know what to do except keep driving and try to get her to her family. Then they could take over and give her what she needed.

She still had the window open, but now she was shivering. I couldn't close it, and I wasn't going to ask her to, so I reached in the back and found the blanket she wrapped around herself when she hung out with me while I messed around with the cars.

"It's going to be okay," I said. No, it wasn't. "You're going to be fine." No, she wasn't.

"Everything's going to be fine." No, no, no. Lies, lies, lies.

She shivered under the blanket and I figured bad words were better than silence. Maybe they would distract her mind, or bring her back. Any emotion could be better than this. I searched for something, anything to say.

"Sometimes when I'm alone I listen to Taylor Swift." I looked to see her reaction, but there wasn't any. "I mean, I know that knocks me down two points on the manly scale, but she's actually got some good stuff. I mean, there's a reason she's so popular and you can't get her songs out of your head, even if you want to. I blame it on Allan, but I've definitely put her songs on when I was alone and sang along. And sometimes in the car. That one about the guy who cheated on her is good." I knew the name of it, but I was trying to get her to talk.

"They're all about guys who cheated on her," she finally said. Guess my little Taylor Swift confession had worked.

"Not all of them. There's a few that are about love."

I listed them off and she agreed about which ones she liked.

That took us a few more miles, and then I started talking about other music, other songs. Music. I could always talk about music.

Katie's musical palette was mostly pop, but she had a good ear, and with a voice like that I knew we could refine it a bit. I named off some bands and talked about their sound and what instruments they used and played her some songs. Yes, I could do this.

The miles clicked by and the closer we got, the more I felt like I could keep this going. She didn't smile or laugh, but she was talking and that was something. She still hadn't cried, but I knew that would come.

When I saw the sign for the exit to the hospital I almost let out a sigh of relief. She looked at the building with her wide eyes and I saw her lower lip tremble. She bit down on it as I zoomed around, trying to find a parking spot. After a few loops, I found one and stopped the car.

"Do you . . . do you want me to come with you?" She pulled the blanket off and let it fall to the floor.

"I don't think I can do it alone." That was all I needed to hear. I jumped out of the car and went to get her door for her. I had to help her undo her seatbelt and she clung to me as we walked toward the entrance.

"I don't think I can do this," she whispered to me as the automatic door swooshed open.

"Yes you can. I'm right here, sweetheart." I squeezed her arm and took a step forward so she had to follow me.

"I'm here . . . " she said when we got to the main desk and the receptionist asked where we needed to go, "I'm here to see my dad. Glenn Hallman." The woman typed something into the computer and gave us a smile. She had no idea. She probably thought we were just visiting.

"Room 301," she said, giving us directions. I listened carefully, because I knew Katie wasn't hearing her.

"Thank you," I said to the woman as I steered Katie toward the elevator. No way was she going to be able to do the stairs.

A couple people joined us in the elevator, talking and laughing as if everything was normal. Their lives were normal, I supposed. Katie huddled into me and I put both arms around her. God, I wished my arms could do more than hold her.

It took a while to walk her down the long hallway to the room. We both stopped outside the door, and Katie stared at it for a long time.

The door was closed, but I knocked. I hadn't planned on coming this far with her, but with her latched onto me, I wasn't really going anywhere.

The door opened and Mrs. Hallman, her face red and blotched, looked out. It was dark and there was a hush that came from inside that sent a chill up and down my spine.

"Mommy," Katie said, reaching one hand out and falling into her mother's arms. I let her make the transfer and stepped aside. I didn't belong here anymore.

Katie

He just looked like he was sleeping. The room was filled with monitors and IVs and other sorts of medical paraphernalia, but they were all silent.

Mom and Kayla and Adam and I all stood around him, as if we were waiting for him to wake up.

I reached out to touch his face and it was cool.

"What happened?" I said in a whisper. My voice was still too loud. Mom's hand gripped mine so hard I knew I would have bruises.

"He was just coming home from work and I was asking him about paying a bill and then he said his chest hurt. I . . . " her voice broke for a moment, but she took a breath and continued, "I called the ambulance and he was still alive when they got him in and the doctors thought he was going to make it, but then . . . " she didn't need to say the rest. *Then he didn't.*

There was another knock at the door and I turned my head, expecting to see Stryker standing behind me. He was gone. Where did he go?

A nurse came in and spoke in a hushed voice. There was another woman behind her in a smart suit.

"I'm sorry, but we're going to need to make a decision about what we're going to do with him. This is Becky, our grief counselor." What did she mean, what they were going to do with him?

Becky stepped forward and started talking in equally hushed tones with Mom.

I looked back at Dad. He didn't even have one of those stupid gowns on. He still had his work clothes. Flannel shirt and khakis. He had a whole closet filled with them. I brushed my fingers on the soft material which had been washed so many times it was thin and had threads hanging here and there. Mom hated that.

"C-can we have some more time?" Mom started to cry again, and I didn't know what to do except keep holding onto her.

The nurse looked genuinely sad. I wondered how many times she'd had this conversation.

Becky stepped forward.

"I am so sorry for your loss, Mrs. Hallman. Why don't you and I sit down and have a little talk?"

"We'll get you some coffee," Kayla said, getting up from her chair and giving Adam a look. He nodded and left the room. She was about to try and take me too, but Mom stopped both of us.

"I'm not leaving him!" she shrieked and the sound shattered the eerie calm. "I'm not leaving him!" She fell next to the bed, letting go of me and reaching for Dad's hand. "I can't leave him," she said, holding his hand in both of hers.

"You can't leave me," she whispered, and I knew she was speaking to him. "How dare you leave me?"

"Why don't we give her a minute," the nurse said, putting one hand on my shoulder and another on Kayla's. I didn't want to leave him, either, but I couldn't be in the room anymore with Mom that way.

I still couldn't cry. Everyone else had done a lot of it; even Adam had red eyes. With an iron grip, the nurse steered us out of the room as Mom sobbed and whispered to Dad and Becky rubbed her shoulder and tried to get her into a chair.

"Does this happen? A lot?" The words were sticky and hard to get out of my mouth.

"Yes," she said, letting go of me. Kayla crushed me in a hug and started to cry.

"I'm so sorry you weren't here," she sobbed.

I didn't have anything to say in response, so I just kept hugging her as she cried on my shoulder. Finally she let go and wiped her eyes.

"Did you drive up?"

"No, Stryker brought me." I looked around and found him leaning against the wall about ten feet away. He was staring off into space and I watched him for a moment before his gaze slid to meet mine.

"Thank you," Kayla said, letting me go and walking toward Stryker before putting her arms around him and hugging him tight. "Thank you so much."

His arms hung limp for a moment, as if he didn't know what to do. Then, hesitantly, he wrapped them around her waist and returned the hug.

When she let him go, he cleared his throat and looked at the floor.

I walked over to him and he looked up.

"Thank you," I said.

"You're welcome." His voice was so quiet I almost didn't hear it. Adam came around the corner then, balancing several cups of steaming coffee.

"Here," Kayla said, handing me one. Adam handed her a napkin and she blew her nose on it.

I should want to cry. When your dad suddenly died of a heart attack, you should want to cry. You should sob until you don't have any tears left. I should be like Mom, or at least like Kayla. I shouldn't feel like this was some sort of elaborate joke, and that any second someone was going to tell me this wasn't real, and then I could go back to normal. I was still waiting.

Stryker watched me as if he was waiting, too.

I held out my hand and he looked down at it as if it was the first time he'd ever seen one. He looked back to my eyes and then took my hand, twisting and locking our fingers together.

"I'm so sorry, Katie."

"Thanks," I said, because that seemed like the thing to say. I sipped the coffee because that seemed like the thing to do and talked to Kayla about the ugly watercolor that hung in the hallway and pretended I couldn't hear Mom sobbing and talking to Becky behind the door.

Kayla and Adam huddled together, talking quietly.

Stryker and I stood silent.

"I don't know what to say. To make you feel better, or to make this somehow less of a shitty situation," he finally said as I finished the last of my terrible coffee.

"You don't have to say anything. I can't even cry, so clearly you're not the only one who doesn't know what to do."

"You can cry or not cry. You can do whatever you want to."

I set the empty cup on the floor. I couldn't be bothered to find a trash can at the moment. "I should cry. I've been trying to, but I can't. How fucked up is that?"

"Like I said, you can do whatever you want." He pulled our linked hands to his lips and kissed the back of mine. It was a simple gesture, but it made me want to smile. If only I could figure out how to make my face do that.

"Can I do anything? Get you anything?" he said.

I shook my head.

"Unless you know how to travel back in time, no." Was I joking? How could I be joking? To his credit, Stryker didn't look shocked.

"I'm sorry, sweetheart. I'm so desperately sorry for you. I wish there was something . . . fuck." He took the hand that wasn't linked with mine and banged it against the wall.

"My dad died. There's nothing you could do." I said it again, in my head.

My dad died. My dad died.

Three words. A bunch of letters strung together in such an order that they meant my dad was dead. He was dead. As in gone, lost, far away, never coming back.

My dad died.

"Oh my God. My dad died."

I said it a few more times and Stryker looked like he wanted to put my hand over my mouth so I'd stop saying it.

"He's dead," I said, looking at Stryker. "He's dead."

There they were. Tears.

Like I'd somehow tapped into a hidden well, they started pouring out of me. A sound tore from my mouth, and I tried to stop it, but I couldn't. I started to fall, but Stryker caught me again, yanking me into his arms, whether to comfort me or stifle the noise, I wasn't sure. It didn't matter because my dad was dead.

Kayla's arms came around my back and I was in a hug sandwich, but it didn't matter because my dad was dead.

And then I didn't remember anything because my dad was dead.

Nineteen

Stryker

I'd been waiting for her to break, or do something, and finally, she did. That was almost worse than the shock, because at least with that, I could still sort of reach her. When the grief and reality finally consumed her, there was no reaching her.

I tried to hand her off to Kayla, but she wouldn't let go of me, so we both sort of held her while she cried and made that sound I'd heard earlier.

Someone must have called another grief counselor, because a second woman in a crisp black jacket and skirt showed up and tried to usher us down the hall to a room where Katie's crying wouldn't disturb the rest of the hospital.

She wouldn't walk, despite our coaxing, so I just picked her up like I had before and carried her into a room that looked like some sort of playroom with lots of plastic toys in a bin and ducks on the wall and plush couches for sinking into. I tried to set her down, but I had to sit with her, so she ended up on my lap, like a child.

I stroked her hair and whispered things in her ear and the grief counselor tried to get her to talk, and finally made the decision that they had to give Katie a sedative.

They took her to an empty room down the hall from Mr. Hallman's and she fought a little before they gave it to her.

"Hey, it's going to be okay, it's going to be okay." I said it over and over, even though neither of us believed it.

Soon, her eyes were drooping closed and her grip on me loosened. When the artificial sleep finally claimed her I sat back on the bed she was in and looked at Kayla.

"She didn't cry at all on the way down. She kept saying that she couldn't and she wanted to." I pushed Katie's hair back so it wasn't in her face.

"I should go check on mom," Kayla said, looking out the door. We hadn't heard anything from the room down the hall in a while.

"Go, it's okay. I'll stay with her. I'm not going anywhere."

"Thank you," Kayla said again before leaving the room. I went back to watching Katie, making sure her breathing was deep and even.

Adam sat down in one of the chairs and stretched his arms over his head.

"I feel like I should know what to do by now, having lost my mom and all my grandparents, but every time I think of something to do or say, it seems wrong," he said.

Couldn't have said it better myself.

I nodded and adjusted Katie's head on the pillow. Her face was calm, as if she'd fallen asleep naturally.

"Kayla's trying to keep it together, but it won't last forever. Eventually it catches up with you. Just takes some people longer than others."

Katie's eyebrows twitched and then went still.

"I have no idea what to do. I've never lost anybody I cared about. Not like this. I'm not exactly close with my family." I wasn't sure how much he knew.

"Yeah, Kayla said you'd had a hard time, but the truth is, nothing can prepare you for something like this. There's no manual or training course. You just have to hold on and not let it take you away."

I hoped it wouldn't take Katie away. She was already so broken. It was too much for one person to handle.

"Are you going to be okay? I know we just met, but we're sort of in the same boat here." He had a point.

"I have no idea. I just want to be okay for her." He nodded. Adam understood.

What he didn't understand was that I'd been on the brink of telling Katie about sleeping with Ric. I'd been about to hurt her again, and then something even bigger swooped in and did it for me.

How could I tell her now? But how could I leave her in the dark? Every time she looked at me with such hope, it killed me. I wasn't the guy she thought I was. I wasn't the guy she needed me to be.

She shifted in her sleep, turning toward me, and I knew that I couldn't tell her anytime soon. Right now I had to be there for her and I'd figure out the rest later.

***

Katie woke up a few hours later, after Mrs. Hallman had sort of calmed down. She'd moved from hysterical to a state like Katie was in earlier. Eerie detachment.

Kayla ended up stepping in and helping with the arrangements, that his wish was to be cremated. She and the first grief counselor, Becky, talked and talked as Mrs. Hallman sat and nodded when they asked her a question. Katie was still groggy, so I kept her in my arms.

Her phone went off and I realized that no one knew where we were. In all the chaos, neither of us had thought to tell Lottie, or anyone else, where we'd gone. I pulled out Katie's phone to find about a million frantic, all-caps text messages and a number of voicemails.

I didn't want to leave Katie, but I had to do something, so I texted Lottie, Trish, Will, Simon, Zan and Audrey what had happened. This was not the kind of thing you sent in a text message, but I couldn't really make a call.

They messaged back, and I tried to answer them as best I could, saying that I would call later with more details.

Talking, talking, talking. So much talking.

And then it was time to leave. Just like that.

I had no idea what the hell I was supposed to do, so I just got Katie to her feet and waited for someone to tell me.

"I guess Africa is going to have to wait," I heard Kayla say to Adam. "You can go back if you want."

"Not without you, and not like this," he said, giving her a kiss on the side of her forehead.

I looked at Katie, at her red eyes and disheveled hair, and I knew I wasn't going anywhere either. Not like this.

"I'm coming with you," I said. "Wherever you go, I'm coming with you, sweetheart."

I drove Katie back to her house and Adam drove Kayla and Mrs. Hallman. It seemed like there should be more to it. Like rain, or a sad song. I guess death isn't like the movies.

There were a few cars in the driveway and the lights were on as if everything were completely normal.

I didn't carry Katie into the house, but she did lean on me as I helped her up the steps. The last time I'd been here, she'd kissed me and I'd drawn on her hand and I'd played the violin and she'd fought with her mom.

As much as it had sucked when I'd had to leave, I wished I could rewind time and go back to it. Even that was better than this.

The house was in chaos, the floor covered in dirt and debris from the paramedics tramping around.

"Oh, you're back," someone said, coming out of the kitchen. It was Katie's aunt, Carol. There were other people in there as well, most of whom I recognized from Thanksgiving.

It was like they were having a grief party.

Everyone tried to come hug Katie after hugging and comforting Mrs. Hallman, who was back to crying again. Kayla went to the kitchen and Adam followed, never leaving her side.

"Tell me what you need, and I'll do it."

"I just want to go to my room," she said, so I took her. It was changed from the last time I'd been in here. The walls were white and bare, empty of the hundreds of smiling photographs that had once covered every available bit of bare wall.

"She did it," she said, going to the wall across from her bed and rubbing her hand on it. "She cleaned it off."

"What?" She turned around and went to sit on her bed.

"I drew all over my wall with marker and she cleaned it off. I took a picture with my phone though."

"Can I see it?" I said, sitting down next to her. I thought she would lean into me again, but she didn't, instead propping her back against the wall. I did the same, our shoulders almost touching.

"It was so stupid. Just a bunch of designs and words. It doesn't matter now because my dad is dead." She turned her head and met my eyes. "My dad is dead."

I thought she was going to break down again, but she didn't, instead closing her eyes and tipping her head all the way back until she was staring at the ceiling.

"I don't remember the last thing he said to me. It was probably I love you, but I don't know. How could I not know? What if I'd said something horrible to him and that was the last thing I said to him, before . . . " She didn't finish.

I had to say something, even if I couldn't find the exact right words. Maybe there weren't any right words.

"He loved you so much, and nothing you could ever say would change that, Katie. Nothing. He thought the world of you. Anyone could see that. You can't think about that stuff, or regrets, or anything like that. You'll just end up crazy and angry and he wouldn't want that for you." Not that I had any right to say what her dad did or didn't want for her, but I knew that blaming herself or being miserable wasn't it.

"I'm still waiting for it to not be true."

"I think that's part of grief. Don't they have those five steps?" I tried to grab at what I'd learned in psychology last year. I was much better at crunching numbers than this kind of thing.

"I know denial is one, and bargaining. I don't remember the others," I said.

"I think I'm definitely in denial."

"Well, that's the first step, so I think you're supposed to be." She sighed.

"Can I get you anything? What have you had to eat?"

"I don't want anything. I feel like I never want to eat again."

"You have to. Please. I'm sure somebody has made something at this point. I don't know much about this kind of thing, but I do know that when someone dies, people cook. Oh, shit," I said, realizing I'd said "dies". "I shouldn't have said that. Sorry."

"He's dead. You can say it out loud. I did. He's dead. Oh, I said it again." She clasped and unclasped her hands. "How can I be in denial if I can say it out loud?"

"Saying it out loud and believing it are two different things," I said, which I probably shouldn't have. I waited for her to slap me, or yell, but she didn't.

She just nodded.

"You're probably right."

Katie

The rest of the night was both the longest and the shortest of my life. There were endless hugs and more tears (hardly any from me) and plans for a funeral and lots of food that no one ate.

At last I was allowed to escape once more to my room. The hospital had prescribed Mom some sleeping pills, so she went to bed, making sure she didn't touch Dad's side when she got under the covers.

Kayla and I went down to the basement with Stryker and Adam, while everyone else upstairs cleaned and tried to do what they could because they couldn't do anything else.

"What's with the furniture?" Stryker said. He hadn't seen it when he'd been here before.

"Mom collects it," I said, noticing a new lamp in the corner that she'd tried to hide. "She has a bit of a problem." Kayla and I lay side by side on the bed, and the guys had to settle for a couple of chairs.

"I feel like we should be doing something," Kayla said, yawning. "Like planning flowers or buying an urn, or something."

"One thing at a time," Adam said, leaning forward in his chair. My phone went off again.

"I've got it," Stryker said, holding out his hand. "I texted them, and they're all freaking out. I was shocked when we got here and they hadn't all driven down."

"Just tell them that I'm fine. No driving necessary."

His fingers went to work and I moved closer to Kayla and took her hand.

"What are we going to do about Mom?" I said, asking the question none of us knew how to answer.

"I don't know. I need to see what the hell I'm supposed to do. I can leave right now. We just need to get through tonight and tomorrow and then we'll go from there, I guess."

How did we do that? How did we go on with our lives now? My life had been a girl with one sister, a mother and a father. That was all I knew how to be. I didn't know how to be a girl who had lost her father.

***

I guess I fell asleep at some point, because when I woke, I looked over to find Kayla asleep next to me, our hands still linked. I looked around, and found Stryker and Adam had cleared a place on the floor and were both asleep on piles of my mom's handmade afghans, Stryker on a Christmas one and Adam on one for Saint Patrick's Day.

The basement was dark and there was no noise from upstairs. Stryker had my phone, so I had no idea what time it was and there were no windows in the basement.

The moment I moved, Kayla woke up.

"Hey," she said, wiping her eyes.

"Hey, do you know what time it is?"

"No idea," she said, sitting up and moving her head to stretch out her neck. "Guess it doesn't matter."

No, it really didn't.

"Why can't I cry more?"

"Everyone deals with things in their own way," she said, nudging me with her shoulder.

"When Zack hurt me, I didn't really cry for that either. Maybe I'm emotionally broken. Maybe I'm one of those people who doesn't feel empathy."

"Okay, I'm going to stop that crazy thought train right now. You're not a sociopath." That was the word for it. Stryker made a noise in his sleep and turned over, but didn't wake up. Adam was softly snoring.

"You're just dealing with it in your own way, and that's okay."

"That's the thing, Kayla. I'm not dealing with it. I still feel like this is one big sick joke, or that this is somehow not true. Because it can't be true. It just can't. Other people lose their fathers when they're my age. Things like this don't happen to us. They happen to other people."

Kayla was quiet for a long time.

"It feels that way for me too."

Oh.

Stryker rolled again and his green eyes popped open, frantically searching for something until he found my face.

"Are you okay?"

"Go back to sleep," I said, not answering the question. He got up from the floor and sat back in the chair. He looked like shit, which meant that I probably looked worse.

"Can I get you anything? I'm up now." It was a lie because he yawned a moment later.

"No, I'm fine."

"That's such a load of shit," Kayla said, laughing a little. "We are so not fine."

"I know," I said, and we both laughed like it was the funniest thing ever. We woke Adam up and he looked at Stryker, who shrugged.

"Everyone has their own way to deal," he said.

***

My mother seemed to have flipped a switch while she was sleeping and the next few days she didn't stop. If she wasn't organizing Dad's service or fielding sympathy calls and cards and flowers and casseroles, she was cleaning or picking out clothes for us to wear to the service or meeting with Dad's lawyer.

She was so busy she didn't even have time to notice that Stryker was still here and that we hadn't spent a night apart.

Sex was the furthest thing from both of our minds (or at least from his, I supposed), but that didn't mean we didn't sleep in the same room. I was never far from him as Mom fluttered around and relatives came and went and I tried to figure out what my life meant without my dad in it.

I was definitely still in denial. I still hadn't really cried since that one time at the hospital.

255

Everyone said that it was okay, but seriously, it wasn't. I also still couldn't go into my parents' room. Mom had cleaned and scrubbed the rest of the house, but she hadn't touched his stuff. Guess I wasn't the only one in denial.

I tried to call and talk to Lottie, but she ended up rambling and then crying and apologizing so much that I told her I had to go, and from then on Stryker kept my phone and was responsible for calling everyone and giving them updates.

I knew he was missing his classes, but he told me not to worry about it, so I didn't. I had enough things to worry about.

Twenty

Stryker

Mr. Hallman's funeral was less than a week after he'd died. Mrs. Hallman had turned into a woman possessed, as if the funeral was some sort of grand event, like a wedding, or a terribly important party. I just kept Katie out of the fray and tried to be invisible, but Mrs. Hallman barely noticed I was there.

I helped Katie zip up the back of her dress in her room, which she hadn't slept in since she'd come home. We usually ended up in the basement, snatching sleep whenever.

"How do I look?" She was gorgeous, even in her sadness.

"Beautiful." I kissed her shoulder and she turned slowly. I'd barely kissed her since we'd gotten back from the hospital and it wasn't just because it didn't seem like the right thing to do in light of her father's death.

I didn't deserve to kiss her; not after what I'd done with Ric. In a stupid way, I thought that she might find out, if she kissed me. Like the truth would be written on my lips.

"You ready?" Katie didn't know it, but everyone was coming down for the funeral. I'd organized what Trish had dubbed the "Grief Committee" when she'd come down to bring me some clothes a few days ago. I told them not to go overboard, but I had no idea what to expect.

The house was full of people. Lots of relatives and friends that I'd become acquainted with. They all gave me strange looks until I explained who I was, which was always awkward. I just told them that I was Katie's friend and let them make their own conclusions, which they were going to do anyway.

Katie's phone buzzed with a message from Trish saying that they were waiting out front.

"Come with me." I took her hand and led her through the living room as Mrs. Hallman yelled at someone about making sure the flowers had arrived at the funeral home.

There they were, all dressed in black, standing on the porch.

"What are you doing here?" Katie said. "I said you didn't have to come."

"Of course we had to come," Audrey said coming forward and giving Katie a hug. Will and Lottie and Trish and Simon and Zan followed, each giving her a hug and their sympathies. I'd heard enough of them by now to know which were genuine and which weren't. These were of the former.

"When are you coming back to school?" Trish said as we shivered on the porch. There wasn't really enough room in the house, but I had an idea.

"Hey, why don't we move this inside? We can go down to the basement." Adam and I had consolidated a lot of the furniture and moved it around so we'd have a place to sleep, and we could probably fit down there.

I led them all through the house, and everyone gave us looks but no one asked any questions.

"Oh my God, it's *Hoarders, The Furniture E*dition," Lottie said when she saw it.

"Don't talk about *Hoarders*," Simon said, shuddering. I'd been right to invite them. Katie almost cracked a smile.

"Oh, sorry," Lottie said. "I should be more respectful."

"No, you should be however you want to be. Everyone's been so damn respectful it makes me want to scream," Katie said, sitting on the bed. "Be normal. I need some normal, because everything else isn't normal."

"I've got it," Simon said, snapping his fingers. "Picnic game." I remembered playing it while waiting outside Katie's hospital room the night Zack attacked her. It seemed as good a plan as any, and Katie actually did smile. I could count on one hand the amount of smiles I'd seen from her in the past few days.

I put my arm around her and she leaned into me.

"Thank you, again," she whispered. "I needed them."

"I know," I said as Simon started the game.

We played until it was time for everyone to go over to the funeral home. We'd all laughed and it had been like a completely normal thing, with the exception of everyone wearing black.

Katie relaxed a little and then tensed back up. I knew she was berating herself for laughing and having a good time on the day of her dad's funeral. Like she wasn't allowed to have fun anymore, which was so beyond wrong, but I couldn't tell her that. She had to figure it out for herself. If there was anything I knew about Katie, it was that she had do things her own way.

In the back of my mind, the guilt for my drunken night with Ric hovered, keeping me up when I tried to sleep and whispering in my ear every time Katie looked at me like she was glad I was here, that she needed me.

I was going to help get her through this and then I'd have to pull myself out of her life. But for right now, I was going to help her get through the next few hours, the next few days, until she could do it on her own again.

Katie

The funeral was nice. The flowers were nice and everyone said nice things and smiled nice and cried nice and it was all nice, nice, nice.

I hated every second of it. All I wanted to do was push one of the windows open and jump, or pull the fire alarm, which was exactly in my line of vision. I wondered what my mother would have said if I'd have done it.

I wished Stryker could have sat with me, but he was stuck a row behind. As much as I was sick of people hugging me and consoling me and touching me, I wished my hand was in his for the service.

I snuck a few looks back at him and he gave me a little smile each time. At one point I heard a cough and glanced back to see him holding his hand over his mouth, and on the back of his hand was drawn, *here 4 U.*

Thank you, I mouthed at him and turned back around. Leave it to Stryker to always have a marker on him.

The rest of my friends were relegated to the very back of the room, but Zan was so tall I could see his dark head of hair every time I turned.

His parents were here, too, also sitting in the back. I'd seen them come in, but I was waiting for the moment when they came through the line to pay their respects. His mother had never liked me. Not that it mattered now.

They played James Taylor, Dad's favorite, as people lined up to hug and tell us how sorry they were.

More words, words, words and talking, talking, talking. I wished I could put them all on mute, like an annoying commercial.

Yes, they were sorry about Dad, but you could tell that every single one of them was glad it wasn't their family, that it wasn't their dad or uncle or brother. They couldn't hide it, when they looked at you. That little glimmer of pity and relief.

After the service we all drove over to the local VFW hall to have a little open house my Mom and Aunt Carol had organized. It was a way to allow people to make more sympathy casseroles stuffed with tuna and peas and sorry for your losses.

I wanted to skip the whole thing, but Mom would have killed me.

"You guys don't have to come," I said as we stood in the parking lot. The air was so cold that it made our lungs and throat hurt when we breathed in, and it smelled like snow. Dad always claimed he could smell the snow, and Mom always said he was crazy.

"Are you kidding? We wouldn't miss it," Lottie said, giving me a little side hug. I actually didn't mind her hugs. She was so tiny that they were never smothering.

"We're all here for you, girl," Trish said and they all agreed.

God, I didn't deserve them and that was the thing that brought my first tears forward in days. During the service I'd pretended because what kind of horrible daughter didn't sob at her dad's funeral?

"Here." Stryker was prepared with a crisp white handkerchief that looked like he'd just taken it out of a package.

"Thanks," I said, taking it. I should probably be with my mom and Kayla and the rest of my family.

"We should probably head over," I said to Stryker.

"You should go with your family. I'll be right behind you." Mom and Kayla walked out of the funeral home and I could tell they were looking for me.

He flashed the words written on his hand and started walking toward his car. I said goodbye to everyone else and walked toward Mom and Kayla, giving each of them hugs.

Only a few days ago my biggest problem was that Mom didn't like Stryker and he was pushing me away. How fast things could change.

Twenty-one

Stryker

We all made it through the open house and then it was time for everyone to get back to school, and it was time for me to go with them.

"So, I'm going to drive Trish back," I said as Katie tossed what was left of the food.

"What?" She looked at me as if I'd just announced I was going to the moon.

"Yeah, I really need to get back to school and . . . everything." It was the lamest of lame excuses. This morning I'd packed up my stuff and loaded up my car with it while she'd been in the shower. Like a fucking coward.

She stared for another second and then shook her head.

"Yeah, yeah, of course. You have to get back to your life."

There was another moment of silence, and it was awkward. After we'd become so close, this seemed very anti-climactic.

"Thank you," she said, tossing something that looked like leftover baby food into the trash can, "for everything. I'll never be able to say it enough, but I don't know what I would have done without you." She set the dish down and gave me a hug.

I tried not to hold her too tight, or pull her too close. She'd been hugged enough today, and if I were her, I wouldn't want another one.

That didn't stop me from leaning down and smelling her hair and letting myself surround her for just a second.

"See you around?" I should win an award for the most moronic goodbye ever spoken.

"Um, yeah. I guess."

"Let me know if you need anything. Anytime."

I let her go and stepped away. She looked like she was going to cry again, so I handed her another handkerchief.

"Thanks, Stryker."

I turned my back and walked away.

***

"You are the dumbest brother ever. Seriously," Trish said as I got in the car. "You are seriously going to leave her now?"

"I don't belong there anymore. I shouldn't really have been there that long. Her mother was going to say something eventually and I didn't want her to have to go through that again."

"You're still a dumbass." She moved the seat back so she could have room for her legs.

"What am I supposed to do, Trish?" She could criticize all she wanted, but I'd like to see her do better.

"Well, first I wouldn't abandon her in her time of need. Second, I would have told her that I loved her."

We were back to that again.

"I don't love her, Trish."

She snorted and rolled her eyes before taking her hair out of the careful bun she'd put it in, to look respectful, I supposed. She hadn't taken out her violet contacts, and she'd worn her black boots, so those sort of negated her effort, but it was a nice try.

"Yeah, you do."

"Look Trish, I'm exhausted and I really, really need a cigarette, so could you just lay off?"

Normally she would have made a snarky comment and just ignored me until she had her say, but I must have looked bad enough for her to back down.

"Fine, fine."

I turned on the radio as loud as it would go and loosened my tie.

"Here," she said, fishing in my glove box for my emergency smokes. She held one out to me and put it in my mouth before lighting it.

"Thanks."

"You should really quit, you know."

Every now and then Trish nagged me to quit, but then she still smoked, so it was a bit of a pot and kettle situation.

"I will if you will." We'd tried that before too. Turned out willpower was not one of our genetic gifts.

"Deal." She held out her hand and we shook on it. "But let me have one last one."

So we each smoked one last cigarette in silence as I drove us back to school.

***

I texted Katie when we got back, just so she'd know we arrived alive. Trish saw me doing it, but made no comment other than raising her eyebrow and giving me a look.

I dropped her back at her apartment and went back to mine. The place felt too big and too silent. Just the sound of my own breathing was loud. I turned on some music, not caring what it was as long as the sound filled up the empty rooms. "Holding on and Letting Go", by Ross Copperman came through the speakers and I almost turned it off, but that would be admitting the song bothered me because it made me think of Katie. I wasn't going to give the song that satisfaction.

My phone rang and I knew without looking at it who it would be.

"Hey," she said, and her voice was thick with tears.

"Hey."

"I miss you. Mom's back to being a sobbing mess and Kayla's trying to get her to eat and my family is smothering me and I just wish you were here. Or I wish I was there. Either way, I wish we were together."

So did I.

"I'm sorry I left, but I didn't want to start anything with your mom."

"I know why you left, but I wish you didn't have to. Things have gotten so . . . complicated." She laughed a little, but it wasn't really funny. "I think I'm still in denial."

"Hey, I'm not judging."

"I know."

"I'm quitting smoking," I said, just for something to say that didn't involve death.

"Really? Have you ever tried before?"

"Trish and I try every now and then, but it never sticks."

"Well, if you need, like, a sponsor or something, I would be happy to fill that role. You know, help you with the pledge."

"The pledge?"

"I accept the things and I can't change and . . . I know there's something about the wisdom to know the difference . . . " I almost laughed.

"That's for Alcoholics Anonymous."

"Does it really matter?"

"I guess not," I said as the song switched to "Rose Tattoo", by Dropkick Murphys.

"Could you play for me?" she said, as if she was asking to borrow a kidney.

"What do you want to hear?"

"Anything."

I turned off Dropkick, put the phone on speaker and picked up my guitar, sifting through my mental jukebox. I wanted something that would make her laugh. Something unexpected. I smiled and started "Lovefool", by The Cardigans. I'd found it through a random internet search once and thought it was catchy.

It took a minute for her to figure out what it was, but I heard her laugh for the first time in way too long. A surprised laugh that she couldn't suppress.

I exaggerated the cuteness of the lyrics, hoping to make her laugh more. It worked.

She was still giggling when I finished.

"That was so random, but so perfect. I heard that one in a movie once and I always liked it." Her laughter died down and I picked the phone up again.

"I thought you'd like that."

She paused and I could hear her thinking.

"I'm sorry. I shouldn't feel like shit about laughing, but I do."

"You're right, you shouldn't. Maybe I'm not the only one who needs to learn the Serenity Prayer. You have to start accepting that you can't change things, and you can't take the blame for everything."

"I know, I know."

"So stop it," I said. "Just stop." My voice was sharp, but she needed to hear it. Everyone else would treat her delicately, but she wasn't. She was tough and she needed someone to call her out on it.

"Are you being a dick again?"

"No, I'm just . . . I don't want you to turn into this sad girl who stops living her life because she's afraid of everything. You're the girl who kissed me because you wanted to see what it was like to make out with a guy who had a lip ring. You're the girl who faced her ex, and the girl who fought her mom for me. I can't lose that girl."

"That girl had a dad. I don't know who I am anymore. That girl is gone and she's not coming back." I knew what she was saying was right, but I didn't want it to be right.

"I just . . . I have to figure things out now. But I don't want to figure them out alone. I want you to be there." I didn't say anything, because I was waiting for more.

"Not like how we first were. Just friends. No sex. I can't deal with all that right now, but I'd like it if we could be friends. Do you think we could do that?"

No, we definitely couldn't go back to being friends, not after everything. At least, I didn't think I could. But, if it was being friends or not having her in my life, I'd take the agony of trying to be her friend.

"I think we can be friends." She let out a breath I felt like she'd been holding for as long as she'd been talking to me.

"Good. I'd really like to be your friend."

"I'll try not to be a dick."

"You can be a dick sometimes. Especially when I need it." This was probably the absolute worst time, but I couldn't go forward without telling her about Ric. Dick move, coming right up.

"Listen—"

She cut me off.

"I know that it's going to be hard to go back. I mean, we started off in the wrong direction to be friends, but I would really like to try, but only if you want to. I don't want you to feel obligated. You've already done so much for me."

Shit. As quick as I'd gotten up the nerve to do it, that nerve had deserted me and it wasn't coming back anytime soon.

"No, I want to be friends. Just friends."

"Just friends."

She told me she'd be coming back soon, that Kayla was going to stay with her mom for a while and Adam was going back to Africa. It wasn't the best solution, but at least she could come back to school and start figuring out who she was now.

"So I guess I'll see you soon, friend."

"Goodnight, friend," I said. "To be continued."

"Dot, dot, dot," she said and hung up.

Katie

There wasn't much more I could do at home, and I was starting to go crazy. Everywhere, there were reminders of Dad. Pictures and tools and socks and even a basket of his laundry. Mom had cleaned most of it, but I still found things here and there. Behind the dryer, and in the dishwasher and on the shelves and randomly in my room.

He was everywhere and nowhere.

Kayla had her hands full with Mom, who went from a busy bee who wouldn't stop moving to a sobbing mess who couldn't do anything. I'd tried helping her, but I just didn't have the knack for it. I wanted to tell her to stop crying because it made me uncomfortable. I wanted to tell her that she had to get her shit together because I was worried about her and I didn't want to go to school without knowing that she was going to be able to make it through the day.

I did grab one of his flannel shirts and shove it in my bag when Mom and Kayla weren't looking. I had plenty of pictures and videos and so forth of my dad, but I wanted something that still had his smell. I also found a few pictures of the two of us and a few other little keepsakes that Mom wouldn't miss.

I still couldn't believe he was dead. I'd said it thousands of times, thinking that if I said it enough, I'd start believing it. Even the service hadn't done it. Even seeing the urn with his ashes in it hadn't done it. I'd taken some of those, too, when everyone had been in bed. They were double Ziploc-bagged at the bottom of my backpack. I was now the creepy girl who stole her dad's ashes. I had no idea what I was going to do with them.

Mom had a million different ideas, but she never stuck with one of them long enough. First it was the beach, then it was the mountains, and then it was at his childhood home, and then it was a little bit in a bunch of places. Her latest scheme was some sort of road trip where we dropped little bits in places that meant something to him. It sounded like something she'd heard in a movie. Some sort of weird bonding experience where we'd all learn something and come out better in the end and ride off into a hopeful sunset in a blue convertible. Too bad life was never like that.

Mom had barely mentioned Stryker other than to say, "That tattooed boy gone now?" I just nodded and let it go. She didn't ask about him again, and I didn't volunteer anything.

"Are you sure you're going to be okay?" I said to Kayla the Wednesday following the funeral. I had used up all my "dead dad" freebie days from classes.

"Yeah, I'm fine. I'll see you on Saturday, right?" I'd planned to come home on the weekends until further notice to give Kayla a break from Mom duty. Not that I'd be much help.

I saw her checking her phone for the millionth time, even though Adam had already landed in Africa and wouldn't have service again.

"It sucks that he had to go back."

"Yeah, but we've got to learn how to deal with stuff like this." She said it, but I could tell she didn't mean it. Since they'd met, they'd barely spent any time apart, and you could see that it was like part of her was missing. Kayla had dated before, but I'd never seen her like this. My normally organized (the apple didn't fall far from the tree) sister was scatterbrained and careless. Some of it had to do with losing Dad and some of it had to do with the fact that part of her heart was thousands of miles away.

"I'm not the kind of girl who can't function without a man. I'm not," she said, taking one of the clean dishes and going to the freezer and putting it in.

"Um, Kay?"

"What?"

"I think that belongs in the cabinet."

She opened the freezer, took the now-chilled plate out and put it in the cabinet with a clatter.

"You didn't see that," she said, grabbing another dish.

"See what?"

"Exactly."

***

"Mom?" She'd gone back to bed after having a crying fit over finding some of Dad's tools in the garage. "I'm leaving."

The room was dark. Kayla had tacked up pieces of fabric over the windows for her. It was a bit like walking into a cave.

She rolled over slowly, barely opening her swollen eyes. Whereas I couldn't cry, she seemed to breaking the world record for most tears shed. If only we could make a trade. I'd be happy to be the sobbing wreck if it meant she could hold it together better.

"Okay." She didn't seem to want to move, so I pulled the covers down and got in with her, shoes and all. It was a testament to how upset she was that she didn't scold me.

I lay my head on the pillow next to hers.

"Are you going to be okay here?" It was a stupid question, but I had to ask it anyway.

"No." Her face collapsed and she started sobbing again. I grabbed one of the many tissue boxes Kayla and I had stashed all over the house.

"Why did this happen? Why did this happen to us?" I handed her a tissue and put my arm around her.

"I don't know. I wish I had a book full of things that I am supposed to say and do, but there isn't one. If we spend all our time wondering why, then we'll waste our lives, and Dad wouldn't want that." I didn't know who I was channeling, but it all sounded good, so I went with it. "Dad wouldn't want you to be sad forever. He was always trying to make you laugh." Even when it ended up just making her madder. Eventually they would stop fighting and she'd crack a smile.

She blew her nose and threw the tissue on the floor. Dear God, she really was in a state.

"You sure it's okay for me to go back? I could stay with you and Kayla for the rest of the week."

She shook her head and wiped her eyes with her hands.

"No, you have to get back to school. Just because I've fallen apart, doesn't mean you have to."

"You haven't fallen apart, Mom."

"Yeah, Katiebug, I have."

"Well, you had a good reason to," I said, using another tissue to wipe her eyes. "You can fall apart all you want. I won't tell."

"Thanks, baby." She hadn't called me that in ages.

I gave her another hug and we lay there for a little longer. We hadn't always gotten along, but that was going to have to change. She was the only parent I had left, and like it or not, she needed me and I needed her back.

Trish had driven my car down for the funeral, so I was able to drive my own car back. I said goodbye to Kayla and promised to see her on Saturday and started the drive back to DU.

I couldn't find a good radio station, so I picked up my phone and put it on speaker, setting it in a little clip on my dashboard. I should have one of those headsets, but I thought they made people look like assholes, so I'd never gotten one.

He picked up on the second ring.

"Hey, I'm driving back and I just thought I would check in with my friend. How are you, friend?"

He sounded like he was in a room full of people.

"I'm good, friend. How are you?" The voices faded, as if he was walking away from them.

"You're not in class, are you?"

"No, I was just getting something to eat."

"When's your next class?"

"Not for a while. I'm all yours, friend."

"Well that is good to hear, friend."

He went on to tell me about all the things that I'd missed on campus, from someone getting thrown out for setting a couch on fire, to the frat that was on probation, to the professor who'd gotten caught smoking pot on campus with a few students.

It was all silly and mundane and distracting enough that I could get out of my own head for a few minutes. It was a blessed relief.

He also filled me in on the crew. Lottie was dying to have me back and had stocked up on ice cream in preparation for lots of *Law and Order* marathons.

Trish had almost gotten fired from her job for mouthing off to her boss, Will and Audrey had finally kissed in public and Simon was trying to convince everyone to participate in some sort of charity event that involved running around campus in your underwear.

"I'm not freezing my junk off, even if it is for charity," he said as I pictured his junk. It was pretty nice junk, and I wouldn't like it if anything happened to it, even if I wasn't going to be using it anytime soon.

It was all well and good to call ourselves friends over the phone, but in person, I had no idea how it was going to go.

"How's your mom?"

"I guess she's as good as can be expected. She goes from sobbing to cleaning like the Queen is coming over, then back to sobbing. I'm going back this weekend so Kayla can have a break."

"Do you feel guilty?" Stryker always had a way of asking the questions I didn't want to answer.

"Yeah. How can I not?"

I waited for him to tell me that I shouldn't, but he sighed.

"You're right."

"Wait, what was that?"

He laughed.

"I said that you're right. A little guilt is okay. It's the big, soul-crushing guilt I'm worried about."

"Well, I'm doing okay so far." If being okay meant having a baggie with my Dad's ashes and not being able to believe he was really gone. I hadn't told Stryker about the first thing.

"Listen, I really want to thank you for everything you've done. I know I can never make it up to you, but I owe you at least a few more Thanksgiving dinners." I'd hoped he would laugh, but he didn't.

"You don't owe me anything, Katie. Anyone else would have done the same thing. It's not like I rode in on a white horse."

"Horses scare me, and no, not everyone would have done the same thing and you know it. Give yourself some credit, Stryker Abraham Grant."

"God, I hate that you know my middle name. It's been the bane of my existence for years."

"It's a perfectly fine middle name. It's a presidential name, and you're trying to change the subject."

"Guilty as charged."

"Look, we don't have to talk about it. I just want you to know."

He sighed again and I could picture him running his hand through his hair.

"Got it."

We talked for a little while longer and I felt like I was taking up too much of his time, being too needy and clingy (again), so I told him I had to stop and get gas.

"See you soon, friend."

"Drive safe, friend."

Twenty-two

Stryker

I half-expected Katie's car to be parked at my apartment when I got back from class, but instead there was Ric, leaning against her car and playing with the holes in her jeans. I'd barely had any contact with her since our tryst, and I was hoping it would stay that way.

"Hey," she said, not moving from her car. "How are you?"

I wasn't in the mood to deal with her.

"What do you want, Ric?"

She looked like she was going to cry, and I felt one pang of sympathy. It wasn't completely her fault that we'd had sex. I'd been a willing, if drunk, participant.

"Sorry, I haven't gotten a lot of sleep," I said. She was shivering. No wonder, she didn't have a coat on and her clothes were always full of holes. "Come on," I said, motioning toward the door. Better to get this over with.

"I'm sorry," she said as we walked up the stairs. "I've just . . . I've liked you for a long time and you never seemed to be into me, so I made a move and now . . . I'm so sorry."

I let her in and went right to the kitchen to make her a cup of tea because it didn't feel like the right kind of situation for coffee.

"I'm sorry too. I was lashing out, or being stupid and you happened to be there. We're both adults and we acted like hormonal teenagers."

She leaned on the counter and wiped her eyes.

"So you're not pissed at me?"

Yes.

"No. It wasn't your fault. Although, the fact that I told you over and over that I wasn't interested should have been a red flag."

"I know, I know," she said accepting the mug of tea I held out to her.

"No, you really don't. I couldn't have been any more clear, Ric. I didn't want to be with you, so why did you keep it up?"

She laughed a little.

"Desperation? Hope? Thinking that one day you'd see that we were perfect for each other?"

"But we're not, Ric. We never would have been."

"But she is?" I didn't need to ask who she was talking about. Her narrowed eyes and the increased bitterness in her voice did that for me.

"This isn't about her. I would feel this way whether she was around or not."

She made a little scoffing sound, and I realized I was never going to get through to her. It was bashing my head against a brick wall. She had issues that had nothing to do with me.

"Look, I just wanted to clear the air because I didn't want you to quit The Band and I'd like it if we could work things out to at least be civil."

She set her tea down, untouched.

"I guess." She pushed herself away from the counter. "Have you told her?"

I hesitated before I said, "No." I thought about trying to lie, but Ric was the kind of girl who would bring it up in front of Katie and then I'd be in an even worse place.

"Hmm," she said, a little smile flitting over her face.

"Her father just died, Ric. I couldn't tell her that right now."

"How convenient."

"It's not like that. Shit, why do you have to make this so difficult?"

"Difficult?" She let out a loud burst of laughter. "Give me a fucking break. You have no idea, Stryk. Your little pink girlfriend who's had everything handed to her on a fucking platter. Yeah, well, the rest of us have had it a lot worse. It's about time she got knocked down a peg." The venom was directed toward Katie, but she should have been shooting it at me.

I crossed the room until I was within a foot of her. "Listen, you don't talk about her that way in my house. Ever. Get the fuck out. There's the door." I pointed to it and turned my back on her.

"If that's the way you want it, fine. Fuck you, Stryker." I heard the door slam behind her. Good riddance.

My phone buzzed a moment later.

Good luck keeping your dirty little secret Stryk. I was going to keep it to myself, but I might just slip and tell someone . . .

I didn't respond, because that was what she wanted me to do. I was actually shocked that it hadn't gotten out already. Trish knew and Zoey knew. I'd caught Trish's eye a couple of times when she'd come down for the funeral and she'd almost brought it up on the phone, but we hadn't had a moment to talk about it. Trish would never squeal on me because she knew it would hurt Katie.

I would be damned if I was going to let Ric manipulate me. Even if she did tell Katie, I wasn't sure if Katie would believe her. Ric didn't have a good track record with her, and Katie would probably figure Ric was being a jealous bitch.

I called Trish.

"Hey, Ric just came by and threatened to tell Katie about us."

"Surprise, surprise. Hell hath no fury, brother."

"Yes, I am familiar with the quote, Trishella, I'm just not sure what I'm supposed to do about it. I have no idea how far she'll take this."

"So what am I supposed to do about it?" she snapped.

"I don't know. Just . . . don't say anything to Katie."

"Do you think I'm the kind of person who would tell her friend that her boyfriend slept with someone else right after her father died of a heart attack?"

"I'm not her boyfriend."

"Whatever, dude. That's just semantics. I'm just saying that I wouldn't tell her. She's got enough shit to deal with right now without worrying about you putting your penis in places it doesn't belong."

"I'm going to tell her."

"Yeah, okay. Let me know how that works out for you. I gotta go, bro. Therapy time is over." She hung up without saying anything else.

Well, I had that base covered.

A moment later, my phone rang again. Damn, I was popular today.

"Hey, it's Lottie."

"Hey, what's up?"

"We're sort of doing this welcome back kind of thing for Katie, and I thought you should be involved."

"What kind of thing are we talking about?"

"Like a get-together-to-take-her-mind-off-of-it thing. We were also hoping, maybe, we could use your apartment? It's bigger than the dorm. I figured you wouldn't mind, but I thought I'd ask before we barged in."

"Yeah, that's fine." I'd have to clean first, that was for sure. I'd left things in disarray when I'd gone to Katie's house and I hadn't gotten them back together yet. "Do you need anything else?"

"Nope. We've got it covered." She gave me some more details and then hung up.

God, I had dug myself a hole and it was like it kept getting deeper and deeper.

Katie

Campus was the same. Why I had expected it to be different, I had no idea, but it was like my world had changed so dramatically, I expected the rest to match. Like the sky should always be cloudy, the weather always cold and miserable, the world gray and lifeless. It would have been easier to accept the truth if it was like that.

I got hug-tackled as soon as I walked into my room by Lottie, who had clearly been waiting for me. My side of the room was all made up and it smelled like she'd just sprayed it with something vanilla-scented.

"I've missed you so much."

"You didn't enjoy having the room all to yourself?" I said, giving her a wink. I would have taken advantage of it, if I were her.

Her blue eyes went wide.

"We didn't—"

"Of course you did. Hell, I would, if I were you." Not that I was going to be having sex anytime soon, and it wasn't just because of Dad. All the reasons I'd used for having sex before didn't seem like good reasons anymore. They weren't even reasons. I just decided I wanted to do it and grabbed whoever was available. It was a miracle I hadn't ended up pregnant. Or worse.

Dad would be so ashamed of me. Would have been so ashamed of me. Now he'd never know. Somehow, that made me even more determined not to do it. Ever again.

"Maybe we did. A little." Such a liar.

"As long as it's not in my bed, you can do whatever you want, girl." I melted back into my pillows and it was such a relief having my pink things around me again. My safe little pink world.

"How are you doing?" I'd gotten used to this question and all its variations. Pasting on a smile and saying I was doing fine was as easy as blinking now. It was complete bullshit, but no one ever seemed to care.

"Fine."

Lottie grabbed a pint of ice cream from the freezer, as if she'd been waiting to do it since I walked in. She handed me a spoon and sat down next to me on my bed. I twisted the lid off and sunk my spoon in the cold, creamy goodness.

"You're getting good at that. Saying you're fine when you're not. You forget, I too am a Master of Fine."

I had forgotten.

She took a deep breath. "After the accident, when Lexie was in the hospital, people would always ask me how she was doing. They didn't want to know that she couldn't remember who her parents were, or how old she was, or that she had to pee in a bed pan. So I got pretty damn good at saying she was doing fine. No one wanted to know those other things. They just want to be reassured. It's like when you ask how someone is; you don't really want to know, you just want them to say they're fine and then you can move on. It's a social courtesy. Like opening a door for someone or saying "bless you" when someone sneezes."

Sticking a giant spoonful of ice cream in her mouth, she shrugged.

"So, how about you tell me how you're actually doing and cut the crap?"

"What do you want me to say? My dad is dead and I can't accept it, and I've got a Ziploc bag with some of his ashes, which I stole, and sometimes I just wish I could fall asleep and not wake up. Is that what you wanted me to say?"

I had to give her credit, she didn't miss a beat.

"You can say whatever you want as long as it's the truth. You stole of some of his ashes?"

"Yeah. I have no idea why. I thought maybe having them with me would help reality sink in, but no luck. I still have this huge part of me that expects him to walk in the door, or call me up, or something. How crazy is that?"

"Not crazy at all. You're talking to a girl who couldn't accept that her best friend was never coming back."

"How is Lexie?" I took another huge bite of the ice cream, enough to give me a brain freeze.

"She's settled, I guess, and her mom's been calling me with updates. I want to go down and see her, but Zan says it isn't a good idea. I know it isn't, but I miss her."

Yet another reminder that Lottie was a much better person than I was.

"I mean, at least she's alive. Wow, that sounded way better in my head than it did out loud. I am so sorry."

"It's okay." Our spoons collided and she moved hers so I could dip in again. "I just keep expecting myself to break, to have this great moment of realization, but I'm still waiting for it to hit me."

"Are you sure you want it to?"

"No, I really don't want it to, because then I'll probably end up worse than Mom."

I gave Lottie a brief rundown of my Mom's insanity.

"Is she seeing someone? Like a counselor?"

"I think Kayla is taking her to some sort of widow's support group."

She paused for a second, digging in the ice cream for the best bite.

"And you? Are you going to see someone?"

The social worker at the hospital had sent us home with brochures and phone numbers of various places where we could get grief counseling. I could always go see Dr. Sandrich.

There was one group especially for children who had lost one or both parents and Kayla wanted us to go together, but I was trying to talk her out of it. I couldn't imagine talking to a roomful of strangers about my dad. And what would I say? That I couldn't cry? I could just imagine their horrified faces.

"Not right now. I just want to get back to things and go from there."

"It might help."

"Did it help you?"

"Uh, no. Not really. But you shouldn't use me as a measure of the effectiveness of therapy." I didn't want to talk about this anymore.

"I really missed you," I said, bumping her shoulder with mine. "You know what I thought when I first saw you?"

"Do I really want to know?"

"I thought that we would never get along. I thought that I should have just sucked it up and lived with one of those bitches from high school. How crazy is that?"

"You know what I thought when I first saw you?" she said.

"I bet I can guess."

"It was, 'fuck, that's a lot of pink.'"

"Surprise, surprise."

I whacked her with a pillow, being careful not to upset the ice cream. She grabbed one and hit me with it and we laughed.

"I got used to it. The pink," she said, gesturing.

"You want to know something else? You were a better friend to me in a few weeks than any one of those bitches were in three years. Wanna talk about something crazy."

"Trish always says that normal people are boring, that normal people don't get remembered. It's the crazies who make history."

"Here's to being crazy."

I raised my spoon and we clinked them together again and fought for the rest of the ice cream.

Twenty-three

Stryker

I could count the times I'd run into Katie on campus on one hand. Of course, one of those times had to be on Thursday after she'd gotten back. I'd thought in the spirit of our newfound friendship that she would come see me, or want me to see her, but she didn't. That girl gave more mixed signals than the government.

I was just coming away from the Starbucks after having caved and bought a crazy expensive coffee to try to give me a jolt. I'd had a hard time sleeping lately. Guilt didn't make a soft pillow.

"Hey, friend." A voice said from behind me. I turned and was met by a tired, but beaming Katie. It had only been a few days since I'd last seen her, but it was almost like seeing her again for the first time. God, she was beautiful. Had I ever appreciated that before?

Her brown hair was up in its usual high ponytail, but it was a little messier than usual. As if she really didn't care. Her pink shirt was loose and I could see her bra straps resting on her shoulders. She wasn't wearing makeup, either, and she had her glasses on.

"Hey, friend," I finally said. I wanted to touch her. Hugging her would be a completely appropriate friend thing to do, right? Yes. There were people glaring at me to move along, but I just gave them a glare back. That made them back off a little.

"What do you want? It's on me." I moved aside so she could order. She looked like she was going to protest, so I said, "Friends can buy each other coffee, can't they?"

She smiled, just a little.

"Sure they can. I'll have a Vanilla Spice Latte."

While we waited for our drinks, she stood next to me and I thought this would be a good time for that hug.

"I'm glad you're back. I'm sorry we left on a weird note." I leaned and put my arms around her. She hesitated, and then her arms went around me. I'd held her so much during those days I spent at her house. That closeness had been so easy, so effortless. It was a reflex. She needed something to hold onto, and I just happened to be there.

I tried not to hold her too tight, or notice how hard her heart was beating, and how her head fit against my chest as if someone had carved a place for it, just for her.

I tried, but I failed.

"I missed you, friend," she whispered as I closed my eyes and breathed her in.

"I missed you."

Our drinks were ready so I had to let go, but I slid my arms down her shoulders, wanting to make the touch last.

"Listen, I have to get to class, but I'll see you later? We should hang out. That's what friends do, right?" she said.

"Right."

"Bye, Stryker. Thanks for the coffee." She touched my shoulder and then turned away and left. I stood there, watching her go, and realizing I could never, ever be just friends with her.

***

Ric sent several more threatening messages, but I ignored them. She was just waiting for me to lash out, which is what I normally would have done in a situation like this. She'd known me for long enough to know my patterns.

Trish showed up at my apartment again, saying that she'd had a fight with her roommate, but I knew it was because she was checking up on me.

"You know, we could always push her down the stairs," she said, looking up from her homework. I was busy writing a paper, so I didn't hear her right away.

"Push who down the stairs?"

"Ric," she said, closing her book with a snap. "You know, just to scare her a little."

"Yeah, I'm pretty sure we'd get arrested for that, and I'd rather not, thank you."

"It was just a suggestion."

"Why do you care so much?"

She made a sound as if I was being a moron for not being able to read her mind.

"Because I don't want evil to triumph over good, and Ric is pure evil."

"I wouldn't go that far, Trish. I think you're being a little overdramatic."

"I don't think I am. Can you imagine how much it's going to hurt Katie right now if she finds out? She's my friend. My concern for her can never be dramatic enough."

Trish didn't make friends easily, she never had. In fact, I didn't think I'd ever seen her get so close with someone before. Her pattern was to push people away with sarcasm and rudeness before they could push her away. But somehow Lottie and Katie and the rest of them had gotten through to her, and now Trish's fierceness was going in a different direction.

"I know, I know. I have to tell her, but not now. Not like this."

"We, my brother, you are in a pickle because of your pickle."

"Jesus, Trish." I threw a pencil at her and she ducked. "You don't have to be in this with me."

"Yeah, I do. You're all I've got." She said it casually, but we both knew it was true. We'd clung to each other since we were very young. We'd been through a lot, and that bonds two people, even more so when they're blood.

"Lucky me," I said, throwing an empty soda can at her.

"Screw you."

My phone buzzed. A message from Katie.

Want to come hang out, friend? My place?

The tiniest part of me wanted to say that I was busy. That I couldn't. It had been hard enough being around her this afternoon, and that was only for a few minutes. Being in her cramped dorm room, surrounded by her? Astronomically more difficult.

But it was only a tiny part.

When?

***

She was wearing an old frumpy t-shirt and shorts when I opened the door, and she wasn't wearing her contacts again. Of course. The universe was setting me up for pure torture.

She looked like the girl who had wrapped her legs around me and kissed me and then fucked me. Only the difference was that this time, I didn't want to fuck her. I wanted to kiss her and touch her stomach and her fingertips and the backs of her knees and everywhere in between. I wanted to memorize every inch of her, every freckle. I wanted to know the map of her body, what made her sigh in pleasure, what she liked, what made her beg for more. I wanted taste her.

With all that running through my mind, I didn't notice that her wall was covered in white sheets of paper. Extra large sheets, like teachers used to draw gigantic letters on for kids to teach them how to read.

"What happened to the pictures?" I assumed they'd met their demise like the others from her room. She'd already gotten rid of a lot of them after Zack had attacked her, but this time she'd cleared them all.

294

She pointed to the trash can and then held something out to me. A marker.

"I think my wall needs a little decorating, don't you? It's all yours." She flopped onto her bed as if she were waiting for me to get to work.

"You aren't going to help?"

"I'd rather watch you. Did you know that you do this thing with your mouth when you draw?" She demonstrated by biting the side of her bottom lip. It probably wasn't nearly as sexy when I did it.

"Is that so?"

"It is."

Fuck, I wanted to kiss her so bad.

"So you thought you could play the friend card and I'd just come and decorate your wall for you without getting anything in return? You drive a hard bargain, sweetheart."

"Do you want another turkey dinner?"

"God, I'm still dealing with the leftovers from the last one."

"Yeah, I think you should probably throw those out."

"Some of it did grow legs and start forming an army to plot my death, so you're probably right." She even made talking about leftovers into something sexy. Or maybe that was just me.

She laughed and there was a beat of silence that stretched longer and longer. I finally took my eyes off her and put them on the blank wall.

"Get to work, Picasso," she said, kicking her leg out and hitting me in the stomach.

"Hey, no violence. I can't work in these conditions." I grabbed her foot when she lashed out again. I held on as she struggled. Fuck the blank wall.

"Let me go," she squealed as I grabbed her other ankle and yanked her toward me.

"I think I'd rather have another canvas," I said, pulling her closer. Her eyes were wide with shock and surprise. "You."

"Stryker," she said, but it was more of a whisper. "We're friends."

"Friends can't wrestle each other?" I knew I was pushing it, but I was having a hard time stopping.

It wasn't until I was nearly on top of her that I realized what I'd done.

"Oh, shit. I am so sorry." I backed away. "I shouldn't have done that, Katie."

She pushed herself up on her elbows, her cheeks a little red.

"No, it's my fault. I was teasing you." She got off the bed and went to turn on some music. "I was flirting with you. I'm sorry."

"Is that what that was?"

"Oh, Jesus. I should not be flirting with you." She put her face in her hands as "Never Let Me Go", by Florence and The Machine came through her iPod speakers. "I should be dealing with the fact that my dad is dead. I shouldn't be thinking about you. Like that."

"Hey, hey." I put my hands on her shoulders. She turned and I wrapped her in a hug again. Effortless. As easy as breathing.

"I'm a horrible, terrible person," she said.

"You know, most of the horrible, terrible people in the world don't believe they're horrible and terrible. You think Hitler looked in the mirror and told himself that? I don't think so."

"What does Hitler have to do with it?"

"Nothing, I was just trying to make a point and screwed it up."

She pulled back and looked up at me. The brown eyes behind those glasses would be my undoing.

"I don't know how to do this anymore," she said.

"Do what?"

"Be."

"Be what?"

"Just . . . human, I guess. It's like I've forgotten how to do everything. Talking and eating and even breathing. None of it is easy anymore."

"I think that's normal."

"How would you know?"

"I just do."

I smoothed her hair back from her face with both hands and put a kiss on her forehead. It was a friend thing to do.

She held onto my forearms locking me in place.

"Fuck me. Please."

Katie

I didn't know what made me say it. I just knew that I wanted to forget for a little while, like we had before. Those times with him, when we'd been naked and sweating and together, I hadn't been thinking about anything. I wanted that again.

He was shocked for only half a second and then I watched his face, waiting for his response. I held him there and begged him with my eyes and my mind and everything else.

Just fuck me.

He closed his eyes and pressed his forehead to mine and then yanked his arms out of my grasp.

"No." Stepping away from me, he shook his head, swiping his hand through his hair. "Jesus, Katie. Why do you do this to me?"

"Do what?"

"You just . . . You say you want to be friends and then you ask me to fuck you and it's back and forth. I never know where I stand and it makes me so fucking crazy I can't even think about anything else." He started pacing the room. "You drive me insane because you never know what you want and you expect me to just accommodate you. And I do it. Every time. You say jump and I get out a goddamn trampoline. When I'm not with you, I'm thinking about you. I can't stop thinking about you and wanting you. I want to walk across this room and do what you want, but I can't. I can't fuck you anymore."

"Why not?"

"I can't just fuck you because I love you!"

I loved going on roller coasters. The moment I lived for was when the car slowly clicked its way up to the very top of the highest point, and then there were those breathless moments when it raced to the bottom and your stomach dropped into your feet and you couldn't catch your breath.

This was just like that, only worse.

"I love you, Katie."

I'd forgotten how to speak. How to take words and put them together in my mind in an order that would make sense and convey what I was feeling. Maybe because I didn't know what I was feeling.

"I know this is the wrong thing to say, at the wrong time. It's all wrong."

Something Lottie said came back to me. Something about how maybe Stryker and I were so wrong for each other that it was right.

"I just . . . I had to tell you. I had to say it out loud."

Words, words would be good right about now. Some words. Any words.

"Are you fucking serious?" Not the best choice of words, but it was a start.

"Yeah. I know, I know. It's . . . crazy." He started pacing again, as if he had to keep moving. "You know what's even crazier? I knew that first time I saw you. In that pink dress. I just . . . I knew. I was watching you during the entire party. You didn't see me, but I was. I couldn't take my eyes off of you. I kept trying to find your flaws, to convince myself you weren't attractive, which backfired because I only wanted you more."

"My flaws?"

"I told myself that your eyes were too big, and you were too short, and . . . well, that was as far as I got."

"Oh."

My stomach still felt like it was going to fall out my body, through the floor and into the room below us.

"But, Katie, there's something you should know." Other than the fact that he loves me? What more could there be?

"I haven't said it back," I said, interrupting whatever thing he'd been about to tell me.

"I know. I didn't expect you to. I didn't expect to say it, but I can't take it back now."

"Do you want me to say it?"

"I want you to say whatever you feel. I always want you to tell me the truth."

What was the truth?

"I can't breathe right now. And I can't feel my fingers or toes. Is that weird? I also feel like I swallowed my heart and it's beating in my throat."

"I'm familiar with the feeling," he said, finally standing still. "I kind of feel like I'm going to die."

"Yeah, me too."

There were several feet of space between us. The truth was that I wanted that space to go away. I wanted to push it aside and not let it come between us. I wanted to beat the shit out of any space that would dare come between us. Was that love?

I made my legs take one step. It was like trying to walk through waist-high water. I took another. He didn't move, waiting for me to come to him.

"I feel like I want us to be friends, but not just friends. I feel like I want us to be best friends. I feel like I want you to be the person I tell everything to. I feel like I could see you every second of every day and it wouldn't be enough. I feel like you are the sexiest, kindest, most wonderful person I've ever met and that I will never be good enough to deserve you, but I'd like to try anyway. I feel like if you weren't there when Dad died that I would have died too. I would have gotten sucked down, like Mom. And loving you is one of the only things keeping me afloat right now."

The words were easy, once I started saying them. They came as if I'd memorized them and recited them hundreds of times, like a favorite song that I would always know the lyrics to.

I stopped with that one last foot of space between us.

"The truth is that I love you too."

His green eyes consumed me, pulling me closer.

"Are you sure?" he said, as if he didn't believe me.

"Yes, you idiot, I'm sure." I tried to smack him in the chest, but he caught my wrist before I made contact and brought my hand to his mouth, kissing my palm.

"Just checking before I did this." He yanked me toward his mouth and our lips crashed together. Like the first time, only so much more. "You ever loved a guy with a lip ring?"

"Nope, this is a first," I said as his hands went into my hair, pulling the clip out and letting it tumble over my shoulders.

"Good."

Instead of consuming my mouth again, he held my face still while he trailed kisses across my forehead, and then down the left side of my face, and around my chin and back up the right side. Tracing my face with kisses. Then he went down my nose and across my eyelids and finally, to my mouth. I held still, my hands on his back. It was torture, being that still and letting him do it. Exquisite, burning torture.

Before he could kiss me again, I took my hands and put them in his hair, holding his face still. My turn.

I went for his eyebrow ring first, and then I used my lips to draw his face, stopping at last with his lips, kissing the ring that had grown warm with the touch of our skin. To his credit, he stayed still, only trembling a bit. His hands did start working their way up my shirt, which made it hard to concentrate on what my lips were supposed to be doing.

"I'm not going to fuck you, sweetheart."

"I know. I don't want you to. I just want this. You and me with no space between us."

"No space."

He slid his tongue into my mouth and we tasted each other as our hands got to work removing our shirts. I went to take my glasses off, but he stopped me.

"Leave them on. They're sexy."

I smiled as we backed our way to my bed. I expected him to toss all the pillows off, but he picked me up and lay me back on them. My sports bra was absolutely hideous, but he didn't seem to care, and it was gone soon enough, thanks to his nimble fingers. Unlike all the times before when we'd been naked and together, this time I wanted him to kiss me, to know me, and I wanted to know him.

My hands gripped his arms and I kissed the ink on his tattoos, kissed his nipples and his hard stomach that quivered under my touch. Good. I wasn't the only one that nearly lost their mind. Stryker was slow, which was agonizing. He left no inch of my skin untouched by his lips and fingers and I still had my shorts on.

I was a quivering mess already and he'd barely made it down my neck. His lips painted my body with kisses, just kisses, but those were enough. I was burning for him and with him and under him.

And then he took one of my nipples into his mouth and I moaned. He was making this all about me, and that wasn't exactly fair, but I wasn't really in a position to stop him. All I could do was hold on and wait my turn.

303

Then he went down my stomach and pulled my shorts down, just a little and kissed the line of my underwear band and then backed off and went for my lips again before doing the same thing, tugging them down just a little more.

"For fuck's sake," I said as he moved his way back up to my lips.

"Patience, sweetheart. I'm going to make this last."

Fuck patience.

I went for his belt before he could stop me, getting it undone and slipping my fingers under the elastic of his boxers. Ha. Two could play that game.

I watched his face with satisfaction as his eyes closed and he bit the corner of his lip like he did when he drew.

"Nope," he said, grabbing my hands and putting them over my head. I was about to protest, but he held my hands with one of his and pulled my shorts off with the other. I didn't put up much of a fight as they went down my hips, my knees and to my feet. I kicked them off.

"Behave," he said, kissing me again, biting my bottom lip and sliding his fingers around my underwear and caressing me. I moaned again as he worked his fingers and his lips. Touching, pulling back, and then touching again.

It was driving me insane, and I was completely helpless. I tried to push myself closer to his mouth, to his hand. I wanted him closer, but he kept pulling back a little.

"Patience," he said as he pushed one finger inside me, removing it so slow I wanted to grab his hand and take charge. He did it again, and then added another finger, driving me to the edge and back again.

"Not yet," he said, nipping my lip again. Like I had some sort of control over what was happening to me. He plunged his fingers into me again, this time harder. Words had deserted me. All I had left was incoherence.

He pulled his fingers away, as if he knew how close I was.

"Stryker!" I was hot and throbbing and frustrated.

"Patience." He finally removed my underwear and his mouth took the place his fingers had vacated. He spread my hips wide to get better access as he started the slow build again. My brain nearly exploded when he moved his mouth back and forth, his lip ring rubbing against me.

It was the roller coaster all over again, but he wouldn't let me go over the edge. He pulled back just in time. My body shook with the need for release, and I was afraid it was going to kill me when he finally took my hands and let me help him remove his pants and boxers.

"Finally," I said as he grabbed a condom from the drawer in my desk. I was wet and ready and I grabbed his dick, but he pushed my hands away.

"Plenty of time for that." I almost screamed at him, but it turned into a moan when he put his fingers inside me again.

This time he took me to the edge and let me fall and I broke around his fingers.

"That's it, sweetheart. Come for me," he said as his lips ravaged me further.

I couldn't help but comply as it went on and on, tearing me apart and putting me together and tearing me apart again. Just when I thought it was over, he threw one of my legs over his shoulder, paused for a moment and plunged into me.

"You and me," he said, pulling out slow and plunging back in.

"No space," I moaned, digging my fingers into his back. He went deep, deeper than he ever had. After every thrust, he waited for a second. No space.

He picked up the pace and I felt myself building again. I pushed myself up to meet him and he met me with force.

I came again, just as strong as before.

"I love you," he said as the world was shattering.

"I love you," I said as I felt him come a few moments later. Our lips met one last time.

You and me.

No space.

Twenty-four

Stryker

It was what I had wanted that very first time I'd met her. Watching her face as I drove her to the edge of pleasure and pulled her back was something so beautiful I didn't think I could ever do it justice with my pen.

Afterward, I lay with her, our sweat mingling and our bodies as close as they could be without being physically connected. She was busy reading my tattoos.

"You figured out what you want yet?" Her skin was still ink free.

"Not yet."

"Well, how about we practice?"

"What do you mean?" I unwrapped my arms from around her and sat up, grabbing a marker from the box on her desk. I'd been planning this ever since I got her naked.

"How about we try out a few. What was something you considered?" I held up the marker and she smiled.

"A butterfly on my shoulder." She pointed.

"Turn over." She rolled onto her back and turned her head so she could watch me. I dragged the marker across her skin, making the outline of a butterfly, as if it was resting on her shoulder. I grabbed a few other colors so I could make it more vibrant. She giggled a little at the touch of the marker. I finished the butterfly and then drew a flower below it, as if the butterfly had stopped on it to rest.

"What next?" I said.

"Um, how about a starfish?"

"Where?"

She turned over. "My hip." She pointed to her left hip and gave me a little smile. I let my eyes trace her body. I'd seen it many times before, but I had a whole new appreciation of it now.

It was so tempting to drop the marker and make her moan like she had earlier. Leaving the cap on the marker, I and slowly drew it over her body, from her collarbone and down her breasts to her bellybutton, where I made a circle and then lower.

"Starfish," she said in a harsh voice, her eyes closed and her hands fisted in her blanket.

"Of course, how could I forget?" I uncapped the marker and started to draw, watching her skin pimple with goosebumps. I drew one starfish and then a clam and then some more shells, starting a seascape on her hip that stretched close to her bellybutton.

"What's next, my sweet canvas?"

"Use your imagination." She seemed to be out of ideas.

"So I can draw whatever I want?"

She grabbed my wrist before I could start drawing again. "Within reason."

I grinned at her and gave her a kiss, which was meant to be quick, but turned heated before she nipped my lip near my lip ring.

"You've got a lot of skin to cover."

***

I covered her shoulders and arms and stomach and back and ass and legs and feet with drawings. Flowers and swirls and stars and quotes that reminded me of her and song lyrics and little things that made me think of her. There was no continuity, except that they all reminded me of her.

I drew hearts on the bottom of her feet and sat back to admire her. She looked over her shoulder, trying to see her back.

"Come on," I said, reaching for her. I picked her up and carried her to the full-length mirror that hung in her closet. I set her down and turned her so she could see.

"Wow," she breathed. "You are freakishly talented."

"An artist is nothing without good materials to work with, and a muse."

She looked away from her beautiful body to meet my eyes. "Oh, so I'm your muse now?"

I touched a poppy I'd drawn on her shoulder in bold red marker.

"Every artist needs one."

"You seemed to do pretty well without me before."

"That was because I didn't know what I was missing."

"Hm," she said, touching my more-permanent ink. "So I guess we're not friends anymore, huh?"

"I beg to differ." I kissed the poppy and picked her up, making her squeal as I tossed her back in bed. "I think you are my very best of best friends."

I kissed her, not being able to hold back anymore.

"You and me," she whispered against my lips.

"No space."

Katie

It wasn't until I woke up in Stryker's arms the next morning that I realized I couldn't go to class the way I was. He'd drawn all the way up around my neck, giving me what looked like a lace necklace, not to mention my arms and hands and legs. Unless I wore a bodysuit, everyone would be able to see it.

"Was this some sort of ploy to get me to not leave this room?" I said when his green eyes finally opened. I would totally paint my walls that color.

"Would that be such a bad thing?" He rolled over me and his dick pressed against me, ready to go again. I stroked him with my hand and he growled in my ear. He tried to remove my hand, but I wouldn't let him.

"Your turn to learn patience, my friend." I kissed my way down his chest as my hand worked and he swore and moaned. It was nice to know that I could affect him as much as he affected me.

I took him to the edge and back with my hands and my mouth, making him mine until I straddled him and we became united again.

***

"I did have class today, you know. And I'm sure that any moment now someone is going to knock on the door and ask me to go to breakfast," I said, still panting. Some of the beautiful drawings were smudged, but I was still covered in them.

"What, you don't want to go around like a walking art project? Afraid of what people will think?"

"No, I just don't want them staring. I can't deal with more people looking at me. It's like being at the funeral all over again."

"Shit, I'm sorry. That was insensitive."

"No, it wasn't. You just forgot, and so did I." Even if it was just for a little while. Knock, knock. Reality calling. "I can't believe I forgot. Oh my God." I sat up and moved away from him.

"Oh my God. My dad is dead and we had sex and you said you loved me and I said it back. Oh God, I'm going to hell." I tried to get out of bed, to get away from him, but he held onto me. I squirmed against him.

"We shouldn't have done this."

"You have got to stop blaming yourself for things, Katie." He shook me a little as he said it. "Do you honestly think your dad would want you to stop living just because he did?"

I knew he wouldn't. I thought back to what he'd said to me when we'd had that chat in the basement. That I was strong and he was proud of me.

"No." He took my moment of weakness to pull me into his chest, right next to his heart.

"What is the point of being alive if you don't live it?" His eyes were bright and his voice was urgent. I'd never seen him like this. "I know you're scared and I'm scared as hell too. That's what love is, being scared as hell, but doing it anyway because it's worth it." He held me so tight, his arms like ropes that tied me to him, tied this moment together.

"You terrify me, sweetheart."

"I terrify you. Me, with the pink obsession? I terrify the guy with the piercings and the tattoos and the, 'I don't give a fuck' attitude?"

"Terrifying things come in pink packages."

I rolled my eyes.

"Well, I'm not scared of you, big bad boy." He unwrapped his arms and held my face.

"I never, ever want you to be scared of me."

"You're not Zack," I said. "You're not anything like him."

"That is the nicest thing you've ever said to me, sweetheart."

Just as he was leaning down for a kiss, there was a pounding on my door.

"Um, you wanna get that? Just tell them I'm not feeling well, maybe?" He climbed over me and put his pants on as I pulled the blanket up to cover myself.

"Oh, hey, Stryk," Simon said. Stryker made sure to keep the door only halfway open so they couldn't see me. "We just wanted to see if Katie was up for breakfast, but . . . never mind."

"She's . . . she's not feeling that great. We'll probably just have something here."

"Sure, yeah, that's . . . that's great." I could hear other voices, but I couldn't tell who they were. "See you later?"

"Sure thing."

"Is she okay?" That was Lottie.

"Yeah, she is." He wasn't facing me, but I could hear the grin in his voice. "She just needs to take an extra day, I think."

"If she needs anything . . . "

"I know. I'll call you, I promise."

He closed the door and I could hear them chattering. More than one of them had a problem with voice volume modulation.

"Thanks for that. I wasn't sure what they'd say about all this." I motioned to the drawings that had stained my sheets a bit.

"Anytime, sweetheart." He took his clothes back off. "Now where were we?"

Twenty-five

Stryker

Katie and I spent the next few hours alternating between getting closer and eating the rest of the ice cream Lottie had stocked up on, and sometimes combining the two, which was the most fun.

"How long do you think it's going to take to wash this off?" The marker had faded from her skin a little, but she was still a walking, talking canvas. "I would like to leave this room at some point and rejoin the world."

"Why? The world is so overrated."

"True, but I think our friends might like to see us."

I kissed her shoulder. "You, maybe. I'm fine with staying in this room with you forever."

"That would be a bit of an issue when the semester is over and summer break comes and we have to move out."

"We could hide in the ceiling and then wait until everyone left and only come out at night to get supplies. Like vampires."

"You have put way too much thought into this. But seriously, I need to shower. I need to . . . do something."

"I have something you can do." I took my hand and slid it down her stomach.

"Fine, if you want, you can come shower with me. I need someone who can reach my back." She got out of bed, then put my hand on her waist.

"I wish we could save it somehow," she said.

"Are you at all opposed to nude photography?" My phone sat on her desk, and I reached for it, turning it on.

"I guess not, as long as these don't end up somehow plastered all over the internet." I was about to answer her when I saw another text from Ric.

Enjoy it while it lasts.

Katie was waiting for me to answer.

"What's up?"

"Oh, nothing. Just . . . Trish, being Trish." Fucking Ric. That was why I'd left my phone off.

"You sure?"

"Yeah, fine."

I looked back at her, putting a smile on my face. She studied me for a second, and I thought she was going to demand that I tell her, but then she smiled.

"Where do you want me?" she said, posing and throwing her head back. God, she was stunning.

I moved the blankets on her bed so she could lay out and took first pictures of her front, moving from her neck on down. I grabbed a lamp to give us better light and she struggled with trying to stay still. I couldn't believe she was letting me do this, and then it hit me.

She trusted me. Not only did she love me, but she trusted me.

Fuck.

She trusted me enough to let me take pictures of her naked and keep them on my phone and not share them. That meant she probably trusted me to not fuck anyone else. Too late.

I took the pictures of her back and her hands and finally, the bottoms of her feet.

"Done."

I kissed them and she squirmed.

"Shower?"

"Only if I can come," I said, making her squirm again as I dug my finger into the arch of her foot.

***

I wrapped her up like a mummy and made sure the coast was clear before we hit the shower. The handicap shower, which was bigger, was known as the 'couples' shower', she said, and more than a few couples had partaken in water conservation.

"Is it working?" She said as I scrubbed her with her most exfoliating soap and this loofah thing she'd brought.

"Sort of." I rubbed harder and her skin turned red, but there was still a little bit of the drawing left behind. She was busy working on her front, checking her arms and stomach to see if it had faded.

"You know, you could have just kept it. Would have come off eventually." I ran my hand down her back and touched her, sliding one finger into her.

She made an incoherent sound and I dropped the loofah.

"Maybe we just need a little more friction," I said.

"Mmmm," she said, bracing herself on the shower wall.

By the time we were done, the pounding water had taken care of most of the drawings.

"Too bad neither of us has a tub, because a good soak would have probably taken care of this, but it wouldn't have been as much fun," I said, pushing her back up against the wall as the water poured down on our heads.

"True," she said, putting her hand on my heart. "I love you."

"I love you, too." So much that I wasn't sure if I could take it, if I could handle how I felt about her. I pressed my forehead to hers and kissed her drenched lips.

"I have to tell you something." I couldn't fill myself up with her until I got rid of Ric.

She stared up at me, and the words wouldn't come.

"I want you to be my girlfriend," I finally said, and I felt her relax in my arms.

"I think I'd like to be your girlfriend."

"Just like?"

"Love. I'd love to be your girlfriend."

Fuck, fuck, fuck.

Katie

Lottie knocked on the door when she came back from class. Stryker and I were working on my wall. Apparently he hadn't used up all his artistic talents on me.

"Oh, hey." She cracked open the door with her eyes closed.

"We're not naked, Lot," I said, jumping down off my bed where I'd been helping Stryker fill in the leaves of a vine he'd been drawing along the top of my wall.

"Oh, I didn't think you were." She opened her eyes and set her bag down.

"Then why were your eyes closed?" Stryker said, swapping markers with me.

"Just being cautious. What are you doing?"

"Changing my wall up a bit since I can't actually paint it."

"Cool. How are you doing?" she said, looking at me.

"I'm . . . good, actually. Not fine."

Lottie smiled and I could tell she'd been worried about me all day.

"So, I got elected to ask, since I'm your roommate, what's the deal here?" She pointed at Stryker and me.

"We are officially together-together," I said.

"Boyfriend/girlfriend?"

Stryker jumped down next to me. "Yes, we are. Right, sweetheart?"

"Yes, my beloved."

He put his arm around me and I leaned into him.

"You're not going to talk like that all the time, are you? Because I think I liked you better as fuck buddies if that's the case."

"Look, I've suffered through you and Zan, so you can deal," I said.

"Fine, fine. Look, I have to text your sister because she's been up my butt about asking since I told her that you had spent the night together."

"She didn't say anything, did she?" Stryker said, his arm tightening around me, just a little.

"Say anything about what?"

He tried to shrug it off. "I don't know. She's Trish."

"True," Lottie said, taking out her phone. About three seconds after she sent the text, my phone rang. I would have been shocked if it hadn't.

"I should probably take this outside. I have a feeling I'm about to get reamed out and emasculated at the same time," he said, laughing a little, but I could tell he was tense. He did that jaw-clench thing that made his face even more attractive.

He closed the door and Lottie seized her moment.

"Well that was unexpected. I mean, I always sort of knew you'd end up together, but I didn't know it would be this quick, and . . . like this. Not that I'm judging you, because I can't throw stones, especially where relationships are concerned—"

"Lottie. It's cool. I swear. Do you remember what a hard time I gave you about Zan? And also that I kept it from you that I slept with him?"

Her face went red.

"Yeah. Right. That."

"It's okay. I feel good, and under the circumstances, that's . . . good. He loves me."

"He said it?"

"Yeah, he did."

"Wow. Just . . . wow."

"Why so shocked?"

"Well, it's just that Stryker doesn't date, seriously, at least according to Trish." He'd told me some about his dating history, but in this instance, I kind of wanted to be kept in the dark. Besides, it was a bit of a pot and kettle situation.

"Not that I'm saying you shouldn't date him."

"I know, Lot. It's okay." I put my hands on her shoulders to stop any future verbal geysers.

"Okay." She let out a deep breath. "Um, so now can I be super happy for you?"

"Yes, you can."

"What's that?" She pointed to a drawing on my neck that hadn't quite faded.

"It's a long story," I said.

***

"How did it go?" I said when Stryker came back from his chat with Trish. He looked like he'd just been told his entire collection of musical instruments had been smashed.

"Oh, you know Trish. She doesn't pull any punches." He tried a smile, but it didn't reach his eyes.

"Is she mad at you?"

"Just mad that she didn't know first. I guess when I make declarations of love from now on, I'm supposed to inform her first." He was still hiding something, but Lottie interrupted.

"You guys want to go to dinner?"

"Seeing as how we've only eaten ice cream today, yes, I could use some real food," he said.

"Ice cream is real food," Lottie said. "Did you eat all of it?" She ran to the mini-fridge and pulled open the now-empty freezer.

"Uh, yeah," he said.

"Sorry."

"No, it's fine," she said, closing the door. "We can always get more."

***

I called Kayla before our dinner to check in on mom. I still couldn't believe that I'd let everything with Stryker happen, but he was right. I couldn't let dad dying ruin the rest of my life.

"She had some soup, so that's something, I guess," she said.

"Can I talk to her?"

"She's not really in a talking mood." She held the phone out and I could hear Mom sobbing. Kayla must have been standing outside her bedroom door.

"Oh."

I wanted so much to tell her about Stryker and that he said he loved me and that we were together, but it seemed disgustingly selfish to bring it up.

"Heard from Adam?"

"Yeah, he finally got the chance to send an email. He's glad to be back, and he feels like shit for leaving me, but it is what it is."

We talked about a few more things and I almost mentioned Stryker, but Kayla did it for me.

"How's everything back there?" she said. I heard water running, and splashing so I assumed she was doing the dishes.

"Good."

"Everyone glad you're back?"

"Are you asking about my friends or about Stryker?"

"The second."

"He's . . . he's good. We're good."

The splashing stopped. "What is this 'we' you speak of?"

"Yeah, there's a 'we' now."

"Are you serious?"

"Uh, yeah."

"When did that happen?"

"Last night." I still hadn't gotten around to fixing up the bed again.

"Katie, you didn't." Here came the lecture. "Do you really think this is the right time?"

"When is it the right time? I didn't plan on it. He said he loved me and I said it too and now we're together. You were all for this not that long ago."

"I know I was . . . it's just that things are different now."

"Because of Dad?"

"I just don't think this is the right time to jump into something. I'm trying to look out for you because I love you. You've been through a lot and I don't want to see you get hurt."

"I'm fine, Kayla."

"I don't want to fight with you, especially not about this. Just . . . be careful and I love you."

"I know, love you too."

I hung up and went back into my room. Stryker and Lottie were debating about who they thought was the killer from an old *Law and Order* we'd been watching. It was definitely the husband's lawyer, but I kept my mouth shut.

"She ream you out too?" Stryker said, leaning on his elbow.

"Sort of. It was more gentle than a reaming. More like a few words of caution."

"I wish my sister knew anything about the word gentle," he said as I sat next to him on my bed and he put his arm around me.

"Is she that upset about us being together?"

His eyes flicked back to the TV. "No, not really."

"Then what is she so upset about?"

Lottie looked away from the show and at Stryker too.

"I told you, she's pissed that I didn't tell her before I told you."

"But she's happy, right?"

"More like bitter that she's still alone."

"Why is it different than when we were together but not really together?" For a guy who was pretty smooth normally, he was having a hard time coming up with a story.

"It's just different." He rolled over so he couldn't look at me.

"Yeah, sure."

As soon as I could, I was going to text Trish and get to the bottom of this. Consuming myself with Stryker's secret was much better than thinking about Dad or his ashes or the fact that I still had all of Zack's gifts under my bed. Stryker kept kicking them whenever he could, but he didn't know what they were. I'd made some vague excuse.

Zack.

I'd thought about him a few times today, but only in contrast to Stryker. When Zack told me he loved me, it was only because he thought he should, like it was an obligation. When I said it to him the first time, I'd been drunk, and I couldn't really take it back. He always followed it with "babe." "I love you, babe," he'd say. I hadn't realized how much I absolutely hated him calling me that until after everything had happened.

He still sent me a text here and there, but they were fewer and farther between. Maybe he was finally getting some help. I thought about asking Zan, but he said he'd cut ties with his family and wasn't keeping up with Zack's comings and goings.

"You guys ready to go?" Lottie said, as there was a knock at the door.

"Yup," I said, grabbing my coat. Stryker jumped up and helped me put it on.

"Where are we going?" I said as Lottie opened the door to reveal the rest of the crew. They all stared at Stryker and me.

"Okay, okay, you can stop staring," Lottie said. "Nothing to see here, just two crazy kids in love." She gave me a wink and Stryker took my hand.

I heard a weird noise and looked for the source. Trish was lasering the evilest of evil eyes directly at Stryker. If looks could kill . . .

I knew Trish well enough to know that it wasn't mere jealousy that was making her look at Stryker as if she wanted to reduce him to a pile of ash, like a vampire in the sunlight.

"Let's go," Simon said, giving Brady a look. "I'm starved."

We all trooped down the hallway with Trish still giving Stryker a death glare.

"Where are we going?" I asked the group in general.

"Caroline's?" Simon said.

Caroline's was one of the nicest places in town, more of a lounge than a bar. It wasn't cheap, either. I always thought of it as a grown-up place.

"Uh, can we all afford that?"

"We're just planning on ordering a shit ton of appetizers and sharing," Will said. "I also have a friend who's a busboy who could bring us some scraps from other people's plates if we get really starved."

"Sounds like a plan," I said.

"You okay with that?" I said to Stryker, hoping no one else would hear.

"As long as I'm with you, I don't care where I am."

"Ditto," I said, and I squeezed his hand, but one look behind at Trish's angry face was all it took to remind me that there was something he was keeping from me and the sooner I figured out what it was, the better.

Twenty-six

Stryker

I really wanted to tell Trish to put her angry face away, because she was making everyone uncomfortable, but I couldn't really do that without making Katie suspicious, so I had to put up with her glare for the entire time we were at Caroline's. While we sat at the fancy tables that had long tapered candles and pure white tablecloths, while soft violin music played in the background. As soon as we all saw the entree prices, and put our eyes back in after they'd fallen out because of how expensive they were, we ordered two of every appetizer, hoping that would be enough.

I tried to kick Trish under the table, but missed and hit Brady. Confusion ensued and I was afraid Simon was going to join Trish and beat me up.

"Hey you, glaring at my boyfriend. What's up?" Katie said as we all fished in our pockets and purses for a tip for our disgruntled waiter. He deserved it after dealing with us.

"Nothing," Trish said, turning off the glare when she looked at Katie. It was like she wasn't aware she'd been doing it. "I'm just pissed at him about something."

"Yeah, I got that. You wanna share with the class?" Everyone was pretending not to eavesdrop but failing miserably.

"He knows. Ask him."

"Oh no, I'm not playing that game, Trish. You two have got some deal and I have the feeling it has to do with me, so spill so you can get over it and we can go back to normal where you guys just fight instead of laying on the silent treatment. It's freaking me out."

"You're not the only one," Lottie said. "What gives, Trish?"

Trish looked around and I thought I was going to have to pull the fire alarm so she wouldn't say what I thought she was going to say, but then she surprised me.

"He told someone my real name," she said, staring down at the tablecloth, which was significantly less-white now, despite all our best efforts.

I breathed a sigh of relief and made a mental note to text Trish and thank her later. I was definitely going to owe her for this one.

"I thought your real name was Patricia," Simon said.

"Yeah, that's what I thought," Audrey said.

"No, it's not Patricia . . . " she said. Damn, she was really taking one in the back for me. I could never call her a shitty sister again.

"Then what is it? We're all on the edge of our seats here," Brady said.

"It's Trishella."

Her announcement was met with a moment of stunned silence and then everyone tried not to laugh and failed.

She crossed her arms and stared at the ceiling. "Go ahead, you can all laugh. Our parents were drug addicts, so they were probably high when they thought of it."

With that, everyone lost it and we all laughed, earning death glares that rivaled Trish's from everyone else in the restaurant.

It broke up the moment as we all walked out, much to the relief of the staff of Caroline's. You could almost hear the audible sigh of relief.

"Was that what she was so pissed about?" Katie asked me as I opened the car door for her.

"Trish really, really hates her name," I said, hoping that would be enough to convince her, but knowing it probably wasn't. Katie was a smart girl, and I'd been a moron to think I could fool her for long. Sooner rather than later, this thing was going to come out.

"She looked like she was going to kill you."

I tried to laugh a little as I got in the driver's seat. "Wouldn't you if Trishella was your name?"

She smiled and turned on the radio. "Yeah, I probably would."

"There you go."

***

Katie and I decided that we needed some time apart, mostly for her to try to catch up with her classwork and to have some girl time to talk about me when I wasn't there. I headed back to my apartment to take another shower and try to figure out the best time to tell Katie about Ric. Once again, there she was, leaning against her car and waiting for me.

Think of the devil and she shall appear.

"Did you have fun with your little pink slut?" This time she wasn't here to apologize. This time she was also drunk. Great. Drunk Ric wasn't anyone I was fond of, not that I was fond of sober Ric either. The more time I spent with Katie, the more I realized how much I really didn't like a lot of the girls I'd hung out with for so long. Compared to Katie they were almost unbearable. And Ric was at the top of that list.

"Don't start Ric. Did you drive here?" I put my key in the door and she followed me, stumbling up the steps.

"Why the fuck do you care?" Drunk Ric had a mouth like a trucker.

"Because as much as I don't like you right now, I don't want you to die."

I picked her up and helped her up the stairs. While it wasn't completely my fault she was in this condition and also pissed at me, I wasn't going to just leave her outside. I'd get her inside, hopefully a little sober and then take her home. She'd have to leave her goddamn car here and come back to get it, but at least she'd get home safe.

After a little work, with her resisting the whole time, I got her to the couch and she flopped down.

"Fuck you," she said into the pillow. I moved her head so she wouldn't suffocate. This could go one of two ways. I could get angry drunk Ric, or emotional drunk Ric. I wasn't sure which one was worse at this point. Angry Ric liked to break things, but Emotional Ric liked to tell me really personal things about her past that I definitely didn't want to know. She also had a habit of throwing herself at people, not that I hadn't dealt with that already.

"You already did, babe," I said, going to the kitchen to get her a glass of water. She also had makeup smeared all over her face, like she'd been having some heavy make-out sessions.

"Where've you been, Ric?"

"None of your business, asshole." I also wet a paper towel so she could clean up a little. "I loved you and you fucked me over."

"Yeah, I know. I'm regretting it more than you know." I sat down next to her and held the glass out. "Drink."

She pushed the glass away. Oh, this was going to be so much fun.

"Come on, Ric. Don't make this harder than it already is."

She squinted her eyes at me, but took the glass, slopping it all over herself.

"Look, I know you're pissed at me, and feel free to take it out on me, but leave Katie out of it. She didn't do anything to you, so just lay off."

"Nice try, Stryk," she said, nearly dropping the glass again. "But that bitch has it coming." Ric pushed me and I snapped. I grabbed both of her arms, hard enough to bruise.

"I swear to God, Ric, if you hurt her, I will make you wish you were never born. You remember what I used to be like, right? Well if you mess with Katie, I'll make that guy look like a fucking boy scout. Got it?" She struggled, trying to get away, but I wanted to make sure she had the message.

She growled and tried to lunge and bite me, but I was ready for her. She knew my patterns, but I knew hers, too.

"Don't even try it, bitch."

I shoved her away from me and stormed out. I needed a smoke.

***

When I came back, Ric was passed out. Well, at least she wasn't talking. Bad news was that I'd have to let her sleep it off. She lived in a seriously sleazy part of town, and I wasn't going to dump her back at her place in this bad of shape. It was a wonder nothing had happened to her yet.

I covered her up and made sure she wouldn't suffocate on the pillows. I also left a bucket, just in case, and went to my room, taking my banjo. I had different instruments for different moods and this felt like a banjo time.

I warmed up with a few chords and then played some bluegrass. When it came to music, I tended to like things that were a little offbeat, or at least had some interesting and complicated instrumentation. Trish used to say that bluegrass was for losers, but that was because she couldn't play an instrument if her life depended on it. I'd tried to teach her a ton of times, but she just didn't grasp the concept. She had a great voice, though, but she wouldn't sing if anyone ever asked her. She'd only do it if she felt like it, which was usually only when she was alone. My theory was that she was afraid she sucked and she enjoyed singing so much that it would ruin it for her forever. And of course, me telling her she didn't suck had no impact.

I missed Katie.

Pulling out my phone, I scrolled through the pictures I'd taken of her. Now, if I could only get those blown up, I could wallpaper my room with them.

She'd kill me, but at least I'd get to have her around me.

I thought about calling just to check in on her, but I couldn't be that guy. Reading between the lines, Zack had been a possessive and controlling, always calling and checking on her and wanting to know where she was at all times. Anything I could do to show her I wasn't him was a good thing, so I settled for playing my banjo and thinking about her and hoping Ric would remember what I said tomorrow and leave us the hell alone.

***

Ric was gone when I got up the next morning, and from a quick look outside, so was her car. Damn. I just hoped she'd been sober enough to get home without having a fender bender. She didn't leave a note or anything, and her calls went straight to voicemail when I tried to check up on her. I was just putting on a new shirt so I could go to her place and make sure she was ok when someone banged on my door.

"Stryker! I swear to God, you never answer your fucking phone!" Trish.

I yanked the door open.

"What? You came to yell at me some more?" Then I saw that she'd been crying. Trish *never* cried. It was a bit like seeing the moon rise in the morning instead of the sun.

"Ric was in an accident early this morning. She . . . um, she didn't survive."

Katie

It was going to take more than a week to catch up on just the reading that I'd missed while I was gone, but my brain wouldn't focus. Things like school seemed so pointless. I mean, what was it for? I didn't even have a major, didn't have any idea what I wanted to study or do with my life. I thought that once I got to college, I'd have some sort of epiphany, like in a movie, and it would all be clear what my true calling was. Yeah, I was still waiting for that call. It had me on hold and the music sucked.

Once my eyes started to swim, Lottie and I called it a night.

"Can you believe Trish's real name?" Lottie said as we both lay in our beds with the lights off. I didn't think either of us felt like sleeping.

"I can't believe that was what she was so pissed about. I mean, really? Trish doesn't seem like the type to get that royally ticked over something like that."

"I don't know, did you see how she got when Nicholas Sparks was brought up? I thought she was going to strangle us all."

"True." Still, there was something nagging me about the way Trish had been treating Stryker.

"Crazy, she gets," Lottie said.

"Amen."

We said goodnight, but I knew I wasn't going to sleep. Most nights I spent in thinking about anything I could to get myself to be tired. I'd started reading when I was home to try to bore myself to sleep, but I'd ended up staying up all night and kind of liking the books. My parents didn't have many in the house, but my dad had a small collection of classics. I'd had to read them in high school and I'd been bored to tears, but maybe it was because I didn't *have* to read them now that I liked them.

Once I heard Lottie's deep breathing, I snuck out of my bed and went to her overstuffed shelves. She had pretty much anything, and I knew from living with her which books were where.

I went for a historical fiction. Lots of ballgowns and gentlemen kissing women on the hand and declaring their undying love with beautiful poetry. That was exactly what I needed. I had a flashlight in my desk for emergencies, and I tucked myself under my covers so the light wouldn't bother Lottie and started reading.

I turned the pages, the hours passed and my eyes stayed open. In the part of my mind that wasn't focused on the book, I thought about Stryker. Would I have slept better if Stryker was here? Probably.

When the daylight started creeping under my covers, I put the book back and settled back on my bed so I could at least get a few hours of sleep. My eyes had barely closed when Lottie's alarm went off and her groan followed a few seconds later.

So much for sleep.

***

"You sure you're ready to be back?" Lottie said as we got dressed. We were all going to breakfast, and I'd texted Stryker to ask him to come, but he hadn't messaged me back, which wasn't unusual. He also wasn't a morning person.

I shoved my foot into one of my calf-high boots and zipped them up. "I don't really have a choice. I need something to fill up my time, and my parents paid for me to be here."

"Good point," she said, tying her sneakers. "When everything happened with Lexie, I made sure I paid extra attention in school and got all her homework ready for her so when she came back, she wouldn't miss a beat. I was going to tutor her, but then . . . it didn't happen. But I got really good grades."

I gave her a little smile and put my other boot on, swearing a little when the zipper got stuck.

Lottie's phone buzzed as she was putting her coat on.

"Oh, crap." She put her hand to her mouth and dropped her backpack. "Oh no."

"What?" I started shoving books into my messenger bag. I was going to have to get a new one soon, because the strap was about to go.

"I texted Trish to invite her to breakfast, but she just messaged me back saying that her friend Ric was in an accident last night." The name made me snap my head up and look at her.

"Ric? What happened?"

"Hold on, I'm calling her." She held the phone up to her ear and bit her thumbnail.

"Trish, what happened?" Pause. "Oh my God. I am so sorry. Do you need anything? No. No. Okay. Call me later, okay?" She hung up and I waited for the verdict, knowing all the while what it was and hoping that it wasn't. Lottie took a long deep breath before she spoke in a small voice that I'd never heard her use.

"She was killed. I guess she was driving home early this morning and she went off the road and hit a tree." She sat down on her bed. I had to sit down too. Yes, I'd only met the girl a couple times, and she had been a bitch, but that didn't mean I wanted her to die. I didn't want anyone to die, not even Zack, although I'd thought I'd wanted that, before everything with Dad. Seeing death up close made me realize it wasn't a thing you wished on anyone.

Lottie stared straight ahead. "I feel like I should do something, but I don't know what. Trish was an absolute wreck. I've never heard her cry before." I didn't know Trish and Ric were close; Stryker had never mentioned anything.

Stryker.

"Did she say anything about Stryker? Is he with her?" I said. Lottie shook her head, still in a daze.

"I'm going to call him." I went outside so I could have some privacy and ran into Will, Simon and Zan coming to get us.

"Hey, how are you doing?" Will said. In another lifetime I would have totally gone for him. In fact, when I first met him, I'd totally pegged him as a potential rebound boyfriend. Now I couldn't imagine it.

"Um, one of Trish's friends was in an accident this morning and she was killed. Lottie's a bit out of it, um, understandably. You might want to go check on her. I'm going to call Stryker."

The boys all went in to take care of Lottie and I called Stryker, going to the very end of the hall where there was a little alcove. The phone rang a bunch of times before he picked up.

"Hey, I just heard about Ric. Are you okay?"

"I'm fine." Oh, there was that word again. I'd never heard him use it, though.

"Yeah, I don't believe that. She was your friend too. Where are you?"

"Home." His voice was tight, like he was holding back. Leave it to Stryker to be one of those guys that turned into a freaking clam when they were suffering from grief. He'd been so open and supportive when I'd been going through it, always trying to get me to talk about it. I was going to do the same for him.

I started walking back toward my room to get my car keys. "I'm coming over."

"No, no. You have to get back to class. I said, I'm fine." He dropped something on the other end and swore.

"Fuck you, you're not fine. Don't you even dare use that word with me, Stryker Grant. I know exactly what it means."

"Katherine, I said I'm fine. Just go to class. I just need you to go to class, okay? Please." His voice cracked, and my heart cracked a little at the same time hearing it.

"Stryker."

"I love you. I'll call you later, okay?"

"I love you, but—"

He hung up before I could say anything else. Dick Stryker had returned, only this time he had a side of Damaged. Simon came out of our room just as I was about to open the door.

"Stryker wouldn't tell me anything. I think he's moping at his apartment, so that's where I'm headed," I said.

"Do you want some company?" In another lifetime I would have gone for him, too. If he liked girls in that other lifetime.

"No, I think I got it. I'm good at dealing with dead people," I said, giving him a smile. "Could you get my purse for me? It's on my bed."

"Oh, yeah, right. Sure." It took him a second to return the smile before he ducked back into the room. My sense of humor had never been particularly dark, but it had taken a turn since everything had happened with Dad.

"Tell Lottie I'll keep her updated," I said when he handed my purse to me a second later.

"Will do." He nodded and closed the door, and I heard Will and Zan talking softly. The crisis response team had assembled and was ready to go. Again.

***

I knew if I just banged on his door, he wouldn't answer, so I used the spare key I knew he hid over the door. He was going to be pissed at himself for showing me where it was, but I was glad he did. It was there for emergencies and this qualified, in my book.

"Stryker?" I opened the door cautiously.

"Goddammit!" he said, slamming something down. I opened the door and he stormed over from the kitchen where I could see a shot glass and a half-full bottle of scotch sitting on the counter.

"I told you to go to class," he said, glaring at me. No, this wasn't Dick Stryker. This was a guy I'd never met. This was angry-damaged Stryker, and he'd also been drinking. Not a good combination.

"Yeah, well, I don't take orders from you, asshole." He stood in the doorway and wouldn't let me come in. "You may not like it, but you were there for me when I needed you, and now I'm gonna be there for you whether you like it or not."

"I don't need you," he said, practically spitting out the words.

"Well, buddy, it kinda seems like you do."

Even six months ago, the way Stryker was talking to me might have sent me running back to my car, but I wasn't that scared girl anymore.

I shoved past him and walked into the apartment to find it in chaos. His instruments were all over the place, as if he'd picked them up to play and then tossed them aside, like an angry toddler with his toys.

"You're going to regret that," I said, picking up a violin bow that was broken in half.

"Jesus, Katie. I really don't need this right now, and not from you."

I turned around to find him going back to the bottle of scotch. Oh no, I was not letting him drown his sorrows. I dived in front of him, getting to the bottle before he could and throwing it in the sink where it shattered.

"What the fuck!" He lunged at me, grabbing my shoulders. His green eyes were bloodshot and puffy. He'd been crying.

"What did you do that for?" He shook my shoulders, but I held my ground. It wasn't like Zack. When I was in the car with him, I'd known to be afraid. I wasn't afraid of Stryker. I knew, with every cell in my body, that he wouldn't hurt me. Ever.

"I'm doing it because someone needed to. Hey, hey, look at me." I touched his face, holding it gently. This boy who seemed so strong was even more fragile than anyone could comprehend.

"You don't have to do this alone. You didn't let me do it alone, and I'm not going to let you. I love you, and we can get through this together. Got it? You and me. No space."

I gripped his face and forced him to look at me before I pulled his face down and kissed him. His lips tasted of scotch and cigarettes and salty tears. He resisted, but I opened my mouth and joined my tongue with his, not letting him pull away. I poured all my love into that kiss, hoping it would break through to him.

His arms went around my back and he pulled me close. Tight, like when he'd been holding me together right after Dad died. I kissed him harder.

I pulled back and kissed his chin, which had a little bit of stubble on it.

"We don't have to talk about it now. How about we go somewhere?" I said, not letting go of his face.

"Where?" he said, his voice raspy.

"I don't know. Anywhere." I searched my brain for somewhere we could go that was close to campus, but that would give me a little time to try to get him back together.

"I'll go anywhere with you."

"Same here," I said, moving my hands down his arms until I was holding both of his. "Come on, let's go somewhere."

He nodded and let me lead him out of the apartment.

Twenty-seven

Stryker

No matter what, she wouldn't leave me, just like I wouldn't leave her. I supposed I should have expected it. What I didn't expect was that even if I was a complete and total asshole, she didn't react. Like I was just a child having a tantrum and she was waiting for me to wear myself out.

"Where are we going?" I said when she shoved me into her Mazda and put my seatbelt on. The irony of the situation was not lost on me.

"I don't know yet. I'm making this up as I go along."

She turned some music on that fed from her iPod and Ed Sheeran's "Kiss Me" seeped through the speakers. It almost made me smile, because I'd put his music on there for her.

"Okay, I know you don't want to talk about it, but we're going to. You made me talk about my Dad, so it's my turn."

"Katie."

"Nope, I'm in charge of this grief committee. You had your turn." She wasn't going to take no for an answer, so I shut my face and tried not to think about how much I wished I was back in my apartment, drinking alone. I didn't deserve a grief committee and I sure as hell didn't deserve Katie.

Katie headed toward downtown. She scanned both sides of the street, looking for something. I had no idea what it was, so I just sat back as the music changed to "Dammit", by blink-182. An oldie, but a goodie.

"Aha!" she said, nearly hitting a parked car. She put on her blinker and turned into a small parking lot at the end of the street. The building looked like it might have been an old church, with a steeple and a bell on top. The sign out front said something about a children's art show. A gallery.

"Come on, Picasso," she said, unbuckling her seatbelt.

"Is he the only artist you can name?"

"No. There's . . . um . . . Monet." She blanked out after that. "Shut up."

We walked up the steps to the gallery and Katie opened the door. It was quiet inside, but soft generic piano music came from hidden speakers.

"Should we just go in?" Katie whispered.

"The door's open, so I think yes," I said at normal volume, stepping around her. I was still a little buzzed from the scotch, so my steps weren't as steady as they normally would have been. Katie took my arm and led me in.

The building was painted all in white to accentuate the art and had tons of windows and good light fixtures. For a small place, it was set up really well.

"Oh, this is so cute," Katie said, dragging me to the right. From a quick glance, they had all sorts of things here, from finger paintings, to a table of pottery pieces to some little dioramas. The first piece was done by Olivia, age 6, and resembled a princess fantasy, if that fantasy were done by a strange little girl.

The princess had a pretty pink dress and a sword in her hand and was plunging it into the heart of what I assumed was a dragon. A guy in armor lay on the ground, his eyes wide open in death. At least I thought so. Maybe he was just lying down for a minute. With his eyes open.

"What do they teach girls these days?" I said.

"What? Princesses can't kill dragons?" she said, smacking my chest in outrage.

I shook my head. "I never said that. It's just a little creepy, that's all. Did you dream about slaying dragons when you were six?"

"No."

"What did you dream about?" I was desperate to know. To think about her instead of . . . instead of Ric.

She moved on to the next painting which was done by a boy and featured something that looked like a snowmobile.

"When I was six? I don't know. A ballerina or something." She wasn't giving me a straight answer.

"No, really. You can tell me. I wanted to be a police officer, if that helps any." She looked at me, surprised.

"A singer," she said, stepping past the snowmobile picture to one that was a zoo panorama.

"Well, that's obvious. Why didn't you ever pursue it?"

She shrugged.

"I don't know. My parents were down on it. I was in chorus in school, but I was in a bunch of other things too and they made me give up one, so I gave up chorus." She looked at the zoo painting, turning her head to the side. "Hey! You're not supposed to be helping me with my issues. I'm supposed to be helping you."

"Talking about you is helping me." It was helping me not think about Ric and what I'd done to her.

She glared at me for a second before she took my hand again.

"I guess. Do you think that's an elephant?"

"Looks more wooly mammoth-y," I said.

We looked through the rest of the art, trying to figure out what some of it was and coming up with ridiculous stories to go along with each of the scenes. She held my hand. Some of the older kids' stuff was pretty good, and you could spot who had natural talent. We were completely alone. I could hear voices downstairs, but they never came up to check on us. Probably figured no one would actually steal a kid's finger painting that wasn't worth anything.

I let myself be surrounded by the art, and Katie and the sweet little moment we were sharing. I shouldn't have. I should have made her leave the second she walked in and drowned my sorrows alone.

I was letting myself have a sweet moment with my girlfriend while Ric was . . .

"I don't want to talk about it right now, but there are some things I need to tell you," I said.

"Shh . . ." she said, putting her finger to my lips. "Not right now. We can do it later. Right now we're looking at . . . um what are we looking at?"

I kissed her finger and slipped it into my mouth, tasting her skin.

"I think it's a flower."

***

"I knew looking at art would make you less asshole-y." She said as we got back in the car.

"Oh, I could still flip the asshole switch."

"I don't think you will. You sober yet?"

"Getting there." I was going to have quite a hangover though.

"We should probably get some water into you." She drove back toward my apartment, but stopped at a fast food place to get us something to eat. I seized the moment to check my phone. I had several messages from Trish, asking where the hell I was and why I wasn't answering my phone.

"We should go check on Trish," I said, hating myself for not doing it sooner. After she'd told me about Ric, she'd said she was going back to her apartment, and I'd been in a such a state, I'd let her.

"Aud's on it. Simon called her."

"Still, she's a bit of a wreck." I'd never seen her like that, and she'd been through a lot.

"Were she and Ric close? I never got the impression that they were."

I turned on the radio and flipped to the alt rock station. "No, not really. They used to have this weird love-hate friendship."

"Huh."

I was also in the dark as to why Trish was so upset over Ric.

"Okay, okay, we'll go see her. I've never been to her place before."

"She'd probably like to keep it that way, but desperate times."

Trish's apartment wasn't as large as mine, but it was a little bit nicer, with the exception of her insane roommate.

Katie parked the car in the only empty space and I showed her where Trish's place was. Her building had two apartments on the first floor, two on the second, and hers was on the second.

Katie knocked softly and the door opened a second later.

"Oh hey, where have you been?" Audrey said, her voice a whisper. "She's in rough shape."

"Yeah, guess the apple doesn't fall far from the tree," Katie said, elbowing me. "Can we come in?"

"Oh, yeah. Of course." She held the door open and we walked in to find Trish wrapped in a blanket on the ugly flowered couch, a pile of used tissues all around her like giant snotty snowflakes.

"Hey, Trish," I said, going over to her and crouching down. "How you holding up?"

"Where the hell have you been?" It was a little hard for her to glare through puffy eyes, but she managed.

"Katie and I just took a walk." It would be weird to try to explain the art gallery interlude. "Are you going to be okay?"

"No, I'm not going to be okay. She died, Stryker. She *died*."

"I know, I know." Trish and I weren't huggers, but I put my arms around her anyway and pulled her head onto my shoulder. Sobs shook her body and she melted into me.

I heard Audrey and Katie whispering behind me, catching each other up.

"Do you want to talk about it?" I said.

"What's there to talk about? She's dead. Just like that. Here one minute and gone the next. Just like Katie's dad. Why do these things happen?"

I rubbed her back. "I don't know, Trish. I don't know."

That was a lie. I knew why Ric had died. She'd died because of me. Because I should have taken her home, or stayed up and watched her, or maybe I shouldn't have been such a world class asshole.

But I kept my mouth shut and just held my little sister while she fell apart.

"Are you sure it's okay to miss class?" Katie said to Audrey.

"Yeah, my professors have been cutting me a lot of slack. It pays to be the teacher's pet sometimes."

"I bet. How do I get in on that?"

"I could teach you." They laughed a little and then went to the kitchen, giving us some privacy.

"Have you talked to anyone else?"

She nodded against my shoulder.

"Baxter is at her place with her mom." Ric's backstory was just about as tragic as Trish's and mine. Dad split, mom married a bunch of jerks and never really cared about her. She dropped out of high school and moved in with whoever would take her, as long as she was out of her mom's house. She worked whatever jobs she could get and barely scraped by. She and Trish had been a lot closer a few years ago, but they'd drifted apart when Ric had started partying really hard. Trish might look like a girl who's seen some hard living, but I kept her away from a lot of it, even while I engaged in it myself.

"It could have been anyone, Stryker. She was just driving home and it killed her. It could have been us."

"But it wasn't. You're okay. I'm okay. We're going to be okay."

Her voice broke again and she convulsed with sobs.

When it came to losing people, Trish and I were pros, but none of them had ever died. Our parents, as horrible as they might have been, were still alive out there, and so were the rest of our relatives. Trish and I had had our fair share of hardships, but death was something that had, by and large, passed us by.

I held her for a long time as I heard Katie and Audrey in the small kitchen. They tried to be quiet, but there was plenty of banging around until they came out with a tray of soup and some grilled cheese sandwiches.

"You should eat something," I said, moving Trish's head. It was strange to see her normal greenish-bluish eyes instead of the violet ones.

"I'm not hungry."

"Well that's too bad because you're going to eat anyway if I have to shove it down your throat." One of the only things that worked with Trish was tough love. Guess I wasn't the only one.

"Bite me," she said, so I nipped her shoulder.

"Don't make me be mean."

"You're already mean."

"Meaner."

Katie and Audrey watched us as if we were interesting animals in a zoo. Tender moments between Trish and me were just about as rare as they came.

I held half of a sandwich out to her and she took a bite.

"That's my girl."

I let her eat the rest of it herself as Audrey and Katie cleaned up some of the tissue mess.

"You guys can go if you want," I said once she was digging into the soup. "I got this."

"No way," Katie said. "You couldn't get rid of me if you wanted to."

"Same here. Even though it means I'm missing the review for a test. I don't care," Audrey chimed in.

Missing something like that was a huge deal to her, and I knew how much it meant.

I had nothing to say but, "Thanks."

Even though I didn't deserve it, Trish did.

We finally convinced Trish to come and stay with me, but first Audrey got her in the shower and said she'd bring her over later. It was a subtle way to give Katie and me some alone time. We went back to my place to clean up and make up the couch for Trish so she would have a place to sleep.

"I've never seen Trish like that," she said. "She's always so strong." Appearances could be deceiving.

"Yeah, she's not good with death."

"She was great when everything happened with Dad."

I took a breath and tried to explain. "That's because she didn't really know him. It's weird, but I think it's because Ric was so young . . ." I couldn't finish.

"Are you going to talk about it now?"

I shook my head. I was completely sober now.

She gave me a little smile. "Do you want me to get naked so you can draw out your feelings on my skin?"

As absolutely sexy and tempting as that was, I couldn't.

"No. I don't think that's a good idea."

She slid her finger down my face and circled it on my chest. "Why not? What does Ric have to do with us?"

More than she knew.

I pushed her hand away. "Look, I don't want to talk about it. I just had to deal with Trish and I just don't want to deal with any more."

"You're getting asshole-y again."

"If only it would work." I tried to move away from her, but she wouldn't let me.

"I don't scare easily," she said, straddling me as I sat on the couch.

"Don't." I put my hands on her hips to try to lift her off, but that was going to be easier said than done. She wiggled just a little, and my body responded. Her body was a tune my body couldn't resist.

"I'm not doing anything. I'm just sitting." She might be just sitting, but everything she did turned me on. She could be just breathing and I'd want her. It was unavoidable.

"Katie, please."

"Okay, fine." She got off me and sat on the other end of the couch, grabbing the remote and turning the television on, flicking through the channels.

"What are you doing?"

"I'm watching TV, what does it look like? Oohh, I love this show." She stopped on what looked like some sort of crime show. A lawyer was screaming in a crowded courtroom about something we'd clearly missed earlier in the episode. She checked the guide and saw that there was another episode after this one finished.

I looked at her, but her eyes were fixed on the TV. This must be some sort of twisted way to get me to cave in and talk, but I had no idea how she thought she was going to accomplish that by ignoring me.

We sat side-by-side as the show finished and the credits rolled. I crossed my arms and tried to think of anything but how much I wanted her and how much I hated myself for thinking about her when I should have been thinking about Ric.

The next episode started and her eyes stayed locked on the television. The minutes dragged by as the body was discovered and the cops were called in. I'd always found it amusing how cops on television were almost always extremely attractive. The cops around campus all had hardcore donut habits, and there wasn't one lady cop to be found, least of all one that looked like a Russian supermodel.

"I will make you a bet," she finally said when the cops started interviewing various suspects. "You pick who you think killed her and I pick one and whoever is right has to buy the other one dinner."

"I already owe you a dinner from the pie-eating contest at Thanksgiving."

She looked away from the TV for a second, her facade dropping for a second. "Well, then I guess you'll just owe me two. Pick your perp."

"Okay . . . Um, that crazy guy who lurked in the alley was definitely suspicious."

She scoffed.

"Please, it's obviously the teenage daughter."

"What? After she cried like that? You're crazy."

She turned to face me.

"Wait and see." She smirked and went back to the television.

Katie

Of course I was right. The teenage girl turned out to have some weird attraction to her dad and when she saw him with his mistress, she snapped. It was sick and twisted, but it was clear from the very beginning that it was her.

"There's another one on," I said, getting up and stretching my arms over my head. "Want to lose another bet?" I'd been right in telling Stryker that I was making this up as I went along, but *Law and Order* marathons had always worked for me, so why not him?

There really needed to be a manual for this sort of thing. Sure, there were plenty of self-help books, but I didn't think they mentioned anything like this.

"What are you doing?" Damn, he was onto me. Not that I was being very subtle.

"Watching you lose a bet, best friend." I sat back down and looked at him.

"No, you're trying to distract me, but you can't do that forever. I have to deal with what I've done some time." He clenched his mouth shut and looked away from me.

"What do you mean, what you've done? How is this your fault?"

He started laughing and got up from the couch, going to his bedroom. I followed him. What the hell?

"What are you talking about?" I leaned in the doorway as he pulled out a cigarette and lighter. I guessed quitting was out of the question at the moment, not that I blamed him. He tried to light it, but his hands were too shaky.

"Let me do it." I hated myself for furthering his addiction to the cancer stick, but he was in such rough shape I figured one more smoke wasn't going to do him in.

I lit it and he inhaled, closing his eyes.

"What have you done, Stryker?" I slipped the lighter into my pocket. If he couldn't light them, he couldn't smoke them.

He shook his head and blew out a cloud of smoke over his shoulder so it didn't go in my face.

"I tried to tell you so many times, and then I couldn't . . . and then you told me you loved me, and I still tried, because you deserved the truth, and then I didn't want to, because I didn't want to wreck everything. Fuck, I just wrecked everything." He sat down on his bed and tore the hand not holding the cigarette through his hair.

"Stryker, you're scaring me," I said, because it was true. "Just tell me what happened and I can help you." I crossed the room and sat next to him, touching his shoulder.

"No!" He said diving away from me and getting to his feet. "You can't do that. I don't deserve it. I don't deserve your compassion. I never did and I never will." I followed him as he stormed back into the living room.

"Talk to me, Stryker. Just talk to me," I said in my calmest voice. I refused to think anything, or make any conclusions until I heard them come from him.

He sucked in another puff from the cigarette.

"And tell you what? That I had sex with Ric? That she showed up drunk last night and I told her that I'd hurt her if she told you about us, and now today she's dead?" I couldn't move. He crossed the room and stood right in front of me. "Is that what you wanted to fucking hear?!" he yelled.

The air was too thick to breathe; it wouldn't go into my lungs.

"Oh, God," he said, putting his face in his hands and dropping the cigarette. I was able to snap out of my momentary shock to stomp it out before it set the apartment on fire.

"Stryker," I said, taking his hands and trying to pull them away from his face, and also trying not to freak out about what he'd just told me. He raised his head, his eyes tear-streaked and hopeless.

"It. Doesn't. Matter."

"How can you say that? She's dead and it's my fault. And I hurt you. How can you say that it doesn't matter? It matters more than anything."

I held his hands and tried to find the right words.

"Because I love you."

"How can you say that?"

It was easy. Simple. As clear and beautiful as a cloudless summer sky.

"Because it's true. It's true whether you slept with Ric, or whether you got drunk and said something you didn't mean, or if you smoke too much, or never pick up your socks, or don't have any money. Love doesn't come and go. It's for always."

He tried to shake his head, but I wouldn't stop looking at him. I leaned and put my forehead to his.

"You and me. No space. Always," I whispered to his lips. He opened his eyes and finally saw me. Saw that I wasn't going anywhere.

"I love you so much, sweetheart. So much that sometimes I can't breathe. I can't think. You're all I've ever wanted, even before I knew I wanted it. I don't deserve you, Katherine."

No, it was really the other way around, but I decided that I'd kiss him instead of arguing. Kissing was always better than arguing.

It was a slow kiss, a burning kiss. The kind of kiss that promised of forever. I wrapped my arms around him and kissed the first and last boy with a lip ring I was ever going to love.

Twenty-eight

Stryker

I let her kiss me, and she let me kiss her back as I cried, bitter tears and regret tears and happy tears. There were so many emotions flooding my mind that I was afraid I was going to burst with them. The world felt like it was about to end.

"I'm so sorry, sweetheart," I said, finally pulling away from her sweet lips. I had to get this all out. It had been slowly killing me.

"Shh, there's nothing to be sorry for. Granted, I'm not thrilled you had sex with her, but it's not going to make me stop loving you. And it's not your fault what happened to her. How could you possibly think that was your fault?" She shook me a little, as if trying to shake the thought out of my head.

I led her to the couch and sat her down, telling her the whole story. About how I'd slept with Ric and the entire time I'd thought of Katie, and how Ric had been threatening to tell on me and how she'd showed up and the awful things I'd said to her and . . . now she was dead. I could never take those words back. They were the last I'd said to her, and that would never change.

She stayed in my lap as I talked, stroking my hair and listening in silence. It felt good to hold her, to have something to ground me while I talked, slicing the words out with the sharpest of knives. They came, little bleeding chunks that left holes, and pain behind. Finally, I was done and we both listened to the silence that filled the room.

"Blame is easy, isn't it? Blaming yourself, blaming someone else," she said, resting her head in the perfect spot on my shoulder. It felt like had been made just for her.

"I wouldn't say it was easy."

"Maybe easy isn't the right word. Maybe . . . it's like you want to do something, and blame is the easiest path to find. It's simple, and it gives you something to do. Something to focus on, because the reality is harder."

"I think you're right." I pulled my fingers through her hair. "Thank you for saving me."

"I didn't save you. If anyone has gotten saved, it's me. That day in the hospital, you were . . . you were everything I needed. I don't know where I'd be if it weren't for you." She took the hand that wasn't in her hair and kissed it.

"How about we just agree that we saved each other?" She tilted her head up.

"Deal?"

"You and me," I said.

"No space."

"Always." She kissed my lips and I believed her. Believed in us.

***

For the second time in two months, I attended a funeral. Ric's was smaller than Mr. Hallman's, and there were significantly more piercings and tattoos present. This time, though, I had a beautiful girl by my side, her hand in mine.

Things are always sadder somehow, when someone young dies. Trish was a wreck again, but she had the whole gang holding her up, and I saw her chatting with some guy in the parking lot afterward. She was smiling and not crying anymore, which was what made me look, even more than the fact that she was talking to a guy.

"Who's that?" Katie whispered to me.

"Um, I think that's Ric's stepbrother, or cousin or something." I remembered seeing him with her family.

"He's cute," she said, looking him up and down. He had electric blue curly hair, which clashed with the crisp black suit he was wearing. I watched Trish talk to him, putting her hand on his arm and laughing.

"Oh my God, is she laughing?" Simon said, letting his eyes leave Brady's for one second.

"Should we call someone?" Will said, putting his coat on Audrey's shoulders, despite her assurances that she wasn't cold. "Like, maybe there's radiation in her apartment and it's caused a brain tumor that is altering her personality. Or maybe it's aliens."

"You always think it's aliens," Lottie said, rolling her eyes. "Have you ever thought of the fact that she might just be attracted to him? That has been known to happen every now and then." She gave Zan a wink and he gave her one back. "I think it's romantic, in a weird way. Has Nicholas Sparks written a book where the couple meets at a funeral?"

"No, but I think there was a movie. You made me watch it once," Will said, snapping his fingers. "You know, with that British guy and the hair."

"Hugh Grant?" Katie said.

"That's it," Will said, snapping his fingers again.

"Well anyway, I think it's great," Katie said. "There's a lid for every pot."

"Do you want to be the lid or the pot, baby?" Simon said to Brady.

"Whichever one you don't want," he said, giving Simon a kiss as we continued to watch Trish.

"You think she knows we're staring at her?" Lottie said. A second later, Trish turned a little, as if to brush her hair back and held her middle finger in our direction.

"Guess that answers that question," I said, as we all looked in different directions. "You ready to go?" I said to Katie.

"I think so. How you holding up? No new attacks of guilt?"

"Just a little one. Nothing major."

"I might have something that can help with that," she said, shoving her arms into my coat and looking up at me.

"Oh, really? A cream, or a pill or something?"

"Ah, no. It involves you . . . and me . . . and no clothing."

"I think I can work with that," I said, kissing her.

I couldn't believe how she'd accepted everything with Ric. I knew it bothered her, but she did her best not to let it. We hadn't really talked about it since, but I knew we needed to. I still had moments, especially in the middle of the night, when I would wake up hating myself for being so happy with Katie, or replaying my last moments with Ric.

Katie suggested I go to her therapist, and I made an appointment. It wasn't going to solve everything, but maybe it could help make things better. She was still having a hard time dealing with her dad's death. I knew she carried around the bag of his ashes in her purse because I'd seen it once when she was searching for some gum, but I hadn't confronted her about it. We both needed more time.

***

Time passed, as it always does. The first snowfall bathed the world in white silence and made driving an even more dangerous exercise, and soon it was time for Christmas.

Katie and I hadn't talked about what we were doing, or more exactly, what I was doing. It was one of the things we'd been avoiding.

"Are you going to sing tonight?" I asked her as we set out the trays of snacks she'd made for Band. She'd come a few times, but I hadn't been able to convince her to sing again. Ric had left a hole and no one seemed ready to fill it yet.

"I don't know," she said, setting out a few plastic cups. She had practically moved in, but I wondered what she would say to making the arrangement more permanent. Lottie didn't stay much in her dorm room either, so it seemed pointless to pay for it when they were both living other places.

"It seems . . . I don't know." She shrugged.

"No one is going to think that you're trying to be a fill-in."

"It just doesn't seem right."

"We'll put it to a vote."

"Stryker," she said, giving me a look. "I don't want you to make a big deal out of it."

"And I don't want you to hide it anymore. You have a beautiful gift and I just want you to share it with everyone."

She came over and put her hands on my shoulders. "Did you read that off a greeting card?"

"Damn. You've discovered my secret. I get all my words of wisdom from Hallmark," I said, kissing her cheek.

"Your secret is safe with me," she said, moving her face so our lips met. A crashing sound downstairs announced the arrival of the rest of The Band.

"Showtime," I said.

Katie

Things had been more than somber with everyone since Ric's death, but nobody really liked to talk about it. It had hit them all hard, especially Allan.

"Hey, how are you?" I said as he came up the stairs, hauling a guitar case and a bottle of alcohol. Great. That was just what we needed. A bunch of sad drunk people.

"I'm good, Pink, how you doing?" He gave me a one-armed hug and a tight smile.

"Stryker wants me to participate tonight, but I don't know if I'm up for it," I said as Perry, Zoey and Theo came up the stairs behind him.

"Why not? From what I heard that one time, you've got pipes."

"I didn't think it was really appropriate. You know, given the circumstances." Baxter had left the group after everything with Ric. Stryker had talked to him, and he said it was just too hard. He'd really loved her.

"Oh come on. If not now, when?" He patted my shoulder and went to set up with everyone else.

"You ready?" Stryker said, putting his violin under his chin. He swapped out his instruments frequently, and he'd been in a violin mood as of late. I claimed my spot next to him on the couch as everyone else caught up and set up their own.

"How about we start off with requests tonight for a change?" Stryker said, swiping his bow across the strings. "Anyone?"

"How about a duet," Allan said, staring pointedly at me. "You two." He pointed at us with his guitar pick. "Mads Langer, 'Beauty of the Dark', duet. You up for it?"

I looked at Stryker, but he didn't look surprised.

"What a good idea, Allan. I'm mad I didn't think of it myself." Stryker turned slowly to face me, a grin on his face. Oh, he so planned this. He'd played the song for me a few days ago, and I'd loved it so much that I'd been listening to it ever since and humming it under my breath.

"You set me up," I said, shoving him a little.

"Hey, anything to hear that gorgeous voice of yours." I looked around and everyone else looked guilty.

I pointed at all of them. "You all suck, by the way."

That response elicited laughter just as we heard footsteps on the stairs before Trish walked through the door with the blue-haired cousin/stepbrother from the funeral. I nearly choked when I saw that they were holding hands.

"Sorry we're late," she said, blushing. The guy, who was still nameless, gave us all a little two-fingered wave.

"Hey, that's my bad. I'm Max."

"Nice to finally meet you, *Max*," Stryker said, and it wasn't my imagination that he gripped his violin extra hard. Haha. Protective big brother strikes again.

"That's my brother, Stryker. You can ignore him. I know I do," Trish said, leading Max into the room and making the other introductions.

"This is Katie," she said when she got to me. I stuck my hand out and he shook it, his eyes widening at the mention of my name.

"So this is Katie. You were right," he said, turning toward Trish and putting his arm over her shoulder. "She does wear a lot of pink." She shrugged and he gave her a kiss on the forehead.

I always thought Will was crazy for thinking about alien abductions or radiation poisoning, but I was beginning to suspect that Trish either had a concussion, or she'd swapped personalities with some other girl. That was the only plausible explanation for this behavior.

"Nice to meet you," I said, watching Trish's personality shift. Oh, she was going to dish later.

All of us had made an attempt to get her to spill about Max, but until now she wouldn't even give us his name or speak about him in any way.

"I hope we're not intruding. Just . . . keep doing what you were doing. We'll be over here," Max said after the introductions, taking a seat on the floor and pulling Trish down after him. She settled against him, and they shared a secret smile.

I gave Stryker a look, and he was giving Trish the Grant Glare. I usually only saw it on her face, but now he wore it like a favorite, well-worn t-shirt.

"Hey," I said, poking him in the ribs. "Your overprotective is showing."

He turned off the glare when he looked at me.

"I don't like him," he hissed at me. "He's . . . got blue hair."

"Yeah, you can never trust those blue-haired guys. As opposed to those guys who bleach their hair."

He looked at me and I tried to do the eyebrow raise, but I didn't think I got it quite right.

"Okay, okay." Everyone else was sort of watching us and also watching Trish and Max, who were in their own little world.

"So, we ready to do our duet?" I was willing to go along with it if it would take some of the heat off Trish. I had to poke him in the chest to get him to focus. Damn. I'd never seen him like that. For all the fighting he and Trish did, I had no idea that he'd be like that when Trish finally found a guy. Yet another side of the mysterious Stryker Abraham Grant.

"Let's rock it," I said, giving him a quick kiss on the cheek. It took a second, but he set his violin under his chin as a hush fell over the room. Why had I agreed to do this again? I was about to stand up and say "never mind" when Stryker started playing, and I had no choice but to start singing.

Stryker came in with me and even without practicing, we followed each other's lead and melded our voices together. It was like making love with him. In some ways it was just as intimate. Another way for us to have no space.

We finished and the room was silent. Then Allan started a slow clap that turned into a round of applause complete with whoops and whistles. I blushed and Stryker put down his violin so he could give me a steamy kiss. I had to pull away before it went any further. Even with a room full of people, I was ready to rip his clothes off and have my way with him.

"Get a room!" someone yelled, and we broke apart.

"Wanna do another?" he said, nibbling on his bottom lip.

"Sure. Can I pick this time?"

"As long as it's not that Beaver kid."

We all laughed.

"Nope. How about 'Stay'?" It was a song that he'd gotten from my collection. I wasn't the only one who needed a musical education. I'd widened his range as well, and that was one of the songs I'd caught him playing more than once. It was also a real duet, with me taking the Rihanna part and him taking the Mikky Ekko parts. Stryker's and my voices were completely different from Rihanna's and Mikky's, but no one seemed to care.

We got another round of applause, and shared another sexy kiss.

"Okay, that's enough of that," Allan said, throwing an empty can at us. "Time for some real music instead of singing intercourse." Everyone else took up their instruments and started playing a new song, and I sat back and watched Stryker do his thing again, but kept one eye on Trish and Max. She caught me watching and gave me a wink. Oh, we were soooo going to have a little chat.

They played a few songs and then it was time for a smoke break and I nabbed Trish before she could escape. Max gave me a kind of scared look and stuttered something about enjoying secondhand smoke and scurried away.

"You have some serious explaining to do, Trishella." Instead of slapping me for using her real name like she probably would have a few weeks ago, she just watched Max walk away.

"What?" she said, tearing her eyes away from his back to finally pay attention to me. The girl was completely gone on him.

I snapped my fingers in front of her face.

"I said that you have some serious explaining to do. When and how being the most pressing questions in my mind right now." She motioned me into the kitchen so we could have some privacy. Stryker had gone out with the smokers to get some secondhand. He was still having trouble quitting, but he'd get there. Plus, he'd probably seen that Max had gone outside and was interrogating him. He was probably about to start the waterboarding any moment.

Trish leaned against the counter and looked down, a little smile on her face.

"Honestly, I don't know. It just . . . happened. I was so upset at the funeral and he came over and made some stupid comment that made me want to punch him, and then I just started crying again and he hugged me. Out of the blue. And I let him, and it felt nice. He started talking about how he'd lost his best friend when they were kids and he knew what it was like. And I don't know . . . I just started talking and he talked and we've been talking ever since." She shrugged.

"Why didn't you tell anyone about him?"

"For the same reason you kept the whole Stryker thing in the dark, Miss Kettle." Oh yeah. I had done that. "I just didn't want a big deal made out of it, which is exactly what happened anyway, but at least I got to give Max some warning ahead of time."

Half of the smoking crowd came back, loud and boisterous, but Stryker and Max weren't a part of the group.

Trish looked concerned. "God, I hope Stryker isn't trying to beat the shit out of him. Max is a third degree black belt in Tai Kwan Do, so I'm pretty sure my brother would be shit out of luck."

"I don't know. Never underestimate a brother trying to protect his little sister."

"He always does that," she said, tossing an empty cup into the trash. "But it's like he doesn't want me to do anything. Even when he's screwing things up, he refuses to let me do the exact same things he's doing himself."

"He doesn't want you to make the same mistakes he has. My sister's the same way." Kayla always used to catch me sneaking out of the house, usually when she was doing the exact same thing. She might have been my parents' golden child, but that didn't mean she had been absolutely perfect. She just hadn't gotten caught.

"There they are," she said as Stryker and Max came back inside. Neither of them had a black eye, and they were talking at a normal volume.

"Everything looks okay," I said.

"I'd better check," she pushed herself away from the counter and went over to Max, putting her arm around his waist. His arm went around her automatically, like he wasn't even thinking about it. As if it was natural.

Stryker said something and then shook his head, and I saw that he was smiling. He shook Max's hand and looked around the room, stopping when he saw me.

Max and Trish went to go sit on the floor again and Stryker came over to me.

"Please don't say you threatened him," I said.

He pretended to be appalled, putting his hand to his chest.

"I am shocked that you think I would do such a thing."

I rolled my eyes.

"Yeah, okay, Stryker. What did you say to him?" He came over and put his arms around me.

"I just said that it was about time my sister trusted someone enough to let them get past her incredibly thick and high walls and I hoped he was worthy of it, even though I doubted it. But I said I'd be watching him."

I smacked him in the chest.

"If you didn't say the last part, the first part would be a lot sweeter. Look at her," I said, turning both of us so we could see Max and Trish together. He'd pushed some of her hair back and she smiled as she told him something.

"She's happy."

"I just hope she stays that way," he said, pulling me close. "I don't want her to have a hard time. I want life to be better for her, you know?"

"Yeah, I do," I said, pushing myself up to give him a kiss. "You're a good brother, Stryker Grant."

"You're a good girlfriend, Katherine Ann Hallman. And a good kisser, and a good singer, and you're *really* good at giving—"

I put my hand on his mouth, because I knew what else he was going to say I was good at, and I didn't want anyone else to overhear.

"That's not for you to advertise, or else I'll never do it again." I removed my hand and gave him a glare for good measure. The threat was enough to get him to press his lips together as if he was sealing them.

"Are we gonna play now?" Allan called as he tried to sit next to Zoey, and she pushed him away with disgust.

"Coming," he said, letting go of me. "Which is what you'll be doing later tonight after everyone leaves. Over and over again," he whispered before walking back to the couch.

Damn him. He played dirty.

It took me a second to get my legs to work so I could get back to the couch and it was a relief to sit down, even though sitting next to Stryker made me really uncomfortable in certain areas. It was torture for the rest of the session, but the sweetest kind.

Twenty-nine

Stryker

"So I think I should pick a major," she said as she lay naked in my bed and I drew a sunburst in the middle of her back. I'd kept my promise from earlier, and she'd reciprocated, so we were both worn out physically. "Don't you think?"

I shrugged one shoulder and looked up from my drawing to meet her eyes.

"Do you want to pick one because you want to, or because there's all this pressure from other people to?"

She thought about it for a second.

"I think it's both. I just . . . I want to know . . . what I want."

I laughed a little.

She smacked my shoulder. "Don't make fun of me."

"I'm not laughing at you. I'm just laughing because that's the human condition. Nobody really knows what they want. They just know what they think they want and then they get it and they realize they don't want it anymore."

"Like what?"

"Money, power, prestige. Mostly money."

"I don't care about money that much."

"I know. That's one of the things I love about you. I don't really care about it either, except that it'd be nice to have enough that I wouldn't have to worry about paying the electric bill."

She yawned. "I should probably get a job now. Mom and Dad mostly footed the bill for everything, and I've been living on my summer babysitting money, but that's almost gone. I don't want to take more money from Mom, because she needs it more than I do. I've thought about dropping out," she said, which made me look up at her again.

"To save money?"

"Yeah, and to take care of her. She's all alone." Katie spent every weekend at home, and it was taking its toll on her. She always came back reluctantly, and it took a day for her to recover emotionally. Kayla had gone back to Africa, and had decided to postpone her wedding for a better time.

I stroked my fingers down her spine.

"Is that what you want?"

She sighed heavily.

"It's not about what I want."

"Fine, then what do you think your dad would want?"

"He'd want me to finish school."

"Then I think you should do that."

"I thought you weren't supposed to tell me what to do."

"I'm not. Just suggesting." I'd said the same thing when I'd told her not to go see Zack.

"Okay, then. If I'm staying, I have to pick a major." I had an idea. If she wanted to pick a major, we were going to pick her a fucking major.

"Stay right there," I said, standing up to get my laptop.

She pushed herself up. "Where are you going?"

"Just a sec." I grabbed it from the kitchen, booting it up on the way back to my bedroom. I went to the DU website scrolled down until I found the list of majors the university offered.

"Okay, how do you feel about accounting?"

"What?" She rolled over and saw me holding my laptop.

"Accounting, yes or no?" I sat down and she moved closer to me.

"Um, no. Not big on math." I went down to the next option.

"Okay, how about Animal Science?"

She shook her head.

"Anthropology?"

"Put that in the maybe column." I grabbed the marker I'd been using to draw on her back and wrote 'anthropology-maybe' below the sun.

"Art education?"

Another head shake. "But that would have been a good one for you, if you weren't already doing your genius thing."

I went down the entire list of majors and she nixed almost all of them, except for a few that I wrote on her back. When we were done, I put the cap back on the marker and admired my work.

"Well Miss Hallman, I think we've got a list. Why don't you make an appointment with a guidance counselor and they can help you out. They're professionals so they know what they're doing."

She made a little snorting noise. "You want me to go in to the guidance office, take off my shirt and say that this is the list of majors I've narrowed my choices down to?" She pointed to her back.

"I meant that we should probably transfer this list to paper and *then* take it in," I said, kissing 'anthropology'.

"Good plan," she breathed as I kissed my way lower on the list before flipping her over and making us both forget about majors for a while.

***

The following Tuesday Katie came back from her meeting with the guidance person with a sad look on her face.

"What's wrong?" I'd been working on a lab, but I threw it aside, even though I was halfway through a tricky calculation.

Her face split into a smile.

"Gotcha. It went fine. Basically they told me that if I'm really not sure, I should just take a bunch of classes for things I'm interested in and go from there. So, I'm signing up for art history, another anthro class, British lit, vocal performance, and food science and nutrition." She flopped down next to me, giving me a quick kiss.

"That's very . . . eclectic."

"I would have taken more classes, but that's a full schedule, and I wasn't sure if I could do more."

She definitely could. I'd seen what she could do when she put just a little effort in. Katie was one of those girls who didn't have to try too hard to get good grades, so she'd just done just enough for years and gotten by.

"So my life makeover is in full swing. Now I just have to find a job." She mimed shooting herself in the head.

"I could always use an assistant. You could hold the flashlight for me," I said, pulling her onto my lap.

She giggled. "Not that that isn't tempting, but I gotta do my own thing. I just don't know what that is. I started looking online."

"You want to make another list?" I stroked her arm.

"I think I can do this one on my own, but there is one part of my makeover I would like you to be with me for."

"And what's that?"

"I was thinking . . . " she said, twirling some of her hair around her finger and staring at it. "I was thinking I'd like to do something with my hair. Like, maybe put some pink in it." She looked at me out of the corner of her eye, searching for my reaction.

"Pink, huh?" I grabbed a few strands and ran them through my fingers. I could picture that. She'd look so cute with pink hair, especially with her glasses.

"You don't think it's dumb, do you?"

"Sweetheart, I would never think you were dumb, and even if I did, I'd never tell you. I might call you an idiot, but I'd never say you were dumb." I kissed her nose. "No, I think you would look beyond adorable with some pink in your hair."

"Okay then." She relaxed against me.

"I have some . . . changes I'd like to make as well, involving you, that I wanted to talk to you about," I said. It was now or never.

"And what might those changes be?"

"I was thinking . . . " Now it was my turn to be nervous. "I was thinking that since you're here so much anyway and Lottie and Zan are thinking about getting their own place, that maybe you might want to move in. Here. With me."

She sat up and turned around. "Move in with you?"

"I know it's really soon, but I thought I would throw it out there. I mean, you already have tampons stashed everywhere, and my bathroom looks like a cosmetics store blew up in it. Not that I'm complaining." I was still at the stage where seeing her stuff around made me happy instead of annoyed. I was sure I'd get to the annoyed part eventually.

"Move in with you." She said it as a statement, not a question. "I . . . Are you sure? I'm just afraid that you'll get sick of me, or find something you don't like about me, and I don't want that to happen."

"What about me? What if you find something you don't like about me?" That was the first thing that had crossed my mind and the reason I'd put off asking her in the first place.

"I guess that's a risk we're just going to have to take," she said, leaning into me for a kiss. "I would love to move in with you. You and me."

"No space."

"Nope, it's going to be *our* space, and it's going to be covered in pink." Her eyes gleamed maniacally.

"God help us."

Thirty

Katie

"Please say that is the last box," Will grumbled as he shoved yet another box into my Mazda. We were moving the majority of my crap into Stryker's today and then the rest at the end of the semester. I hadn't told Mom yet because I didn't think it was something she needed to be worried about at the moment. She was doing a little better with the help of her support group, and she'd become close with another woman who had also lost her husband suddenly. Still, I didn't want to mess with the careful equilibrium we'd established by telling her that I'd moved in with Stryker.

"That is the last box," I said, shutting the trunk. Lottie had roped Will and Simon into helping me. Zan would have been there, but he had a class, as did Stryker. Or so they said. I had my suspicions.

"You sure about this?" Will said, crossing his arms and leaning on the back of the car.

"Not really, but there's only one way to find out. I mean, we've already been through so much."

"True." He glanced over at Lottie and Simon, who were playing rock, paper, scissors for no apparent reason.

"Hey, how are you and Aud?"

He shrugged.

"I don't know. She's . . . I always feel like she's hiding something from me, you know? Like she lets me get close enough and then shuts the door in my face. It's driving me crazy." He yanked his hand through is hair, which didn't do much. Will always looked like he'd come from the beach, with his blonde wind-blown hair.

"That sucks."

"Tell me about it."

Simon and Lottie had started what looked like a slap fight.

"Sometimes I don't know about those two," Will said, shaking his head as I got my keys out.

"So I'll see you guys later. Thanks so much for all the help." It seemed anti-climactic for me to be leaving like this, but they all seemed to have things to do. Supposedly.

"Bye, roommie. I'll miss you," Lottie said, giving me a hug.

"I'll see you tonight, you idiot. Remember? Girls' night?" As much as I wanted to spend the night having no-space time with Stryker, I still needed my girl time. Especially now that Trish could dish on her new guy.

"Right," she said, not looking at me as she let go. "So, I should get to that thing. That I'm doing. You know."

"Riiigggghhhttt," I said, getting into the driver's side. She was a terrible liar. Something was up, but I sort of knew that already. None of them could keep a secret very well. Not even Stryker.

Driving back to his, I mean our, apartment wasn't easy because I couldn't see out my back window. When I pulled into the lot, there were more than a few cars that I recognized. The least they could have done was park down the street, but they weren't that stealthy. Amateurs.

"Knock, knock," I said loudly at the bottom of the stairs. Frantic movement ensued and then Stryker appeared, looking flustered.

"Hey, best friend. What you doing up there?" I said.

"Oh, um, nothing." He made sure to close the door behind him.

"Sure." I let him kiss me for a really long time. Clearly, he was trying to stall me, and it was working. His hands worked themselves under my jacket and shirt, hot and demanding.

"Are you trying to have your way with me right here, right now?"

"Maybe," he said, kissing down my neck. He was very good at distracting when he put his mind to it.

"Uh huh," I said, biting my lip as my legs threatened to buckle. "And this has nothing to do with the surprise you guys are trying to get together upstairs." My words were all garbled, but he got the gist, raising his head from my neck.

"Were we that obvious?"

"Well, Lottie couldn't keep something like this a secret to save her life, so yeah." He rested his head on my shoulder.

"Damn."

"Nice try, though." I patted his head and he sighed, which tickled.

I nearly jumped when a very fake-sounding bird call emanated from Stryker's partially open door. He called back, sounding very much like a wounded seagull.

"You are ridiculous," I said as he led me up the stairs. He stopped me and put his hand on the door, and I heard some scurrying feet. Stryker waited a second longer and then swung the door open.

"Surprise!" Unlike with Lottie's car, they all yelled it at the same time. Simon had practiced with them, no doubt. They were here, Simon, Brady, Lottie, Zan, Will, Audrey, Trish and Max. All smiling at me like idiots. God, I adored them.

"Oh my God, you guys," I said, pretending I had no idea. There was a huge pink banner that said, CONGRATS ON LIVING IN SIN TOGETHER in white lettering.

"Thanks for that," I said, giving Stryker a look. He just raised his hands in defeat.

"It was Trish's idea."

Of course it was.

She grinned from ear to ear, but at least Max had the decency to look sheepish, blushing under all that blue hair.

"We also have another little surprise for you," Lottie said, coming around from behind the couch. "So you know how we are not going to be living in the same room for next semester, which made me crazy sad."

"Uh huh." I had no idea where she was going with this.

"Weeeelllll, there just happens to be an available apartment right below this one," she said, giving me a huge wink.

"You didn't," I said, looking at Zan, who gave me one of his rare smiles.

She put her arms in the air in celebration. "We did!"

"And guess who is getting her own place, just down the street, and away from her psychotic roommate? This girl," Trish said, raising her hand.

"Thank God," Max said. "I didn't think I could stand her staring at me every time I came over. I was afraid she was plotting to murder me in my sleep, or at least use me as a human sacrifice."

"Don't worry, I had a knife and a Taser under my bed. You're safe," Trish said, patting his arm.

"I love how prepared you are," he said.

Simon made gagging noises, but he was wrapped around Brady, so he couldn't really say much.

"So, who wants to help bring all my stuff up from my car?" I said and they all groaned in unison. They must have practiced that too.

***

As soon as we got all my crap up the stairs, Lottie announced that she wanted to get her stuff moved as well. Apparently Zan had already moved his things, by himself, in one trip. But he was a guy, and he was kind of a minimalist anyway. They thought my stuff was bad, but Lottie had all those books.

"Can't we just . . . not and say we did?" Will said as we consumed the cupcakes Audrey had brought over for the party.

"Look, if we could just Portkey the stuff here, I would totally do that, but we can't," Lottie said.

"Wish we could," Audrey said. "It would make things so much easier."

Stryker swiped some frosting off his cupcake and held it out to me. I licked it off and someone made a disgusted sound. Oh, like they hadn't all done it already.

"There's another part of this little surprise," Trish said, getting up from Max's lap. "Stryker mentioned your wish to change your hair up, so I brought some supplies." She grabbed her backpack and dumped it out on the coffee table. Bottles and combs and other things fell out.

"You ready to be pink?" I picked up the box that had a smiling girl with brilliant pink hair on the front. Well, I wasn't ready to be *that* pink, but a few streaks were definitely doable.

"Um, you sure you know what you're doing?" I said.

"Who do you think does my hair, and his?" She pointed to Stryker. "I've been doing it for years, and I haven't messed up yet."

"There was that one time . . . " Stryker said.

She glared at him. "Okay once, I messed up once."

"What happened?" Max said.

Trish looked at the ceiling. "I may have made Stryker's hair the color of snot."

"I think it was more dirty canary. Either way, it was pretty bad," Stryker said, shuddering. "Never again."

"But that's not going to happen to you. So, are you ready?" She took the box from me and grinned.

"Guess so," I said, even though it was kind of a lie. No time like now.

I'd only ever had highlights done, so doing the pink was a whole different thing. First Trish had to bleach the pieces that I wanted, which made my eyes burn, and then she had to put the color on. There was a lot of waiting, and holding still, and people staring at me, and more waiting for the end results. I opted for a few streaks in the front, and then a few more here and there throughout. Trish seemed to know what she was doing, so I trusted her enough to take charge.

She wouldn't let me see anything until she'd washed the dye out in Stryker's sink and blow-dried my entire head. I couldn't remember the last time I'd flat-ironed it. I'd sort of stopped doing a lot of that stuff. I also hadn't been tanning in forever. I used to go like clockwork, but it seemed like both a stupid and dangerous waste of money now.

"You're done, gorgeous," Trish said, turning me around.

"Let us see!" Lottie said, banging on the bathroom door.

"Well, it's . . . " I said, searching for the right word.

"Pink," Trish finished for me.

The girl looking back at me from the mirror looked . . . older? More . . . in charge? I tucked one of the streaks behind my ear and smiled. It was pink and it was *awesome*.

"My mom is going to freak." This couldn't be any worse than Kayla's tattoo. At least this wasn't permanent.

Lottie banged on the door again.

"I'm coming out," I said, looking once more in the mirror. There was something missing. I quickly fished in my bag for my glasses, after popping out my contacts. I always kept extra solution at Stryker's because he liked the glasses better than my contacts.

"Genius," Trish said when I put my glasses on. "It's like in those movies where the girl takes off her glasses and all of a sudden she's super hot. Only you're the opposite of that."

"Right," I said, trying to figure out if that was a compliment or an insult and deciding it was a compliment.

There was another bang on the door, so I took a deep breath, opened the door dramatically and struck a pose.

"Tada!" I was met with a round of applause and a kiss from Stryker.

"Hey, Pinky. You look amazing."

"Thanks."

Everyone said how good it looked and touched it and oohhhed and ahhhed. Even if it looked like crap, they probably would have done so with as much enthusiasm. They were also all starving, and would have done anything to hurry up the process so they could all go eat.

"Shoot. I think I left my phone back at the dorm," I said, after searching for it in my purse and my car. "I think it's on my desk. I'll go grab it and be right back, okay?"

Everyone was restless and hungry, but I promised I'd be back ASAP. Stryker offered to come with me, but I figured it was just an excuse to pull over somewhere so we could make out, and everyone was hungry enough as it was.

"I swear, I'll be right back and then we have aaallll night. Just think about that," I said, reaching my hand in his pocket and giving him a little squeeze when no one was looking.

"Fine," he said, his voice rough.

"Be back soon," I said, waving to everyone. They were all busy starting another round of the Picnic game. I shook my head and walked down the stairs.

***

I was so distracted by my new pink hair and thinking about moving in with Stryker that I almost didn't see him waiting outside the dorm's entrance.

"Katie."

I looked up and there he was, wearing a pressed shirt and expensive jeans, and a serious look I'd never seen before.

"Zack," I said, as if saying his name would make him disappear, like in a dream.

He didn't.

I stopped walking with at least twenty feet of space between us.

"What do you want from me? What are you doing here?" I fished in my purse for the pepper spray I'd gotten a while back, just in case of moments like this. I reached for it, but he didn't move closer to me. My hand brushed the Ziploc bag of Dad's ashes before I withdrew it.

"I just . . . shit, I practiced this."

I crossed my arms, tucking the pepper spray against my palm so he couldn't see it.

"Zack, you had your chances to say everything. I just want you to leave me alone." I tried to be stern, but my voice shook a little.

"I know, I know." He took a step closer, and I took one back.

"I just wanted to tell you that," he took a deep breath and looked up at me, his eyes clear. "I just wanted to tell you that I'm sorry, and that I'm getting help. I just wanted you to know that."

Part of me wanted to tell him that was great, but another, larger part wanted to tell him that it was too little, too late. He'd broken anything we had together beyond repair. The only hope I could have for him now was that he wouldn't do it to any other girls. That was the only hope I could ever have for him anymore.

"Good. Now you can leave me alone," I said.

"But . . . " He sort of reached toward me, but didn't step closer.

I put one hand up to stop him. "Look, you came to say what you needed to say. I'm going to go in the building right now and the next time you see me, it will be in court. Bye, Zack." He was standing between me and the building, but I wasn't going to let that stop me. He was never going to stand between me and anything else. Ever.

I started walking and was about to reach for the front door when he planted himself in front of me.

"But you're not hearing me, babe. I really need you to hear me. What did you do to your hair? And why are you wearing your glasses?" There it was. That word, and the desperation in his eyes. He reached for me, and that was it.

I simultaneously sprayed him and kneed him in the groin.

He screamed and dropped to the ground, and I went for the door as fast as I could, yanking it open and running for the stairs. It was unlikely he was going to follow me, but I wasn't going to take any chances. My hands shook as I unlocked my door and went for my phone, which was exactly where I thought it would be.

I gave the operator the details as I pushed several boxes of books she'd been packing up in front of the door and sat on them, heart pounding.

The operator told me that the cops were on their way, so I called Stryker.

"I thought you were going straight there and back. What's taking so long?" He tried to make his tone joking, but I could hear the worried edge in it. We didn't have twindar, but Stryker always seemed to worry about me when I wasn't with him. Maybe because of all the death that had been around us lately.

"Zack's here. I'm okay, though. He tried to touch me, but I pepper sprayed him and kicked him and now I'm in my room with the door locked. I called the cops and they're on their way. So I'm fine, really." My voice sounded like it didn't belong to me.

Stryker let forth a string of curses and I heard a commotion in the background.

"I'm coming to get you. Hold on. Just stay on the phone with me." He put his hand over the phone and I heard muffled talking. They were probably all coming to my rescue now. I listened to them with one ear and trained the other on the hallway. I'd told the cops which room I was in so they could find me.

"Are you still there?" Stryker said as I heard more chatter and car doors slamming.

"I'm here." Sort of.

Tires squealed. "Just stay with me, sweetheart. I will never let him hurt you."

"I know."

He said a bunch of other things, but I didn't hear most of them. I felt floaty, like a balloon that was only lightly tethered to the ground.

I waited and waited and waited.

Finally, voices sounded down the hall. Adult voices. Police voices. Then there was a banging on my door, followed but a flutter of other voices that I recognized.

"Katie?! Are you okay?" Stryker said, trying to open the locked door. Ah, that question that never had an answer. "Just tell me if you're in there, sweetheart."

"I'm here," I said, getting off the boxes and pushing them out of the way. I opened the door and was met by quite a group. Three cops and five friends.

"Oh, Katie," Stryker said, reaching out for me. I shook my head.

"I'm okay. I just . . . " I looked at all of them. "I want to fucking *kill* him, the bastard." My weird floaty feeling was gone, replaced with something that burned hotter and brighter.

Rage.

"Where is he?" I said to one of the cops. "I have a few things I'd like to tell him."

The cop looked at me with a stunned expression.

"We, uh, took him into custody. I don't think you should see him right now." He tried to put his hand on my shoulder, but I shrugged it off.

"No, I'm not done with him yet. I'm going to make him regret everything he did to me." I tried to lunge past the crowd, which wasn't the brightest thing to do because about six sets of arms were there to stop me.

"Let me go!" I said, trying to shove my way through and failing. "I'm going to make him wish he was never born." I growled, and another set of hands clasped my face, forcing me to look into a set of lovely green eyes.

"You already got him. You got him. He doesn't have any power over you. He never did. He is nothing. Nothing, compared to you, do you understand, Katie? He's nothing." He pulled me into his arms and whispered the last part into my ear as he crushed me into his chest.

"Nothing, nothing, nothing." Rocking me back and forth, he said it over and over. I was sure the cops were giving us strange looks, but they stepped back.

"I hate him," I whispered into his pounding heart.

"I know, I know. I hate him too. The only reason I'm not killing him for you is because I'm holding you. You're the only thing keeping me from making a big mistake and ending up in jail." His voice shook a little as the cops talked back and forth about what to do. I knew from experience that I'd have to give a statement and so forth. It was going to be a long night. I wished I could rewind and go back to when I was so excited about my hair.

Stryker held me for as long as it took for both of us to calm down enough that we didn't both bolt.

"Can I give my statement tomorrow? I'm really tired," I said to one of the cops.

He said something into his radio. "Are you sure? It's best to get everything while it's fresh in your mind."

"Oh, it will still be fresh tomorrow."

"Are you sure?" I appreciated his concern, but I couldn't do it tonight.

I nodded. "Yes. I just want to go home with my boyfriend." I squeezed Stryker's hand.

"Okay, well just come in tomorrow when you're ready. He's not going to be bothering you anymore tonight." He gave me his card and I thanked them for their quick response.

We all stood silently in the hallway. Then Simon's stomach growled so loud we all heard it.

He blushed. "What? My stomach didn't know there was a crisis. I can't help it."

"Sorry guys," I said, leaning against Stryker.

"Are you kidding? What do you have to be sorry for?" Simon said. "I'm sorry about my stomach. Shut up stomach," he said, tilting his head down as if he was talking to it.

"Let's go back home and order pizza. What do you think?" Stryker said.

"Good idea," I said, letting him lead me back toward the stairs.

"If he ever lays a finger on you—" Stryker started to say.

"He won't. I'll break his hands off first," I said. "Nobody will ever make me feel that way again, least of all Zack."

I leaned my head on his shoulder. "That's my girl."

Thirty-one

Stryker

She put on a brave front, but I woke up in the middle of the night to find her whimpering in her sleep. I was still on edge about the whole thing, so I wasn't sleeping at all.

"Katie, wake up." I shook her shoulder and her eyes popped open.

Looking left and right she searched for me. "Whaaa?"

"You were dreaming, sweetheart. It's okay." She wiped her eyes and sat up.

"It's nothing. I'm fine."

"Do you want some tea or something?" I'd do anything I could to try to make it better, or at least not suck so much.

"Yeah, sure." She closed her eyes and sat back, breathing as if she'd just run a mile.

I made her some tea in the microwave and brought it back. She was messing with her hair.

"I'm sorry I woke you," she said as I handed her the mug.

"You didn't. I was already awake. I couldn't sleep after . . . everything."

She sipped the tea and moved so she could lean against me. I put my arm around her and my chin on the top of her head.

"I just feel like I'll never be free of him. That he's always going to be lurking in the back of my mind. He'll be that thing I'm afraid of when the house is quiet and I'm alone and I let my mind go to a dark place."

I sighed, wishing I knew what to say, what to do to change it. But we all had our demons, and we all carried them with us. That was just part of life.

"He's always going to be a part of you, of your past. It happened and in the absence of a time machine to go back and change things, that's always going to be the case. The only thing you can control is how you respond to it. There are so many people that wouldn't be able to pick themselves up after what you've been through. Those people wouldn't even bother to get out of bed, let alone give their heart to someone else after what he did to it. But you did. You do. Every day. And that's all you can do. Be strong, move forward."

"You and me," she said, turning to give me a kiss.

"Even without me. You are strong, and you will survive. Always."

"But I'd rather do it with you."

I kissed her back. "Me too."

***

The alarm rang much too early, but I did end up getting some sleep, wrapped around Katie. Both of us had class, but we skipped to go make her statement. She figured that was a valid excuse, and I concurred. We also dodged calls and texts from the group, asking how we were, and we were somehow able to sneak past Lottie and Zan's new apartment without them being the wiser.

"They're so sweet, and they mean well. There's just so many of them," Katie said as we got back in her car after giving her statement.

"I've never had this many people concerned about my welfare before. It's stifling." She nodded. "Hey, do you want me to drop you off at class?"

She shook her head.

"We're just doing reviews in most of my classes, so I don't really need to be there. What about you?"

"Same." A smile started growing on her face. "What did you have in mind?"

"Just a little something. I'm going to be gone aaaallll weekend."

"I think I'm picking up what you're putting down and I like it." I smiled as she put her hand on mine on the shifter.

We couldn't get to the bedroom fast enough.

Katie

Mom's reaction to my hair wasn't nearly as dramatic as I expected. Before Dad died, it probably would have been. Her eyes just went wide and she sighed and shook her head like when I was little and I spilled something.

I didn't tell her about Zack showing up at my dorm, but she found out anyway through the grapevine. Her reaction to that was more intense. So much so that she installed a security system, including a motion detector that turned on the outside lights. I thought it was overkill, but with her living alone, it probably wasn't such a bad idea.

I emailed Kayla and gave her the low down, and she messaged back right away that she was coming home early for Christmas and bringing Adam, and that they were going to take some time off and stay with mom for a few months. At least until the next semester was over and I'd be home for the summer.

Right. Home for the summer. I emailed Kayla back saying that was great. I had a whole other semester to figure out what I was going to do this summer. I'd worry about that later.

The rest of the weekend I spent picking up on the slack, including paying bills and doing a few loads of laundry.

I caught Mom crying over her wedding album just before I was due to leave and go back to school on Sunday night.

"Mom?" Most of the time I pretended like I didn't hear her crying because she worked so hard to hide it. I'd cried a little here and there, but nothing like I should be. Guess that denial thing was still going strong.

"Oh, I'm sorry." She shoved the album away and wiped her eyes with her hand.

"No, it's okay. You have every right to cry." I grabbed the newly-replenished tissues and handed them to her.

"I just keep expecting things to get better, you know?" She blew her nose and I sat down beside her, looking at the pictures of my then-young parents, gazing adoringly at each other. They'd had their tough times, but I never doubted their love for one another.

"Everyone says it will get better, but I still feel like a part of me is missing."

"That's because a part of you is. When you love someone, you give them a little piece of yourself to keep. When they die, or they leave, they take it with them." Even Zack had taken a little bit of me with him. "When you lose someone, you have to learn how to live without that missing piece."

She sighed and blew her nose again.

"When did you get so smart?"

"Just recently." I took the used tissue from her and chucked it in the trash, closing the album with my other hand. "Listen, I have to get back, but I'll be here for break next week. All I have are finals, and then I'll be home, and Kayla will be here, okay?"

"You don't have to take care of me." She slid the album back into its place on her dresser.

"Of course I do." I got up and gave her a hug. "You're my mother."

"I just can't imagine what Christmas is going to be like. I don't even want to think about it. Nothing's going to be the same."

"I know."

She hugged me back and then touched my hair.

"Pink, huh? It looks cute on you." She ran some of the newly-pink hair through her fingers. I was still getting used to it, but I was still thrilled with how it turned out. I felt more . . . me with it.

"Thanks."

Mom let out a sigh, pushing my hair over my shoulders.

"So, is that boy going to be around? The one that brought you to the hospital?"

Mom still couldn't remember his name.

"Stryker?"

She nodded.

"Is he allowed to be around?"

"Well, I just thought that you said he didn't have a place to go for Thanksgiving, so he might not have a place to go at Christmas, and he was so great when everything happened that you might want to invite him over." She put on a smile as I tried to figure out if it was opposite day.

"I'll, um, I'll ask him." It hadn't occurred to me to even ask Mom if he could come. Stryker and I hadn't talked about Christmas plans, mostly on purpose because I knew he didn't really have anywhere else to go. Trish was teaming up with Lottie again, and everyone else had somewhere too.

"Thanks, Mom. I love you."

"Love you too, baby."

***

Winter dropped the hammer down on us with a vengeance and we had snowstorm after snowstorm, causing classes to be cancelled right before finals. Stryker called off Band, but the rest of our crew braved the bad weather and came over instead.

"You still owe me dinner out," I said as we popped two pizzas into the oven.

"I'm aware, I'm aware. I just don't know if they're going to let us back into Caroline's, ever, and that's the nicest place that's close."

"You don't have to take me to the nicest place. Just a place with food and a decent atmosphere."

"But I want to give you fancy," he said, pouting a little. Damn, that was sexy.

I set the timer and turned around.

"I don't need fancy. I just need you."

He leaned in to kiss me just as the door burst open, bringing with it arctic air and the rest of our snow-covered crew.

"Son of a bitch, it's cold out there," Trish said, blowing on her non-gloved hands.

"Hon, you should wear gloves," Max said, taking her hands in his and rubbing them.

"Yeah, yeah."

Stryker had almost gotten over the fact that his sister was dating Max, but every now and then I caught him giving Max a look like he wanted to disembowel him for touching Trish.

"Be nice," I said, brushing my fingers across his chest. "He could be your future brother-in-law."

Stryker shuddered.

"There's something I don't want to think about for at least twenty years."

"Good luck with that," I said, watching Trish and Max giving each other googly eyes.

I still hadn't asked him about Christmas. I wasn't sure why, exactly. Maybe I was afraid that he'd feel obligated to come, and I really didn't know how things were going to go, with Dad gone. There was a very good chance Mom was going to go to a really dark place and it would be one giant disaster. He'd seen enough of my family disasters to last a lifetime.

Stryker beat me to the punch.

"How do you think your mom's going to do? With Christmas and everything?"

He handed me a beer from the fridge, grabbing one for himself.

"Results are inconclusive. It could go either way." I popped the top and took a sip as everyone else piled in, bringing bags of groceries. "But, um, you are invited to come. You know, only if you want."

He paused with the bottle halfway to his lips.

"Really? I don't want to impose or anything. I know this is a hard time—" I interrupted him.

"No, no, not at all. I'd love to have you there. You were so good before, and . . . it would suck a lot less with you around."

He smiled at me. "Good."

"Good." I raised my beer and he clinked it with his.

Thirty-two

Stryker

I'd been nervous for Thanksgiving with Katie's family, but that was nothing to how I felt about Christmas.

"Should I bring a tie? Do you think I should bring a tie?" I said to Katie as I packed a bag. I was only planning on staying for a week or so, to feel things out, even though our winter break was nearly a month long. I didn't want to overstay my welcome.

"You are being way too neurotic," Katie said, leaning on my suitcase so I couldn't put anything more in it. "No one is going to care if you wear a tie, although, I like that black thin one you have in your closet."

I went and grabbed the only black skinny tie I owned.

"This one?"

"That's the one." She took it from me, folded it and placed it in the suitcase. "I think you need to be done now." She zipped it shut and lay on top of it so I couldn't access it, even if I wanted to.

"Why are you so nervous? You've been to my house a bunch of times. You've seen us at our worst and still came out alive."

"That was . . . different. I was there because I had a place to fill. You were so sad and I wanted to be there for you. But you don't need me like that anymore. You're strong enough."

I shrugged.

Katie got up from our bed and stood in front of me, a little smile on her face.

"You're an idiot. You're. An. Idiot." I'd said the exact same thing to her once. "I do need you. I need you because sometimes I feel like you're the one thing that holds me together. I start thinking about all the bad things in my life and then I think of you, and all the bad things don't seem so bad anymore."

I put my arms around her.

"But the real question is, should I bring another tie?"

***

This time, Katie drove, and we didn't need a GPS. I also had her hand in mine. She had to take it slow as a few snowflakes drifted down and melted as quick as they hit the pavement.

"You think we're going to get a white Christmas?" she said, dropping her speed down as the snow got heavier. Pretty soon it would start to stick. I just hoped we got there before that happened. I didn't exactly trust the Mazda's ability to navigate a snowy road.

"That would be nice. Haven't had one of those in a long time," I said, peering up at the grey sky.

"When I was a kid and it snowed, Dad used to take this thing and make reindeer footprints on the lawn. That was how I discovered that Santa wasn't real. I caught him doing them one night. He was so upset that year."

I loved hearing about her Christmas memories. They beat the hell out of mine.

"I guess there won't be anyone to do it now."

"Why can't you do it?"

"I don't know. I guess I could."

"Make you a deal. If it snows, we'll go out and do it together." I squeezed her hand and she squeezed back.

"Deal."

***

The other thing that gave me pause was Katie's Christmas present. I had two, actually. One to give her in front of her family and one that I'd give her in private. I'd made both of them, and I was beyond nervous that she'd like them. One could be construed as semi-creepy, and that was the one I was going to give her when we were alone.

I had no idea what she had planned for me, but I knew she was up to something, because I'd caught her whispering on the phone when she thought I was doing something else. I didn't really care if she gave me anything. Having her safe and in my arms was enough.

"Well hello again," Kayla said, opening the door and giving Katie a huge hug. As soon as they let go, Kayla grabbed me and gave me one too. Well that was unexpected.

"Hey, man," Adam said, giving me a handshake.

"Oh my God," Katie said, staring at Kayla.

"What?" she said, giving Adam a nervous look that he shared. I looked at Kayla, but didn't get it.

"You're pregnant," Katie said, removing her hand from her mouth. "You are freaking pregnant!"

"Keep your voice down," Kayla said, grabbing Katie's arm and yanking us back out on the porch. I had no choice but to follow, and Adam closed the door behind us.

"I haven't told mom yet, you moron. Besides, we just found out. How did you even know?"

"Look at you." She looked exactly the same to me. I even let my eyes travel to her stomach, but it looked just as flat as ever. "I can totally see it."

"Where?" Kayla flattened her shirt over her stomach.

"Right there." Katie pointed to an invisible bump that only she could see.

"If it's any consolation, I can't see anything," I said as Kayla smoothed her hands over the invisible bump.

"I told her that, but she's been paranoid," Adam said. "I'm telling you, sweetie, you can't see anything." He put his hands around her and kissed the side of her face.

"Well, congratulations anyway," I said, poking Katie, who was still gaping at Kayla.

"Thanks," Adam said. "We didn't plan it, but then some of the best things are unplanned, aren't they?"

"Amen to that," I said.

Katie still seemed like she was in shock.

"You're pregnant?" she whispered, looking at Kayla.

"Yeah, I am." Kayla said, starting to cry. "You're gonna be an auntie."

Then Katie burst into tears and they hugged and cried and laughed. Adam and I just looked at each other. Sometimes there was no understanding the Hallman women. Didn't mean we wouldn't try.

The front door opened and Mrs. Hallman poked her head out.

"What are you all doing out here? What's wrong?" She was immediately alarmed because of the tears.

Kayla sighed and looked at Adam.

"Well, I was going to wait until Christmas, but I guess now is a good a time as any." She took Adam's hand and pulled him close. "We're going to have a baby." She beamed and waited for the reaction.

"You're pregnant?" Mrs. Hallman clutched her chest and looked like she was going to faint. Katie reached out and grabbed her so she didn't fall. "Oh my God, you're *pregnant*?" Like daughters, like mother, she burst into tears and threw herself at Kayla and at Adam. Lots more tears and hugging ensued.

"So you're happy?" Kayla said. "I know we're not married . . ."

"Oh, who cares?! I'm going to be a grandmother. Oh, Kayla! Come on, let's get you into the house."

"Mom, I'm fine."

"The cold isn't good for you, come on." Rolling her eyes behind her mother's back, Kayla let herself be led inside and the rest of us followed.

Unlike Thanksgiving, the house was nearly bare of decorations. There was an undecorated tree, and not much else, which surprised me. Or maybe it wasn't surprising, giving the absence of Mr. Hallman.

Mrs. Hallman led Kayla into the kitchen and forced her to sit down and have some tea, before slamming her with questions about the baby and how far along she was and everything else. Katie and I slipped away so I could get my things and put them in her room. She'd said that it would be okay for me to stay in her room, but I wasn't going to hold my breath. I could always bunk down in the basement if I had to.

"Kayla's a big one for the surprises, isn't she? First it was the engagement, now this."

"Yeah, I can't believe it. I knew she wanted kids, but I'm pretty sure it wasn't this soon." She sat down on her bed, lay back and closed her eyes. "I wonder if this means she's going to come home. That would be good."

"Yeah, it would take some of the pressure off you."

"I shouldn't even think of it as pressure. I shouldn't think of it that way. I should want to do it. She's my mom, Stryker."

"I know, I know." I lay down next her, squishing myself against her on the twin bed. "Listen, I have a present for you, but I wanted to give it to you when it was just the two of us. I know it's not Christmas, but I want to give it to you now, if that's ok."

She turned on her side to face me, smiling.

"Okay. Give it to me."

"Geez, demanding much?" I bit her shoulder as I got up and fished in my bag. I'd pre-wrapped her presents in paper I'd drawn on myself.

"Stryker. It's so pretty." I'd duplicated a lot of the drawings I'd made on her body. "I almost don't want to unwrap it. Almost."

I sat down beside her and tried not to freak out as she slowly unpeeled the wrapping from her present.

"Oh, Stryker." She revealed a wooden box that I'd painted on. Then she turned it and saw what the painting was. "Oh my God."

"I may or may not have stolen that picture from your house last time I was here."

I'd painted a picture of her father on the top of the box, from a photograph that I'd commandeered from an album last time I was at her house. I had the feeling I'd need it at some point, even if it was just to give to her. Mr. Hallman sat on the recliner and smiled, waving at the camera. It must have been taken quite a few years ago, because his hair was definitely darker than when I'd met him.

She opened the velvet-lined box and brushed the inside.

"I thought you could use something better than a Ziploc bag. And you can close it and carry it around with you. See?" I pointed to the little lock on the front of it.

"This is . . . this is one of the sweetest and most creepy things anyone has ever done for me."

"Is it more on the sweet side or more on the creepy side?" I was hoping for the former.

"It's a little bit of both, but I absolutely love it. Thank you so much." She reached for her purse and took out the bag of ashes that she always carried with her, putting them in the box and locking it shut. She smiled down at the portrait on the front.

"Now he's with me all the time."

I put my arm around her.

"Exactly." I wiped a tear from her cheek. "Merry Christmas, sweetheart."

Thirty-three

Katie

After Kayla's announcement and Stryker's present, things were sort of uneventful. Mom had flipped the nice switch and treated Stryker like he was a member of the family. She even asked about him and they had an entire civilized conversation, which was crazy.

"I think she likes you," I said that night as we lay in bed. Mom had given me a look when I'd said we were going to bed, but she hadn't said anything as Stryker followed me.

"Well, that's a nice step up from loathing me, so I'll take it." He was busy drawing on my arm.

"So you gave me a present, so I'm going to give you one." He'd been pretty sneaky with his, but I was pretty sure he had no idea about mine.

"It doesn't involve you getting naked, docs it?" He raised his eyebrows suggestively.

"Uh, no. That's not a present. That's a normal night."

"It's a gift, as far as I'm concerned."

I rolled my eyes and went to get my bag.

"So the wrapping isn't as pretty as yours, seeing as how I can't make my own, but it's the thought that counts, right?" I'd found wrapping paper online that was covered in musical instruments, and I'd used it for all his presents.

I wanted to just tear the paper off for him, but I let him slowly unwrap it until he got down to the box. He popped it open and took out the card inside, reading it slowly.

"It's a gift certificate for the art supply place. It's not a box for your parents' ashes with their faces painted on it, but I thought you could get some really good supplies and—"

He looked up from the card and stopped my flow of words with a kiss.

"I love it, and I love you. So, so much. It's perfect."

"I love you too, best friend. There's another little something under that card." He pulled out the second part of that gift. It was one of those hokey charms that was half of the heart, and it said 'Best' on it.

"I've got the other one," I said, pulling the chain out from under my shirt, showing him the other half that said, 'Friend'. I was surprised he hadn't noticed it yet. "You don't have to wear it as a necklace or anything, if that's emasculating."

He pulled it out and slipped it around his neck.

"My best friend gave me this. Just try and take it off me." He held onto it, daring me.

"Never," I said, shaking my head.

And now a sneak peek at No Attachments, now available from author Tiffany King!

Chapter 1: Why lightweights shouldn't drink

Ashton

"Come on, go," my friend, Tressa said, trying to push me out of my chair. "What good is a bucket list if you're too chicken to do any of it?"

"Zip it," I said out of the corner of my mouth as I apprehensively eyed the situation in front of me. It seemed like a good idea on paper, but actually committing to it suddenly made me nauseous. I took a long pull from my beer, hoping that would help calm my nerves. "God, that's disgusting." I grimaced as the foul liquid poured down my throat. "I don't know how people drink this crap," I complained, slamming the bottle back down on the table a little harder than I should have.

"You're stalling, Ash. Besides, this was your idea. Pick up a random stranger and bang his socks off," Tressa quipped. "You need to seize the opportunity before someone else does, otherwise you'll be SOL, and your only choice will be Old Man Jones over there," she added, making our friend Brittni snort loudly.

"Shush," I said, elbowing her in the gut. Tressa had one volume level—loud. Her words traveled from our table to the many other patrons throughout the only bar in this sleepy little town. Joe's was the hotspot here in Woodfalls, and Friday was your only good chance to meet someone if you were single and on the prowl because Saturday was family karaoke night.

"Ow, bitch," Tressa said, rubbing her stomach. "It's not like the grumpy old fart can hear us anyway," she said loudly in his direction.

"Gahhhh, shush, Tressa. He's going to hear you," I said, sliding back down in my seat.

"Chillax, drama queen. He doesn't even have his hearing aid in. Watch," she said, shooting me a mischievous grin. "Hey, Mr. Jones, I really want to blow you," she said loudly.

She managed to get the attention of about a dozen guys with that one, including Mr. Jones, who whirled around, studying us with his beady black eyes. His grey bushy eyebrows came together in a unibrow that looked like a giant caterpillar on his forehead.

Brittni snorted again as she shook with laughter. I squirmed uncomfortably on the hard wooden bench, fighting the urge to point at Tressa like we were in kindergarten and had gotten busted for throwing spitballs or something.

Tressa returned his stare head-on, smiling sardonically until he turned back around.

"Sheesh, girl, you're lucky he didn't take you up your offer," I said, stifling my own laughter.

"Hey, you never know what he's sportin' in those dusty old overalls." Tressa winked.

"Gross," I shrieked.

Tressa just shrugged, unconcerned. I couldn't help admiring her self-assuredness. She didn't care what people thought about her. She was loud and seriously inappropriate, but hilarious as hell, despite the tight leash her boyfriend tried to keep her on. We'd only been friends for four months, but I had grown quite fond of her in the short period of time. Both she and Brittni had welcomed me into their friendship circle without a second thought. They acted like I belonged. Not because they felt sorry for me or pitied me like everyone else had done for so many years, but because they genuinely seemed to like me. Brittni wasn't as flamboyant or inappropriate as Tressa, but she had a wickedly dry sense of humor that kept people on their toes. And then there was me. I wasn't completely sure what I brought to the group, but that's why I was here. Somewhere over the last five years, I'd forgotten who I really was.

"Alright, time to stop stalling. Get off your ass and pick up that tall, dark, he-can-have-my-panties-any-day seximist," Tressa said pointedly, looking at the stranger we'd been eyeing for the last fifteen minutes.

"Maybe I should do something else on my list," I said, pulling a rumpled slip of paper out of my bag while desperately trying to ignore the butterflies that had suddenly decided to hang out in my stomach. I gently smoothed out the creases as I contemplated the items scrawled on the paper.

"You're kidding, right? This town has a population of like negative ten, and he's the hottest thing to walk in here in forever. When are you going to have the opportunity to have one night of hot wild sex with a stranger like that again?"

"That's my point. Don't you find it a little weird that we don't know this guy? This town is pretty much off the beaten path. He could be some mass murder. How do you know he wouldn't put my head in his freezer or something?"

"Sweetheart, after a night with him, you'll want a freezer to cool you off," Tressa said, eyeing him with open admiration. "Besides, if you don't make your move, I'm totally claiming him," she added, adjusting her shirt so the tops of her ample breasts peaked out from the thin camisole she was wearing under her button-up see-through shirt.

"So, you wouldn't mind that you don't know him and that he could very well chop up your body into a million pieces? Not to mention what Jackson would say if he found out," I said, reminding her of her boyfriend.

"Wow, seriously, chill, Ash. She's just trying to give you a spark. Besides, you were a stranger here once too, and you didn't show your true crazy for a couple days," Brittni teased. "Now get up there and sex that possible serial killer up."

"You two are a riot," I said, choking down the last of my beer that tasted like elephant piss, or at least what I would assume elephant pee would taste like. "Alright, wish me luck," I added, finally sliding out of the booth. "If he chops me up into little pieces, neither of you get those boots of mine you want so bad," I threatened. I made my way up to the counter where the object of our interest was perched. Considering my shaky legs, I wasn't exactly as subtle as a prowling jungle cat. Tressa was right. Finding a perfect candidate for a one-night stand was slim to none in a town the size of Woodfalls. Strangers were far and few between. Couple that with the fact that he was drop-dead gorgeous and his sudden appearance was like a gift from god. Not that good-looking was a prerequisite. The only requirement I had set was that he know nothing about me or my past. I wanted one night where someone wanted me for me, not because they felt sorry for me.

"Hey, Joe, can I get a shot?" I asked, sliding onto the barstool next to the tall-dark-panty-dropping-worthy hunk.

"Sure thing, Ashton. How'd you like your beer?" Joe asked, drying a small shot glass with a cotton towel he had tucked into his apron.

"It tasted like pee," I confessed.

Joe threw his head back as a loud roar of laughter erupted out of him. "Drink a lot of pee, do you?" he asked.

I opened my mouth to answer him sarcastically when the object of my fascination let out a low rumble of laughter. Seizing my opportunity, I gulped down the bourbon Joe had placed in front of me and swiveled around to face the stranger next to me. The liquor burned its way down my throat, leaving a fiery trail all the way to my belly, but it was eclipsed by the liquid fire that burned through me when my eyes finally met his.

"Can I get you another?" he asked softly in a radio DJ-like voice that you would hear on a lonely Saturday night, encouraging listeners to call in with their favorite weepy love songs.

"Sure." I eyed my empty glass as my body responded to his sexier-than-sin voice. I was a sucker for a deep voice — or an accent, especially British or Australian accents. Neither though, could compare to his rich deep voice that seemed to vibrate through me. I realized in that instant I had left a crucial item off my bucket list. Having an intimate conversation with someone with a voice like his should have topped my list.

"You all right?" he asked, looking bemused as Joe placed another shot in front of me. I started to answer his question and mentally kicked myself when I realized I'd been staring at him like he was a tall glass of water on a hot summer day. Matter of fact, I was about ninety-nine point nine percent sure I may have licked my lips in anticipation.

"Absolutely. How 'bout you?" I asked, trying for a seductive throaty voice that just went wrong. "Thanks for the drink," I added, sucking down the liquid confidence in an attempt to calm my frazzled nerves.

His bemused expression turned to outright amusement as he took in my watery eyes that had resulted from my quick gulping of the whiskey shot. "Another?" he asked with raised eyebrows.

"Why not," I answered, though the room was already tilting slightly. I could count on one hand the amount of times I'd actually had a drink growing up. They all centered on the time my life had slipped drastically off course. I'd gone hog wild for a couple of weeks until I realized drowning my sorrows in alcohol only made me sick, and didn't solve anything anyway. After that it wasn't a viable option. Needless to say, my time in high school and college had been pretty lackluster.

Tall, Dark and Dreamy chuckled softly beside me as he flagged down Joe for another round. Holding up his own shot glass, he waited until I raised mine to meet his, and then winked at me as we clinked glasses. "Damn," my breath hitched. I was a sucker for winking too. Something about it made my stomach tighten up in anticipation and my breath quicken. Not to mention having Mr. Seximist behind the wink made other areas tighten up too, while a certain other area began to throb. It took me a moment to distinguish the throbbing as desire. My one and only sexual encounter had been four years ago, after prom, and it didn't last long enough to ever cross over into the desire category. It was the means to an end. I had wanted to feel normal just for one night, and by the end of the dance, I finally coaxed Shawn Johnson into ending my virgin status once and for all. He'd resisted the idea at first, but my constant touches and whispered comments finally muddled his brain enough that he caved. The actual act lasted less than two minutes and hurt like a bitch, but in the end, I was glad I'd gone through with it.

It was ironic that one wink by Mr. Voice had me crossing my legs in an attempt to distill the ache that was slowly beginning to radiate between my legs. He'd managed to excite me more in three minutes of flirting than Shawn had done in an entire evening of slow dancing, grinding and sloppy kisses.

I was pulled away from my thoughts by a low chuckle. "Son of a bitch, not again," I thought, blanching inwardly. He busted me gawking at him like a lovesick teenager again. "Okay, pull it together," I reminded myself. "Focus on why you're here." I welcomed the warm buzz from yet another shot of bourbon and the uncharacteristic confidence that came with it. Licking the last drop of amber liquid off my bottom lip, I watched with satisfaction as his eyes settled on my lips. I could do this.

"You know, you keep winking at girls like that and one of them is bound to take it as an invitation," I said.

"Sweetheart, I only wink at the girls I'm interested in," he answered smoothly, tipping his own glass to his lips.

The desire I had been trying in vain to control unfurled inside me, making my nipples harden beneath the black lace bra I had the uncanny foresight to don that evening. The dull ache between my legs morphed into a steady throbbing that even my crossed legs could not ease.

"Is that so?" I asked, arching my eyebrow in what I hoped was a seductive manor.

"It's a fact, sweetheart," he whispered close to my ear.

I clamped my lips together so I wouldn't embarrass myself by moaning out loud as his warm breath rustled the hair at the nape of my neck. I resisted the urge to sweep my long dark hair out of the way to give him more access.

"You're pretty cocky," I said as he signaled Joe for another round. My head was already spinning, but I figured another one couldn't hurt.

"Not cocky, sweetheart, confident," he answered huskily, reaching for our drinks with one hand when Joe brought them over.

I reached over to relieve him of my glass, but before I could retract my hand with my drink in it, he snagged my pinkie with his. Looking at our now linked hands, I watched as he slowly raised my hand to his mouth. I gripped the glass tightly as he brushed his lips across my knuckles before releasing my hand.

Suddenly, the drink felt ten times heavier with the sudden absence of his hand. I worked to keep the glass upright in my shaky hand as I raised it to my lips. Gulping the contents, I set the glass down and took in his slightly blurred features.

"You okay?" he asked as I swayed slightly on my barstool.

"Absolutely. I do this all the time," I lied.

"I'm sure," he mocked, softly signaling Joe for another round.

"You can bank—" my retort was cut short when my cellphone chirped in my purse.

"I need to use the ladies' room," I breathed, rising unsteadily to my feet as the floor tilted slightly beneath me. "I'll be right back."

"Do you need some help?" he asked, cocking his eyebrow at me.

"Um, I'm pretty sure I know how to pee on my own," I answered, feeling flustered.

He chuckled. "I meant getting to the bathroom. You looked like you were a bit unsteady there."

"I'm good," I clarified before strutting away. It took all my willpower to keep my gait steady as I made my way across the scuffed wooden floors to the bathroom. Tressa and Brittni were leaning against the bathroom counter waiting for me when I entered. It was all part of the plan we had set up. They were here for the status update.

"So, is he a serial killer?" Brittni asked as I headed for one of the stalls.

"Hold on, I really do have to pee."

"He looks like he's into you," she added, switching on the faucet so I could pee in peace.

"Of course he's into her. She's smoking hot," Tressa interrupted. "I bet he's already suffering from a case of blue balls," she added laughing as I heard the smacking of flesh.

"Do you always have to be so crude?" Brittni asked disgusted as I flushed the toilet and opened the stall door.

"He's not the only one," I muttered, filling the palm of my hand with soap before sticking them under the faucet that was still running.

"Ooh, things a little damp downstairs?"

"Oh my god, Tressa, seriously?" Brittni said, taking another swipe at her.

"That's one way to say it. Put it this way, he'd slide in pretty damn easy right now if you know what I mean," I giggled, bracing my hands on the counter as the floor beneath me continued to sway.

"You okay, slick?" Brittni asked, really looking at me for the first time since I'd entered the bathroom.

"Fine," I answered, moving my eyes from the slow rolling floor.

"She's buzzing," Tressa crowed, taking in my glassy eyes and flushed cheeks.

"I sure am," I cracked up, not entirely sure why I found it so funny.

"Are you sure you're up for this, you lightweight?" Brittni asked, placing her hands on my shoulders so she could study me critically.

"I'm fine, Mom," I teased. "I just decided to take the liquid courage route."

"So, you're going through with it?" she asked, looking worried.

"Duh, that was the plan," Tressa chastised.

"I know, but I thought she'd chicken out," Brittni retorted like I wasn't even there.

"Hey, standing right in front of you," I said, waving my hands exuberantly in front of them like I was trying to land a plane or something to that effect. "Besides, I have to do it, it's on my list," I pointed out.

"Right, it's on your list. I still think it's ridiculous for someone our age to have a bucket list."

"I told you a million times. It's for a study I'm doing for the master's program I'm hoping to get into," I lied, smiling brightly at her. "It's a study on living life to its fullest in a limited time frame."

"So you've said a hundred times. I just think a study on males that have the best pecks or dreamiest eyes would have been more productive."

"That's so cliché and overdone. Having a nice six-pack usually translates to 'conceited asshole,'" I answered, sweeping the lip gloss Tressa handed me across my lips. "Thanks," I told her, handing the wand back. I tried not to focus on the irony of my new friends having no qualms about sharing their makeup with me. Back home, most people refused to touch anything I had touched. They were all assholes. What I had wasn't contagious.

"You better get back out there before Mr. Blue Balls thinks you ditched him," Tressa interrupted, giving my back a light shove toward the bathroom door. "Text us if he turns out to be an asshole."

"And make sure he bags his junk," Brittni piped in.

Giggling at their advice, I twisted around before exiting the bathroom and threw my arms impulsively around both their necks. "I love you guys," I said, knocking their heads together from my exuberance.

"Okay, we love you too," Brittni complained, trying to extract my arms.

"Yep, she's toasted," Tressa commented, rubbing her head where it had knocked against Brittni's.

"Maybe we should hang around to make sure she doesn't embarrass herself," Brittni mused.

"No way, you guys promised," I reminded them. "If I'm doing this, I'm going in without a safety net.

"Fine, but your scrawny ass better text us first thing tomorrow morning, or we're sending out the armed forces to take down Mr. Seximist," Brittni warned, giving me a quick hard hug.

"Don't worry, Brit, he looks harmless enough. Besides, I've taken at least twenty pictures on my phone. We'll nail that bastard's ass to the wall if he hurts her," Tressa said from behind me as I pushed open the bathroom door.

"Don't worry, my head will make a beautiful mantle piece," I threw over my shoulder as I sashayed across the room toward the bar.

"Hey stranger," I said, boldly sliding onto my barstool.

"Whoa there," Mr. Hotness said as my ass misjudged the middle of the seat and teetered on the edge, making the legs of the stool wobble. Hotness reached over and grasped my arm to steady me.

"You're hot."

"Why thank you," he said chuckling.

"I mean, your hands are hot...no, I mean, your touch is hot...shit. Never mind," I mumbled as he chuckled next to me.

"It's not the first time I've been called hot, sweetheart."

"Vanity isn't a virtue," I pointed out, picking up the shot glass that had magically filled itself in my absence. "So, what do you do Mr. I Know I'm Hot?" I asked, realizing that in all our flirting we'd neglected to exchange names.

"Nathan," he answered, holding out his hand for me to shake.

"Ashton," I parroted as his hand engulfed mine. His touch was sure and sensual at the same time, making my poor hand feel bereft once he let go.

"I'm a freelance journalist."

"Freelance journalist? What does that entail?" I asked intrigued.

"Lots of traveling and a knack for being able to dig out the truth. I've been fortunate enough to be able to pick my assignments," he answered, turning on his barstool to face me. His knees knocked against mine, which my body was keenly aware of as our legs settled, intimately touching each other. "I'm actually on my way to my next assignment. What about you?"

"Right now, I'm working at Smith's General Store over on the corner of Main and Stetson," I answered defensively, waiting for his judgments. I didn't bother to mention the barely dried ink on my B.A. in Human Psychology, or the fact that up until four months ago, I had been planning my internship at the local hospital back home. Those were need-to-know facts that he didn't need to know.

"I think I met the owner when I arrived today. Fran, right? She's quite an old card," he replied warmly, surprising me.

"Yeah, she is. Don't let her age fool you. She's sharper than people a quarter of her age. That store has been in her family for more than a hundred years. Each generation it's passed down to the next. Fran should have passed it down like fifteen years ago, but she claims hell will freeze over before she allows her 'sniveling, no-good, lazy nephew to run it into the ground.' She says she reckons she'll stay until she breathes her last breath or her nephew finally decides to man up. She says she won't be holding her breath on the latter…" I rambled on. Obviously, the multiple shots had turned my tongue into a nonstop chattering mess.

"That sounds like the person I met," he said, chuckling softly. "So, have you lived here all your life?" he asked as Joe set another round in front of us.

Running my finger around the small base of the shot glass, I weighed his question, contemplating how I wanted to answer. "No. I moved here four months ago after my dad died," I lied, giving him the standard answer I'd given everyone else when I moved to town.

"Really?" he asked, studying me critically.

I was slightly taken aback by his response. I'd been greeted with nothing but sympathy when I'd let the lie slip on previous occasions. I always felt a twinge of guilt over it, but knew in the end it was necessary. "It was quite sudden," I answered defensively.

"I'm sorry for your loss," he replied, finally offering up the words that I had grown accustomed to hearing.

"Thanks," I said, not sure if his sympathy was genuine. Maybe he really was some psycho who traveled through small towns collecting heads and storing them in his trunk. I sucked down the contents of my glass once again. My brain was teetering on the edge of remaining focused on the noticeably rock-hard pecs beneath his shirt and becoming drowned by the liquor party that was flowing through my bloodstream. My tongue became numb while the buzzing in my head intensified, making me wish I could rest it on the bar. I contemplated climbing up on the bar so I could lie down, but even that seemed like way too much work. Instead, I tried to focus on my last coherent thought, knowing it had something to do with my head.

"Are you going to put your trunk in my head?" I asked, finally able to make my tongue work.

"Excuse me?" he asked amused.

"Wait. I mean, are you going to put your trunk in me?" I asked, though the question still seemed slightly off.

"Is that what the kids are calling it now?" he asked with open amusement.

"Wait. What did I say?" I asked, shaking my head in a feeble attempt to clear it.

"Well, darling, you asked if I was going to stick my trunk in you. Is that an invitation?"

"Well, shit. I meant, are you going to put my head in your trunk?" I asked slowly, making sure the word placement was correct.

"Just your head?"

"Unless you keep the whole body, but won't your trunk get full if you keep the whole body?" I reasoned, pleased that I was able to form a coherent question even if it was related to my decapitation.

"I'm more a breast kind of guy," he said, smirking.

Laughter bubbled up out of me. "So, your trunk is full of boobies?" I asked, giggling uncontrollably.

"Boobies?" he snorted. "I haven't heard that word in like twenty years.

"Twenty years? How old are you?" I asked, giggling again at the idea that my one-night stand would be with an old man.

"Twenty-nine. What about you?"

"Twenty-nine? That's not old."

"Who said I was old?"

"Didn't you?" I asked confused on why I had thought he was old.

"I only said I haven't heard them called 'boobies' in twenty years. It's actually closer to sixteen years to be precise."

"So, 'boobies' is a thirteen-year-old-boy word?" I snickered again, not surprised at all. I'd been known to crack up over word choices for years. It was official. I had the mind of a thirteen-year-old boy.

After that, the conversation took on a hazy quality as Nathan ordered more drinks. I lost track of what my thirteen-year-old mind said, but I was pretty sure I asked Nathan to put his trunk in me again, which is what I was going for before the booze messed it up.

Chapter 2: The big head versus the little head

Nathan

I couldn't help contemplating my actions that evening as I carried her motionless body into the small cottage in the woods. If lightning struck me at that moment, I could see where it was justified. The moment I entered the bar, I seemed to ignore every rule I'd ever set. My rules were simple enough that a fucking two-year-old could follow them. Find my target, evaluate the situation, contact the parties concerned, find my target, evaluate the situation, contact the parties...I never deviated from this routine for a reason. I had a job to do. A job I was good at. A job free from personal attachments. It was a routine that suited me well. Of course, the delicate brunette I held in my arms contradicted all of it.

I shifted her slightly in my arms, suppressing a chuckle as she let out a loud snore when her head rolled backward over my arm. I pulled her more securely against my chest as I carried her through the only doorway into the cottage. I didn't want to admit to myself how much time I'd invested that evening thinking about what she would feel like pressed against me. Of course, carrying her like this wasn't the kind of pressing I had in mind. Her delicate frame made it easy to shoulder her weight, and she had a firm body, I could feel that even through her clothes. It'd be embarrassing as fuck right now if she woke up and saw the hard-on I had just from holding her. Unable to resist, I inhaled her heady perfume one last time before gently placing her on the bed. For a brief crazy moment, I considered crawling into bed next to her. It had been years since I'd felt the urge to actually stay in a bed with a woman any longer than it took to have sex with her. You couldn't call it "making love" since it was never intimate enough for that. Hell, it wasn't even "fucking" since even that required emotion. It was just sex. Nothing but two bodies coming together to scratch an itch.

I backed away from the bed and left the room before I could cave to the urge. She was an assignment, not a means to scratch an itch. Besides, it was a dick move to mix business with pleasure, and a threshold I never crossed. It was time for me to leave anyway. I had made contact with my target, and by tomorrow my job would be done. Instead of heading for the front door though, I walked to the far side of the room where a small functional kitchen was located. I'm not sure why I bothered going to the trouble, but I filled a glass with water and palmed the bottle of aspirin off the top of the refrigerator where it was sandwiched between a bag of powdered mini doughnuts and a stack of magazines. I focused on remaining professional as I returned to the room where the spitfire temptress was still snoring. Helping her through her given hangover would only make my job easier in the morning. It would help expedite the job. Glancing down at her unconscious body, I decided I might as well make her as comfortable as I could, so I sat the water and aspirin on the nightstand and got to work pulling off her jeans and shirt. "You're not a perv," I kept telling myself. "You're just trying to make her more comfortable." Of course, tell that to the other particular part of my body that was responding to her creamy smooth skin and brutal curves. With one last reluctant look and an apology to my painfully throbbing boys, I pulled the quilt over her and exited the room.

I locked the cottage door behind me and headed purposefully toward my trusty Range Rover before I could change my mind and climb between the crisp sheets with her.

The drive back to my hotel was short given the town's size. Two stop signs after pulling off the dirt road that led to Ashton's small but charming cottage, I pulled into the parking lot of the only hotel in town. It was actually more of a motel, but I guess they figured slapping the title of "hotel" onto the sign made it more legitimate. As long as the room was clean and the staff stayed out of my way, it suited my purposes. The last thing I needed was for some nosey maid to riffle through my papers and find out why I was really in town.

The hotel was cemetery quiet as I climbed out of the Range Rover and locked it behind me. The late hour combined with the stillness around me provided a ghost town-like aura. It felt strange to be out here in the middle of nowhere. Ever since I arrived here I'd been wondering why a rich girl like Ashton had picked this town to hide. I would have expected the glitzy lights of New York or the party atmosphere of Chicago to appeal to her, but instead she'd chosen Woodfalls. I'd seen her type over the years: rich, easily bored, with big time diva complexes. Woodfalls was too tame for someone like that.

I pushed the motel room door open with my foot after sliding the key into the lock, making sure the "Do Not Disturb" sign remained on the door. Once I switched on the lights, Ashton's face greeted me from the multiple images hanging on the wall. Each image depicted her in a different setting and pose, all courtesy of my client. Studying the pictures of her smiling, I couldn't help noting how the images didn't do her eyes justice. They couldn't capture the same sparkle I had witnessed earlier that evening. Just remembering how she'd smiled at me with her bright shiny eyes made me want her even more.

"This is ridiculous," I thought, shaking my head in disgust. I backed up to the edge of my bed and sank down onto the sagging mattress. What the hell was I doing? Lusting after a target was unacceptable. I was hired to make contact, observe, and report back to my client. That was it. I wasn't hired to sniff at her ass like a dog in heat — no matter how appealing that might be.

Striding to the bathroom, I stripped off my clothes in aggravation and cranked the shower to its coldest setting, hoping a cold shower would shock my system. Five minutes later, I stood with a towel around my waist, glaring at the traitor between my legs. It's not like I was sexually deprived. Something about Ashton just appealed to me. Well, not just something. It was everything. She was smoking hot.

My cellphone vibrated on the nightstand, pulling my mind from the gutter I couldn't seem to get out of. It was a little late for this call, but considering I neglected to check in today, I wasn't too surprised.

"Yes, sir," I answered.

"Did you find her?" the voice on the other end asked, offering up no greeting.

The words of affirmation were on the edge of my tongue, but I surprised myself by answering negatively. "Not yet, sir. I have a lead though. It should only be a matter of time before I locate her."

"You gave the impression the last time we conversed that you were following a lead."

"It's the same lead," I lied. "It's only a matter of time before I pinpoint her location."

"The sooner, the better," he grumbled, hanging up without any further words.

I returned the phone to the nightstand and slid back against the pillows. That was unsettling. I'd never lied to a client before. For three weeks I'd been on Ashton's trail. I should have been happy to finally close up the case and head back to my condo in Tampa for some much needed R&R. Just that morning I'd been dreaming about taking several months off to catch up on some fishing and scuba diving. This case was ready to be wrapped within twenty-four hours, but now, suddenly, I was dragging it out. All for her. From the moment I laid eyes on Ashton I've been acting like a complete jackass, letting my little head outthink my big head. As soon as I walked in the bar tonight, I was taken in by her. I'd scanned the smoke-filled room, spotting her with her friends, joking and carrying on in the far corner. It was obvious the moment they noticed my presence as their voices came out in short bursts of excited chatter followed by whispering. I figured it was only a matter of time until I was approached. Bar scenes didn't get their hook-up stigma for no reason. Eight years ago, it would have been my buddies and me in the far corner of the bar playing the game. All of us banking on getting laid that night. More times than not, we'd all gone home alone. We were young, dumb, testosterone-crazed maniacs that most chicks wouldn't touch with a ten-foot pole.

Then I met Jessica and fell head over heels in love with her. She was poised, polished and challenged me to be better. Jessica wasn't into the whole club scene, so I gave it up, without a fuss. My buddies were pissed, claiming I was pussywhipped, but I didn't care. What did I need the clubs for anymore? I'd found the perfect girl. A year later, I realized perfection was nothing but an illusion. She shredded me to the point I swore I'd never let a woman have that power over me again. I jumped back into the bar scene a changed man. I couldn't have cared less about trying to get any girl's attention. Instead, I made them come to me. The guys thought I was crazy, but my aloof attitude worked better than any of the stupid one-liners or any other shit we used to do. I always laid my rules out in the open to avoid any future complications, and most of the time, the relationship would end amicably. Only one had called me a bastard, but I held steadfast to my rule. No attachments. Take it or leave it.

I kept my eyes on the trio in the corner through the mirror over the bar, waiting to see who would make the first move. I had several game plans in place. If I was approached by one of them, I would suggest buying a round for her and her friends so I could get close to my target. If they chickened out and never made their move, I'd order a round anyway and see if I could strike up a conversation that way. One thing was certain. I would not walk away tonight without making contact.

It took fifteen minutes for the group of girls to finally make their move. Much to my astonishment, it was Ashton instead of her heavily-endowed friend who approached me. After listening to her boisterous friend, I would have bet money that she would be my first contact with the group. The night was shaping up to be filled with surprises. My good fortune continued as Ashton awkwardly began to flirt with me. Seizing the opportunity, I ordered a round of drinks to see if that would loosen her tongue further. Much to my pleasure, the whiskey not only loosened her tongue, providing me with information, but it also provided a glimpse into something more. Her voice washed over me like a seductive caress, laced with an equal share of innocence and wisdom that hinted at a hidden inner pain. Something was bothering her, but regardless, whatever it was didn't concern me. It wasn't my job to rescue her. She was just an assignment, nothing more.

With each round of drinks though, that fact continued to dissipate. The more she talked, the more I was pulled in. Even her fumbled attempt at sexual banter was endearing and erotic at the same time. When she asked if I wanted to put my trunk in her, I got rock hard and wanted to hoist her up on the counter and take her right there in front of everyone.

I reached over for my cellphone to check the time and was shocked when I realized I had been lying there, thinking about her for the last hour. I reached over and flipped the light switch, plunging the room into darkness. As I contemplated my next move, the sane part of me knew I should call my client first thing in the morning and hand over Ashton's location, but the slightly insane side considered the possibility of waiting a few days to see if I could flush out why she had run away. The irrationality of this thought wasn't lost on me. It shouldn't matter why she'd run off. I was paid to locate her, plain and simple. It wasn't my business to ask questions. The fact that I had the sudden urge to hunt down my client instead, and bury my fist in his face for ever hurting her, shook me to the core. It had been years since a woman had this effect on me.

Insanity. That's all it was. I would turn her in tomorrow. It was the only way to get my mind back on track. I had no problems keeping the women I dated at arm's length for the last six years. I wasn't about to screw that up over some girl I'd been tracking for the last three weeks.

Cover created by **Okay Creations**
Edited by Hollie Westring
All rights reserved. Published by A.T. Publishing LLC

YA Titles by Tiffany King

The Saving Angels Series

Meant to Be (Book 1)

Forgotten Souls (Book 2)

The Ascended (Book 3)

Wishing For Someday Soon

Forever Changed

Unlikely Allies

Miss Me Not

Jordyn: A Daemon Hunter Novel Book 1

Where to find Tiffany King
www.authortiffanyjking.blogspot.com

Twitter: @AuthorTiffany
Facebook: Tiffany King
Goodreads: Tiffany King

Thanks go, firstly, to my family for not thinking I was crazy to quit my job to write full time and for always thinking that I'm way cooler and more talented than I actually am and for listening to me ramble on about the publishing industry during Christmas.

Second, to my besties, Caroline, Colleen, Liz and Rachel, you are the cheeses to my macaroni. I love all your faces.

Third, to my editor, Jen, who SOMEHOW found the time to do an amazing job, even with her brand new baby.

Fourth, to my beta, Laura, my soul twin. There are no words for how I creepy love you.

Fifth, to my online community, including Magan Vernon and the rest of the Indelible ladies. You make me feel like I'm not alone, and that means more than I can say.

Sixth, to all the book bloggers who have or ever will support me. You are aca-mazing and supportive and I am not worthy of you.

Seventh, to all my readers (it sounds pretentious to call you fans), YOU are the reason I can do what I do. I wish I could invite all of you over to my house and feed you cookies baked with love and too much chocolate. YOU ARE ALL MY BESTEST FRIENDS.

About the Author:

Chelsea M. Cameron is a YA/NA New York Times/USA Today Best Selling author from Maine. Lover of things random and ridiculous, Jane Austen/Charlotte and Emily Bronte Fangirl, red velvet cake enthusiast, obsessive tea drinker, vegetarian, former cheerleader and world's worst video gamer. When not writing, she enjoys watching infomercials, singing in the car and tweeting. She has a degree in journalism from the University of Maine, Orono that she promptly abandoned to write about the people in her own head. More often than not, these people turn out to be just as weird as she is.

Visit her blog: chelseamcameron.com, follow her on twitter: @chel_c_cam, or on Facebook.

Other books by Chelsea M. Cameron

Nocturnal (Book One in The Noctalis Chronicles)
Nightmare (Book Two in The Noctalis Chronicles)
Neither (Book Three in The Noctalis Chronicles)
Whisper (Book One in The Whisper Trilogy)
My Favorite Mistake (available from Harlequin)
Deeper We Fall (Fall and Rise, Book One)

Printed in Great Britain
by Amazon.co.uk, Ltd.,
Marston Gate.